THE NEW YORK YANQUIS

◆

THE NEW YORK YANQUIS

YANQUIS

Bill Granger

ARCADE PUBLISHING • NEW YORK

FIRST EDITION

This is a work of fiction. Names, characters, places, and incidents are
either the product of the author's imagination or used fictitiously.

Library of Congress Cataloging-in-Publication Data

Granger, Bill.
    The New York Yanquis / by Bill Granger. — 1st ed.
      p.   cm.
    ISBN 1-55970-289-3
    1. New York Yankees (Baseball team) — Fiction.   2. Baseball play-
ers — New York (N.Y.) — Fiction.   3. Cuban Americans — New
York (N.Y.) — Fiction.   4. Baseball teams — New York (N.Y.) —
Fiction.   I. Title.
PS3557.R256N4 1995
813'.54 — dc20   94-39262

Published in the United States by Arcade Publishing, Inc.
Distributed by Little, Brown and Company

10 9 8 7 6 5 4 3 2 1

BP

PRINTED IN THE UNITED STATES OF AMERICA

This is dedicated to the memory of the late Bill Veeck, the best thing to happen to baseball since they made it round. Thanks for the afternoons we spent together in Miller's Pub under the El tracks, drinking beer and figuring out the way of the world.

THE NEW YORK YANQUIS

◆

Preface

I don't even know what a preface is, but Bill Granger and the editor who read this thing said it was necessary to explain myself. I thought a story this long explains its own self, but they are in the business and they probably know what they're talking about.

Well, it all started after the last baseball strike, and since everyone wrote about that to death, I don't have to bring it up. After the strike, nothing changed much except the owners were just as greedy as ever and so were we, the ball players. That means, I suppose, that I should explain my position, but I don't really care to. I just played baseball is all and kept my mouth shut until now.

I told this stuff to Granger and he had the easy part of just taking it down the way I told it and typing it up. Here and there, he corrected my way of talking, and here and there I let him. Then the editor read it over and he corrected here and there and sometimes made me hot, like when he didn't know what a "red ass" was. This is about baseball, for the love of God, not about the English language. I think I said that to someone, and pretty soon they just went away.

I don't go on and on about what happened to Raul Guevara after the season because my agent, Sid, told me that's another story and if they want to know, they should pay more. I agreed with that. No use putting water on the table if they don't ask for it. A waitress in New York told me that one and it stuck.

What can I tell you about the strike except what you already know? What can I tell you about guys like Bremenhaven except what you already feel about guys like Bremenhaven? But I tell you one thing, when I look back on it, that year which I am describing here was a hoot.

Sincerely yours,
Ryan Patrick Shawn

P.S. Charlene made me put in my middle name. I didn't let her see the story as it was written because she would have wanted to leave some stuff out. Never show anyone what they don't need to see.

1

The thing began when Bremenhaven's accountant showed him what he was spending in salaries to finish third in the American League East. Fifty million dollars.

I pitched last in the last game of the season, after it was lost anyway.

Hoak Wilson was nursing a 1-0 lead in the eighth when the White Sox decided to go on a last-ditch salary drive. After the second homer of the inning, old Hoak just stared into the darkness of the dugout, pleading with his eyes for Sparky to take him out of the game.

Who says Sparky doesn't have a heart? Sparky dropped a dime to the bullpen and the next thing was I was on the mound, trying to staunch the bleeding. The Chicagos were up 4 to 1 at that point and it never got any worse. Or any better.

It was a lousy finish to a lousy season. The fans still in the park were too tired to even boo when Dave Belfry popped up to finish the thing off. Not that we would have heard them because there were too few of them to make much noise.

After the game, I showered up and packed my stuff in a ditty bag and said good-bye to Sparky in his office and good-bye to the clubhouse man, Sam, which was an envelope with $300 in it.

When you finish a shitty season with a shitty game, well, there's not much sentiment left to squeeze. You pack your bag and go home and hope you'll be invited to Florida in the spring.

Except this was my last good-bye. I felt it in my thirty-eight-year-old bones.

Time for Ryan Shawn to hang it up, catch the last train to Clarksville, *hasta la vista.*

I had had my innings and won nearly 160 games over the years. I was planning my retirement at least three years before that last game. Auto dealer named Jack Wade in Houston was going to give me a job selling cars and promoting the firm, and it was better than a sharp stick in the eye. Besides, my girlfriend, as she then was, Charlene Cleaver, lived in Houston and whatever I was going to do, I wasn't planning on going back home to El Paso. You ever get out of El Paso, you stay out, take my word on it.

So I was surprised when old George came down the runway just as I was leaving and asked me to talk to him.

George Bremenhaven, who owned the Yankees, liked to think he was a hands-on kind of owner, but the truth was he didn't give a rat's ass about the players. I'm not saying this with any kind of bitterness, because if you want to know the truth, the players didn't give a shit about him either. So it surprised me to see George in the weight room, trying to banter. He even tried banter on Sam, but Sam wasn't buying it and emphasized his distance by dumping a bunch of used towels on the floor between them.

"I want to talk to you, Ryan," George said to the next victim of his bonhomie mood, and I winced only a little. "Come on up to my box."

George was grinning at me as we went up to his box hanging over the open-air boxes below. I had never been in the owner's box before and it struck me as crude, with a little icebox and a couple of television sets tuned to catch the action you couldn't see just by looking out the plate-glass window down to the field. He opened the icebox and asked me if I wanted a beer and I said sure, and then he gave me a green bottle. No, it wasn't Heineken; George was never that generous. Rolling Rock, as I recall. It must have been on sale that week.

George said, "You know, Ryan, Sparky called you in one inning too late."

"Year's been like that, George," I said, man-to-man, using his first name. I settled on a cushioned chair that George probably smuggled out of a Holiday Inn someplace. In fact, the whole suite that was his private box looked a lot like a lot of motel rooms I've been in.

"I know the year's been like that and I'm gonna change that," George said.

I studied the man while he let the silence hang there. He was drinking something in a martini glass that I supposed was a martini. He has a round sort of face, puffy, and the only sharp things on his body are his eyes and his suit. Nice suit. Bad eyes that make you feel you're getting an IRS audit.

There we were, the only two people left in the world, surrounded by 60,000 empty seats. Actually, it is now 57,000 and something seats, but who was counting except George? Sixty thousand seats sounds just right for a great old place like the Stadium. Nothing is as empty as Yankee Stadium after a losing game. The neighborhood is sort of crummy, but I been in crummier ballpark neighborhoods, believe me. When people get it into their minds that a neighborhood is bad, it stays bad even when it gets better. I think it was the reason the ballplayers split so fast. That and it being autumn. It had been a cool day and cooler night and my arm twinged when I was warming up. Getting old. I sipped the Rolling Rock and just waited. When you're a relief pitcher, you learn to wait until the other guy makes a mistake. He wants to foul off twenty pitches, you let him. Just wait the son of a bitch out.

"You speak Spanish, don't you?" George said.

I just stared at him. I couldn't have been more amazed if he had just announced he was the Queen of France. I can deal with non sequiturs with the best of them, but this was more like walking into a phone booth and finding out you're standing in the oracle at Delphi. Or finding out it's already occupied by Superman. (Got that oracle thing out of college.)

"Don't you?"

He's got eyes like a Gila monster. Little glinty eyes that are colder than the desert floor at midnight. Or a woman's good-bye.

"Yeah, I speak some."

"You study it in school, when you went to Arizona?"

"You come from down where I come from, you speak Spanish just to survive. I guess it's the same the other way around. I mean, from across the river. At Ciudad El Paso."

"You come from El Paso," George said. He sipped on his drink some more.

"Yep." I don't really talk that way but I let out a "yep" every now and then to satisfy people's preconceptions.

"You going back to El Paso for the winter?"

For the winter. This was a peculiar turn of phrase applied to a thirty-eight-year-old relief pitcher soon to begin selling Buicks and Hondas in Houston. "For the winter" sort of implied there might be spring coming and winter was just a temporary setback instead of a permanent condition. I studied the question the way we relief pitchers like to study our baseballs before we fling them.

At this point, I didn't know all the things I know now. I didn't know, for instance, that George had toted up his payroll and decided on drastic action or that he had met with his old friend who was now secretary of state or that he had once slept in the Lincoln bedroom at the White House or that he had actually seen Lincoln's ghost. None of those things.

"You made what this year?" George said.

I may be a dumb ball player, but I'm not dumb enough to believe that George didn't know exactly what I made. I thought about telling him that, but I didn't. I've seen George when he's rattled and it isn't pleasant.

"I don't remember exactly," I said.

"Six hundred fifty thousand," George said.

"I'll take your word for it."

"You plan on coming back next year?"

"You plan on inviting me?"

"Three hundred thousand," George said.

Now George knew and I knew that I had an agent out there somewhere and it wasn't seemly for an owner to start negotiating with a ball player with no one around except all those empty seats.

"Take it or leave it," George said.

This is the new style of negotiating in the nineties, sort of like IBM firing ten thousand workers who were hired for life and calling it downsizing. One day you make a living wage and the next day you're selling pencils. My Daddy always told me about the Great Depression and the dust storms and all of it, and I believed every word, but we both thought at the time we were talking about the past, like talking about jousts and knights in armor and guys wearing powdered wigs. Just goes to show you.

"Well, I'll have to consider it. With Sid. My agent," I said.

"Fuck Sid, fuck agents. I'm up to here with agents. Fuck them all," George said. The Gila monster's eyes flickered then. I wouldn't have been surprised if his tongue had darted out and stabbed a fly.

"The trouble is, George, I'm not very good at negotiating these things. I could probably do it for someone else, but not for myself. I'm just too personally involved."

"I paid fifty million dollars in payroll this season to finish third," George said. "If I paid fifty million to be in the World Series, that would be one thing. I thought that's what I was paying for, to be in the Series. But no. I paid fifty million dollars for twenty-five assholes to finish third, fucking third. New York does not stand for third. They love that shit in Chicago, fucking Cubs could finish in Triple A and they'd be standing in line to throw their money into Wrigley Field, but I am in New York, this is New York all around you, Ryan, this is not third place, not for a fifty-million-dollar payroll. What do you think the last baseball strike was all about? We have to take control of the game before you people ruin it."

"I just play, George, I don't ruin nothing," I said.

"That's what they all do. They all play, the greedy bastards," he screamed. "I walk in the locker room and they got their boom boxes on and they dance their watusi jitterbugs when they should be concentrating —"

"Maybe you should get us chess boards," I said.

Nothing I said was getting through. He was standing now, gesturing, walking around that Motel 6 room of a box, staring out at all those empty seats like the empty stadium was the sea and he was King Lear.

"Money! Money is ruining this game! In the old days, a ball player was happy to have something to do in the summer and if he got paid for it, all the better! But not any more, no he needs BMWs and broads and Johnny Walker Black Label not Red and a fucking farm in Florida or some such godforsaken place!"

"I live in Houston in a motel," I said. I wasn't being humble. I was trying to distract the bull because that little vein in his forehead was swelling up. It would have been alright if the damned thing ever burst but it didn't, it just made everyone else miserable.

"You're bums, illiterate fucking bums, all of you!" George said, not looking directly at me. I suppose he meant not me personally but in the collective.

"We finished third! Third! The *New York Times,* I'm surprised they still carry the box score. You know what the *Daily News* said this morning? No, I forget, you probably don't read. I read. The *Daily News,* the rotten bastards, the *News* says, GEORGE BOMBS AGAIN!"

He said it exactly that way, with capital letters, just like a headline. I just sat there, deciding whether I could take another sip of Rolling Rock before he turned to look at me. I snuck it.

"Oh, you arrogant scum, you strike baseball, you blow the World Series even, you break little boys' hearts for your filthy paychecks!"

"George," I began.

"Shuddup, Ryan. You should talk! You had 10 saves and a 5.36 ERA and that sucks, Ryan, that sucking sound you hear is six hundred fifty thousand of my — MY — dollars going into your pocket for shit. For total unvarnished unpolished unimpeachable shit."

Well, I figured I would go out quietly, not with a bang and not with a whimper neither. George didn't look like he was going to die of a stroke so there was no point in sticking around. I think an employee can tolerate a certain amount of abuse from a boss, but not so he'd make a habit of it. I put down the Rolling Rock and got up quietly and started for the exits.

For just a moment, I saw all those empty seats in the old place and tried to feel the way George must feel, but then I thought, fuck it. Empathy was wasted on a prick like George Bremenhaven. Never have sympathy for an owner.

"Where you going, Ryan?"

"Texas."

"Is that your answer?"

"What was the question?"

"Three hundred thousand."

"Doesn't have a question mark at the end of it, so I figured it wasn't a question."

"And that's your answer?"

"What was the question?"

"You asshole, I'm offering you a one-year, last-hurrah contract for three hundred thousand dollars."

"Shit, you got guys on the team make three million a year for lingering on the DL list half the season," I said.

"Those days are over, Ryan. There's a new reality in baseball. The fans are sick and tired of paying thirty bucks a pop to watch losers shuffle off into third place."

"We drew pretty well till toward the end," I said. "You got your television money. It wasn't all expenses, George. Ball players are just one of the unavoidable costs that go with owning a major league team. They must've told you that at Owners' School before you bought the Yankees."

He glared at me then, but he didn't say anything. Maybe he saw I was getting personally pissed off, which is not the way I usually am. I do a professional piss-off, but that's to scare the shit out of the batter. I wasn't doing that now.

When he started talking again, he started soft and low.

"Ryan, I want to keep you. Like Ishmael. You're going to tell everything you saw and heard and did when George Bremenhaven declared a one-man revolution and seized his team back from the bloodthirsty, bloodsucking, scum bag agents and players and unions and showed he could win the pennant on his own terms."

It's true I spent three years at Arizona State before I got into the minors and I did officially major in English, although it was mostly fooling around. I knew who Ishmael was, but I didn't know then that George was really planning something and not just spouting off. So I just opened the door of the skybox and said, "S'long, George."

"Ryan, there isn't a team that is going to give you a better offer."

"Sure there is," I said, as if I believed it.

"I need you next year," he said.

I just looked at him.

"Six hundred thousand. But the proviso is you don't tell anyone what you're getting, not anyone."

"George, my agent will know and the union will know, all kinds of people get information."

"Not if you don't tell them."

"Six hundred fifty," I said.

"Six and a quarter," he said.

I couldn't believe it. I thought this time next week I'd be selling Buick Regals for a three-hundred-dollar-a-week draw and now the old crocodile was giving me one more ride on the merry-go-round. I thought I should call Sid and just check it out with him, but Sid hadn't been returning my calls promptly like he did when I was twenty-nine and burning up the league with the lowest ERA in baseball. Damn, I was beginning to think like George and that was a scary thought. Fuck Sid.

"Draw the contract," I said.

"Where will you be in the morning?" he said.

"I was gonna be in Texas," I said.

"Fuck Texas. Texas'll wait. And while you're waiting, practice up on your Spanish."

"Why?" I asked.

"Because, Ryan, I gotta have one ballplayer who speaks English," George said.

That didn't make any sense to me at the time. I thought George was going off the deep end again, jumping into a martini and swimming his crazy old way from rim to rim.

I wanted to just stare at him like the cold-blooded old reliever I am, but I couldn't.

"What are you talking about, George?" I finally said.

And those Gila eyes twinkled at me and that Gila tongue darted out and stabbed a fly.

"Cuba," he said, like that explained everything.

2

For a couple of days after that, I didn't hear a word from George, although he'd said he'd call me as soon as the contract was ready. It's like waiting for the check that's always in the mail.

I called him a couple of times and got his private secretary, Miss Viola Foster. She was nice on the phone, but she said Mr. Bremenhaven was away on business in Washington. She would tell him I called; I believed her. George was just doing one of his disappearing things and it annoyed heck out of me. It also annoyed me that I was sticking around New York, taking it, because of the thought of working another year for just a $25,000 salary cut.

I even believed George was down in Washington, D.C. on business, other business, not baseball business.

The trouble was that Washington didn't have a baseball team, and that Baltimore was the closest city in the playoffs. I watched some of the games on television at night with a six-pack of MGD close at hand. I thought about George. Every owner worth his weight in gold — and they all are, no matter how they poor-mouth — was at one or the other playoff game. Baseball owners have a weird social life, like umpires. Owners can't fraternize with anyone except other owners and they jump at any chance to hang out with the other guys in the Owners' Club. Umpires stick together because they don't fraternize with ballplayers and they need someone to eat with at night on the road.

One thought led to another while I was drinking beer and surfing through the games on television. I thought about speaking Spanish. And I thought a disturbing lot about Charlene Cleaver, who was waiting for me down in Houston.

I called her the first night after the last game of the season. She was disappointed, she said. She had made reservations for us for dinner at Tony's and now would have to cancel them. I said for $625,000 for another ride in the Bigs, I'd make up the dinner to her.

This was the wrong thing to say. Or maybe I put it in the wrong way. George had upset me some and I let our conversation carry over to Charlene by the tone in my voice.

"I happen to know $625,000 is a lot of money," Charlene said. Then nobody said anything for a moment. "What does Sid say?"

She talks about Sid Cohen like they are co-conspirators and I am the conspiratee. I resent the hell out of it. Charlene and I were close, but, I thought then, not that close. Same with Sid.

I have to admit here that Charlene is a prattler at times and goes off on her own tangents, which, combined with her stunning good looks, might lead some people to think there is no brain behind those pretty eyes. But there is. When we first started going together, I showed off my wallet to her, in a manner of speaking. Talked about my CDs and how I would be fixed when I retired and so forth. She set me straight on that.

I remember the first loving words out of her mouth that night. I kissed her long and deep, and she said, "Latin American funds."

I was so intoxicated by her at the time that it took me a moment to react. "What did you say?"

"Latin American funds are returning twenty-five percent the last I looked. What do your CDs return?"

One thing led to another. One kiss led to another to an invitation to share breakfast with her at her place. And I started listening close to Charlene after that, transferring out of my CDs and into strange things like Latin American mutual funds and some gaming stocks. Damned if she wasn't right about all that stuff I never paid much attention to.

But she wasn't Sid Cohen. I had cut this deal for myself by myself.

I tried a silence-breaker. "Charlene —" I began.

"Anybody works for a living 'stead of playing baseball knows what that kind of money is. I might have to work fourteen, fifteen years to see that kind of money, Ryan Patrick, so don't high-hat me. But what does Sid say?"

"I didn't talk to Sid."

"Oh. I see," she said.

"Honey, I just wanted to point out the obvious. If I was to tell you I had a chance to make twenty-five dollars an hour shoveling shit in some god-forsaken place like Albuquerque, you'd give me a kiss and pack my lunch before I left. But I tell you I got another chance on the merry-go-round, you sound like you ain't happy."

"I'm *not* happy," she said, stating her feelings and correcting my English in the same three-word sentence. "I miss you."

"Hell, I miss you, honey," I said.

"I was just thinking about you comin' up the drive."

Charlene don't have no drive. She lives in an apartment building.

"I was thinkin' it, too," I lied.

"Was you?" Sometimes she slips like that. She went to community college, not a regular four-year place, but she works hard to root out that East Texas way of talking.

"I was."

When we start talking like characters out of "Li'l Abner," it is a sign that the squall is passing.

"Isn't that less money than you made last year?" Charlene said.

"A bit."

"Why's that?"

"Why's what?"

"Why're you getting paid less?"

"I'm lucky to be paid," I said.

"I know that," she said. "I mean, why would he pay you again? You ain't that good, not anymore."

"You never complained."

"I don't mean about that," she giggled.

"He don't pay me for that," I said, sort of sly and giggly myself.

"I miss you, honey."

"I miss you. Couple of days here, settle this contract up, and I'll be heading home, Charlene. Come up that driveway, you better look out, girl."

"You been good, Ryan?"

"I been good."

"I know you're lying when you say it."

"I ain't lying, Charlene. I'm sittin' here in my box in Fort Blessed Lee, New Jersey, dosing myself with Miller beer and taking cold showers morning and night."

Giggles.

"I mean it, honey. You're worth waitin' for."

I did mean that and maybe it showed in my voice because her tone got cooey and soft. Actually, Charlene Cleaver was the first serious girlfriend I had had in some time.

She was very pretty, which goes without saying, but she was very smart as well. I ain't half-dumb, so I know smart. She studied to be a nutrition-ist at Houston West Community, said nutrition was a growth field in the years to come. Looks like she was right if you half-read *USA Today* most mornings, all that stuff about B's and C's and E's and bulk fiber, which is one of my favorites. She had a good job with Rice University Hospital working on improving the diet habits of Texans, which is a lifetime job in itself. It's a lot like selling grizzly bears on a low-fat salad diet when they would much rather chomp on hikers and campers.

Part of my loving her was letting her work on me. I still drank beer when watching the ball games. Every now and then, I fell over a rack of ribs, too, but I also partook of at least six servings daily of vegetables and fruit, and there were whole parts of weeks passing without me taking in any animal meat at all, not even a cheeseburger.

We talked some cuddly talk that carried some explicit sexual language and hung up at last telling each other we loved each other and what we were going to do to each other when we saw each other again.

Charlene is tall and leggy, but that doesn't stop her from wearing slacks most of the time when you know her bare legs would send half of Hous-ton into a catatonic state. I admire her for that. Also for letting me see her legs from time to time. And knowing all that shit about NAFTA and its ef-fects on Latin American mutual funds. If you ask me, there is far too much book-judging by covers, especially when it comes to women. The cover is so pretty, you forget the words inside.

I tried Sid, my agent, on the second day, partly because when Charlene makes an offhand hint the way she did about Sid, it works on me like an itch. She wanted me to talk to Sid and it was probably a good idea. But his office said he was in Hawaii with his newest best buddy, a quarterback named Bret Branson.

Bret Branson. Why is it that football quarterbacks all have these soft and pretty names that make ugly-named linemen want to chew them up? It's like taunting them.

I left my number with Sid's service, but I figured Sid would get the message and think I was calling him about shopping me around and he wasn't ready yet to talk to me about how I was unsalable. The hell with him.

On the third day, when Baltimore beat the Angels for a second time, George dumped Tommy Tradup. I knew he must have loved it because of the way he did it. Called Tommy into his office at the Stadium and said he wasn't going to even niggle about a new contract, that Tommy was history with the Yankees.

You have to understand something about baseball. For a player of Tommy's caliber — if you trade him, you trade him for someone else. Tommy hit .321 that year with 34 homers and 102 ribbies. This is a solid performer and George was letting him go, not even waiting for the winter trades.

George is not a dope. He is mean, vindictive, and a complete asshole, but those are qualities shared by most of the club owners. Howsoever, George was dumping a salary and it didn't make any sense unless there was a lot more going on that I didn't understand.

While I was hanging around that week, waiting for George to call me with the contract, I did my usual sight-seeing.

I have a studio apartment in Fort Lee, New Jersey, just across the Hudson River from Manhattan. It's a nice view of the city and the prices there are about half, so I keep the studio year-round. I was not going to renew the lease that fall, but that changed when George offered me another year at the Dance.

I've got a Buick Park Avenue only four years old that Jack Wade sold me down in Houston, and I park it in the open lot of the Holiday Inn up the street from my building. They never check the lot to see who's parked there, so it doesn't cost me anything. One nice morning, I drove across the George Washington Bridge into the city and down the West Side Highway to Midtown.

Maybe it's my Texas eye and appreciation for absurdity, but there are things to love about that city. Like the West Side Highway, which used to go downtown, that now stops at Midtown because the rest of it collapsed a few years ago and everyone thought it would be a good idea not to rebuild it. So they didn't and the traffic just funnels into the city at 56th Street through this gauntlet of black men wielding spray bottles, towels, and window sponges. They insist on washing your car windshield whether you want them to or not, sometimes even when it's raining. This is car washing through intimidation and it annoys the suburbanites backed up at the lights off the West Side Highway. The car washers usually give me a pass because I got Texas plates and Texas people are crazy about their cars and about not wanting strangers to lay hands on their windshields.

I park in a pay garage on 56th Street. It costs more to park in Manhattan for a day than it does to rent a room at the Motel 6 in Amarillo, which tells you something about both places. After I park the car, I get this spring in my step and go out on the sidewalk to see the parade. It is held every day of the year. I just wander all over that island, watching the parade. It steps off with a bang on Mondays and it's dried-up, pale-faced, and crushed in the shoulders by Friday afternoons. Never saw people work so hard as New Yorkers. It makes me tired to watch them, but it's a pleasant kind of tired, the way you get when you were a kid in summer and spent the whole day jumping in the swimming hole with your buddies, getting burned deep to a lobster shade and, after everyone is called home, just falling asleep under cool sheets, dreaming little fever dreams. I think about things like that, watching people running around working so hard.

You might think a hick like me goes to country-western bars or wears cowboy boots on Broadway. True, I do wear boots in Texas, but when in Rome, dress in togas. I leave it to the New York fellas to wear snakeskin boots under their three-piece suits and to top it off with black cowboy hats. I generally wear a nice little corduroy sports coat with leather on the elbows. You might mistake me for a college professor. Charlene says it is the expression I wear when I'm watching the parade that makes me look like a college teacher she once had, I think it was in modern American literature.

"What expression?" I asked her once.

"Bemusement. Not unfriendly, just sort of amused and uncomprehending at the same time," she said.

"You mean I don't get it?"

"I mean more like no one else gets it, but that's all right, you're just there to see the show," she said. When she talks like that, she gets very thoughtful and still. It's like she's seeing something else when she says it, not me listening to her.

I walked all around the town and drank a couple of MGDs and went back to get my car out of the garage and drove uptown to the GW Bridge just before rush hour. It was a cool day and the lights were all lit on the Palisades on the New Jersey side.

When I got back to my little apartment, I saw the message machine was lit. I rolled the tape and the only one on it was George.

"Where the hell are you, Ryan? You suddenly pulling a doublecross on me? I thought we had a contract worked out, you son of a bitch, what am I doing here with paper in my hand, what am I, chopped liver?"

With that, the recording recorded a slam as in a phone being abused. Here I've been hanging around for three days and he decides to call me when I'm hanging out in Manhattan. Fuck him.

Baltimore won the third game and advanced to the next round of the playoffs that night. I saw it on my 25-inch Mitsubishi. I turned in at eleven and George called me at one.

"So what's going on, you trying to cut another deal for yourself?"

I mumbled. It's what I do at one in the morning.

"You drunk, Ryan?"

"Are you, George? It's one o'clock."

"Why didn't you call me?"

"Miss Foster'll tell you I called you twice, looking for my contract. I decided to take the afternoon off. Drove over to Manhattan and wandered around for a while."

"You were here? In the city? When I was here trying to reach you?"

His questions had a rising tone as though I lived in Venezuela and he was my best buddy and I had passed through New York without giving him a call. George gets away with his crazy act, of course, because he's rich.

I decided not to say anything. After a moment of silence, George continued in a less-aggrieved tone of voice.

"I want to see you tomorrow morning in my office at ten."

"You got my contract, George?"

"We can talk," George said.

"What does that mean, George?"

"We can talk. You're awfully anxious about that contract, Ryan."

"George, you offer me a contract for one year and I take it. So I'm hanging around now because you wanted me to hang around and I now get the feeling maybe we're not talking about a contract."

"What makes you think that?"

"George, I've got a mind to get in my car around dawn and just aim it for Texas," I said.

"Why? What have I said to make you do a thing like that? It's your fucking agent, Sid, that son of a bitch is trying to torpedo —"

"George, I haven't talked to Sid."

"Then what is it?"

"It's you, George. It's one in the morning, George."

"Look, put Texas on hold until tomorrow at ten. In my office."

"In the ballpark."

"No, no, no. My office on Park."

"You gonna have the contract?"

"Trust me," George said. "And nighty-night."

He hung up and left me sitting there, wide awake. 1:21 A.M. I got up and went to the icebox and took out a can of Miller Genuine Draft beer and opened it. I took the beer to the window. It was only a studio, but there was a sort of half-ass view of Manhattan and the bridge and the river. I do some of my best thinking there, looking at the city.

Sixteen years in the Bigs was a good career. The only way I'd see Cooperstown was to buy a bus ticket, but, what the hell, I was a major leaguer and there were a lot of boys who'd played baseball and never got as far as Single A in the minors. I had a major league pension coming and wasn't a spendthrift, so a lot of money was in mutual funds and such. I wouldn't starve even if it turned out I couldn't sell Buicks. Charlene was talking about us opening up a healthy food fast-food restaurant, although I didn't know that most of Texas was ready for that just yet. We might just have to go to Santa Fe on that one and sell tofu to the movie stars buying up New Mexico.

I thought my way through a half-can of beer and I saw the truth of things. I didn't want to let go. Not yet. Just let me hang on one more time. Go out on the mound in the seventh and hear the crowd and see the sharp faces on those shiny young batters. Be part of the parade. Let me feel it again. Hell, George, I'd pay you, and you know it, you son of a bitch. You know it.

3

Miss Viola Foster is a middle-aged lady of grace and style who was really too good for a crude turd like George Bremenhaven. She gave me a nice smile when I opened the door to the suite and said it was nice to see me, as though she meant it. She took me into the inner sanctum and asked me if I wanted coffee, and I said no. I said it automatically because I was staring at Sam, the clubhouse manager.

Sam was inherited by George from the previous owners of the Yankees. Sam is in charge of equipment, packing, shipping, seeing we get our supplies of uniforms, bats, and balls, and all the other necessary little jobs that let ball players concentrate on important things, like their hangnails and navels.

I bet Sam had never been in George's midtown office before.

The office is on the thirtieth floor of the sandy-colored building just below Grand Central Station on Park Avenue. It was a nice morning for it, whatever "it" was going to be. The men loped along the sidewalks playing their briefcases against their knees like tambourines and the ladies had that crisp autumn look that takes over the city in October and hangs on smartly until it snows.

"Hey, Sam," I said. He nodded at me and said nothing. Sam never wastes a word when a silence is better.

George came around his fat rosewood desk like a maître d' and grabbed my hand. I expected to be shown a table, but instead he led me to a stuffed leather chair opposite Sam and indicated I should sit. I sat and the leather squeaked as I settled in.

"First, I trust you, Ryan."

I waited for the next shoe.

"Second, I been talking to Sam here about assuming extra duties next season. We're all going to have to pull our oars together to get this thing done."

"Pull our oars," I repeated.

"Shoulder to the wheel," George said.

"One or the other," I said.

George said, "Sam, talk to him."

Sam looked at George with a miserable expression. Anyone in the club-house knew that Sam hated George Bremenhaven almost more than the players. This was an instinctive class thing on Sam's part. His name is Sam Ortiz and when he was twelve he was picking strawberries in California and he and his migrant folks were living in ten-by-ten unheated shacks on the edges of the big fields. I wouldn't be surprised if Sam was a Commu-nist, except Mexicans tend not to be, in my experience.

"Go ahead," George said with that grim little look on his puffy fat face. His lips get so tight they almost disappear.

So the next thing, Sam turns to me and says in Spanish:

— This cocksucking son of a whore wants me to test you on your Span-ish. He calls me in the middle of the night and he says to me I have to talk Spanish to you to see if you can speak Spanish to me. What in the name of God is this about?

— I don't know, Sam (I replied in Spanish). Four days ago, he says he wants to keep me around for another year because I speak Spanish and now he wants to test me. Why don't we ask him?

— Good idea.

"George," I said in English. "What the hell is this about?"

"What did you say to each other?"

"I asked him if he still fucks chickens and he said I had a venereal dis-ease, he could see it in my eyes," I said.

"Is that what you said? What kind of a thing is that to say?"

"What do you want us to do, George? Dance the Mexican hat dance? Sing La Cucaracha?"

"I wanna know you know how to speak Spanish," George said.

I looked at Sam and said:

— This son of a whore has gone crazy.

"I know that word, *loco*. You think I'm crazy, Ryan?"

"We both think you're crazy, George."

"You know, I could go out in this city right now and I could buy Span-ish interpreters a dime a dozen. Every courtroom's got them, every Puerto Rican grocery, every —"

"George, your veins are starting to stand out and that carotid artery is gonna fill your ears with blood in a minute. Just calm down and tell us what you want."

He was quiet for a second. I looked at Sam and he looked at me. We waited.

"I get rid of Hoak Wilson at noon. One million in cash and assumption of his contract. I've already made three point five million and got rid of twenty-two million in contracts and obligations. My accountant is going crazy, this is the best news the Yankees have had since Joe DiMaggio."

"I'm happy for you, George."

"Naw, you're not happy, but I don't care. I'm happy. You're just lucky. Lucky you grew up in Texas and learned to speak spic with the Mexicans. I mean, Spanish."

Sam said nothing. I could have made a corrective cluck, but it wasn't worth it. George didn't mean anything; he just talks that way.

"Why's it lucky, George?"

He stared at me. And then glanced at Sam. "He speak Spanish okay, Sam?"

"He's okay," Sam said in his way, shrugging his shoulders. He wasn't my buddy and I didn't expect him to go out of his way for me.

George glared at Sam with his Gila eyes as though he could laser the truth out of him. Then he said, "Okay, Sam. That's it. See you around later."

Sam sat there.

"Come on, Sam. I got things to do. To discuss."

"That's it?" Sam finally said. He started to rise.

"Yeah, you got work back at the Stadium and I got things to do. Just keep this under your hat, okay?"

Sam shrugged again.

"Understand?" George warned him.

"*Si,*" Sam said. If he had a sombrero, he would have held it across his belly to show respect for *el patron.* Sam pulls that Mexican peasant thing when he wants to show his contempt for you. I could see he didn't understand a damned thing. Neither did I.

Sam opened the door and went out, closing it behind him.

George pranced around his desk on those surprisingly small feet and grabbed at a pile of papers.

"Sign these," he said.

"Whoa," I said, holding up my hand. "I gotta read them first."

"It's all boilerplate, the usual crap. See, this is the last contract you signed and this is the one you're going to sign. The same."

"Except for less money," I said.

"You agreed."

"I agreed. But what's this?"

"An agreement not to disclose confidential information. It's becoming very routine in the business world."

"Not disclose what, George?"

"Confidential information."

"Like what, George?"

"Confidential information that you don't have yet but you may acquire in the course of your duties with the New York American League baseball club," he said.

"Why, you gonna raise ticket prices and not tell anyone until they show up at the stadium?"

"Bigger than that, Ryan."

"You're going to move to New Jersey."

"Sign it."

"I don't know," I said, scanning the sheets of paper.

"Look, if you're going to be Boswell to my Johnson, I need to trust you."

"You going to write a dictionary? Maybe a Spanish-English dictionary?"

"I'm going to reinvent baseball," George said.

Major league ball club owners talk this way as they teeter along from crisis to crisis. Read the sports pages today and the baseball news is all about how much someone is making or some owner is losing or attendance or television, anything but marks on a scorecard or the sound of a bat.

"Sort of like a new Charlie Finley."

"Charlie would have loved this idea."

"What idea?"

"Sign the fucking form, Ryan."

Shit. I was intrigued enough to sign it. I also signed the contract and made George sign his. We were a team again.

George gave me my copies and he slipped his into a drawer of his desk that locked.

"Don't we need a witness?" I said.

"I'll fake that later," he said. "Now, Ryan. The secret. It's worth it, all this fooling around. But it stays secret until after the winter meetings in Las Vegas, until I can finally dump all the players I want to dump."

"How many is that, George?" My voice was sort of quiet. Baseball is a brutal kind of business and you're here today and traded tomorrow. Still, you play with those guys, live with them on the road, they're flesh and blood and they have families and friends and hopes and fears. You wouldn't know it to read about them in some of the sports columns. Or listen to an owner.

"Twenty-four. Everyone but you, Ryan. I told you, you survive like Ishmael."

"And you're going to kill a white whale, George?"

"Something like that."

"Like what?"

"Where are the best ball players in the world? Besides here?"

"I don't know. Maybe Japan."

"Too little. No power."

"Venezuela. Mexico."

"You're getting warmer."

"I was never good at this kind of questioning, that's why I got bad class-discussion marks in school. You want an answer, you furnish it."

"Cuba."

I let that sink in.

"Cuba, what?" I said.

"Cuba, Cuba," he said.

"You're going to buy some ball players in Cuba? I thought we didn't trade with Cuba, something like that."

"Reality is setting in, in the world and in Washington, even in Havana."

"And what is reality?"

"Castro wants dollars. And recognition. And he wants the U.S. to lift trade embargoes. Funny thing is, so do we. But the administration doesn't want a backlash here so it has to proceed with caution."

"I didn't know you knew so many famous people."

"I do. I was just in Washington. Spent the night at the White House. You know where I slept?"

I thought of several smart-ass answers but offered none of them. I was fascinated by the lizard in the blue suit across from me.

"In Lincoln's bedroom."

"How is it?"

"I saw his ghost."

"Did you."

"You don't believe me?"

"I believe you, George, if you believe you."

"He just stared at me and then he nodded once and disappeared."

"Maybe he had to go to the bathroom."

"I was dreaming about Cuba and what I want to do and he knew it. Lincoln. You know, aside from everything else, this is a good thing I'm doing. A good thing for our Hispanic friends."

"Like that spic, Sam," I said. I shouldn't have bothered. It just rolled off that chubby blue suit.

"The deal is done, but it has to stay secret until I get rid of my payroll," George said. "You signed a confidentiality agreement and I can have your ass in prison if you breathe a word of this to anyone. But I've got to have, you know, be in at the beginning, be able to give testimony on it when the time is right."

"What?"

"Twenty-four Cubans. The twenty-four best Cuban baseball players. The best. The best ball players from one of the best baseball countries in the world. They've been living under Castro for more than thirty years, but they can play baseball. Castro plays baseball. It's the national sport."

I was understanding every word, but they weren't really registering deep. I took a breath and then another.

"Next spring in Florida, Castro airlifts in twenty-four elite baseball players to play for the New York Yankees. You realize how much this cuts my payroll? I'm arranging for them to have rooms all together on a floor in the East Side Hotel."

This was the name of a well-known SRO and welfare hotel on the east side of Manhattan. Its ambience is halfway between a YMCA residence and a West Texas county jail. It turned out later that George owns this high-rise semi-slum.

"George —"

"The deal costs me five million, half to the Cuban government, the rest to the ball players. Man, do you realize these kids who probably didn't even have shoes when they were kids are going to have $100,000 a year each?"

"The union —"

"Fuck the fucking players' union, this is bigger than them and there's nothing they can do about it if the players' green cards are sanctioned by the State Department. Man, they are going to have jobs. What's the matter, are you prejudiced against Cubans?"

"George, you really thought this thing out?"

"This thing is a done deal, Ryan."

"I don't like this, I feel like I've been let in a conspiracy."

"You been let in a last chance to rob me of another $625,000, Ryan. This ain't shoveling shit in Louisiana, boy, this is real money and I know it and so do you. In fact, I know you know it, which is why you agreed to it."

He had me there.

I looked at the contracts in my hand and folded them and put them in my sports coat. George might be crazy, but there were enough lunatics running the game these days to make anything seem sensible.

"What about the press?" I said. "The fans?"

"Fuck the fans and fuck the reporters. The fans will come if there's a winning team on the field, and the reporters, as long as they get their free passes and their lunches comped, they're irrelevant. Besides, this is a liberal town, Ryan, we're not in West Bumfuck, Texas. I can see the editorials streaming out of the *New York Times* hailing me for my bold opening to Cuba and to restoring normalized relations blah-blah-blah."

"Nobody who's a fan reads editorials, George. They read the sports pages."

"Let them read. I'm going to have a good team, better than the one I'm getting rid of, maybe the best team in baseball, and all in one year and all for a tenth of what I'm paying out now. Salaries and egos, that's all I got on the field."

"And what do you want from me?"

"I want you to be present at the creation," George said. "And I want you to *parlez* with them."

"Surely you're kidding."

"I don't call $625 thou a year kidding, Ryan. If you failed your Spanish test with Sam Ortiz, you would be in your fucking Buick now heading across the river to pick up your clothes and drive back to Texas. Believe me when I say it."

"I believe you, George."

"Besides, there are some on the team now speak Spanish. But I don't trust them. They're spics, and when they all get together, talking their Spanish jive, they're tighter than clams in champagne. I need an Anglo on the team, sort of an identity thing, the leader of the rebels. Like John Wayne when he led all those Filipinos in that movie. You can be a spokesman for the players."

Pimping for a bunch of Cuban scabs.

Man, Ryan, you must want it bad enough to sell your mother's cow.

I looked at George and I couldn't express how low I was feeling just then. I almost was ready to throw the contract on his desk and walk away from the whole mess. Go down to Houston and sell cars for Jack Wade. Talk it out with Charlene Cleaver, who could probably make sense of it for me and make me feel better.

George. I would have liked to have had the courage just then to pop him one in the middle of his white pudding face. But then what? I'd just see someone else come in to replace me. The grand gesture looks good in movies, but it seldom works in real life, I find. You want to quit, they say here's your coat and hat. You want to be arrested over principle, hell, they arrest you and throw you in a cell with a three-hundred-pound colored ax murderer who hasn't had pussy in six months.

I always have felt the need to stand up for something like a principle, but I've never gotten to it. Well, not never. There was Kathleen Day in fifth grade and I stood up to Booker Longtree, who was teasing on her to the point of making her cry on the playground. I took him on for Kathleen Day. Booker beat the shit out of me, and when I got home Daddy did the same for fighting. I tried to tell him it wasn't a fight, more like a slaughter, but Daddy wasn't much on fine points of law. My last stand for principle.

"You got a problem with anything I said, Ryan?" George asked. He was pushing it now because he knew he'd won.

"You getting anyone good, George? From your buddy Fidel?"

"The best players money can buy."

"You had those."

"And they got fat and lazy and they didn't care if they finished first or third. That's the trouble with baseball today."

"Everything's the trouble with baseball today, George."

"I got me lean tigers who love the game and play in the dirt and get cheered by peasants just like them. And they hardly make any money."

"Castro tell you this?"

"I know they ain't making a hundred grand a year."

"Castro sent us those boat people that time, bunch of guys he had in prison. They came over here and did bad things here, too."

"Castro had the Soviet Union bankrolling him then. He's got too many fields of sugar canes now."

"And he needs a field of dreams," I said.

George beamed. It was his most hideous smile.

"I like that, Ryan. I really do. From field of canes to field of dreams. I like that, it appeals to . . . to what would you say? Sentiment? To something inspiring?"

Inspiring.

When would I learn to keep my absurd sense of poetry leashed?

4

I felt bad enough after meeting with George that I went straight back to my studio apartment in Fort Lee and packed.

I packed my clothes and a couple of books that travel with me and threw out the perishables in the icebox.

There were six cans of MGD left and I left three of them in case I came back late to the apartment and the liquor stores were closed. Threw my shit in the trunk of the Park Avenue. Except for the three cans of beer. They lasted me across New Jersey. When it was late afternoon, I had gotten through the Poconos when I was stopped by a goddamned state cop. Speeding laws are sick in the East. The limit is 55 miles per hour on these big, wide interstate highways all across New York and New Jersey and even Pennsylvania. Nothing gets halfway sensible until you reach Ohio, and it doesn't get honestly good until Oklahoma and Texas.

I told the Pennsylvania trooper that my mother died and I was coming home, all the way back to El Paso. A lie like that sounds terrible, but I've explained I never had any principle, except for that time in fifth grade when Booker beat it out of me. Besides, my mother did die, a little after I was born, and I never forgave her for doing it.

The cop probably didn't believe me, but he let me go with a warning and I watched my step the rest of the way across Interstate 80. Watching your step in the East on the interstates means going just as fast as the trucks will let you. They go 70, you go 70. They slow down, you slow down.

I pulled off the first exit in Ohio and called Deke Williams in Chicago.

Deke (Catfish) Williams was a long reliever with the Yankees in the early eighties, when I broke in. I was a starter, but Deke taught me the stuff. If he hadn't taught me the stuff, I would have been out of the Bigs in a year or two because I didn't have the speed to start.

"But you mean, boy, and ain't half dumb, so listen up," old Deke had said. Nobody ever called him Catfish even though he listed his name that way and wanted to be called Catfish. He thought it would make him a character. But he was just Deke to everyone, even the clubhouse manager. I tried to call him Catfish to please him, but he saw through that and said I was patronizing him. You couldn't win with Deke.

I can say he was a friend. And I needed one.

"Where you at, boy?" Deke said on the long-distance line from Chicago. He was owner of three "Catfish Williams" rib shacks and, well, catfish houses in the black neighborhoods of Chicago. I did mention he was a colored man?

"Boy, you got four hundred miles till you at Sweet Home Chicago, you be driving all night 'fore you get here. Get a Holiday Inn some place with that buzzer in the bed and start out at dawn — you be here 'bout when I'll be wakin' up. You drive all night, you get here when I'm goin' to sleep."

It made sense. I agreed. Ten minutes later, I was all alone in a motel room with a fresh six-pack of Miller Genuine and two Big Macs and one giant order of fries. I turned on the TV, ate my supper, and drank two of the beers. Then I called Charlene in Houston. She wasn't in and that annoyed me because, like most men, I expect women to sort of hover around the phone, waiting for their man to call them. That's a male instinct, and I'm modern enough to realize how chauvinist it sounds. But I'm honest enough to admit that I have the failing, along with every other swinging dick ever born.

I called her after two more beers and she still wasn't in. I calculated that it was close to midnight in Houston. I calculated I didn't want to calculate anymore.

I woke up at dawn, showered, and combed my hair. I checked out and turned down the offer of a free *USA Today* at the front desk. It was a cool dawn and the fields around the motel were soft with white fog. I drove to the McDonald's of the night before and got a coffee and an apple bran muffin. Charlene would have been proud of me.

I spent the next six hours or so going to Chicago. There is not much to say about Ohio and Indiana, at least as they look zooming along Interstate 80-90. It was one in the afternoon Central Time when I got lost on the South Side of Chicago and called Deke for help.

"Where you at now?" Deke said. There was a yawn in his voice.

I told him it was a liquor store at 747 East 47th Street.

"Shit, boy, you in the ghetto."

"I thought you lived down here."

"I do business down there, I live up here. Just stay inside and try not to look too white, I be right down."

Well, it isn't easy not looking white when that's what you are and everyone around you is noting the fact. The guy who ran the liquor store carried a pistol on his waist and that was as far as it went. Couple of drunks came in and took me for a policeman and asked me to arrest some woman across the street. Two kids wearing White Sox caps at an angle came in and ordered a bottle of Johnny Walker Black and told the guy with the pistol to put it "on account."

Then Deke came in.

Deke taught me the split-fingered fastball and a slider and how to play chin music with a batter crowding my zone. "Don't be 'fraid to knock him down — knock him out dead if need be and always stand your ground if he comes for you on the mound," Deke would say. He was right about everything. Including me being mean enough to be a good relief pitcher.

Relief pitcher is like a grunt in the marines. You never see him until you need him. Nobody asks a grunt how he killed someone on the battlefield, they just want to know he did it. The way no one wants to know how steaks come from steers. Deke taught me all that and it made me a survivor.

Deke was wearing a camel hair coat and a jewel in the lobe of his left ear. He came into that liquor store and there was instant respect all around.

"Hey, boy," Deke said. "What's a white boy like you doin' lost down here in the hood?" Playing with me.

"Catfish," I said for the first and last time.

"Hey, Irish Hillbilly. Come on outta here," Deke said, and he wrapped me up in a camel hair bear hug.

"That your car? With those Texas plates on it? Shit, you got more luck than brains."

"Yeah, George says I'm lucky, too," I said. We were on the sidewalk. The street is mean and shabby and looks bombed out. Reminds me some of the neighborhood around Yankee Stadium.

Deke said, "Well, you don't want to leave that car here, not if you want it back. You follow me."

I followed him across his city. Deke was born and raised in the housing projects, and somehow he got on. Played Triple A in Louisiana for two years, which is a story by itself, and then jumped to the Bigs with the White Sox. Got traded to the Yanks in a six-player swap and finished up there. Deke is Cooperstown, record for saves in a season, lifetime 2.59 ERA, a couple of other trophies of note. I'm just grateful he took notice of me when I came up. And took some pity on the strength of my fastball.

We parked in a lot next to an Italian restaurant somewhere near the Loop. Deke waited for me while I locked the car and joined him at the entrance.

Good food and good beer, and when I was beginning to feel full, I told him everything I promised George not to tell anyone. Deke just listened while he spooned his linguine, and when it was finished, he grunted. At the story and at the empty plate in front of him.

"You need money that bad?"

"I never met anyone could turn down $600,000 without at least wincing a little bit."

"What you think the other players gonna do when George brings in these wetbacks don' even speak English to knock down their wages? Huh? And what you think it's gonna mean to you?"

"Gonna mean I'll be eatin' on the road with the umpires," I said.

"Sheet. Umpires won't even have nothin' to do with you. Little owner's pet you turn into being," Deke said. "How you know no one else woulda picked up your contract?"

"Sid was shoppin' me all season, quiet-like, and no one was even sniffing in my direction. I supposed that's the reason Sid didn't return my calls."

"Then you negotiate your own contract for even less money than you made last year and for a lot more headaches. Man, these wetbacks ain't even gonna be your friend, knowin' you the Anglo reports to the owner."

"They ain't wetbacks, Deke."

"I know what they are," Deke said. He took a piece of Italian bread and tore it in half. He had a large diamond ring on his pinkie finger and gold chains around his neck. He got out of the Bigs in 1984 or '85; he was a man destined to do all right.

"The only friend you got in the world of baseball right now is George Bremenhaven," Deke Williams said. "That is a sad commentary on you, your character, and your future."

"I tried to call Charlene Cleaver last night from the motel room and she was plain out," I said.

Deke gave me the cold-eyed look. "You feelin' sorry for yourself, boy?"

"Semi," I admitted.

"You pulled that swamp over on yourself. No one made you do it," Deke said.

"It didn't look that bad at the time."

"How's it look now?"

"I could make a . . . well, public statement."

"From what you told me, the government be all over your sorry pink ass if you do that. Why you think George wants you to keep this under your hat? This is about the government, boy, and you don't fuck with the government. Ole George, man, he sleeps with Abe Lincoln. You know what the government do when they decide they wan' you? Check your IRS, check how often you fucked your mama, man, there ain't nothin' they can't do to you. You fucked, boy."

"I drove nine hundred miles to have you tell me that?"

"I woulda done it over the phone if you'd let me. No, wait. I ain't gonna talk to you over no phone no more till you out of this. Government, the first thing they do is tap your phone, sort of as natural as pissing first thing in the morning."

"What should I do?"

Deke thought about it. The Italian waiter asked him if he wanted anything else and he said something about Amaretto. I said I wanted another bottle of beer. I was full of food and still on edge, the way I get before a big night game. They ought to only play baseball in the daytime, the way the Cubs used to do. You eat too much before night games and it upsets you.

Deke said, "You go down to Texas, see your honeylamb, and don't get her involved in this thing. Just stay low for the winter, let George do what George is gonna do. Maybe the shit'll hit the fan for George and his friends in the government. Them Cubans down in Miami might burn the town down, they find out the government was making a deal with Fie-Del Castro."

I hadn't thought of that. There were Cubans in Miami, lots of them, and they made people like Pat Buchanan look soft on communism. If it came out that the government was doing a back-door deal to import Communist baseball players, not just to any team but to the God Bless America New York Yankees, well. . . .

"You're making me feel better, Deke."

"You can feel slightly better but not good enough to rooster strut," Deke said. "You just find yourself a hole in Houston — and I'm sure there are plenty — and you hide in it."

Deke paid with a platinum American Express card and we sashayed into the parking lot like two millionaires after a long lunch. I was even feeling sleepy, but that didn't last long. Deke gave the parking attendant ten bucks to keep a careful eye on my Buick with the Texas plates. And he took me on the town.

I've never had a bad time in Chicago except the night the White Sox took off on me and I gave up a grand slam and another homer before Sparky put me out of my misery. And that wasn't the whole night, just the working part of it.

Well, to make it short, I didn't have a bad time in Chicago again. It lasted until five in the morning at a blues joint on the South Side where Deke and several ladies at a round table tried to pretend I wasn't white. But I was and I fell asleep on them, and the next thing I know, I was in Deke's condo on the Gold Coast, sleeping it off in the spare bedroom. Deke was right about sleeping until early afternoon. It's the only sensible thing to do if you're going to stay up all night.

Deke made coffee and grits and runny eggs around two P.M. and told me what to do again, and I took a cab to my car in the parking lot. The car was still there and I gave the attendant another ten on top of Deke's ten, and I was out of Chicago just before the afternoon rush hour.

Went by the St. Louis Arch around sundown and kept traveling until the tiredness hit me again around Columbia, Missouri.

Charlene Cleaver answered her phone on the second ring. I was naked and warm from a shower and lying in a bed with a coin-operated vibrator that made the mattress wiggle.

"I tried to get you a couple of times last night," I said in a casual way.

"I was out," she said, just as casual.

"I figured either that or you can turn off the ringer on your phone."

"Why would I want to do that?"

"Well, that was just a joke," I said.

"You still in New Jersey?"

"Actually, Missouri. Be in Texas tomorrow."

"Really?"

That "really" was kind of cool, I thought. It had the tone that receptionists use when they are not paid a lot of money but have to deal with people while wearing high heels and makeup because the bosses want it that way. Sort of hostile and yet polite.

"You mad at something, Charlene?"

"Not angry at nothing. Figured you'd be sitting up in New York the rest of the winter," she said. She was explaining and complaining at the same time.

"Charlene. I just wanted to sign the contract."

"Says in the *Post* that your owner is dismantling the team. How come he isn't dismantling you, Ryan?"

"I dunno," I said.

"Says in the *Post* that some season ticket holders are withdrawing from buying seats next season because George Bremenhaven is getting rid of the best players."

"Well, he's doing that, all right."

There was another of those long-distance silences. Even though I know the phones are all wired with fiber optics and really don't hum on the lines anymore, I can still hear that old-fashioned long-distance hum when no one is speaking.

"But he's going to sign you."

"He signed me."

"You talk to Sid?"

There she went again with that Sid shit. "I can't get hold of him."

"So it's another year you're on the road."

"One more year."

"So you're coming down to Texas for the winter."

"That's the idea. Winter in New Jersey doesn't thrill me."

"Well, I guess we'll all see you when you get here."

"What's making you mad, Charlene?"

"Dogs get mad, people get angry."

"All right, angry then."

"Nothing," Charlene said.

"Charlene," I explained, "I had to get the ink on that contract before George changed his mind."

"Ryan Patrick, I think your friend George is going insane," Charlene said.

"He's been there for years. I told you that before. But money is money. And he ain't my friend, I only work there."

"And you got your money and now you'll have to sleep with it," she said.

When she's upset, her metaphors get sloppy. I said, "I talk to you four days ago and you had to cancel a dinner reservation at Tony's. You honestly blame me for sticking around New York for a couple of days to get assured of a job for next year?"

"Jack Wade offered you a job."

That was it. Or part of it. I just forgot about Jack Wade in all this. And Jack and Charlene went to college together, I think. Jack was married, but that rarely matters with car dealers. On the other hand, maybe it was something else besides Jack Wade.

"You didn't want me to sign again?"

"What does it ever matter what I want, Ryan?"

"We'd have that much more to open that restaurant," I said.

"Don't patronize me, Ryan," she said.

There is nothing more miserable than being in the middle of Missouri at night talking by phone to your woman who is seven hundred miles away and she's pissed at you. So I told her that.

"There you go, Ryan. Feeling sorry for yourself. Look around you, Ryan. The world is full of people who could use a little pity. You're a major league baseball player making more money for each game you're in than most people make in a year of working. You can feel sorry for them."

"Like Jack Wade," I said.

"Like him."

"Jack Wade can take care of hisself. Hey, Charlene, I did what you said, I put more money into Latin America."

"That's nice," she said. "You still got that Canadian steel?"

"I guess so, it hasn't come up in my thinking so I must still have it."

"I'd dump it if I had it," she said.

That's what I mean, she's always thinking on three tracks at once.

"Well, then I'll get rid of it."

"You do what you want, Ryan Patrick. You always have. No one can tell you nothing." Back to Track Number One, train now leaving.

"Not even poor li'l old Charlene Cleaver."

"Charlene don't ever need a man's pity," Charlene said, and that was it. She didn't slam the phone down, but she might as well have, it was that final. I knew if I called back now, I wouldn't get through. I think I saw where the conversation had been heading — right into a train wreck — but sometimes you hurry it along to get to the punch line anyway.

And when I finally fell asleep that night in Missouri, I dreamed of Charlene and Deke in the same dream with George. Sam was in the dream, too. They were all telling me what a sorry-ass dope I was and how every bad thing that was going to happen was my own fault. And some of the dream was in Spanish, which made me wake up sweating.

I didn't know — did not have a clue then — that Charlene was mad at me for reasons completely different from anything I imagined. It was just as well I didn't know, because I would have ended up driving all night just to be with her.

5

George dumped a bunch of players in the next ten days while the World Series was engrossing the rest of the country. Not a trade. A dump. Contracts were up and he just dumped them. The New York newspapers were hounding him, but George mostly let Miss Foster take care of the reporters. He was spotted in Chicago with his pal from the White Sox, but before anyone could get to him, he was down in Kansas City with another owner and pal, and so it went, day after day, with George slicing skin off his payroll with the subtlety of a hunter gutting deer.

I did not get a warm welcome in Houston from anybody. Got in about eight P.M. after a grueling drive on a bad, rainy day. I rented a studio at the Longhorn Arms and sent out my laundry and called Charlene. She didn't answer. I put on my cowboy boots and went down to Mickey's Place and drank some beer and tried to get in the mood of being back in Texas. Texas, if I had to explain it, is sly and full of itself. Sort of like China used to be, the center of the world. It can get on your nerves, but Texans don't mean nothing by it, it just goes with the spaces they live in. Being in Texas is wearing boots without feeling like you're wearing a costume on Halloween. The country music was about Budweiser and losing a good woman and Budweiser again. It made me sad for myself. I went to the pay phone and called Charlene. Still no answer. It was about midnight then and I decided I could either sleep in my car or try out my bed at the Longhorn Arms. I opted for the bed and slept till morning.

It was raining and dreary and it made my pitching arm ache. I drank some coffee and ate a bowl of chili at Ernie's Cafe, then I went by Jack Wade's store. "Store" is what the auto dealers call their showrooms when they're talking to each other. I tried to pick up those terms.

Jack was in because it was only eleven and Jack never went out to lunch before 11:20 A.M. He also never came back once he was gone to lunch unless he ran into someone at a bar who wanted desperately to buy a Honda right then and there.

Jack was about thirty-five, which was Charlene's age, and he was hefty and soft-looking, except for the eyes. Every owner in the world has the same eyes. Jack and George were born to be owners of men.

"Nice of you to come by," Jack said in his drawl, the one that is heard on commercials on cable all night long. He didn't hold out his hand while I settled my bones on a straight chair in his office. He just sat there, belly sprawled out in that squeaky swivel chair, going back and forth. On the walls, he had a picture of himself with former governor Anne Richards and another with present governor Jeb Bush. I wonder if he switched them around depending on whether he was selling a Republican or a yellow dog Democrat.

"I had me some bidness to clean up in New York," I said. I said "bidness" because Jack likes to think talking funny is a sign of sincerity. If he was from Georgia, you wouldn't have been able to understand a word he said because Georgia people are hanging in there with their accents, no matter how much television they watch. Texas does yawls and all, but every passing year, another kid loses his critters and druthers. We all are going to end up talking like they do in Omaha on the 800 telephone line.

"You all ready to start, Ry?"

"Well, Jack, that's it. I got me a contract for another year."

"Is that a fact? Seen in the *Chronicle* it was, that your crazy Jew boss in New York is gonna dismantle the team. How come is it he isn't dismantling you 'long with those others?"

"Not a Jew, Bremenhaven," I said. "German."

"Same difference," said Jack Wade. "Why is that? I mean, you getting a new contract? I thought you thought you was at the end of the trail, pardner."

"Turns out I wasn't," I said. I might owe explanations to Charlene, but I'd be goddamned if I would owe one to Jack Wade.

"Well." He cleared his throat. "Just as well, pardner. Just as well. I don't think I could've used you now."

That went through me like a butcher knife in a watermelon. I said, "Why's that?"

"I didn't know about your tax problem," Jack said, leaning back in his swivel chair.

"I got no tax problem."

"Is that right?"

"That's right."

"You got no tax problem."

"Why you think I got a tax problem?"

"Why I think that is that when the tax man come by a day ago and sat down with me and we close the door, the Yankee son of a bitch I thought was looking me over was looking you over. He wanted to know what I paid you last winter both over and under the counter and that the gummint appreciated my cooperation. Then he tol' me not to tell no one, just keep it under my hat."

"Like you're doing," I said.

"Well, shit, it's a free country. Besides, he shook me up so much I was over at Ernie's before noon and Ernie says that when the gummint comes lookin' for someone, you best not have nothin' to do with that someone. And besides, you never did call me from New York City. I don't know what you been doin' up there. And then I seen Charlene on Post Street and tol' her about the gummint and you and your tax trouble and she just buttoned up like she was frozen and walked away. I offered to buy her a drink for old times."

"And she didn't take it."

"Not that I recall," Jack said. It was as certain as Jack ever is about what happens in late afternoon, let alone at night.

"Well, Jack, I'll tell you one thing. I ain't got no tax problem with the gummint."

"Let me give you a word of advice, Ryan. If the gummint says you got a tax problem with them, you got a problem."

"I ain't."

"I don't care," Jack said. "I just don't want to get involved in it. I got a bidness to run and I can't have a baseball player as my P.R. man who is wanted for fraud or something by the U.S. gummint. It might attract a certain clientele but it would drive just as many away."

When I left Jack, I didn't even say good-bye. I was plain mad — angry — and confused, and just a little bit thinking about Deke Williams telling me that the government got me by the balls now with that confidential thing I signed for George and how he wasn't going to call me on the telephone anymore for fear it might be tapped.

I drove out to Rice University Hospital, which is a big complex where they do routine miracles of healing and research. I admire it greatly and more so since Charlene showed me around one day to the good things being done there. Charlene was due to be working. I parked in the visitors' lot and walked three or four miles through the complex to the building where Charlene hung out.

I saw her when I stepped off the elevator.

It's a special, even warm kind of thing to spy on someone you are crazy for when they don't know you're there. She was writing something down and biting her lip the way she does sometimes and I just wanted to give her a kiss long enough to last till morning.

"Charlene," I said instead.

She looked up at me and said nothing for a moment. Then she put down her pen and got up. She was wearing brown slacks and a brown sort of blouse with pleats and her black hair was tied back with a red piece of rope or yarn. She has incredible skin, which I won't go into describing because I can't. I can say her eyes are gray and they go from the edge of blue to the edge of an Arctic kind of ocean, depending on what she's thinking about. Her eyes were about medium at this moment.

She stepped from behind her desk and came around to me, but she didn't give me a hug, which I expected her to do. "Come on, Ryan," she said.

She led me to a cafeteria at the end of the hall where we got coffee and carried it to an empty table. We sat down at almost the same time. I told her she looked beautiful. It had been five weeks since I last saw her.

"When did you get in?"

I told her, and told her about going to see Jack Wade, but I didn't tell her about Jack Wade and the tax man. And I didn't tell her about Deke Williams and his conspiracy theory of government.

"What are you going to do?"

"I guess get a job for the winter," I said.

"But not with Jack."

"He rethought the whole thing and figured he couldn't use me right now," I said, making it light and easy. Telling the truth is just frying eggs in bacon grease. Lying is making an omelette. "No hard feelings. I figure maybe I can get back on with Bruce Construction, if they're doing anything."

"Back to the hammer and saw."

"Honest work," I said.

"It's that," she said. There was trouble in her gray eyes still. She wasn't exactly here at the table with me, she was somewhere out of the hospital, I figured.

"Charlene, I been honest with you," I lied. "I really miss you and I'm glad to be back in Houston but I got to know if you got someone else on the line now and if I'm a thing of your past."

"Why would you say that?"

"Because I been trying to reach you and you're always out."

"You think I should hang around a telephone on the chance you might take time out from your busy social life and call?"

"What has gotten into you, Charlene? Five weeks ago, we was lovey and dovey. A week ago when I called telling you I was staying in New York a couple of days, we were still cooing and doing each other. Now, the last couple of nights, I been on the road coming home, it's all changed."

"Maybe it all changed a while ago," Charlene said. "Maybe you were just stringing me along. And then you tell me you're rehired by the team just when everyone else is getting fired."

"What's got into your head?"

"Miss Roxanne Devon," she said. Just like that. As if it meant anything to me.

"Who?"

"Come off it," Charlene said.

"I never heard of such a person in my life," I said.

"Roxanne Devon is not a common name."

"Not to me. It would of stood out if I had met anyone with a name like that."

"She lives in New Jersey and she wrote me. I got the letter Tuesday and she was telling me about you and her and how she was now shocked to find out that you had a woman on the side in Houston. It was some letter," Charlene said. She said it in an even voice with only a little sarcasm thrown in.

"You believe that?"

"What should I believe? What's convenient for you, Ryan?"

"Charlene, I have had girlfriends and girlfriends, which is only natural because I am thirty-eight years old and of the heterosexual persuasion but you are it and you have been it for the year we've known each other. There ain't no Roxanne or Tanya or Mary or Janie or anyone else and I resent your thinking there would be," I said.

"Then why would this person out of the blue send me a letter?"

All I could think of was Deke and George and the tax man and that terrible moment when I groveled for George in his office and agreed to stay on the Yankees one more year as his official Spanish interpreter.

I knew this was all tied in somehow, but I couldn't explain it. Not now, not to Charlene. She'd just get caught up in the same mess, wouldn't she?

"Charlene, you try to call this Roxanne woman up?"

Charlene stared at me for a moment and then shook her head. "What could I say to her?"

"There ain't no Roxanne," I said.

"What if there is?"

That was a thought. What if there was? I mean, how clever was whoever was doing this for whatever reason?

Then I thought of George. And the people in the White House, including the ghost of Abe Lincoln. No. They weren't that smart, this was just preliminary bullying, like Booker did on that playground when I was in fifth grade. On the other hand, Booker did end up beating the shit out of me.

I took her to the pay telephone in one of the lounges and we placed a long distance call to the information operator in Brunswick, New Jersey, which is where Miss Roxanne Devon was supposed to live. We tried an "R. Devon" and then any kind of Devon with initials. The operator said there was no such listing and Charlene replaced the phone and looked at me.

I grinned at her. "Thank God we can still believe in the phone company."

6

Now we're going to have to switch around in this story for it to make any sense about the way it turned out in the end. Raul Guevara told me all this much later, but at the time I was in Houston, trying to fix things up with Charlene, and George was running a fire sale on the team, Raul was having his own adventures.

I can tell you for a fact that Havana is not the way I expected it to be, not when I finally saw it. It had the old American cars and it had a lot of crummy-looking buildings, but it had something else, something about the people. They still have style, Raul explained. Even if they wear rags, they wear them with style. He was right there.

Raul said about this time — we are talking about at the end of the World Series in late October — he was playing ball.

The way Raul explained it later, I got the picture. Playing ball in Cuba is like waltzing on a battlefield with the orchestra going on despite all the gunfire. Not that there's gunfire in Havana. It's just so fucking poor is all, yet the Cubans got this thing about baseball — it just goes on and on and it's glamour, it's probably like the way it was in the 1930s here when Babe Ruth and Lou Gehrig were doing their dances at Yankee Stadium and the country was outside the walls, selling apples on street corners to itself.

Raul. I can see him on that hot, humid Cuban night with the sweat soaking his uniform and that limber-easy swing of his. Not a big dude, don't have muscles on muscles. Just all the muscles he needs. And the eye. He sees a thing on the ball and he don't have to wait to communicate it to his arms or wrists or his back, with the way his back rears back and slouches into a reaching swing.

On this night, he hit two home runs and drove in four runs. I could even hear the bat, the way he described it to me. Ever notice how some ball players start out trotting toward first base even before the ball is halfway out of the park because they know it's gone? It's because of the sound and

♦ 42 ♦

the feel of the bat on the ball. You hit the ball square and it just implodes on you, on the bat, just takes the wind out of itself and goes thump or something. I don't have that swing — thank God I'm a pitcher — but I seen it in plenty of others. Raul said he was hitting that way that night and his team won and they were all falling over each other on the way out of the dugout to the lockers. He was feeling good when he got back to the clubhouse to strip off his uniform and take a shower.

The good feeling did not last as long as it should have. Raoul said there were two men waiting in the clubhouse and they said he was going to go with them after his shower.

They had cards that said it didn't matter what their names were, they were from government house.

What a miserable shower that must have been, with two goons waiting for you, both of them still wearing sunglasses even though it was nearly midnight.

After his shower, he shaved slowly and then put on his clean clothes. He wore his clothes with style, even though he was a poor kid from the outback. Havana had taught him style in the two years he was playing there. Raul has big square shoulders and a slight build and sort of olive drab eyes. He told the men he was ready, and he wondered what he was ready for.

They all crammed into an East German Trabant, which is a two-cycle car like a motorcycle and is mostly glued together with plastic panels. It makes a VW Beetle look like a Cadillac. Old Fidel, he sure got shit for his bargain with the devil — you'd think for a smart guy he would've at least looked at the kind of cars they would end up sending him for being a Communist. Well, they rattled through Havana that night, over to one of the few buildings with lights on.

Let me tell you, it is scary in a city at night with no lights on in the buildings. You wonder where the bad people are. And for all I know, the bad people wonder where you are.

All the while, Raul kept asking the goons what was going on and they kept saying nothing. *Nada.*

When they got to the government house, the men untangled themselves from the Trabant like three clowns getting out of the car in the center ring and went up the steps. Raul said he had a charley horse from the way he had to sit in back and I believed it, having ridden in a Trabant since then and being two inches shorter than Raul.

When they got inside, they went up another set of marble steps to a landing and down a hall to a big wooden door, the kind of door that is built that big just to intimidate the shit out of you. I mean, nobody needs a door that big for anything. Raul said he was intimidated, but he carries himself with such natural dignity for someone only twenty-three years old that I doubt it showed at the time.

They made him wait alone in an office for a long time. He studied the office while he waited. There was a photo of Fidel on one wall and another of Che and one of Fidel cutting sugar cane with the peasantry.

Then they came for him around one in the morning and took him down another hall to a bigger room.

He sat down in a bigger chair with ornate arms and red cushions. He asked for a glass of water and the goons ignored him.

About two in the morning, Raul looked up and there was Fidel himself sweeping into the room with a small entourage of toadies.

Raul had never seen him up close, just at the May Day rally and once when he came out to the park to throw out the first ball, but Fidel had been in and out so fast that it didn't count. Now he was in the same room with Raul, and Raul said Fidel lit it up until it hurt his eyes, like all the lights going on in a dark bar at last call. (Raul didn't say nothing about last call or a dark bar, but I imagined it my own way.) Raul stood up by instinct and the president came around a desk and gave him a big bear hug, chattering away as he did it.

Castro has a tenor voice sort of roughened by the cigars he smoked for a long time. Raul recalled that Castro said:

— Hey, big man, what a game tonight, I saw your first homer before I had to leave, big man. You are sweet, Raul, you swing like Ted Williams could swing in his prime. What do you think of that?

— Many thanks, Mr. President (Raul said). I was lucky tonight.

— Was lucky? You ARE lucky, Raul, this is your lucky night, son. Talk about luck, you are the luckiest man in Havana tonight and I am so happy for you.

— Why? What has happened?

— Hey, you, let me tell the story and you just listen, okay? You know what has happened? I am always looking out for people like you, great people rising up in Cuba, the flowers of the revolution now bearing fruit.

Raul said at this point he wasn't following the president very well, but that Castro had removed his hands and arms from the bear hug and was letting Raul stand alone.

— Raul, little Raul, we are going to show the world now what they have been missing for thirty years while the Americans followed their pig-headed plan to destroy Cuba. Well, we're not destroyed, we're just catching our second wind, true, Raul?

— Yes, it's true (Raul said).

— Time now to show the world on the stage of the world what we are made of, what our young men can do when the challenge is thrown down in a fair and square way.

— Yes.

— Do you know what is the stage of the world, do you, little Raul? You are so young, you were not even born then, when I went on the stage of the world. Do you know where it is?

— No, Mr. President, I do not know.

— Of course not. You are a humble child of humble farming people and only your great talent and determination have worked to give you the chance to go on the world stage which I, your president, have arranged for you because my life is devoted to the flower of the revolution, to all the flowers.

Raul said he waited while this went on for a while. Then Castro interrupted himself to ask a question.

— So you don't know where the world's stage is?

— No, Mr. President.

— Then I will tell you.

— Yes, excellency.

— No, no, not excellency, that is for the bourgeoisie. President. The stage is New York City.

— What?

— New York City.

— I've heard of it. Yes. I know what you mean. New York. A city.

— Well, thank God for that, it would be no good to go some place you have never heard of it, would it?

Raul said Castro laughed then, and I can imagine it, but Raul said he was too nervous to do anything but just stand there.

— So (Castro said) what do you say?

— About what, Mr. President?

Castro frowned.

— About what I have proposed.

— What have you proposed, Mr. President?

— Aren't you listening, you cloth-eared bumpkin?

— I'm listening, Excellency. I'm just confused.

— You are going to be a Yankee.

Raul said he thought he would pass out. Someone had spoken lies against him and this was a cruel sort of joke, they were going to send him to prison, maybe for years. He thought of his beloved fiancée Maria Velasquez then and of a thousand other things and he wondered if he would be allowed to play baseball in prison.

— No, no, President, I am not a Yankee . . .

— I did not say that, bumpkin, little Raul, I said you were going to be. You are going to be a New York Yankee. You and a brave, handpicked contingent from Cuba will go to North America and show the gringos that we have the finest ball players in all the world. You are going to lead Cuba to glory as a Yankee, Raul. You are going to help Cuba win the World Series.

— As a Yankee?

— That's temporary. In time, when Havana is admitted to the major leagues, we will be able to stay home and invite the world to us to see our brave young men battle the enemies. (He paused.) But for now, a small step, you will become a Yankee.

— I don't want to go to New York. To be a Yankee. I want to be here.

Raul said Castro frowned for a moment and then said:

— I know, I know. Defectors. Traitors to the Revolution. We have too many of them, but I don't worry about you. Or the others. When we played in that disgusting lick-spittle Costa Rica, the gymnasts defected and that discus thrower. Pah. Not one of my baseball players would betray the Revolution, even though the worms of Costa Rica taunted them to betrayal. I am not concerned, my little one, not at all. You will be a Cubano in New York and you will show New York what Cuba's greatness really is.

And that is the way it started rolling down the hill. I take Raul's word for it because he was there and no one says it wasn't true, so I suppose it was. Besides, when Raul talked about it, it was straightforward like frying eggs, and everyone knows that lies are made like omelettes.

7

The Series finally ended on television. Reception was lousy because I didn't have cable. There was snow on the TV and there was snow in the air up north. Counting spring training and all, baseball just goes on too long, like a bore at a party who thinks he's Chevy Chase or something. I think baseball should end itself before it gets too cold to play, but I guess I'm just a purist.

I settled into life in Houston, a life of leisure as it turned out, because the construction business didn't need any bodies that winter. I sort of hung out during the day when Charlene Cleaver was working over at Rice. We went out a lot. I got her that dinner at Tony's more than once. We ate our way across Houston and there were a lot of salads in the mix because I was on my best behavior. Saturdays, we drove half across Texas sometimes to see a football game or do the same thing down into Louisiana, which is closer. Looking back on me with Charlene, I'd have to say I was a perfect gentleman.

That's not exactly true. Charlene and I are lovers, and we did the things you do when you're lovers. She didn't much like my place and I didn't blame her because the Longhorn Arms is strictly utilitarian living. The bed is too soft, the television doesn't have a remote, and you eat off the credenza if you're eating in your room. They let you have an automatic coffee maker and there's a hotplate and an icebox. I had beer in the icebox, a can of Colombian coffee, a jar of peanut butter, and a loaf of bread. I also bought a toaster to make the bread edible with the peanut butter, but I couldn't use the toaster and the coffee maker at the same time, which made breakfast a matter of timing.

Making love to Charlene in her place was like being on vacation. First of all, she's got a nice apartment. And then, anyplace with Charlene naked is like being on the best vacation you ever had in your life. She'd do this thing of strutting around stark raving naked but doing domestic things like poaching some eggs and it just about drove me crazy. Part of the game was that I was supposed to be ignoring the fact that she was naked and so I would just sit there in my Jockeys and say things like "Pass the salt" and she'd lean over the table and let her lovely breasts rest there a moment while she reached for the salt and passed it. Then she'd say, "Pepper?" and that was the end of eating and we'd both be giggling at how bad we were.

I guess I'm saying it was like old times with Charlene, and that's better than sunshine. But it wasn't, too. There was still that darned secret agreement with George that stuck in my throat everytime I thought to tell her. I didn't want her to get involved in this, but it was there, between us, and I think Charlene knew it, too.

It wasn't until the end of November that I told Charlene. It was just after Thanksgiving. She went to her mama's for Thanksgiving and didn't ask me to come along. Charlene is cautious some about men because she's had a few bad ones. When she got that phony letter from Miss Roxanne Devon of Brunswick, New Jersey, she just figured I was another one, so I suppose there was a certain amount of suspicion in her about me all that winter. I understood it, but it didn't make it any easier.

I spent Thanksgiving Day in Ernie's Cafe eating sliced turkey, mashed potatoes and gravy, and string beans. And a salad, which shows I was thinking about Charlene.

She came back on Friday because she had been thinking about me. We were lovers again, and it was so wonderful, it hurt. It's the style now to talk about all those intimate things, but I don't do that, never have. The only thing that's fair game is what any fool on the street can plainly see. Not a man in East Texas wouldn't give up his comfort for a night with Charlene, and that's so evidently the fact that it's hardly worth repeating.

I don't know what it was, the making love or just the warm and runny of being with Charlene, but I told her about Cuba around midnight or one in the morning when we were lounging around in various states of undress. I recall I was wearing her pink bathrobe with the frills on it and not feeling the least bit foolish, and she was wearing my polo shirt and nothing else. We were drinking the last of a fine bottle of Merlot, sitting at her kitchen table.

"You look cute in that robe," Charlene said.

"Hell, I'll go out and buy a dozen of them in different colors," I said.

"No. Pink is your color, definitely."

It was that kind of goofy, giggly talk that led up to it. I was getting in deep with Charlene, I thought briefly, the way you think it might be better to turn back instead of trying to swim all the way across the lake. Then you swim on. If we didn't have this instinct to risk our hides, we'd never get anywhere. And besides, I'd been buttoned up too long.

I told her all about the George plan, the thing with the Cubans. Of course, at this time I didn't know about Raul and Castro or any of that, because that came later.

When I was finished, Charlene just sat there the longest time. Just sat with her fingers on the stem of her wine glass, kind of twirling the wine glass around.

Then she laughed.

Damn. I was expecting anything except that.

Maybe it was because I was wearing her pink fluffy robe, but I could see the humor in it while she kept laughing and tears started in her gray eyes.

I cracked a smile and then let out a couple of chuckles and then it was all I could do not to laugh too, so I did.

When we finished our giggles, we looked at each other and she grabbed my hand.

"Poor old Ryan Patrick Shawn. Now you're swimming with the sharks," she said.

"Well, I been working for old George a while, I think I can handle myself."

"George Bremenhaven is in deep trouble," she said.

"Well, more power to him. I hope the ship goes down. All I know is, I got a contract."

"That's why you got a contract, then," she said, talking to herself. "He gives away his best players and the other owners scarf them up at a discount and that's why they give the go-ahead for George to follow through on his crazy scheme. It makes sense. They benefit and they figure George ends up holding the bag for them."

"I don't get that at all," I said, resenting not getting what she was saying.

"He undermines the salary structure, league arbitration, everything. He tilts the game by freeing up his old cast of characters, 'cept for you of course."

"Well, it's a secret."

"And you weren't supposed to tell me what you told me."

"Well, I trust you. I waited this long 'cause I didn't want any trouble for you."

"And this fellow, Deke Williams in Chicago?"

"Deke ain't gonna say nothin' to no one. He taught me all I know."

"He taught you about that? The thing in the bedroom?"

"No, I learned that on my own."

"Your mouth is so sweet. I think you get turned on wearing my bathrobe."

"I do when you're wearing my shirt."

She stared at me, sort of smiling but not smiling at the same time.

"You don't suppose there's something wrong with us?"

"There's always something wrong with everyone, that's normal. What ain't normal are the people pointing out there's something wrong with you."

We were quiet then for a while, pondering old Ryan's philosophical point. I often think I should have been a philosopher, if you could find anyone who would pay me for it. Took a course or two in philosophy at Arizona State. I liked the existentialists best, because they had the best scam: None of it means nothing except that it just is, so what's the next question?

"George used you as a goat twice," Charlene said, shaking her head, suddenly turned serious.

"I don't understand that anymore than I understood George when he asked me the first time if I spoke Spanish."

"First, you're the Judas goat, leading all those little lambs from Cuba into his slaughterhouse. Then, if anything goes wrong, you're the scape-goat. He'll figure out a way to get everyone's hatred directed at you."

"Why would anyone hate me?"

"Teacher's pet."

"Ah, I can handle that. I been called worse things in my life."

"Traitor. To your fellow ball players."

"I have been thinking on that. But a relief pitcher ain't got a lot of friends to start with, so I can handle it as long as they keep putting TV sets in the hotel rooms on road trips."

"And the Cubans? They aren't going to trust you, Ryan."

"I wouldn't, either. But I'm not going to betray them to George, you know. Besides, what are they gonna do? Invade New York? March on the Pentagon? Smuggle in cigars? Canadians do that already."

"I wonder," Charlene said. "I've wondered a lot since I got that letter from Miss Roxanne Devon."

"That was a phony letter, we proved it with the phone company."

"I know it's a phony now. From what you just told me. You see? This was all George Bremenhaven, sending me that letter. He doesn't want to see you get attached to anyone or anything to queer his deal. And you're attached to me."

That's when I thought of Jack Wade and the IRS man. So I told Charlene and she just shook her head.

"Poor old Ryan. You're already in the slops up to your knees and you're just beginning to realize it."

"I realize a lot of things," I said. That was pure defense and we both knew it. Charlene said nothing, waiting for me to collect myself. Realize a lot of things? I didn't. Not a damned thing until then. "I got a mind to fly to New York and bust George in the face."

She stared at me. The eyes were cool, the way they'd look at someone ordering a Big Mac.

"Do it, then," she said quietly.

"I just might."

"You won't."

"Why won't I? I just might."

"Ryan. You're gonna do what George wants you to do."

It was hopelessly true and Charlene was too smart not to see it.

"Charlene. He owns the team. They're all that way, the owners. And we're the same way. This ain't sandlot, we're playing for big bucks. We all talk about respect, but what we're talking when we say it is about getting a sweeter contract than some other mope on the team. We got a union, but it basically is every man for himself. The best thing the union ever had going for it was the collective dumbness of the owners. Take arbitration, that's a hoot in itself. Owners fucked themselves up good on that one. So George is dumb and selfish. For $625,000, I'll be dumb and selfish one more year."

"Then what? You'll never get a job in baseball again."

I hadn't thought of that at all. It showed I was right about the dumb part. But Charlene was dead on — if things turned out sour, I'd be the goat and I couldn't get a job scouting class A ball.

Well, who said I would have anyway?

That question comes from the Resentful Ryan when he gets up against it. It's a cousin to Self-Pitying Ryan. What did I need baseball for?

Which got back to why I signed for another year under George's terms. I could say it was the money, and it was, but it was something else. I can't explain the Bigs from the inside out because it is a parade like no other parade you ever seen, and you're in the center of it. You go into Yankee Stadium and, man oh man, there are 60,000 people who actually paid to come out and see you, who sit there eating hot dogs to watch you scratch your nuts or spit or warm up in the bull pen. Not that I think I'm the center of attention; I'm just part of the center of the parade. Sometimes, after a game, you can't get down at all. You drink beer and just sit there in your sweaty old suit and just think about it, about winning or losing, about the high of it or the low of it, depending. It is an addiction that you know is going to be cured when you're too old to play, and then you hope to carry it on by doing something else in the game. That's why you see those old farts coming around the clubhouse before a game with their golf shirts on and their Florida tans and gray hair and crinkled eyes; they just want to be part of it again for a moment, like smoking a joint again when you used to smoke one every day.

"Shit, I wasn't coaching material anyway. I'll go out like Catfish, open me a restaurant, learn the trade."

"Catfish?"

"Deke Williams," I explained. Then I explained Catfish to her and that made her smile a little, even though her eyes were sad.

"I bet he doesn't serve healthy food," she said.

"Not a lick of it, except for greens. Although I thought catfish was supposed to be good for you."

"Not fried catfish."

"Hmmph," I said.

"Not ribs."

"Well, it tastes good. I ate a salad at Ernie's Cafe yesterday with the traditional Thanksgiving dinner of sliced turkey in gravy with mashed potatoes and string beans."

"Poor baby. I should have brought you home to Mama, but I wasn't sure about you, even yesterday. I was just missing you so much that I said, 'Charlene, go ahead, make a fool of yourself for this man.'"

"Because you still believed that phony letter."

"And because you were acting goofy. I mean, you didn't want to talk about Jack Wade and not taking the job selling cars and, I don't know, you were just moping like a milk cow after milking's done."

"Charlene, I was the way you say I was back then because I didn't want to get you involved in the mess I been making for myself."

"I believe you."

It was like she had said she loved me. Exactly like that. Later, when we were finally getting to sleep after another round in bed, I thought that I had got that part of it right anyway.

8

You can imagine how discombobulated Raul was that winter, playing ball and thinking of going to New York City. He got an old guide-book to New York in the central library in Havana and he went over it with a fine-tooth comb. The book was about thirty-five years out of date and didn't bear a lot of resemblance to New York as she is now — I mean, there was something about the "wonderful, safe, efficient" subway system, which was a hoot by itself — and about the Empire State being the tallest building in the world and about the football Giants playing in the Polo Grounds. Man.

But it was all that Raul had to go on. You see, he hadn't ever set foot off Cuba except for those inter-American games in Costa Rica, and he was homesick for it without even leaving it.

One of the things that was impressed upon him by old Fidel was he could say nothing — nothing — to anyone about this before it happened and was announced by the Supreme Leader.

So he couldn't tell Maria.

Maria Elena Velasquez was a daughter of the middle class in Cuba, which is supposed to be about having no classes in their society. She had a good education and, despite everything, she had fallen in love with a ball player like Raul. Her father was a doctor and her mother was a university teacher, and though her father liked baseball, he didn't like it that much.

Raul, I have to explain, is a sweet and shy boy who is very polite. He's light in the body and his skin is sort of translucent brown, if you can follow that. He has stunning olive-drab eyes and a power swing that is surprising coming out of that light body. He put on a few pounds in New York eating unhealthy food, but he was never going to be a Babe Ruth or Frank Thomas in bulk.

The polite part of him got him inside the Velasquez household, finally.

He was deferential to both the Señor and the Señora, and they could not deny his charm. Or his obvious love for Maria. They just wanted to make sure that the love was held this side of respect until something legal came along. I don't blame them. I'd feel the same way if I had a daughter. I know it's a double standard in light of my relationship with Charlene — what would her mama say? — but that's the way the world works, on double standards. It's the only thing we can rely on.

The secret Raul carried around with him that winter affected his play, and he was only hitting .387 by the end of the season. Everyone noticed it, including El Supremo, but he let it pass because the big announcement was due any day now. The winter meetings of the major leagues were being held in Los Angeles and it was there that George Bremenhaven sort of stunned the sporting world. But more about this part later.

The secret weighed on him the way it had weighed on me. Maybe more. But I was thirty-eight years old and I just dropped the weight on others, including Charlene Cleaver and Deke Williams. Raul was twenty-three and Cuba is scarier than it is in America, especially when your leader tells you to keep something secret and he's got a prison system to back it up, not to mention firing squads and whatever else they have down there.

Maria Elena Velasquez was troubled by Raul's behavior that winter and by him hitting only .387, because she was a big baseball fan. She went to every game she could.

It was how they met. After a game one night, in a Havana cafe that stayed open late, she and her father had gone to the game together and they were eating one of those midnight suppers when Raul and a couple of his teammates came in to do the same. Her father wanted Raul's autograph but he asked for it in the usual way of grown men. He pretended it was for his daughter.

Raul took one look at the daughter at the far table and fell in love. He told me that and I believe him. When you're an instinctive great hitter like Raul, you learn to trust your instincts. Why shouldn't people fall in love at first sight anyway?

So Raul went to the table and personally handed her the autograph, and the father, Señor Doctor Alejandro Velasquez, politely asked him to join them, figuring he wouldn't.

He did.

— Señorita (Raul began) I am so sorry I can only offer you my name on a piece of paper. It is a worthless gift and I am ashamed to . . .

— No more flowery words (Maria interrupted). The gift is kind.

She patted the back of his hand then, something old man Velasquez did not like to see. Maria Elena had great presence in the company of men, even with her father.

— Then the next time I see you (Raul said), I'll bring a garden of bougainvillea instead of flowery words.

— Be careful of the thorns (she said).

— I would be happy to be scratched all over by thorns. The beauty of the bougainvillea is worth a little pain. All beauty is.

Well, it went on and on like this right from the start and I can't remember all that Raul told me they said because a lot of it sounds too fantastic for translation, and it probably is. It probably isn't all true, either. When you think you've been really eloquent, you probably were just drunk. I've found that true in my case anyway.

They talked and talked over cups of coffee and bottles of beer. Like any ball player who works at the game, Raul could drink beer after a game until the cows come home and not be affected by it. Some hydrate with ice water, but I like flavored ice water myself. So does Raul.

They talked about Raul's life as a boy on a *finca* in the countryside. That means farm. He was an unremarkable child, one of six, except for this baseball thing. Fortunately, it could be spotted because Cuba is a country full of baseball scouts, the way everyone in New York is an architecture critic.

Maria Elena was just beautiful and was just twenty-one. She had a long, thin nose set just right in her face and those full lips and a generous cast to her brown eyes. She wore glasses, too, which showed she was smart. Charlene wears glasses, too, but only to read. She had a sense of humor. She told jokes and listened to them. She was a captivating speaker. She she she. Raul could not praise her enough to me later, to explain all the things he ended up doing.

The old man, the doctor, was getting pretty tired of this boy by the end of the evening, but he couldn't seem to cut his way through the youngsters' mutual admiration society. He said he had an operation in the morning, and that was supposed to be the end of it.

It had just started.

It took about six months for Maria Elena's parents to recognize the facts of life and go into phase two, a strategic retreat that involved leaving behind booby traps for the advancing trooper. Nothing seemed to work.

Polite Raul showed up for dinner Sunday nights at the Velasquez house.

He didn't really know about knives and forks in their proper order, but he wasn't a slob, and even Mrs. Velasquez gave him a pass on table etiquette. Another dud booby trap.

Polite Raul took Miss Maria Elena by the hand and did an elegant promenade on non-baseball evenings in Havana before the lights began shutting down. There is passion in the air in Havana, I have to give it that, and you can feel it even if you are an Anglo.

But that winter before the announcement of George and Fidel's revolution was a bad one for the young lovers. It strained them so severely that the Señor Doctor and his wife saw hope that the whole thing would self-destruct and that they wouldn't have to worry about their dud booby traps.

And the romance might have ended. But it turned out it lasted long enough — until the winter meetings of major league baseball were held, up in cloudy Los Angeles. I can tell you that after the meetings and after George and after Fidel and after everyone else in the world let the beans out of the bag, it was hopeless from the standpoint of being Maria's parents. Nothing would stop Raul and Maria then.

9

"Before I throw this open to questions, I have an announcement to make," George Bremenhaven said on that gray L.A. morning.

I can tell you what the weather was because I was there. George asked me to come. Ordered. All of this at one in the morning, the usual hour for a George Bremenhaven phone call. The man has the social life of wallpaper. I stumbled around my tongue and told him I didn't want to go to Los Angeles even to see Michelle Pfeiffer and he made it clear I couldn't refuse. Charlene was right. I was already in his web, which he had just barely started spinning. But I was stuck.

All right. I went to L.A. for two reasons. One was that George popped for the room and air fare. The other was that I was curious about what was going to happen to Dr. Johnson next. Boswell needs eyewitness facts, not watching everything on C-Span.

No, the third reason was that I still had it half in mind to bam George for setting me up. Charlene had got under my skin with what she'd said about me, about George making me the scapegoat and the Judas goat, and I thought if I saw George, it might just remind me to pop him in the chops.

I didn't, of course. George, if he cared, probably knew that.

Another thing I have to explain about George is that he's a Republican and the guys in the White House were Democrats. I figured that out by myself before I ever went to L.A. He was a patsy for them in just the way I was a patsy for George.

(I picked up that "patsy" from old movies, not that they talk that way anymore in New York City. Even the cab drivers in New York ain't colorful, unless you consider scary colorful. They're all foreigners anyway; they only speak in foreign, so maybe if I understood foreign, they'd be colorful. You go down Broadway, you don't see guys and dolls and people who talk like that. You see colored guys selling junk jewelry on the sidewalk and towel-heads running delis. Where's the color in that? The whole country is bent on speaking like they speak in Omaha. I read one time that all the 800-numbers are in Omaha because Omaha people are smart and speak clear English, which means no accent when they answer the phone, so there's nothing to offend anyone from any part of the country. Take Johnny Carson, he's from Nebraska, but if I were to ask you where he was from, you'd have a hard time remembering because he doesn't sound like he's from any place at all. Who would have thought it came down to talking like Omaha?)

That tangent comes from thinking about George and everything George puts everyone through. It makes you crazy.

To get back to it: George made me have dinner with him that night in the hotel and the closest I came to punching him was telling him about the letter from Miss Roxanne Devon to Charlene Cleaver and about the IRS man coming around Jack Wade at the dealership.

"I don't know anything about that shit," George said, eating a very unhealthy charbroiled steak. He stabbed a piece of the steak and made it disappear. While he was chewing, I said very calmly:

"You're full of shit, George. You're just the kind of evil son of a bitch who would do something like that. Like this kid I knew, pulled the wings off butterflies. To see what they would do when they couldn't fly anymore."

"You are not a butterfly, Ryan. You're an employee."

"Why'd you want to mess me up with Charlene?"

"Why would I want to do that? And what about this Roxanne Devon, you fucking her?"

"There ain't no Roxanne Devon, which you know anyway. And where would you get a name like that?"

"I had an aunt named Roxanne once." He tried to look wistful then, like one of those kids drawn on eating plates that get sold to collectors for anything but eating. "She's dead. I always liked that name," George said, chomping another piece of steak.

"Why Jack Wade?"

"Who?"

"George, I know you did it."

"Prove it."

"It's a federal offense to pretend to be a federal officer . . . I think."

"Is it really?"

"George, you have a reputation for cavorting with unsavory people. I mean, besides your fellow owners."

"That's not true," he said. He was getting whiter in the face and he was chewing harder, which means I was getting to him. I relaxed a little and turned on a smile.

"So you were afraid I would go back to Houston and stay there and tell you the hell with the contract."

"I wasn't afraid, Ryan. You're too in love with baseball and money to do something like that. Besides, you'd be lousy selling cars, believe me."

"How would you know?"

"I wouldn't buy a car from you."

"I wouldn't sell you one."

"On principle, right?"

"Something like that."

"Ryan, you don't have any principles. Look, you're here, eating my food, drinking my wine. A man of principle wouldn't do that."

"You're drinking a martini and I'm not eating steak."

"Same thing."

"George, why'd you invite me here?"

"Why do you think?"

"Because you've just about sold off the team with no sign of hiring anyone."

"More than half. Just got a couple more. My lawyers are looking into the Cookie Coletti contract. I think I can can him without paying for it."

"George, you are really a shit."

"That's the second time you've said that. Normally, once would be enough, I would have let you walk. But I'm generous tonight. It must be the wine."

"George, that's a martini."

"Same thing. How can you be Boswell if you don't hang around Johnson?"

"If I knew I was gonna have to spend social time with you, I would have asked for a raise."

That rolled right off. Another chomp of steak. The steak actually looked good, not that there was anything wrong with the redfish, but the steak actually looked very, very good. Why the hell hadn't I ordered a steak? Charlene wasn't here, she wouldn't know. Except it might stay on my breath.

"But you didn't ask for a raise. The reason you didn't was that your agent Sid was trying to shop you last season and you got no takers. And you still want to be in the Show."

"Well, that's water slopped out of the trough. What are you going to do, George? You make that announcement that I think you're going to make and you're going to be dog meat."

"Really? Among whom?" He said it just like that, with arrogance and coolness in his voice.

"Everyone. The fans, press — I told you that before."

"Listen, Ryan. I'm going to reveal something to you that no owner has ever told one of his employees."

He paused for dramatic effect.

"I don't give a shit. Because I know fans and I know press. Who are the beloved owners? Bill Veeck? Right. Never won shit, so he turned on the charm."

"He won in Cleveland. And the '59 White Sox."

"Same thing." That didn't make sense, but George wasn't paying attention now. He was fixing his little Gila monster eyes on me and not letting go.

"I know fans, Ryan. You finish third, you're a bum. You appear in the field and they boo you even if you were announcing a fund to save a kid with cancer. It goes with owning. But win and they might not love you, but they respect you. They back off. They say, 'Well, that old George Bremenhaven is a son of a bitch, but he gets things done.' Fans pile up all their resentments in life on the owner of the team they follow. That's a fact. Win, and your shit doesn't stink. Lose nobly and they'll bury you in a concrete bridge in New Jersey.

"Now, media. Press — the sporting press — is just the same, only more vicious. You get a winner, especially in New York, they'd let you walk down Fifth Avenue in a dress and find a way to explain it was the latest in macho fashion. Lose and they can't wait to get you, even get you indicted, encourage lone gunmen to stalk you, burn your house, shoot your dog. Press are vicious and they're so used to it, they don't know they are. They think they're the good guys, the arrogant cocksuckers. Even if you win, like I said, you can't really take all the credit for it, even if you deserve it.

"It's a no-win situation, Ryan, which any owner knows from the start. So we don't play that game. You don't like the way I run a team, buy me out. You listen to the shit on WFAN in New York? Whiny little losers call in whose high point in life is to go to the Stadium and boo the millionaire players and then get on talk radio to pretend they'd be better owners. I don't listen to whiners, Ryan, or take advice from cheerleaders, so that's why I don't give a shit what the press or the fans think about me."

It was quite a tirade, but he delivered it in a low voice so it didn't get circulated around the room. I wished I had ordered steak, I was feeling that miserable. Like an ex-smoker facing a crisis without a weed nearby.

All I could say was, "Well, George, I got no part of it. Just send me my check on time."

"You got no part of it? Man, you're in it up to your asshole," George said with a non-amusing chuckle. Charlene had said something similar.

"I don't see how. I don't own the team. I don't tell you what to do."

"But you're my number one boy, Ryan, on and off the field."

"I think I'll just throw up quietly, here, in place," I said.

"Come on, get some balls," George said. "It won't be that bad, I promise you."

Like all promises, especially from owners, this one was flawed in ways I didn't even guess at that night.

The next morning, George did his announcement in the Century Room in the hotel. There was a good crowd from the press, because he had put out sweet rolls and a wet bar. Also because the sporting press wanted to see what it was that George could explain he was doing all fall, getting rid of players.

I sort of slunk in, toward the back. Besides the press, there were scouts from the other owners with their own tape recorders. No one from the League was there that I could see, but that didn't mean anything because I don't rub shoulders with the bureaucracy.

Not usually. Except that time I took Catfish's advice about playing chin music on this first baseman from Kansas City and ended up beaning him instead. Well, the son of a bitch was practically hanging over the plate — what could I have done and kept my self-respect? But I got a hearing and a fine anyway and five games suspension. On the other hand, I didn't have a lot of hitters crowding me the rest of the year.

"Ladies and gentlemen, this is a historic moment for major league baseball. We wish to help our government in its quest to pursue a rational foreign policy in a new world age," George began, reading from a paper.

This set the crowd buzzing. It was exactly the way I felt when George first asked me if I spoke Spanish. I'm sure some of the reporters were hoping that George was about to deep-six himself or reveal he wore ladies' underwear. I was hoping.

"In full cooperation with the State Department, we are going to be the first in opening a new bridge to our one-time friend and long-time enemy. I am announcing the end of the cold war in Latin America."

This is pure George, if you've never heard him. He's like an ocean liner that sails into a dock hard and insists the dock was in the wrong place.

"This spring, we will introduce the American public to the most exciting concept ever in baseball history," he rambled on. "The public, the ordinary fan, has complained for years that baseball has become too high-priced for the ordinary fan, and I have listened to the man in the street and I agree with him wholeheartedly. We don't need million-dollar ball players to play million-dollar baseball. What we need are people whose love for the game transcends mere money. We don't need more bloodsucking agents sending ticket prices soaring. So, the first thing I want to announce is a ten percent reduction starting next April in ticket and season ticket prices at Yankee Stadium in the Greatest City in the World." He paused for effect, and then, like he was there, said, "New York!" This does not get much of a response in the rest of the country, but George wouldn't know that. On the other hand, he was reducing ticket prices. No one ever did that.

"Mr. Bremenhaven," a reporter began.

"Just shut up a second, willya? Gimme a chance to finish," George said.

He went on, "Through the offices of our State Department and in negotiation with the government of Cuba, New York next year will have the most exciting baseball team since the 1927 Yankees. I am bringing to this country for the first time in decades the best and brightest of the young men who play baseball in Cuba, the greatest baseball nation in the world after our own great nation. This is not about ideologies but about sports. Although I trust that those young Cubans will see the wonders of America and the wonders of New York and be able to go back home next fall with stories to tell their grandchildren about America."

Man, the guy was on a roll, he was piling up nonsense on nonsense the way he did when he really believed in something. This seems to be a common trait among true believers.

"The New York Yankees organization is committed to excellence, no matter how much it costs. We are committed to the common fan and the price he has to pay. We are committed to global peace and the diplomatic resolution of our differences. We are committed to winning the American League pennant, not in five years or three years or someday soon, but next year! We are committed to bringing together on one team the best and the brightest, the finest and fairest, of what everyone knows is the baseball-lovingest nation in the world except for our own. Now, are there questions?"

Only about ten million. I love it when I see a bunch of reporters step on one another's lines trying to be first. Sort of like watching people waiting at a luggage carousel after a five-hour coast-to-coaster that came in ten minutes after midnight.

George was ready. He was really enjoying it. Yes, he said, he was committed and he was getting rid of his old team not to save money but to commit to excellence. Guy sounded like a teacher I had once.

"How can we deal with Cuba, when we don't have diplomatic relations with Cuba?"

"We are not dealing with Cuba directly. We are dealing with third parties in Mexico City, our allies in the great North American Free Trade Association. That's what this is about. About a day when our children will be able to walk the streets of Havana —"

"They can't walk the streets of Miami," said a smart-ass from *Newsday*.

"I don't care about Miami, I care about the Greatest City in the World," George said, flushing.

"Who authorized this?" said the *Daily News*.

"I authorized this," George said, seizing the mantle of government. "I own the Yankees."

"I mean, who says we can deal with Cuba?"

"Didn't you hear anything, you fucking asshole? I said we're dealing with Mexico."

"For Cuban ball players."

"Are you a racist?" George said.

"Are you crazy?" the *Daily News* responded.

So it went on and on and the questions got narrower and narrower and I was sort of half-dozing, standing there with a paper cup of coffee in my hand.

"How will you communicate with all these players, who you say don't even speak English?"

It was the guy from the *Los Angeles Times*. It was a smirky question. The New York *Daily News* guy had asked the same thing before but in a different, furious way that just made George go off the deep end and answer it with no answer at all. The L.A. guy didn't really care, but everyone likes to watch a train wreck as long as he isn't in it.

"I'm glad you asked. Standing over there with that cup of coffee — heh, I hope it's coffee — heh heh — is the man to answer your questions, because I want to announce that I have re-signed my star reliever Ryan

Shawn, a good old boy from Texas who has been with the Yankee organization for the past eleven years. You want to answer him, Ryan?"

No, you miserable son of a bitch, you sandbagging sack of shit. I spilled some coffee on the front of my slacks.

The press turned like the Marine Corps band doing a right wheel. It was that precise.

I was certainly the center of attention at that moment and I hated it.

"Uh," I began.

Now, ball players learn how to talk to the sports press right off. All you say is stuff like "We can do better" and "Team has no *I* in it" and "I've been working my way out of this thing" — crap that doesn't mean anything. But this press was going to be vicious no matter what I said.

"Uh, George there, uh, Mr. Bremenhaven, he wants me to help translate on the field."

"Do you speak Spanish?" asked the *Kansas City Star* guy, the same son of a bitch who once said I was a beanball hitman just because I plonked the first baseman on the Royals. Cheerleading son of a bitch.

"Well, it'd be a little hard to translate on the field if I didn't, wouldn't it?"

That was the wrong thing to say. The rule is that the press gang can smart-mouth you but you can't do the same back.

"What I meant was," the snot from K.C. said, "the Cubans speak a form of Castilian Spanish, affected somewhat, with a tendency to lisp. This is attributed to the affectation of the upper classes in Spain to speak in the manner of Philip the Second, who lisped badly. So what I meant was, there's Spanish and there's Spanish. Just because you understand Mexicans doesn't mean you'd understand Castilians."

"Shit, pardner, I don't even understand you," I said. Now that got a laugh because it had to and there are a few press guys, here and there, who still got a sense of humor. But I was going to pay for it, I knew it.

"How do you feel about dealing with Communists?"

"I dunno, I never have."

"But you're going to. Do you feel you're betraying your fellow baseball players?"

"Some of them are Communists."

"Which ones?"

"Sy Edelman with Kansas City, for one," I said, naming the first baseman I had beaned long ago.

"You know that for a fact?"

"It's why I beaned him," I said. "Doin' my bit." But it was wrong, what I was saying. I was trying to keep it light, but these boys who write about sports, they want everything heavy. Who gives a shit who's a Communist? There are no atheists on pitcher's mounds. Or something.

I got it two or three times in a row about didn't I feel I betrayed my old teammates by staying and how long did I know about this plan, and was I a Democrat or Republican. Bam, bam, bam, like coming in to do long relief in the fifth and losing the lead on doubles to three sorry-ass hitters at the bottom of the lineup. Makes you want to throw up. About the only thing they didn't ask me was how long my dong was.

Finally, to save myself, I did the only thing I could think of: I headed for the tunnel, which in this case was the double door at the back of the conference room. I even dropped my cup of coffee, which, thank God, was coffee or some writer would have had it analyzed to see if I was drunk at eleven in the morning.

Leaving was also the wrong thing to do because it looked like I was evading questions. I was, but not for the reasons they thought. Hell, I was never so good that I had to face the high-profile media. Just drop in a quote like "I was lucky out there today" every now and then. They scared hell out of me, was all. I looked back once and saw George up there, having the time of his life watching me get it.

Judas goat.

I needed to call Charlene real bad and cry in her beer. I needed to see what I could do next to get myself out of this.

10

I didn't think my picture in the *Houston Post* looked very flattering. It showed me spilling my coffee, and the headline said something about Texas Boy Betrays Baseball for Castro, or something along those lines.

I saw the paper the next day because I hightailed it out of the Century Plaza right after George sandbagged me. George didn't hightail it anywhere. The son of a bitch enjoyed the attention. He was on *Nightline* with old Ted Koppel that night and, since he was in Los Angeles anyway, he went on the Jay Leno show. He was on TV more than anyone since Bill Clinton explained Gennifer Flowers.

He was wonderful.

You and I know that George is a shit, a right-wing money-grubbing bastard who probably steals from orphans, but he was standing there with an American flag on his lapel, talking about giving honest and hardworking Cubans a chance to sample true Western-style democracy. He was doing it all for the good of the game and for the good of the common fan. He kept saying ticket prices were going down at Yankee Stadium next year. He'd save ninety percent on his payroll and end up cutting ticket prices ten percent but never confuse the press with real numbers, I've learned.

The flight back from L.A. to Texas is semi-short, but it seemed long to me. I was in a slinking mood. I slunk away from the stewardesses when they asked me if I wanted anything, and when we landed, I slunk into the city. Felt like I was ashamed of something. I took the cab to Charlene's apartment. Damned if she wasn't out again. She was starting to make a habit of being out, and I was out of sorts about it. So I walked around a while and then got another cab back to the Longhorn Arms and found my car. Then I did what Texans do when they want to pace a bit: I drove like a bat out of hell.

Went out of the city headed toward Galveston. When you're feeling down and dirty in Houston, you head for Galveston. The road was made for roadhouses and pickup trucks in the parking lots. Found me a few. Played some Willie, then some Waylon, thought about busting George in the chops, thought about where Charlene was. It was a cool night and I had the windows open and felt the breeze slapping me in the face. Willie said not to grow up to be cowboys and Waylon said he was the highwayman. That made me feel better and better. Then I ended up at a roadhouse where everyone wore a cowboy hat, even the girls. I was the only one dressed funny — Eastern-looking funny — and I was so full of my own thoughts that I didn't realize it.

People were semi-polite and gave me room at the bar. I drank a bottle of beer and then another one. They had the country music channel on the big screen and they were running an old tape of the Judds. I watched and listened and then went out to call Charlene on the pay phone. This time I got her. Asked her where she'd been and she said it was none of my business. Then she asked me where I was and I told her the truth, which was I wasn't exactly sure, but it was someplace on the road to Galveston.

Then she said she saw me on television on the news and it had made her sick.

And then she said I should hurry home.

It was like morning coming up and I wasn't hung over, just the sound of her voice made it better. Hurry home. I hurried right along.

So we watched Ted Koppel together that night and the next morning, she went out and got the papers, even the *New York Times* and the *Wall Street Journal.* Imagine, they had stories, too. Well, maybe the *Times* you could understand, the team being in New York and all. But the *Journal* did this story about the economic impact on a breakthrough with Cuba, a lot of stuff I didn't understand and I suspect the writer didn't understand either.

As I said, I didn't look good in the *Houston Post.*

"Makes me look like a fool," I said to Charlene.

"Honey, this is just starting."

We turned on the TV and there was old George, still at it, on the "Today Show" with Bryant Gumbel. Son of a bitch might be old and full of gout, but he had legs. Made it on the red-eye all the way across the country and he looked as fresh as a morning meadow.

" . . . I think a lot of credit has to go to Ryan Shawn for volunteering to help our new team make the transition from being the best in Cuba to the best in the American League," George was saying. "This is a great step toward world peace and it starts with baseball. Imagine that, Bryant."

I spilled my coffee for the second time in twenty-four hours.

Charlene said "Wipe it up" absentmindedly, watching TV. I went in the kitchen and got a paper towel and wiped the rug until the dark stain was a dry dark stain.

"You'd better stay here. I can go over and get your clothes from the Longhorn Arms."

"Why would you have to do that?"

"Ryan, this here is the tip of the iceberg. They're gonna be camping out on you over there, the media. You didn't seem to handle yourself too well yesterday, and I don't expect you took a Dale Carnegie course since then. So I just figure I could give you a little breathing room."

"I don't need to hide behind no woman's skirt," I said.

She giggled. "Not when you're wearing her pink fluffy robe."

Damn. You can never get sympathy from a woman unless it's to her advantage to give it. Kindness, yes. Women deal in kindness as an everyday thing. But sympathy, no.

I marched off to the bathroom and took a long, soapy shower. I had brought my bag, the one I took to Los Angeles, and I shaved and changed underclothes and socks. Then I slipped into my jeans and a fresh polo shirt and went out to the front room of Charlene's place. She was sitting there on the couch watching "Good Morning America" where a guy named Orestes Montez was denouncing George Bremenhaven.

"The Cuban community of Miami has devoted itself to bringing true democracy back to our native land, and now this baseball owner, for selfish reasons, has stabbed us in the back," is some of what Orestes was saying. I didn't want to hear any more. I kissed Charlene on the forehead. She looked up.

"You going to the Longhorn Arms?" she said.

"I ain't got no reason not to. I ain't done nothing wrong," I said.

"That don't matter, what you did. I read this story in the *Post* and you come across as halfway a Communist and halfway a Benedict Arnold in a cowboy hat."

"That's just a newspaper, Charlene, it don't mean the end of the world."

"Watch yourself the next time you go into a Billy Bob Bar, make sure someone don't crack your skull with a bottle of Bud."

"You're exaggerating, Charlene. Anyway it's football season and folks in Texas don't get that riled up about baseball."

"They get riled up about Mexicans coming up to take their jobs away from them," she said.

"These are Cubans. For Christ's sake, Charlene, can't you even tell the difference? Ain't taking no shitkicker's job anyway, this is just about baseball players."

"When you were washing your sins away in the bathroom, they had the head of the player's union on 'Today.' He said you sold out your teammates and the entire American League."

"He's as full of shit as a Christmas goose," I said. "George was gonna get rid of his payroll one way or another, like that fella did down in San Diego not that many years ago."

"You think ball players are overpaid?"

"'Course I do, but I'm taking as long as they're giving. Man's worth what someone is willing to pay him."

"You are going to have a lonely life next season. At home and on the road," Charlene said.

"Well, I wasn't expecting any sympathy from you."

"Good, 'cause I ain't in the sympathy business. I might have been if you'd gone off back to New York at Thanksgiving and popped George Bremenhaven like you said you were gonna do, but you didn't, so you've made your bed and now you're stuck in it."

"Charlene, you really think I should've turned down $625,000, which is enough money to set us up in the business of our choosing? This ain't gonna last two-three days."

"Honey, sometimes I think you're about half-smart and sometimes you're dumber than a sack of oats. It's the sack of oats I'm thinking of now. This ain't gonna end, not a week, not a month from now. George Bremenhaven picked his chump right, if you ask me."

"Well, I didn't, Charlene," I said. It was a pretty weak comeback but that's because I had started out looking for sympathy when there was none to be had. Men are always making that mistake.

"Fine, Ryan Patrick. You go on home now and get the shit beat out of you like I said it was gonna happen, because it will. You go on. I don't need your trouble when you don't have the brains to do any different. I see it now. Thank God we didn't have children — I'd keep wondering which one took after your stupid side."

That did it.

I was out of there and stomping down the hall and taking the stairs to the parking lot without waiting for the elevator. Then I saw the Channel 7 van across the street with the antenna dish on top and something that looked like an automatic weapon sticking out of it. I didn't care. I got in my Buick Park Avenue and sent it into reverse so hard I took 10,000 miles off my 50,000-mile tires in two seconds. Then into forward and damned near plowed into the side of the van getting out of there.

The van started chasing me.

I was being chased by a goddamned television station van right there in the morning light of downtown Houston. Around us, the usual caravan of cars was trying to pass through various eyes of needles on their way to work, and me and this television van was doing Starsky and Hutch or something.

Why was I running anyway? I wasn't a criminal.

And then I thought of Jack Wade and the IRS man. Maybe George really had deep connections with Washington, D.C., and maybe he could get some revenue man to come down and put the fear on Jack Wade, the jelly doughnut son of a bitch.

You can see how upset I was. I was blaming everyone for what essentially was my trouble, brought on by my own greed and desire. I am normally much more rational and thoughtful, but I am putting this down exactly the way it was to show that I was no hero in what happened, that I had many, many moments of weakness.

I finally made it over to the Longhorn Arms and was in my room before the television van found me. The trouble was, there were two other television vans in the parking lot and a car with some guys from the *Chronicle*. They had staked me out but missed me when I drove up because they didn't know what kind of a car they were looking for. The Channel 7 driver told them, and I was surrounded.

Calmly, I packed my big bag and took two cans of MGD out of the icebox and put them in the bag as well. Then I pulled on my black cowboy hat and my long leather coat. I also made sure I had my checkbook and two or three other things I wouldn't normally carry for a short trip to Los Angeles. All the while, I was thinking about getting sympathy from someone, even if I had to pay for it. I decided I needed it that bad. So I made a call to my agent, Sid.

He was in. Himself.

"Well, cowboy," he said, "you've screwed yourself up. In one way. You should have consulted me before you did what you did with George."

"You weren't in the mood to be consulted," I said. "You were tripping over the daisies with that queer quarterback in Hawaii, I recall."

"On the other hand," Sid said. "I can see a TV movie in this. I think a feature is too big. On the other hand, there might be a book if we could find a writer."

"I can't do that stuff. I gotta get out of this thing, Sid."

"You signed a contract."

"I can always retire."

"Sure. You could have done that at first. Now it's harder, but you can do it. You can call a press conference and retire."

"Except George is working somehow, you know, with the government in this thing."

"So?"

"Well, an IRS agent came by —"

"I don't want to know from IRS agents."

"Jesus, Sid, what kind of an agent are you?"

"An ex-agent, as I recall. I recall you became your own agent when you signed that contract. So I became an 'ex.' I don't recall you sending me ten percent."

Sid always talked in a calm voice. It's an agent's voice. Agents don't yell or scream, not the good ones. Agents just sit there like a poker player, peeking at the cards, shoving out the cartwheels to the center of the green felt.

"I'll send you ten percent."

"I don't want your ten percent. I didn't earn it."

Sid Cohen is like this. He is putting me through a guilt trip. The trouble was, I was feeling guilty about everything on the theory that I must have been guilty of something.

"Sid, what should I do?"

"Hey, enjoy the ride. I wish I had been there to make it with you."

"I can't go back on George, he might be able to use the government against me. But I can't stand this, day after day. There's three TV vans in the parking lot right now. I just packed my bag."

"Packed your bag? Where you going?"

"Tahiti. I dunno. I gotta get out of here. My girl and I just had a fight and I don't know why and there ain't nothing but trouble for me right now in Houston."

"Well, it would be better if you told your side of things."

"What is my side, exactly?"

"I haven't figured it all out yet, but I will," Sid said.

"Sid." My voice was grateful.

"You want me to be your agent again?"

"Sid," I said.

"I could earn that ten percent," he said.

"Sid," I said.

"On the other hand, I could have gotten you a better contract. George needed you more than you needed him."

"Sid, that isn't true. George said he could have picked up a Spanish interpreter any place in New York for peanuts."

"Oh, I see. Someone to be on the field, position players, make signals in Spanish, be in the locker room after the game. Sure. What did he have in mind? A courtroom interpreter? A Mexican grocer?"

"He sort of went along those lines."

"Ryan, ball players play ball, agents think. I'm thinking right now and the meter is running. We have to come to an understanding."

"I understand," I said.

There was a knock at the door.

"They're here, for Christ's sake," I said.

"The television guys. Good. You're pathetic on television, Ryan, did I tell you?"

"I saw me, you don't have to tell me."

"What you have to do is issue a prepared statement shifting all this back in George's lap. And the State Department's lap, too."

"Saying what?"

They were now banging on the door.

"Saying what?" I said again.

"I can't hear you, what is that racket?"

"I told you, it's the reporters."

"Are they going to bang the door down?"

"I don't know, Sid, maybe they are. What should I do?"

"You have a gun?"

Sid Cohen is based in L.A. and they are very crazy about guns in that town. Everyone has a gun, and not a shotgun or rifle but a handgun, so they can shoot at each other. Never met anyone hunted with a pistol except my Uncle Dave, who never hit anything but a tree and this farmer once. But Sid is not a gun nut, and I thought he asked me because he has all these prejudices about you, depending on where you come from. I'm from Texas so I wear a gun. That's their mentality in L.A. when it really is L.A. we have to be scared of.

"No, Sid, I ain't got no gun. What d'you think I should do, shoot one of them reporters?"

"That would put a different spin on the story, all right," he said in his thoughtful voice. "No. I just wanted to be sure that if they broke the door down they wouldn't find anything incriminating like a gun. They already have you labeled as a Commie; you don't have to be a gun nut, too. Tell you what. I'm flying to Chicago this afternoon to talk with the Cubs, why don't you meet me there? You could hide out there for a couple of days and I could figure out a strategy for you."

"I got my car," I said.

"You ever hear of airplanes?"

"I still got my car," I said.

"Leave the car at the airport, Ryan. They all have parking lots. Even in Texas. Get a plane for Chicago."

"But then they'll know I'm in Chicago," I said.

"The reporters? Simple. Book a flight through to New York with a stopover in Chicago. Slip off the plane in Chicago."

"But what do I do with the rest of the ticket?" I said.

"Donate it to your favorite fucking charity!" Sid was shouting. "I'm not paid enough to think of everything!"

"Take it easy, Sid."

"I'll be at the Drake Hotel tonight. I meet with the Cubs tomorrow all day. I can see you tonight and we can work out a statement. I'll draw up a draft on the flight to O'Hare."

"Can you get me out of this, Sid?"

"Maybe, maybe not."

Silence. Sid was letting me twist.

"Sid."

"The only thing I can guarantee . . . ," Sid said.

"Yeah?"

" . . . is we can put George Bremenhaven in the middle of it. The arrogant cocksucker, he thinks he's going to get rid of agents by trading with Cuba, he's got another think coming."

And I was relieved all of a sudden, despite the pounding at the door and despite the fight with Charlene.

It never occurred to me that this might be personal for agents as well.

11

Chasing out to the airport was a hoot, me and the three TV vans, but I got there a good ten minutes before them and took the first plane to anywhere. First fun I'd had in days, punching along at 90 and 100, watching them old vans in my rearviews fall behind.

Anywhere turned out to be Kansas City, which figures. I thought of looking up that wise-ass reporter who showed off his fancy knowledge of different kinds of Spanish, but I didn't. In fact, it amused me more now. I bet George didn't know when he hired me that I only spoke Spanish with Mexicans and that Mexican Spanish wasn't like Cuban Spanish.

While I waited around in the K.C. airport for the next plane to Chicago, I tried to think of everything I knew about Cubans.

I knew about Castro. Everyone knew about him. Wore a beard, smoked cigars, wore an army uniform to bed at night, and gave long speeches. He played baseball once. Pitcher. But I didn't know anything else.

Ricky Ricardo. Lucy's husband. Now I was getting someplace. Come to think of it, he spoke lousy English all his life. Part of the fun of watching the "I Love Lucy" reruns was trying to figure out what Ricky was saying. How could someone spend all those years in America and not speak better English?

Take Mexicans. They pick up English fast and good, and you give a Mexican enough rope and he'll talk better English than they do in Detroit.

So maybe the smart-ass from the *Kansas City Star* who once wanted to hang me for accidentally beaning one of their players was right. Maybe George had hired me on to do something I couldn't do — speak Spanish with Cubans the same way they can't speak English to us, even if they've been here a million years.

That thought kept me tickled all the way to Chicago. I took a cab downtown to the Drake Hotel and checked in without even looking at the room rate. I looked up Sid, but he wasn't in yet so I left a message for him.

Next, I called Charlene at work to ask her to forgive me. But she was taking the day off. I called her at her apartment, but she was taking the day off from there, too.

Then I had a sudden and brilliant and sickening inspiration.

I called her at Ernie's Cafe.

She came to the phone. She sounded fuzzy around the edges, which I know is the way she sounds when she's been crawling around inside a bottle of Smirnoff long enough. She is not a drunk, but she can drink when she wants to.

"Where are you?" she said.

"Chicago."

"Why?"

"I'm gonna meet with Sid here."

"And do what?"

"I dunno. Sid hasn't figured it out yet."

"Fuck Sid," she said. I could hear the weave in her voice.

"Charlene. You drinking alone?"

"I drink with whoever I want."

"Who you drinking with?"

"Jack Wade, if you want to know."

That's what I mean about having an inspiration that was both intelligent and sickening.

"I wish you wouldn't."

"Ryan Patrick, I am free, white, and over twenty-one, and I drink with whoever I want and wherever I want."

"Just don't go to bed with him," I said. This was the wrong thing to say. I knew it when I said it. There was a long silence.

And then: "We were talking about you, you shit."

"Charlene, I called to tell you I was sorry."

"That ain't saying 'I'm sorry,' saying don't sleep with the first man buys you a drink in Ernie's Cafe, man you knew since college, man with a wife and two little children."

"It's just that he's a car salesman," I said.

"And it's just that you're a broken-down ball player who everyone in the country right now thinks is a Communist and a scab. If I didn't know better and know you're just dumb, I'd think it, too."

"So what does Jack think?"

"Jack thinks you need a lawyer."

"Sid is a lawyer."

"He's an agent more than a lawyer."

"Well, I don't need two lawyers."

"I didn't say you needed one lawyer. I said Jack said you need a lawyer. I told Jack he was full of shit," Charlene said. "I said what you need to do is cut your losses and go out and resign and maybe punch George in the nose for the hell of it to do what you should've done last Thanksgiving if you remember I told you."

She was stringing her words together as carefully as a drunk putting popcorn kernel by kernel on a needle and thread to form a decoration for the Christmas tree.

"Charlene, I feel terrible about everything, just everything. But mostly, I feel terrible about walking out on you that way."

This produced more silence. Was she figuring I hadn't said enough? Or too much? It is hard to tell with a woman's silence which is intended.

I said, "Can you just let me apologize?"

"I thought you just did that."

"Well, I didn't hear nothing from your end."

"Like what?"

"Like, you accept my apology."

"No, you didn't."

"Does that mean you didn't?"

"It don't mean anything."

"I wish you would go home, Charlene, and get a good night's sleep and I'll call you in the morning."

"You do? I figure to go on drinking until I can't stand up and depend on Jack to take me home."

"That would be a mistake. I wouldn't trust Jack to take Mother Teresa home."

"That's a terrible thing to say, Ryan. You judge everyone by your own standards, which are none too high. Or so it seems from everything I been reading about you in the papers and on the TV. They say you beaned a ball player once and got suspended. You never told me that."

"Charlene, you know me more than a year. You know —"

"I know that you told me some things and I know that you convinced me there is no Miss Roxanne Devon of Brunswick, New Jersey. I don't know any more than that."

"You know I love you."

Now, I am not a glib talker and I do not go out of my way to say "I love you" to ladies I meet and even might go to bed with. The ladies and I have an understanding that if we meet up after a game someplace — say like Toronto, after a game — we have a couple of hours to decide to do it or not. Mostly the ladies decide by the look of me and whether there's kink in me and whether I hold my liquor, and I decide if the girl is honestly sincere about having fun or one of those naggy kinds of groupies who'll end up selling her story to the *National Enquirer.* I haven't done that for a while — like I told Charlene, it was the truth — but I used to. I am thirty-eight years old, after all. I ain't a stud, but I ain't a virgin. And I never told Charlene I loved her before — well, maybe once — so I guess I meant it.

"I don't know that, Ryan," she said after a moment. Her voice was soft then, and sober-sounding, though that was impossible if she had been drinking with Jack Wade a whole boozy afternoon.

"Well, I mean it."

"You never said it before."

"Which proves I mean it."

"Like the telephone operator proves there's no Miss Roxanne Devon of Brunswick, New Jersey."

"I don't know what to say," I said.

"It's all right. Don't say anything. I'm going home now. Call me in the morning," she said.

It was good enough. Not great. But good enough.

"Safe home," I said.

"I'll be fine."

"If you can't drive, let Jack drive you."

"You think I'm crazy?"

"Is he that drunk?" I said.

"Ryan. He's a car salesman," she said, and hung up.

12

Sid Cohen is tan, tall, has a great toupee — the kind you can wear in a pool that is all tied to your real hair — and wears sunglasses all the time. He never says "baby" to you, because it doesn't fit the role of a sports agent. Other than that, he is pure Santa Monica in Los Angeles and is not to be trusted kissing babies.

I mostly got along with Sid in my salad years in the league because when he went out on the edge, I pulled him back in. Some players get with agents who think they're representing King Kong. There are no King Kongs except for maybe a Michael Jordan or Shaquille or Bonds, or a couple of others. The rest of us are higher-grade replacement parts from Mr. Goodwrench or we're down-and-dirty knockoffs from the discounters. Notice I mentioned basketball players being among the King Kongs. Big difference with 12 men on a team compared with 25, like in baseball, or 47, like in football. The stars get fewer, the bigger the night sky.

I knew that and made Sid know that I knew that. Sid always said I held myself back, but I kept making money, which is more than some wannabes made sitting out the seasons.

We met at a table in the Coq d'Or, which is a brassy little bar on the ground floor of my hotel. I had a beer and Sid had an iced tea and a salad. Angelenos in the show biz business eat very little of substance and never really look healthy except to one another. If they were cows in Texas, they'd be shot in a pit and burned.

"You looking good, Sid," I said. It was omelette time again.

"Hmmph," Sid said, gnawing at his lettuce. It was winter in Chicago and the salad did not meet California standards. Sid chewed on grimly like a rabbit in a wire cage waiting to be potluck. It was all the rabbit knew how to do, even though it was going to come to no good end. I felt so sorry for myself I ordered a steak on toast and a mound of french fries because Charlene wasn't around to smell meat on my breath.

"I gave it a lot of careful thought on the plane. I even keyboarded myself a few notes. What you're going to do is say you had no idea that George worked out a secret deal to trade off the whole team and import Cubans and that you want to resign, but that you have signed a valid contract and you can't back out on it. You know, blah blah, your word is your bond and blah blah blah," Sid began.

"But that isn't the way it was," I said.

Sid looked up at me sharp across his salad. "Who am I talking to? Diogenes?"

"Well, for one thing, there was Sam the equipment man. A couple of days after the season was over, George brought him into the office and had him speak Spanish at me, to see if I spoke Spanish."

"You're telling me George told him what was going on?"

"No, I don't think so. George just told him to try out my Spanish."

"So?"

"So what if Sam says anything about that?"

"Why would he?"

"Same reason people go on the Phil Donahue show, to make fools of themselves just to get on the TV."

"I know Phil Donahue and I know he doesn't want to put a Mexican equipment man on his show. Unless he wears a dress in the locker room."

"Well —"

"Look. Don't tell me Sam wears a dress in the locker room, I would have heard. George wanted to know if you spoke Spanish. You pass his test. You ask him why. He says, I can't tell you. He says, sign a contract. You sign a contract. Adios. The next thing you know, George tells you to go to L.A. You go to L.A. — and, I might add, you don't even give me the courtesy of a phone call to tell me you're in town — and the next thing you know, George is announcing the end of baseball as we know it and implying that you're part of the conspiracy. Now, that's not true."

"That's sort of not true."

"It's not true for reasons of clarification."

"All right, it's sort of not true for that reason."

"Not sort of. We've got to get 'sort of' out of your vocabulary if you ever are going to do anything. I'll hold a press conference Thursday, after I meet with the Cubs tomorrow. We'll do it in New York. You'll stand up and —"

"I ain't ever gonna do no press conference again."

"That's right. I forgot. You're terrible. All right. We'll issue a press release and I'll do the press conference and say you are in seclusion with your family."

"I don't have no family left, not anywhere. Except for Uncle Dave in the Panhandle, he's three bricks shy of a load. I'm not sure he wasn't adopted by my grandfather, because they never spoke about where he come from."

"It's an expression, Ryan, don't get tedious with me. Being 'in seclusion with your family' means you're going through the grieving process, and the press likes that, believe me. It shows you're human even if you're a Commie lover and a beanball pitcher."

"I told you about beaning that guy in Kansas City, he was practically hanging over the plate with that goofy pumpkin head of his."

Sid held up his forkful of lettuce. "Joke, Ryan. Chill out."

"I can't chill out when that son of a bitch has made me a goat."

"Oh, George? He hasn't managed to do that yet. What we have to do is damage control. And then we go back into the burned-out hulk and do damage assessment."

"I sound like a building."

"It's like that. And I'm the fireman putting out the fire."

"Then what?"

"We wait on the pleasure of the Yankees. On George. On whether this mild protest from Miami goes into a full court press and the government backs down and revokes the permits for the Cubanos. In which case, George is holding a sack of shit. This is a gamble on George's part, Ryan, not a done deal. I made a couple of calls to people inside the Beltway. The Democrats want to make the bold move, but they would just as soon have a Republican creep do it for them if they can get the eventual credit. An old Democratic trick is to get Republicans to do their foreign policy work for them. Nixon in China, Bush saving the oil states. If it turns south, they cut loose and George will have no payroll, but also no team. Unless you can pitch and catch at the same time."

"What about the other owners?"

"If this works, George is a genius, he's their hero, the first guy to seriously show how to stomp the player's union since the strike. If it doesn't work, they force him to sell the franchise to the next sucker in line. They are actively neutral, believe me, but they are secretly cheering for George."

Sid cut another piece of lettuce. Northern salads have lots of lettuce, a reason it's so hard to order a salad seriously.

"The Cubans in Miami are a smaller problem. Everyone hates everyone else in Miami — it's what holds the city together. They're like lobsters in a pot. Every time one climbs up to get out the other lobsters pull him back in. The Haitians hate the Cubans, they all hate the Anglos, naturally everyone hates the Jews, it's a mess. Which can work to the Administration's advantage. It's unlikely the Cubans are going to burn down the city, since they seem to own so much of it. The Haitians might be confused enough to riot, but who cares, Haitians are always rioting. Besides, they speak French. The Miami contingent is a wild card but a small one."

"What about the player's union?"

"Well, I'm going to try to get you in their good graces again — you know, kiss and make up and stand by your man. What's done is done insofar as getting rid of the old lineup. . . . This salad sucks, you know that?"

"I ordered steak."

"It'll kill you."

"I feel self-destructive."

"Don't let me down."

"I won't, Sid."

"You did once."

"I won't, Sid."

"The union can be made to see it's getting no sympathy going after you, they have to keep their focus on George. The solution is pretty simple."

"Solution?"

"George wants to break the union, demolish the agents, end arbitration, et cetera, all the things the owners always want. Remember the Big Strike. And he wants to do it in the name of international peace and brotherhood, which is a neat trick."

"So what's the solution, Sid?" I said again.

Sid put down his fork and covered the remains of his salad with a red napkin. I thought he might say a prayer over the departed, but he said something else.

"Get rid of George."

And he was smiling.

13

I was right about one or two things that would happen next, but so was George.

Sid Cohen issued a statement Wednesday that made me a victim of management greed and a good guy promoting international healing. It was good enough for a lot of papers that weren't necessarily mad at me — or angry, as Charlene would say — but were distracted at first by George.

I was right about the editorials. The liberal papers weighed in with editorials endorsing the combination of baseball and the State Department to end squabbling in the Caribbean, and even the *New York Times* picked up George's line about baseball ending the cold war. I was also right that it wouldn't matter on the sports pages of the selfsame newspapers, where everyone was still upset. A columnist in the *New York Times* sports section practically had a stroke in print about a field full of Castro Cubans, as if politics had anything to do with baseball. Only everything.

Next day, Fidel Castro made a six-hour speech in Havana and introduced every ball player who would be going to New York. It was covered by CNN and C-Span.

I thought the *New York Post* and the *Daily News* got it right, though. On the same day, both papers had as their headlines the same words: NEW YORK YANQUIS!

You couldn't get those papers in Chicago, but Sid sent them to me by Federal Express. George was up to his ass in alligators for a few weeks while the season ticket cancellations came in. One lawyer filed a class action suit on behalf of season ticket holders who felt cheated by the shoddiness of the product George was going to be putting on the field next season. What clients want to go out and see the Havana Nine on the field in the House That Ruth Built?

It was a mistake on their part. George went on public television and denounced the unconscious racism of the fans who wouldn't turn out to see

Latino ball players. He denounced the union for the same reason. This put both groups in a box, even though everyone knew that George was about as unconsciously racist as they came. In a way, I admired his using political correctness to lie his way out of something that was so obvious, though I didn't let it blind me into admiring the son of a bitch in general, just in particular.

New York Yanquis. Damn. The people I admire in the print media are the guys who write the headlines.

I could even see George restitching the uniforms with that name, *Yanquis.* He's a bastard, but he's got a stubborn streak in him. This was about money to him, at least it was at first. But maybe after he saw Lincoln's ghost that night in the White House and Lincoln gave him the thumbs up on the way to the bathroom for a midnight tinkle, maybe he — George, not Abe — started believing his own lies.

I couldn't blow the whistle on George without blowing the whistle on myself, and getting fired in the process. So I said nothing.

After a week of hiding out in Chicago — I spent a couple of hilarious nights on the dark side of town with Deke and company — I went back down to Houston. It was all right. Everyone had lost interest in me for the time being. It was January, and Charlene and I had missed Christmas. Texas A&M missed another bowl bid. San Francisco was set to go to the Super Bowl in New Orleans at the end of the month, so you might say football was over.

Missing Christmas. At least *I* had. She'd spent Christmas at her mama's and baked cookies. I believed it, but I couldn't see it, exactly. Besides, the cookies were all eaten up. I took her to Tony's again, but she wouldn't let me come up to her apartment. We were strained, you might say.

And then, January 14th it was, this guy shows up on my doorstep at the Longhorn Arms with George.

This guy was a bean pole on which was hanging a gray suit. George was a fatty in a blue suit. They were a pair, though, and I counted my fingers after we shook hands.

There are two places to sit down in my room. On the bed or on the single chair by the credenza where I eat breakfast. The gray suit didn't sit down, but George flopped on the bed like he lived there.

George looked around the room and then fingered the material of the bedspread. He looked at me. "This is a dump, Ryan."

"Just a room," I said.

"Barely," George replied. "Where do you keep all your money? In shoeboxes?"

I didn't say a thing.

George said, "I got something for you to do."

"What's that, George? Last time you had something for me to do, I was tied to a can."

"You know you don't even have a passport?"

Another strange thing to say. I replied by saying nothing. I sat on the straight chair backward, legs spraddled and resting my arms on the back.

"Grown man, thirty-eight years old, doesn't have a passport?"

"I never had need for one," I said.

"All the money you've made, you never wanted to see another country?"

"Been in Toronto. Ciudad Juarez. As far as I wanted to go," I said.

"Well, Ryan. Well." He seemed to be searching for words, but this was a feint.

"That was a dirty trick you pulled with your slime-bucket agent Sid Cohen, saying I fooled you. I never fooled you."

"Is that right?"

"I could let hard times be hard times, but I'm not a hard guy. I'm a guy trying to do what my country needs me to do. Trying to do the right thing for a lot of poor spics who just want a chance to play the American game."

"George, you just want to cut the payroll and cheap your way to a pennant."

"That's American, isn't it?"

He had me there.

"Ryan, Mr. Baxter here is with the State Department. He arranged a passport for you." He pointed at the bean pole.

"Why?"

"For Cuba, of course."

"I'm not going to Cuba."

"Ryan, someone has to evaluate the team that Señor Fidel picked out for me."

"This wasn't no part of the deal," I said.

"The deal is you're my employee," he said.

"I ain't never been to Cuba."

"No. They require a passport. You never had one before. Mr. Baxter got you one."

I admit I have a reverence for government objects. Saw the Constitution once under glass. That was one. Went down to D.C. for a day trip when we were playing the Orioles up the road. Saw the Lincoln Memorial, that was something. Couldn't make sense of the Washington Monument, though. Got there too late for the White House tour. But I saw the Constitution.

The dollar bill. That's another thing that looks government to me. And important. And this passport, with its blue cover and seal and all, and inside, a picture of me that had a seal across it to make me official — it was like a deputy sheriff's badge. I just looked at it and all the blank pages that followed it. It was a beautiful thing and made me proud of myself. Then I realized something: I still didn't want to go to Cuba.

"I don't wanna go."

"I don't want a pig in the poke. Neither does the government," George said. "We want you to evaluate the players and if you turn thumbs down on someone, he doesn't get to go to New York."

"I'm no scout."

"Not yet," George said.

That was a teaser. Charlene said I had no future left in baseball. But what if it was known that I scouted this team and it turned out well? Well?

I started to calculate. If it turned out well, I could parlay this into something the year after next, maybe shop around to a decent club that would forget I betrayed the whole baseball world by carting in a bunch of wetbacks from Cuba. I realized I was even starting to think the way Charlene and George talked, but as I say, when in Rome. It made you wonder if there was ever a time when you weren't in one Rome or another, wearing that toga and pretending you'd go back home and put on regular cowboy boots someday when the toga days were over.

"This is over and above what we were talking about, when I signed the contract," I said.

"No it isn't," George said.

I just sat there, staring at him. Mr. Baxter looked uncomfortable in the room.

"You want a can of beer?" I said in general.

Baxter shook his head. George said, "You have any vodka?"

"No, George. Just beer."

"I haven't had a beer in twenty-five years," he said.

"You want one?"

"No. It bloats me."

I just looked at him. Then I got up and went to the icebox and pulled out a can of Miller's and popped the tab. It tasted cold and I made a slurping-burping sound with the swallow. I went back to the straight chair and sat on it the wrong way again.

"You always drink in the morning?" George said.

"You were the one wanted vodka," I said.

"You got to take care of yourself."

"George, how much you want to give me to be your scout?"

"I don't have to give you anything, you're already on the payroll."

"To play baseball."

"Five thousand dollars. And your expenses."

"Twenty-five thousand. Brings me back to par."

"You greedy cocksucker, I can get someone else to look at the team in Cuba."

"You oughta, then."

"Look, I thought we were in this together."

"You keep reminding me that I'm the Indian and you're the chief. I like to keep it that way."

"Are you and that son of a bitch Sid Cohen cooking up something else?"

"George, you wanted me to go to L.A. for the winter meetings and I did and you sandbagged me right in front of the nation's medias. I'm already thinking that twenty-five thousand more is too little for whatever is going to happen. If I go down there and bring the team back and they stink up the Stadium, you'll put the blame on me."

"Would I do that?"

Silence. We both knew the answer.

"Ten thousand," he said.

I shook my head.

"I thought you told me once you're no good dealing for yourself."

"I'm getting better. The more time I spend with you, the better I get."

"You are screwing up a beautiful deal. We're two weeks from spring training and I got to get moving," George said.

"Thirty-five thousand. Now that I think about it, this is going to be a lot of trouble for very little money for me."

"No, no, no. You said twenty-five thousand."

And that was that. We made the deal right there and George signed an agreement and Mr. Baxter put down his signature as a witness, though I could see he didn't want to. The contract was written on the stationery of the Longhorn Arms, by hand, but my writing is very neat and legible because I went to the Catholic school in El Paso and the nuns were insane on the subject of handwriting.

"Now give me some expenses," I said.

George peeled ten hundred-dollar bills off his roll. His roll is big enough to have a custom clip holding it together. In the middle of the clip is a diamond, I guess in case George gets down to his last few hundred and he needs to pawn it.

"A thousand dollars?"

"And your airline tickets. Mr. Baxter?"

Here was an employee of the State Department and he was doing major lackey work already for George. They had probably only been together for a couple of hours. George certainly has his way with retainers. Baxter gave me the tickets and George said, "You only need a couple of days in Havana. Put them through a camp, see how they handle things. Then call me in New York and bring 'em down to Sarasota through Mexico City and get this show on the road."

"Tickets say I leave day after tomorrow."

"That's it," George said.

I knew there was something wrong with all this. George practically gave me that extra twenty-five. But money has always blinded me to my own best self-interest.

That night I took Charlene out to a Mexican restaurant that was full of hot food and thirsty drinkers. Charlene can eat. I admire that in a woman. She doesn't pick around or say she doesn't do onions or something, the way some women do. She tucks in and even gets salsa on her chin in the process.

I told her about going to Cuba and she didn't seem real enthused. For that matter, neither was I. The reason I don't go to foreign countries and never got a passport is that I don't want to be in a place where no one speaks English. Told that to a team buddy once and he asked me why the hell had I stayed with a New York team, then? He said he'd only found three or four people in the whole city who spoke English, or pretended to. But he was from Omaha originally and they think everyone doesn't speak English who ain't from Omaha.

"You ought to talk to Sid before you go," Charlene said, wiping some food from her upper lip where it was stuck. "You think by now you'd of realized that George is not your friend."

"I didn't think he was my friend ever," I said. I get riled when Charlene questions my intelligence. Any man would. "I just made me another twenty-five thousand dollars. And it's just baseball work anyway, what I'm paid to do."

"Go to Communist Cuba and pick out his team, right? Just baseball work?"

"Charlene, I'm a pitcher. I know a hitter when I see one. I know a pitcher when I see one. If I was an outfielder, it'd be different. Pitchers and catchers are the smartest players on the team. They make the best coaches and managers."

"You think you're going to be a coach when this is over?"

"Maybe. Maybe a scout. I'd like scouting, go out and watch some games and make notes and file my expenses every month."

"What if you scout wrong?"

"Well, I won't. If I see someone can't play in the Bigs, I'll tell George and we won't take him."

Charlene sneered and put down her tortilla to make a point. "You're gonna go to Castro and say, 'This boy ain't got it, Fidel.' And Castro's been standing there backing down America for more than thirty years and he's gonna doff his hat and say, 'Sorry, Mr. Shawn, sir, is there someone else I can get for you?' Shit. In your dreams."

I hadn't exactly thought of that. Maybe I should call Sid on this thing. But it was a done deal.

"And suddenly, in the middle of January, George and this Mr. Baxter, whoever he is, fly down here and knock on your door and give you a bonus and a brand-new passport to fly down to Cuba for you to evaluate? Why didn't he call you up to New York? Why didn't he call Sid? Ryan Patrick Shawn, I am beginning to have grave doubts about your genetic code."

"What does that mean?"

"You said you loved me once," Charlene said.

"I do. You never heard me take it back."

"I never heard you say it again, either."

"All right. I love you, Charlene."

"Sometime you could say it without me dragging it out of you."

"All right."

We sat there a moment and I saw Charlene had a head of steam and I was letting it settle down a little. She picked up her glass of beer and drank some, to cool the palate.

"Charlene?"

She just glared at me.

"I love you."

She kept glaring, but it got less intense.

"I love you," I said, holding her eyes in mine.

"What if we had kids? I want kids, but I don't want dumb kids. I ain't dumb and I never thought you were before. But what if there's a streak of dumbness runs through you, through your genes? Then we have a kid and he's gurgling and cute and crawling around the crib and I keep wondering, is this the dumb one or is he going to be like me?"

"I ain't dumb, Charlene. I went to college."

"You could prove it once in a while. George has got so many tricks he needs more than two sleeves. You keep falling for the same gags over and over again. This team is going to have your fingerprints all over it and George will say, when it goes wrong, that he was misled by you."

"He can say what he wants, but I got the extra money."

"And then, when the year is over, the Colorado Rockies or the Marlins or the Rangers or someone is gonna say, 'Hey, you know that real dumb player on the Yankees what sold George a load of Cuban horsemeat? Let's see if we can get him to do the same for us. Be a scout. Be a coach. Hell, we'll make him manager.' You think they're gonna say that?"

"You ever think I might know what I'm doing around an infield? You ever think that, Charlene? I played this game man and boy for thirty years and I know a little bit about it. Just a little. It don't matter if they lisp or wear dresses or carry those little red books the Chinese always had, they still gotta play baseball the same as anyone else. Same bat, same glove, same pill. I got eyes, I can see if someone is no good. I'll call George and tell him —"

"What if George disappears on you again like he's done times before?"

Damn. Another thing I hadn't thought of.

"See what I mean, Ryan? You don't think to the next jump. You gotta do better'n that with someone like George Bremenhaven."

"I'll call Sid."

"And lock the barn door."

"Charlene, you never told me you wanted to have kids."

"I'm thirty-five years old and I want to be a mama. I been thinking for a while that you were the one, because I liked you. But these last few months, you are either acting squirrelly or you are acting dumb. I'm beginning to believe this is not acting."

"I want to play baseball," I explained.

She stared at me then like she'd seen me for the first time. And then she did a surprising thing. She patted my hand on the table.

"Poor baby. That's what it is, isn't it? You just want to play baseball," she said.

"Yep," I said.

"Ryan, Ryan." She said my name twice in that tone women use when they're trying to convince you that men are children. It's the Big Mama voice, and I resent it.

"About having kids, I wouldn't worry there. Uncle Dave, up in the Panhandle, I think he was adopted by my grandfather so he's not natural kin to us."

"I wasn't thinking about anyone else except you."

"So would you throw a kid out of your house because he wanted to be a player in the Bigs?"

"I would consider it carefully," she said.

"If we were going to have kids, it would involve getting married. I don't believe in that Hollywood stuff where you get married as the last thing."

"Neither do I."

It was my turn to stare.

She stared back and I flinched first. When you're thirty-eight years old and been playing a boy's game for a living all these years, you kind of think young. I never thought about marriage. I mean, for me personally.

"You'll want to give that some thought," Charlene said, letting me off the hook. "So will I. Did you ever have an IQ test?"

"I suppose, I don't know. They give you one to go to college, don't they?"

"We might need an IQ test. I just don't want to make a mistake because I'd be stuck with it," she said.

"Why don't you make it an HIV test while you're at it, Charlene?"

"Why, are you gay? You do like wearing that pink bathrobe of mine."

"I wear your robe because it's the only warm thing you got and when we're lounging around your drafty old apartment in our altogether, I get cold. I don't wanna be cold so I put on your robe. I'll go out and buy myself a regular robe and hang it in your closet except that I ain't seen your closet or the inside of your apartment for more than a month."

"Are you shouting at me, Ryan Patrick? I won't stand to be shouted at by any man," Charlene shouted.

People in the restaurant started to look 'round at us and then turn away, sly-like, the way people do when they're catching a show.

"I'm just saying there's no reason to worry about me wearing your clothes because you don't let me come to see you anymore," I said.

It's amazing how your voice carries in a place with tile on the floor and walls. Like singing in a shower, makes you sound good or, at least, loud.

"Is there something wrong, Señor?"

The waiter was large and wore a Pancho Villa mustache. At that point, I realized we might possibly be making a spectacle of ourselves. I looked at Charlene and saw she realized the same thing.

"No, no, *por favor* the bill," I said and he went away.

Charlene stared at me a moment and then laughed. She laughed and laughed and I didn't get it.

"Do you speak Spanish, isn't that what George asked you?"

"Yeah. That's what started it," I said, still not getting it. Charlene just had a fit of the giggles and couldn't stop it.

"'*Por favor,* the bill?'"

"Well, we're in Texas, honey —"

"*Por favor,* the bill. Where'd you get your command of language? Reading Doritos bags?"

So, naturally, I had to start laughing, too. It was a good thing because we might have stayed mad — angry — at each other if I hadn't said it that way and Charlene hadn't been smart enough to pick up on it. I'm not too worried about dumb being in my genes, it's just that I don't always see the worst in other folks the way I should.

And there was another bonus that night.

I got to wear Charlene's bathrobe again. And a couple of other things happened before.

14

They took me out to the ball game the night I arrived in Havana. The park was not big league but they came out to see a ball game. The way things go in the States, a lot of the people who show up at the games are there because they can afford to be. They're the skybox crowd, and when the skyboxes overflow, you find them down the first and third base lines in what used to be boxes and are still called that, although the real boxes are skyboxes.

They were hooting and hollering and carrying on and this was before the game even started.

My escort was a smiley little fellow with a mustache who spoke English just like Ricky Ricardo. He pointed out the players on the roster sheet who were going to be going to New York.

We ate something like beans and rice on a tortilla and it tasted good, but it was a little too hot for me. I started sweating and asked Mr. Martinez for a beer, *por favor.* He was my guide. My rusty Spanish was coming back bit by bit and Martinez understood me enough to send someone to fetch an ice-cold. On the other hand, it's hard to screw up *cerveza fria.*

Quite a trip down: Houston to Mexico City and then a short hop to Havana International, as they call it.

It wasn't a real warm night, not at all, but the humidity was just lying there like a bump on a log, building up to something that was going to be rain.

First guy up was not on my roster, but I watched him anyway. He walked on four pitches, which told me nothing. The next guy was on the roster, listed as infield material. He stroked a clean single to right even though he batted right-handed and the first guy, Munoz, legged it to third on the throw. The next guy up was Raul.

George told me to keep an especial eye on this kid.

The pitcher was a blazer. Threw it high and inside, just to get respect, and Raul sort of ducked out of the way without acknowledging that the pitcher might want to take his head clean off. He did a couple of swings outside the box and got back into his stance way too fast. A major leaguer takes his time. Dusts his hands on the resin, looks at his bat as though he's never seen one before — you know, all the tricks. Makes the pitcher think too much about the next pitch. But Raul was back in the box like greased lightning.

The next was high and outside and Raul shouldn't have done it. It was a ball, but Raul couldn't wait, maybe he had a train to catch.

He stroked the ball like Willie Mosconi shooting pool. Just that clean and certain, like it was no trouble at all. The pitch was high and outside, but Raul just reached over and plucked it out of the catcher's mitt and batted it down the first base line, fair by two feet, all the way to the outfield wall. Two runs scored and Raul stood on second not even breathing hard. The crowd started throwing things up in the air.

Damn. I was feeling like throwing things myself and I didn't have anything but a bottle of beer and it was still half-full. The kid shouldn't have done what he did, he should've waited on the next pitch, but it was like he had his own timetable and it had nothing to do with anyone else.

Raul hit three for four that night, which is a .750 clip. Mr. Martinez said Raul was the best player in Cuba, and he beamed when he said it.

The kid looked light to me, but his wrists must have been made of steel cables. He slugged the way Ted Williams slugged, rearing back to let the power of the swing flow through the wrists and sort of letting the bat dictate the power of the drive. It's like one of those rides in the carnival where the faster the center pole turns, the higher and faster the cars on the periphery ride. Raul swung that bat and I was seeing a medieval knight swinging a mace at the end of a chain.

I was semi-impressed by it. And very tired when Mr. Martinez took me to my room at the Hilton, which is no longer a part of the Hilton chain, of course. Sort of a Comrade Hilton now.

I loved those old cars on the street. City was full of them. The air was bad from auto pollution and the streets tended to be narrow, but the cars were as wide as Wilshire Boulevard. Damn, I love old cars, I don't know why they don't make them anymore.

I figured when we started trading with Cuba in a big way, those old cars would be part of it. There are car collectors in this country who would pony up to get some of those rust-free specimens that were a dime a dozen on Havana streets.

The streets were mostly dark, by the way, which Mr. Martinez explained was part of the ongoing shortages, but he wasn't complaining. I could understand why.

The room was a hotel room, all right, and the air conditioner, which was in the window, worked. It kept me awake half the night, but I didn't dare turn it off. The rain started around one in the morning and the rain danced on the metal box hanging outside the window. I like the sound of rain on metal, I think everyone does. Rain in Texas is manna mostly, unless we get too much of it, and that seldom happened when I was a kid down in El Paso. Rain made you wanna run out in the red dirt road and dance in your clothes until you were soaked. Rain was warm when I was a kid. I bet myself, before I fell asleep, that rain in Havana was warm, too.

I spent three days watching them all on the practice field, but I didn't show my stuff until the last day. It's tricky evaluating minor league talent when you don't know the starting point of what you're looking for, but I was learning the ropes. I watched the players when they were involved in the action and that tells you a lot. Some players, especially outfielders, even in the Bigs, stand around during a game like they just happened to be there waiting for a bus. They don't go on their toes, they barely follow the play, they want to be so cool that they outcool themselves. In other words, they don't come to concentrate on the game.

That was not the problem in Havana. These boys played like boys. They talked all the time, the infield chattered like the inside of a Texas jail at lights out. Yak, yak, yak Spanish, mile a minute.

About this lisping thing. It is annoying at first; you miss certain words even if you speak Spanish as well as I do. Still, we had players up from Panama and Venezuela who didn't lisp, so I could parlez in the locker room if I felt like it, but I seldom did. The other thing is slang. Cubans use slang all the time and it was hard to pick up.

The last afternoon, I took the mound because I wanted to see what these boys would do when they tried a rough sample of major league pitching. Not that I am a Nolan Ryan or even a Deke Williams, but I earned my pay over the past sixteen years.

Raul.

He didn't look like much to me from 60 feet 6 inches away, but looks can be deceiving. Ask anyone ever had to pitch to Molitor.

I remembered the way Raul had stroked that pitcher my first night in Havana. I wasn't fastball, wasn't even a fastballer when I was young. I could do a decent 85 miles an hour, but you only earn a ticket to Des

Moines with that kind of pitch. I was a thinker and I was thinking, standing on the mound. The ball felt wet in my hand because of sweating. Must have been the humidity. Might have had something to do with facing Raul, *mano y mano,* 60 feet 6 inches away.

I decided to try some chin music, just to tune him up.

I threw it inside, letter high, and he hit the deck in a cloud of dust. When you throw inside on purpose, don't fake it. Dumb shit wants to stand there, let him get plunked in the ribs. That's the way I throw. Deke taught me.

I heard a lot of yakking behind me, but I just took the ball back from the catcher and paid it no mind.

The catcher was a kid named Orestes Manguez and he had an arm. But there was no reason for him to burn it back to me, just because he and Raul were roommates. So I called him out to the mound.

— Orestes (I said in Spanish), batter's gotta learn to deal with the brushback in the Bigs.

— Yes.

— You can throw the ball hard as you want to me, but I don't want no hard feelings. This is just business.

— What?

— Baseball. This is just business. I'm making a judgment here on what your buddy can do.

— He can stick the ball right up your fat Yanqui ass, sir.

— We're all Yankees now (I said, making a nice pun).

But Orestes wasn't smiling. He grumped his way back across the plate, assumed the squat, and Raul aimed his bat at me and then regripped it with both hands.

High and away.

My intention was to get him to reach for it, tap it into the infield.

Pop. He popped that son of a bitch toward right and I turned to watch the line drive descend. It didn't. Just kept getting higher the longer it traveled. Cleared the wire fence in the outfield by ten feet and the players — those in the field behind me and those lounging behind the plate — started dancing and laughing and yakking it up. I never seen a happier bunch of ball players since I was a kid and we were doing it for the love of the game.

Raul just stood there, grinning at me.

So I tried again. I have a good slider left over from my tutelage days under Catfish. Understand, I'd been idle all winter and might be a little rusty, but I gave it my best shot.

Slider slid the way it was supposed to.

All Raul did with it is what he did before. Only this time it was center field, rising on the line just like a shot fired at a squadron of ducks. A low-flying duck would have been grounded by that ball — I swear it was going 90 miles an hour when it cleared the fence.

When someone hits a ball out as fast as you managed to throw it in, there is something very serious about his hitting.

I must have shook my head in wonder because everyone started cracking up and pointing at me and yakking. To show I was a good sport, I pulled off my glove and threw it down and shook my head again. That got them off again. Then I walked to the plate.

I was going to shake hands with Raul, tell him he had a good stroke.

But when I dropped my glove, he dropped his bat and turned and walked back toward the dugout of the practice field. It wasn't a dugout, exactly, just a covered area over a long wooden bench. The bats were in a rack at the side of the bench.

— Shit, man, I was just going to say you got a sweet swing.

— Fuck you (Raul said), you just got a lousy pitch, is all. I can't believe you're good enough to play for a major league team.

This got everyone laughing again and making mocking gestures. This one clown, Tio, took a glove and threw it down and stomped on it, up and down, and shook his head in mock fury and this got the players all crazy with the giggles again.

Felt my face getting flush, but then I thought better about it. The hell with them.

We stayed at it. The Cuban kids had moxie, which is a New York word I personally like.

Well, I did manage to prove to myself that I still had enough to win one for the gipper. I struck out the clown Tio on three pitches and I managed to get Orestes to ground out, except the second baseman threw the ball a mile over the first baseman's head.

— You boys are a bit sloppy in the field (I said to none of them and all of them).

— They're just nervous (Raul said).

I stared at him a moment to see if this was another Cuban joke. But Raul wasn't giving any indication.

— They oughta be. Old Fidel there, he says these boys are the best, that's the way he sold them to George. If they can't pick up a grounder out of the dirt, they are going to be the laughingstock of New York City.

— New York will not laugh.

— That's what you say. (I shrugged.)

Raul came over from the dugout and stood about this far from me. His face was serious, and when he was serious he looked just as young as he was. It was a different look he got when he was batting. This was a twenty-three-year-old look.

— Tell me, Señor Shawn, have you been up in the Empire State Building?

— What's that got to do with handling a grounder?

— It is the tallest building in the world.

— Not anymore.

— I have read this.

— I don't really give a shit.

— What's your problem, Señor?

— My problem is your problem. Can't Jimenez play shortstop?

Raul just stared at me a moment before replying:

— This business. "Business," you said. Why is Doctor Castro sending us to North America?

— Beats the shit out of me. Believe me, you boys are not the popular choice.

— Is there danger?

— Naw. We only kill umpires.

— That's a joke, but I am not joking, Señor.

— C'mon and play ball.

Raul trotted to the outfield then and I settled back to spray a few out there with a fungo bat, just to make sure that the boys actually did know a thing or two about fielding.

It went all right. Raul is not Jimmy Piersall in the outfield when it comes to flat-out fielding, but he was all right, as good as Doak Walker had been for us at considerably more money. Damn. I was even beginning to think the way George talked, and that bothered me. The other thing was, the guys were taking it seriously. They were on their toes in the outfield, even when the sun started falling and we had been at it long enough to make us all look like drowned rats. I was giving it to them good on the hitting and fielding and the rest of it and they were taking it with a measuring spoon, like medicine.

That night I was taken to a big white building in the center of the city by my guide Martinez, who said I would be received by the Supremo himself.

I was wearing a white polo shirt and dark slacks and sneakers because it seemed to me the heat demanded that no one overdress himself. We took Mr. Martinez's Trabant to the white building and I thought my back would give way before my legs numbed up.

We untangled ourselves from the car and went up some steps and through a couple of doors and halls and then we were in a big room with a lovely carpet on the floor and a lot of paintings on the walls. A couple were portraits of Fidel and his merry men in the mountains during the armed part of the revolution. There was also a Cezanne, which I knew was a Cezanne because it was signed Cezanne.

Around ten P.M., Castro and his entourage came into the room and I just stood there, not knowing what I was supposed to do or say. This is usually the best thing if you really don't know what to do next. It's what rabbits do.

Castro smelled of Old Spice when he came around to give me a hug. I did notice that men hugged a lot in Cuba, but mostly each other. I attribute nothing to this, just note it.

— Señor Shawnus (he said), I hope you have enjoyed your visit to Cuba and you have seen how excellent is the baseball which we play.

— It is excellent, Mr. President. I enjoyed it more than I can say. And Mr. Martinez here was very kind to me to show me the city and everything.

— The hotel room. Did you like the hotel room?

— I liked it very much. It's just like a hotel room in the States.

— Don't patronize me, Señor. I've lived in the States and I would much rather live in Cuba.

— I know what you mean, sir. I am not patronizing no one. I am just saying what I saw, sir. I like your city and your people.

— Then why do you declare unceasing war on us, day after day, trying to bleed us to death?

That stopped me for a moment. The only time I ever thought of Cuba in my life before this whole thing started was wondering why Ricky Ricardo couldn't speak better English and now I was being turned into the United States. I didn't want to get into a fight here over anything. George sent me down to get him some scab ballplayers and I was just doing my job.

— I'm just a baseball player, Mr. President. I don't declare war on no one except the Baltimore Orioles and the Boston Red Sox.

"Oh, speak English," Fidel said. "I can barely understand a word you said. Your Spanish is terrible, you're going to have to learn to speak it better."

"I been trying to lisp it the last three days," I said. I was getting a little irritated with the attitude. Everyone was so sure their shit didn't stink that they didn't even notice what a slum they were living in. These people acted like they were French. The nice thing about Americans was we use language to understand one another. If a Mexican says something in English I don't get, I ask him again and he tries harder until I understand him, even down to using hand signals. The Cubans acted like Spanish was a joke I didn't get, and I say that's rude of them.

"Do you mean to insult me and my countrymen?" Fidel asked. He has very large eyes, brown, but you wouldn't want to get them lit up the way they were lighting up then. I backed off, even literally.

"I didn't mean no nothing, Mr. President. This is a great honor for me to be sent here, to see your best baseball players play and to see your wonderful city. I hope I can come again, sir, when the season is over up north."

"When the season is over, you will still be playing, Señor Shawnus. In the World Series. Because my brave youths are the best baseball players in all the world and now the world will see that. I have accepted your government's humble petition to make amends for the past thirty-five years, years of insults and plots and acts of war, because I am a man of peace and honor."

I never saw someone as full of himself as old Castro. Not even George. Not even Tommy Tradup who was the best hitter we had last year before George sold him. Tommy thought hitting a home run earned him two women per night so he'd just hang out in Elaine's until they'd come to their senses and adore him. But Castro had an excuse, because no one was saying no to him for all those years until the Russians fell in on themselves.

"I don't know what to say," I said.

"You say 'thank you,'" he said.

"Thank you," I said.

"On behalf of a grateful American government."

"President, I don't know nothing about this stuff, about what's going on with you and us, I just know I was supposed to come down here and escort your ball players to the Yankee spring camp in Fort Lauderdale. I'm just a simple baseball player."

"With a lousy slider," he said then.

"What?"

"My Raul humiliated you today when you tried to bean him. You have a reputation as a beanball pitcher, and when you tried to bean our best player, he became very, very angry. To that point, he was willing to accept you for what you are, an old baseball player who thinks he can speak pure Spanish, which you obviously cannot. But when you anger a Cubano, you stir up a nest of vipers, and this little viper struck back and showed you how pathetic your intimidation is."

This diatribe seemed to have exhausted him and he reverted to Spanish.

— You, I hold you, responsible for the safety and the well-being of those twenty-four boys who will go to the spring camp in Florida. You and the government. If you harm those boys or let the fanatics in Miami harm them, then it will be on your head. I will follow you wherever you try to hide, whatever hole you crawl into, and I will deal with you. Remember that Fidel is watching you, Señor.

This did not set well with me at all.

And then I thought of Charlene warning me about this.

And Sid. When I called Sid the next morning after my night with Charlene, he was practically hysterical and told me I was crazy to go to Cuba in George's place. Funny how people who give me advice all say the same things.

I tried to soothe him.

— El Presidente, I want you to know the health and welfare of your ball players, of my teammates, is a prime concern to me personally.

— I know it is. It has to be.

That was it. That last line was it. He turned away like he was dismissing a waiter and moved back across the room with this gaggle of people around him and left me and Mr. Martinez alone with just a security guard to glare at us. What had I done to offend anyone? Did Castro really think when his boys played their first game in the Bigs that someone wouldn't brushback a hitter? How was I responsible for that?

I went back to the hotel and took another shower. The water ran slow, but I managed to get wet enough to stand in front of the air conditioner until I started to feel shivery all over. Then I toweled off and tried to call George in New York. For the third straight day, the lines were overloaded, the operator told me. I thanked her and went to bed. I never did get to sleep that night, which explains why I was so groggy in the morning.

The players looked groggy, too, assembled with their bags at the airport. It must have been a fine howdedo, their last night in Havana. I felt a little sympathy for them — they were just kids going to America where everyone spoke a different language and people drove tiny new cars.

But not too much sympathy. Especially for Raul. He was clinging to this girl like he was going to Vietnam to fight or something, and I thought that was a little melodramatic. She covered him with kisses and she was sure something to look at. So I looked at her until Orestes, the catcher, came over and asked me what I thought I was staring at.

I might have to take shit from Castro, but I was damned if I had to take it from Orestes.

— What do you think? Lovely young thang over there with Raul.

— That is his intended, Señor.

— I hope he has good intentions.

— Are you insulting that woman, Señor? Or my friend, Raul?

— I ain't insulting nobody. I never insult anyone this early in the morning. I could make an exception in your case, however.

— You better watch yourself, Señor.

— You mind your own business, Orestes.

He just stood his ground, glaring at me, and I looked away, back to the girl and Raul, just to see what he would do. But he didn't do anything. There were security guards everywhere in the almost empty airport and Mr. Martinez was nowhere to be seen. I wanted to say good-bye to him; he had been kind to a stranger.

Instead, we boarded a plane.

The girl hanging on Raul walked him across the tarmac and then a soldier barred her from going any farther. I thought Raul wouldn't go any farther either, but I wasn't going to say anything. This was George's show and I was just the tour guide.

We walked up the ramp to the twin-engine prop job and Raul made it halfway up when the girl cried out to him.

— I love you, beloved. I love you and I miss you already. I love you.

He turned and I thought he would bolt back down the ramp steps, but there was a security guard standing at the bottom. He looked at the guard. The guard shook his head slowly and I guess Raul got the message. He trudged up the last steps like he was walking to the chair.

The plane bumped up and out of Cuba and I looked out the window. The countryside was green and there were mountains in the east. I thought I saw Guantanamo Bay but, never having seen it on the ground, I sure couldn't swear to it from the air.

We touched down at Mexico City an hour and twenty minutes later. We went through customs fairly fast and there were TV cameras but they were kept at a distance. I thought I saw Mr. Baxter, George's State Department friend, but I might have been mistaken.

We picked up a guy named Romero there. He wore a tropical suit already plastered with sweat and a dirty white shirt and tie. I asked him who he was and he said nothing in a particular way of saying nothing — he just stared at me and then walked past me. He sat down in a front seat of the plane and did a head count on the players. They saw him. So he was big brother, I thought, the chaperone. I felt relieved to have the chaperone along; whatever happened would be his problem, not mine. That's the way I thought then.

The plane lifted out of the smog bowl of Mexico City (which would make L.A. look clean) and headed sort of north and east toward Lauderdale.

We touched down in a shade over two hours.

Then the fun really began.

15

The New York Yanquis. Papers everywhere were calling us that.

George didn't like that part of it, but he liked the publicity just fine. For a club with twenty-four rookies and one over-the-hiller (me), he was getting more ink than the Bulls in Michael Jordan days.

Sparky Hershberg was back as manager, still without a clue in Spanish, and Sam Ortiz, the clubhouse manager, was now promoted to sit in the dugout with him or stand by the sidelines and interpret for him.

The young warriors from Havana treated Sam with mild contempt for a few days until they found out that getting along with the clubhouse man is more important than getting along with the owner.

Sam worked it by first showering them with the luxuries of the Bigs. Big, fluffy, clean towels by the dozen. Locker space. Soap and shampoo for showers. Taking care of their bags, getting them to the right rooms at the hotel, making sure the icebox was stocked with mineral water and Coke and beer.

Then he started punishing the guys who patronized him. Orestes learned first when Sam stranded him at the practice field and Orestes had to walk back to the hotel, asking directions most humbly of anyone who looked like he might know Spanish. There are not a lot of people in Fort Lauderdale who look like they might know Spanish, and those who do are generally the hired help. Orestes was pulling his Spanish grandee on them and they resented it; they might have to take that kind of shit from Anglos who paid their paycheck but be damned if they were going to take it from another greaser.

Orestes got the idea.

Protestors were there from Miami from the git-go, but the cops handled it because there were plenty of FBI guys around, too. The FBI guys walked around in suits with white shirts and ties and talked into their lapels a lot and wore hearing aids. It was all very distracting between that and no one speaking English and the curious but unfriendly national media coming down every day to see the monkeys in the zoo.

I was working on Ryan Shawn's problems, which were several. Raul had been right. Something was wrong with my slider. I stayed on the field longer than anyone else just to play catch with Billy Bacon, the pitching coach.

At night, after a couple of beers and a steak and salad, I went back to my room and immersed myself in television English. All that Spanish I was using day after day was taking a toll on me.

We did an exhibition with the White Sox.

The Chicagos were mean about everything. The pitcher threw so many inside that the umpire — it was Flaherty — had to go out to the mound and explain it was only a fucking exhibition game.

The Sox gave us the dog. No reason to slap someone twice with the ball on a steal of second. They had beat Tio, but when Tio stood up to dust off his togs, the second baseman slapped him with the gloved ball again for good luck. This pissed off Tio and he said something in Spanish and the next thing you knew, everyone was out of the dugout.

Major league fighting is not like hockey in that no one ever gets hurt, unless it's by accident. Flaherty threw out Tio and the Sox second baseman and me. That left it for Sam to interpret for Sparky. I don't know what Sam said to Sparky, but it wasn't much good. We came out on the losing end, but the Sox wouldn't let it go, they were yelling insults at us all the way off the field. Orestes wanted to go back and fight, but I shoved him hard into the tunnel and told him no one paid extra for a fight, this wasn't hockey. They were teaching the Cubanos a thing or two, the fucking Sox sons of bitches. Nothing personal except it was all personal. Even the Panamanian shortstop on the Sox joined in on dogging the Cubans.

The Cubans got their dander up at last and took it out on the Indians, who came over to play us a friendly one in the afternoon.

The Cleveland tribe was just its usual lackadaisical self with it being so early in spring training and them thinking that in a few short weeks they would be freezing their cookies off up in northern Ohio.

Raul came up in the first inning because I had him batting number three. I say "I" because I was working through Sparky, who deeply resented ending up his career as chief cook and bottle washer to a bunch of Communist foreigners. He got himself in such a funk that he refused to talk to anyone except me. And he only talked to me to complain about what George had done to him. Sparky was becoming even more of a pain in the ass than he usually was.

Raul took a strike and looked insulted and complained to the umpire. The ump didn't speak Spanish and Raul didn't speak English but the ump got the gist of it and warned him. He said it loud, the way you have to talk to foreigners.

"You wanna get thrown outta this game, Commie?"

Now that was unfair. I said to Sparky, "You gotta go out and bitch for Raul."

"Raul?"

"The kid at the plate."

"I thought that one was Orestes."

"Orestes bats eighth."

"I can't keep these assholes straight."

Strike two. Raul just glared at the umpire this time.

The next one was high and dry. Raul reared back and whipped his wrists and the bat came around faster than a chopper blade. Splat. I told you about that sound a home run makes when it's clean? It made that sound.

The ball tore a line through the middle of the infield and the pitcher saved his own life by hugging the dirt. Ever see a sweet liner about six feet off the ground just blazing ahead? The ball just soared from there, like it was launched from a catapult. Just kept climbing into that lazy, hazy Florida sunshine sky. The center fielder ran back to the fence for exercise because everyone in the place knew where that ball was going.

Raul, the crazy son of a bitch, dogged the Cleveland pitcher, barely trotting around the bases, practically walking. And he wasn't looking at the ball, just staring at the pitcher, putting the sign on him.

I want to skip ahead now to the next time Raul came up. Same pitcher, same game. This time he took a tumble in the dirt, which is normal for a first pitch after giving up a home run the last time. Just routine meanness. Then Raul spit — first time I seen him spit — and waited. Didn't take a practice swing or nothing. Just waited. The pitcher — it was Sanderson — did a big windup, all arms and legs, and laid it down a little too low. Raul swung and popped a line down the first base side. He rounded first when any fool could see he only had a blazing single. But he didn't stop and didn't listen and the right fielder grabbed the ball on the second hop and flung it into second where the second baseman was waiting.

He shouldn't have been.

Raul slid into second about the time the ball got there and about the same moment that Raul's spikes tore a chunk out of the second baseman's calf. He went down with a yowl and dropped the ball and then all hell broke loose.

The shortstop for Cleveland was offended by the slide and told Raul he was a dirty Communist cocksucker but, again, he wasted it because it was in English.

Raul grinned at him, and at the second baseman writhing around the vicinity of the bag, and that was the end of that.

The shortstop charged him and the umpire backed off so that he could more clearly assess the carnage to come. As is the rule of baseball, any fight must immediately be joined by everyone on both teams. I looked out and it seemed a long way to second. I try never to be the first guy to pile on because punches are still being thrown at that point. I like to jog to a fight in a nonchalant way and find someone easy at the outside of the fray to jump on.

I turned and saw Sparky just sitting there and I said something like "Hey, Sparky, let's go fight."

Sparky just looked at me. "Fuck those greasers, I ain't fighting for them."

Well, the old rah-rah spirit had to be upheld so I upheld it myself by trotting out to the infield just as Raul and the shortstop had disappeared under a pile of bodies.

The ugly thing was that the Cubans didn't seem to understand the rules of combat. They thought a fight was really a fight.

They were kicking, gouging, and biting up a storm, and the home plate ump, Bill Donnelly, shouted to me, "Somebody is gonna get seriously hurt out of this."

So I started shouting in Spanish.

— Stop fighting, stop it!

Nada.

— The police have machine guns!

That started slowing it.

— They are going to kill everyone!

It was still roiling but calming a bit.

— Heads down, they're getting ready to shoot!

Well, sanity more or less got the upper hand and when the bodies were cleared up, nobody was really that badly hurt except the Cleveland backup catcher, who got a finger in his eye. Everyone got thrown out of the game, of course, and letters were sent to the league office and the newspapers made too much of a fuss about it. But the reaction, I saw, was already setting in. Say what you want bad about Americans, they hate being seen as unfair and the way the other teams were dogging the Cuban kids, well, it just wasn't baseball. There was even an editorial about this in the *Miami Herald* and I thought it augured good for us. After all, the Cuban kids couldn't help it if Doctor Castro and George Bremenhaven were cooking up secret deals — they were just kids who wanted to play ball, and what was more American than that?

The whole time, George pulled his disappearing act. Never made a show.

Spring training was not pleasant the way it usually is. The crowd was big at games, but it was a quiet crowd, full of curious people who had never seen a Cuban play baseball before. The park holds seven, eight thousand and they must have been uncomfortable, sitting on their hands for nine innings at a stretch. The other teams had at least stopped putting this thing on a nuclear threat basis. We were all in Florida just to play ball and get tan and not overexert ourselves. Every team had a hothead or two, and some of the Cuban kids got regular baseball slurs, but the other players saw that this thing was not the missile crisis. They resented the Cubans as scabs, but they had come to play ball.

The quiet crowds, though, that got to me. The people paid their money and bought tickets and went through the metal detectors — the FBI guys insisted on that — but then they just sat on their hands. I hoped it wasn't going to be that way all year.

I told all this to Charlene when I called her at night. She was still in the habit of being out some nights, but I was learning that Charlene was not going to be anybody's little housewife and was coming and going as she pleased. But when we talked, it was real pleasant. I didn't tell her what Castro said to me, but I did tell her he smelled like Old Spice. That made her get the giggles. She has a nice, deep-in-the-throat giggle that has appreciation for your wit written all over it. I counted myself a lucky man in that, at least.

The cops arrested a half-dozen Miami Cuban exiles one night when they staged a demonstration in the lobby of our hotel, but I didn't pay any attention to that and neither did anyone else. The Cubans on the Yankees were getting to be old hat. The only one who was clearly destined to get ink in the future was Raul.

Damn. Arrogant son of a bitch though he was, he could hit a ball. Not just home runs but singles and doubles and triples and liners and towering drives. The man seemed determined never to let an appearance at the plate pass that he didn't whack into the ball. Throw outside the zone and he'd reach across the plate with those long arms and just flick that ball over the second baseman's head into center, bouncing fifty feet in front of the outfielder. Whack, whack, whack. I hate to say it was a pleasure to watch him hit, but it was.

The real thorn in my side was Romero, Castro's spy and the designated chaperone. He counted all the time. He counted the kids on the bus to the park and counted them on the bus on the way back. He counted them in their rooms. He had a room at the end of the hall and his light was always on and his door was always open. Little fucking bean counter. I tried to talk to him one time and it was no go. Then, when the agent for the player's association came by, I tried to explain to the players they had to join the union. They said OK. The rep said OK. Romero didn't get it.

"You call yourself a Communist and you ain't gonna let them join the union? What kind of a Communist are you?" I said in plain English.

Romero just glared at me with lazy, bad eyes.

The players' rep was Bill Ofmeyer from headquarters. He said, "Whaddaya mean, Communists? We aren't Communists."

"I know you ain't Communists, I was just making a point with Castro's toady here. Hey, Romero, you want Castro to get the dog for sending in scabs to break the union?"

Romero didn't understand this at all so I tried again in more formal Spanish.

— Señor, I was told nothing about this (Romero said).

— Fine, fine, I'll handle it.

I turned to Ofmeyer and said, "Whadda they gotta do?"

"Sign up," he said.

I personally took the papers around to the boys and made them sign. I said they had to sign to play. Señor Romero watched this and made out that he was reading the form, but he couldn't read English any better than I could read Spanish. He said he would have to call El Supremo. I said he could call his Aunt Tillie, they'd still had to sign with the union. In the end, they did.

I did get together one night with Tommy Tradup and we became semi-hilarious in the bar at my hotel. The team stays at the Palm Aire Hotel, which is nice digs and has a nice little bar. More important, the Cuban kids didn't drink there because it cost too much. Instead, they bought six-packs and drank in their rooms and watched the Spanish station out of Miami.

I was never close to Tommy when we were teammates, but we did hoist a few from time to time because when you're on a long road trip, even teammates can substitute for friends. This night was one of those times, and Tommy didn't turn mean on me until he'd had his sixth stinger.

"Your new friend, Raul, he's an uppity spic bastard, isn't he?" Tommy said.

"No more than you, hoss. All you hitters got the disease. All the great ones," I added, stroking him down the way you do a horse.

"That cunt is gonna find out that we play the game different here," Tommy said. He sneered. He was a mean drunk. I had forgotten that. I should have been counting his stingers for him.

"Well, I'm sure he'll learn. He's just a rook, Tommy."

"You, you fuckin' traitor, I expect you to say that."

"Now, hold on, Tommy. You ask me to have a beer with you and then you insult me. You don't wanna do that." I said this calm, looking down the dark bar at the bartender, wishing I was back in my room. I didn't need this shit.

"You fuckin' rummy pitcher, you suck George's cock and whatcha do now, the same for that cunt?"

See, when a drunk gets mean, he swears and the words seem to lose their impact through the alcoholic haze, so they just pile them on, one after another, much like a baseball brawl. After a while, words fail them and that's when the bottles start flying. I wasn't in a flying mood myself and I started to look at my watch as though time meant something to me.

"I gotta run, Tommy," I said.

"Fuck that, stay for another drink," he said.

"Can't. Got to call my girl."

"Aw, you ain't got a girl, you just sucking cock these days."

"Tommy, don't be saying things you don't mean."

"I do mean them," he said.

"Then don't say them anyway."

"Oh, yeah. You wanna stop me saying things I don't mean?"

This is the moment when Clint Eastwood gets that squinty tic in his eye or John Wayne hauls back and the fight commences. Except I am not in a movie and I am neither of those guys.

"Grow up," I said and turned.

He conked me on the back of my head with my own empty beer bottle. The bottle did not break, thank goodness. But it hurt like hell so I turned around, as though he had tapped me on the shoulder.

He still held the bottle by the neck.

"Put the bottle down, Tommy."

He dropped it on the bar and it broke. This got the bartender's attention and he edged down toward our end. (Where was he a couple of minutes earlier?)

"You got trouble, take it out of here," he said.

Tommy said, "Go fuck yourself, monkeyface."

I didn't say a thing. I just turned and started out of the lounge. Tommy held on to the bar for the good reason that he needed to, but I could hear him all the way into the lobby.

"You lie down with Cubans, you wake up with fleas. Remember that, you son of a bitch!"

It made about as much sense as anything did.

16

We escaped from the Grapefruit League with an 11 and 14 record, which was fairly miserable.

The New York sports media is as vicious as they come and they bared their collective teeth at the sorry lot of us as we descended the American Airlines charter at LaGuardia. The team bus was waiting. I was glad to see it still spelled *Yankees* the regular way. Microphones cluttered the arrivals area inside the terminal, but not for us. They were commandeered by our supreme leader, George himself, finally ducking out of hiding.

The Cubans dutifully marched aboard the bus, but I opted for a cab. I told the guy the address in Fort Lee and he grimaced and cursed and said it would cost me $40 and it was a trip out of his way and all the blah-blah I hear every time I take a cab to Fort Lee.

I wanted to get home in the worst way. I wanted to see if the drive-away car service demon had delivered my car without denting it or stealing the lighter. I wanted to turn on the TV just to hear some more English. The bilingual thing was giving me a headache every day.

Mostly, I just wanted to get away from baseball. It was the first time in my life I was beginning to feel like that, and it bothered me. One-hundred-sixty-two games with these kids who now had about twelve words of English between them — and one of those was *cerveza,* which isn't English to begin with. It wasn't that they couldn't learn English. Some were actually smart. It was that they refused to. If Mexicans had been that arrogant, they'd still be living on the wrong side of the Rio Grande to this day and we wouldn't have any cooks in our Italian restaurants.

There was a dent in the right front fender, but the lighter was still in its slot. The anonymous kid who had driven the car up from Texas had parked it in the pay lot of the apartment building. I'd move the car later. I was beat.

There was a plastic garbage bag full of mail accumulated over the winter. I took it along with my bags into the elevator.

It was good to be home, even if home was just a studio in a high-rise on the Hudson River looking over at Manhattan.

The beer I left in the icebox was still there and I had one and just sat in my armchair with my feet up on the windowsill and looked at the city. It was late on an April afternoon and the light was fine, angling low behind me and making the city shine.

I started thinking about something and stopped when I realized I was thinking in Spanish. I never realized before what a struggle two languages were when you were working with people in another language. Made me wonder how those immigrants managed to hold up while struggling to make a living.

The phone rang.

I answered on the third ring.

"You son of a bitch, what are you trying to pull on me now? I was at the airport."

"I saw you, George. I thought you had matters well in hand."

"You son of a bitch, I was going to introduce you."

"I figured that. That's why I'm here now."

"I give you an extra twenty-five thousand on your contract and you pull this shit on me, ducking your responsibilities."

"I've got no responsibility to talk to the media and act like your Charlie McCarthy."

"What the fuck is wrong with this team? You guys stunk up the Grapefruit League this spring."

"It's only spring training, George. They're just learning to work together."

"The fucking opening day is three days away, what kind of shit are you pulling? I could lose a fortune on this thing."

"You could hardly lose a fortune since you traded away your fifty-million-dollar personnel roster."

"Except for you, you broken-down son of a bitch. I kept you."

"Yeah. Now I wish you hadn't."

"You gonna quit on me? You and that cocksucker agent Sid cooking up —"

"George, I can see you now, those arteries pounding and your eyes bulging out of your head. I won't tell you to calm down because I'd just as soon you had a stroke, then maybe you'd stop calling me all the time to hear yourself think out loud."

"I own you, Ryan, I own you!"

"People don't own people except in certain parts of the Middle East and Africa. So you've got a contract, is all you've got."

"And the contract says you got to help me with these Cubanos. They got their rooms at the East Side Hotel and they start complaining right away about the sheets and the beds and the bugs."

"Get an exterminator."

"I spoiled them. I spoiled them in Florida, put them up at that hotel. This is New York, this isn't Florida. People live like this here, don't they get it?"

"When I first came up, I was in that East Side hotel you own, George. I'd rather live in a Chinese prison than live there."

"Oh, Mr. Bigshot now with his $650,000 contract —"

"George, you want to settle this now? You call up Sid and make him a reasonable buyout offer and I'll walk tomorrow. I'm tired of your shit and I'm tired of getting a headache every day listening to those kids and I'm tired of interpreting for Sparky when Sam goes and hides in the club-house. Even Sam gets tired of them."

Silence.

Now George became conversational in tone: "What's wrong, Ryan? With the team?"

"Time will tell." It is my all-time favorite sports cliché.

"What's that mean?"

"It means you got to give them time and treat them right."

"All right. I'll send over an exterminator."

"That's a start."

"What if this thing doesn't jell? In a month or so."

"Then we'll finish lower than you expected."

"I expect to win the pennant, nothing less. New York expects nothing less."

"It's good to have great expectations."

"You see any bright spot in any of this? Sparky looks like he's on dope, I can't get a straight answer from him. I should fire his ass and get some-one else."

"It isn't Sparky. Sparky is fifty-six years old. He's used to talking to ball players, not talking through his clubhouse manager. They're a decent bunch of players —"

"You were supposed to weed out the bad ones."

"Some are better than others. What did you expect, twenty-four super-men?"

"Yes. I expected twenty-four supermen and one washed-up reliever."

"Well, you got part of your expectations."

"You mean you."

"I mean the kid — Raul. He's genuine, George, he'll learn his way the first go-round of games, but it'll be the hitter learning, not the pitchers learning how to pitch to him. Because you can't. You can walk him to get around him, but if you put it anywhere near the plate at any speed with any curve, he'll hit you. He's a natural born hitter and he's only twenty-three. You stole him."

That pleased George, to think he'd made a good theft.

"Anyone else?"

"Pitcher named Ramon Suarez, he's as hard a thrower as I've seen since Nolan, but he's twenty-two and gets steamed up when things don't always go his way. Billy Bacon is trying to show him some tricks with a slider but he's kind of stubborn about his own style. What they really need, all of them, is to loosen up. I think that between Castro and you they're a little insecure."

"Insecurity in an employee is a good thing," George said.

I didn't say anything. George was an old leopard and he wasn't going to learn new spots.

"What about the catcher, Orestes?"

"You coulda done better keeping a veteran there, settle down the pitchers."

"Too late now," George said. "You've got something nice to say about everyone. You sound like Sparky."

"George, spring training is just not the place to form a new team. They got to play with each other — they came from different teams, you know. They got to learn to adjust to each other, to the weaknesses as well as the strengths. How long you been around baseball, anyway?"

"I got a good mind to fire your ass right now."

"Go ahead. The checks can be sent to me at Houston."

"But I won't."

"Why?"

And he sounded just like Sid that night in Chicago.

"I need you right now, Ryan. You're useful."

Damn. Just like Sid said he would say if you pressed him on it. He needed me more than I needed him.

17

George had to do something. When he gets antsy, the way he did, he's a whirl of motion, just keeps moving. I could see the signs of it because I had been with him a while. What he decided to do is to have an inspirational meeting in the locker room.

The team was suiting up for a practice session, the first time they had tried the game in the shadows of the old ball yard. There was the usual locker room chaos. One of the kids had a radio and the music was too loud and tinny, like it came out of a can. Two of the players were buck naked, standing on a bench and doing some sort of dance step, swaying like chorus dancers. I seen all this shit before and now it depressed me, whereas before I never took notice of it. Some of the players used to prepare for a game by playing gin rummy, but these kids didn't have any cards on them.

George came into the room about eleven in the morning and the first thing he did was shut off the radio. One of the kids — the one they called Tio, which means "uncle" in Spanish — went over to the radio and turned it back on.

George, just as calm as anything, pulled the plug on the radio and picked it up by the handle and smashed it into the concrete wall. It was an attention-getter, no doubt about it.

Tio went over to the broken radio and picked up the parts of it in his two hands and began to weep. I knew from before he could do this on cue. He was the class clown and it was pretty good, even when it got tiresome. Like throwing down his glove and stomping on it every time I came on the field.

George didn't know what to make of it so he got mad. I don't mean *angry,* either.

"Ryan, I want to talk to these assholes and I can't find Sam," George shouted at me.

I was dressed already, right down to my spikes. I looked around but Sam was hiding good. I went over to George and said, "Maybe you can hold your inspirational chat until we have a workout. Take the piss out of them, they'll be more receptive to a sermon."

"I'm not a wet nurse," George said, looking exactly like the duchess in *Through the Looking Glass.* "Listen up, *hombres!*"

— This is the owner of the team, men. George Bremenhaven (I said in Spanish).

— He broke my fucking radio, this son of a whore.

— Who the hell does he think he is?

— He's the owner (I said to the crowd crowding around George).

I said to George, "Looks like a lynch mob."

"Tell them I'm the señor who signs the paychecks and if they don't like it, they can take the bus back to Cuba."

— Men, the owner here says if you don't quiet down and listen, he's going to send everyone back to Cuba.

That seemed to have the wrong effect.

— He can send me back right now (Raul said).

— Man, I said, what would El Supremo say?

That had the right effect. Everyone fell silent, contemplating Castro. George thought it was a show of respect for him and I didn't explain. Then I saw Romero, Castro's fink, standing in the tunnel outside the locker room door. I walked across the locker room to the door and my spikes were the only sound. I smiled at Romero. And slammed the metal door in his face.

That provoked a couple of smiles from the troops. And made George smile for a moment before he began.

"Men, we stunk up spring training, but today we have a new start on a brand-new season," George said.

He waited for me to translate.

— Men, this horse's ass means to preach you a sermon. He is going to tell you a lot of shit about playing for the great New York Yankees and about tradition and all that. Just be quiet and listen. The sooner we listen, the sooner he'll leave.

I nodded to George.

"Men, you're the building blocks of a new Yankee tradition, reaching across the hemisphere for a new era," George said.

— Men, George says his mother was not a whore because she never charged for it.

Tio caught on. The others were dumbfounded. Tio smiled at me for the first time, a genuine smile, not a smirk aimed at the dumb gringo pitcher with the broken slider.

I was very, very sober. We all waited on George.

"Men, we all of us have to show the rest of the league what we're made of. We're the brothers in history of Ruth, Gehrig, DiMaggio, Reggie Jackson."

— Men, he is now reciting the names of famous Yankees past — Ruth, Gehrig, DiMaggio, Reggie Jackson. Don't pay any mind to it.

"Men, I want fire in this team. I want fire in your bellies. You aren't just playing for Castro or Cuba, you are playing for something greater — the New York Yankees!"

I groaned at that.

George looked at me and waited for me to translate.

— Men, Castro will cut off your gonads if you are sent back in disgrace to Cuba from the New York Yankees. He told me as much when I met him.

— You met him? (Raul asked).

— Sure did. Bearded fellow, smelled of Old Spice.

— Old Spice? (Tio asked). What is Old Spice?

— Cheap aftershave lotion.

— He don't shave ever (Tio said).

— Maybe he likes the smell.

George said, "You mind carrying on your conversation some other time? I got things to say."

"George, why don't you just wrap it up. This is giving me a headache. I can't keep all these conversations in my head."

"All right, men. It's up to you. Be proud of your tradition, you are wearing the pinstripes now and a whole world is watching you. More important, the greatest city on earth is watching you."

— Men, George is finally wrapping up his bullshit. Now is the time to give him a big cheer. It will make him happy and it will make us happy because he will finally go away.

I looked pleadingly at them and they stared me down. And then, out of the blue, Tio began to applaud wildly, shouting and clapping, and the others, sensing the joke, started to do the same. Clapping and laughing and jumping up and down. It was like a room full of Harpo Marxes all doing a number on this Margaret Dumont in a three-piece suit. George and I went outside to the therapy room.

THE NEW YORK YANQUIS

"Well, George, you certainly inspired them," I said.

"I did, didn't I?" George said.

"Brought a lump to my throat, I can tell you."

"Stop being so cynical, Ryan. These are kids, simple farm kids, and they can be moved if you press the right buttons. They're just looking for an authority figure to tell them to do their best."

"I guess that's right," I said. "I wouldn't know, never having been one."

"That's what I got rid of a fifty-million-dollar payroll for. To get some enthusiasm and team spirit back in the game," George said.

"Team doesn't have an *I* in it," I said.

"You don't believe that, but I do," George said. "This is bigger than anyone's ego."

Not bigger than George's, of course. I sort of shuffled him out of there because the kids were still cheering hysterically and I was afraid even George would begin to understand it was all a joke. We closed the clubhouse door together and went into the tunnel that runs under the stands. George didn't even hear the laughter that was starting to build in the locker room.

George said, "I've been thinking all night about this, about the team and lighting a firecracker under them and about what you said."

I don't like it when George starts quoting me to me. I try never to say anything of consequence to him.

"About Sparky being too old," he said.

"I never said that," I said.

"Sure, don't you remember? You pointed out to me he was fifty-six years old. A fifty-six-year-old gringo who doesn't speak a word of Spanish. I made a mistake, Ryan. I let sentiment guide me instead of good judgment."

George and sentiment have never been on the same street together before. Not even in the same town.

"Ryan, I want you to manage this team," he said.

"No, George, you don't. I don't know how to manage nothing bigger than my checkbook."

"I made up my mind this morning. I'm getting rid of Sparky."

"Well, you ain't gettin' rid of him on account of me."

"I called Sid on my way over here. I told him and he's waiting on a call from you," George said. "You give him a jingle and I'll go and tell Sparky. God, I hate telling someone he's through."

George hated no such thing. Nothing like telling a man he was fired. It gave George the same feeling a hunter gets when he bags a white-tailed deer on the first day of the season.

"George, the season ain't even started yet," I said. I was pleading less for Sparky than for myself. George was putting me in the equipment bag again and I was going to get hurt in there, bumped around by bats and bases and all.

"Sid and I talked price. You can be a player-manager like Pete Rose."

"I ain't like Pete Rose, for Christ's sake. What am I gonna do, put myself in as a reliever?"

"When it comes down to it," he said.

"Managers got to pay their dues, George. Work in the minors a while, do some coaching. I can't just take over a team. Especially a team like this, bunch of raw recruits out of some Communist country. They ain't just wet behind the ears, they're wet all over."

"Ryan, if I did things the way things are always done, I'd never get anything done. I do things the way I do things, my own way. I always have and I always will." He was fading into his Frank Sinatra imitation and there was no stopping him.

I said, "George, let me think on it."

"You call Sid Cohen right now in L.A. and he'll give you the details. I've called a press conference for two P.M." With that, he turned on his little tasselled loafers and went through the nearest door, doubtless humming to himself. Scooby-dooby-do.

I called Sid.

"What did you agree to?" I said.

"I don't agree to things, except George called me and told me what he was going to do and I asked him how much he intended to pay you. Ryan, you are going to be a 1.2-million-dollar man this season."

"I'll make a fool of myself."

"Probably."

"Which would ruin my chance of getting a decent coaching job with anyone."

"Your chances, Ryan, are nil to begin with. Every team in the league is on the Yankees' case because of what George did. And you, you schmuck, agree to go to Cuba and bring his scabs home with you. Frankly, I don't see how you can do yourself much more damage."

"So I should finish the job, is that it, Sid?"

"You should take the only chance you have. Go out and win one for yourself."

"How's that?"

"Is this team any good? I was watching Chris Berman on ESPN. He doesn't seem enamored."

"He gets paid not to be enamored. Besides, he's in love with himself."

"What about it, Ryan? Can they do themselves any good?"

"I dunno."

"Can they finish third?"

"I dunno."

"Let's say you manage them to third place. I don't think anyone would fault the job you did. Say, finish with a .500 average. That would put you in a different light your rookie season as a manager."

"I don't know how to manage."

"Half of them don't. But you know how to speak Spanish. That puts you one up on Sparky. George said that Sparky depends on the clubhouse manager to be his interpreter. That's pretty pathetic, you have to agree."

"Language is a problem, tell me about it. I been taking Excedrin. I was watching 'The Mary Tyler Moore Show' last night and I started translating it into Spanish in my head. I don't know how they can do that for a living day after day over at the UN building."

"It's a gift. Take the money, Ryan. And do yourself some good."

"George says I put the idea in his head. I don't want to be the man who fired Sparky."

"Sparky has a two-year contract, he'll be all right. He can go down to Kentucky and raise race horses."

"So George is willing to pay me $550,000 to manage on top of the $650,000 to pitch?"

"Don't get an exaggerated sense of your own importance, Ryan. This is business. He's still got you by the short hairs, even more when you take the job, but you've got no alternative I can see, other than flat-out quitting."

"I was thinking along those lines yesterday," I said.

"You'd walk away from that kind of money?"

Silence.

"No, I guess not."

"Guess not? I should say not. Figure you pay half of that in taxes and my ten percent, you'd still walk away with about a half-million dollars. For what? Putting up with some shit for the next six months."

When I broke into the Bigs, I got $30,000. I've been careful about money all my life, which comes from being raised poor and knowing you were poor. Money is just counting to some people, but to me it's real. I never forgot the first time I read a Scrooge McDuck comic and saw that critter jumping into piles of coins in his vault. I could relate to it. Sid was right; his sense of knowing what I would do for money was uncanny.

"All right, Sid," I said.

"Listen, Ryan, listen. This isn't going to stop here. I can work on a bio for you, tell your side of the story of the year of the Yanquis — Q - U - I - S. Something along that line."

"I can't write."

"It's the last thing you have to know how to do to get published, believe me," Sid said. "You tell George we've got a deal and I'll send along the contract when I get it."

"I hope this thing semi-works out," I said.

"It will, Ryan," Sid promised.

At least it sounded like a promise. Maybe it was only a wish like crossing your fingers but I was a desperate man all of a sudden and I would grab at the first straw that floated along like it was a life raft. One last year in the Bigs was all I wanted, and it seemed that that was getting a lot more complicated the more it went along.

18

The next day became the worst day I ever had in baseball. It was the worst day since old Booker beat the crap out of me in fourth grade, in fact, and then I went home and got more of the same from my old man.

It was exactly like getting beat up.

First, I got beat up at the press conference. That lasted about a half-hour. Then I had to talk to this guy on the Spanish radio network. At least he didn't try to make me out to be something that I wasn't, which was a fancy Spanish speaker. It was just basic stuff and I could understand him good and he let me take my time with my answers. Then someone who was a producer for WFAN told me I had to go on the air and I did and they beat me up some more about this "Latino team," as they put it.

Then I found out that Orestes was interviewed for Telemundo, which is a big Spanish television news network, and he said that I was a lousy pitcher and would probably make a lousy manager.

So I did what I had to do.

I had to get their respect and trust and that wasn't going to be easy because they saw that I was George's link to the team and that I was more George's boy than theirs.

I went to Kill 'Em Dead on Ninth Avenue and ordered an exterminator for the East Side Hotel. I rode with the exterminator in his panel van and we parked in front of the place. You'd think we were bringing the welfare checks — we were greeted like royalty. The exterminator packed on his gear, including a tank he wore on his back, and we went up to the twelfth floor where the kids were living. It was a hell of a dump, worse than I remembered it from that day I stayed there long ago.

The cockroaches were doing the Mexican hat dance all over everything. I could see how this would get people down.

"This is really shit," the exterminator said in his best medical judgment manner. Like Marcus Welby.

"Bomb 'em," I said.

"You're not supposed to bomb 'em," he said. "You bomb 'em and they just run to other floors of the hotel."

"I don't give a shit about the other floors."

"Look, we sell a service that —"

"I really want them out of here," I said.

So we closed the windows and I told the boys what I was going to do as best I could. They got the drift, which means they put on their street clothes and went downstairs while the exterminator set off six or seven sulphur bombs in the halls and the rooms.

The roaches did what they had to do. They scattered to the floors below and above the twelfth.

"This doesn't do much for the rest of the building," the exterminator said to me, as if I cared. I told him to send the bill to George Bremenhaven, care of the Yankees.

That night, I ordered up a dozen pizzas and two cases of beer and the players went back to their rooms and watched me like I was their jailer. Romero came by to do his head count. He was staying at the Essex House, a fact I noted to the assembled players. They resented it, the way I wanted them to, but they still resented me, too.

I wasn't finished.

"Orestes," I said.

— What do you want?

— I want to beat you up. But I don't suppose that would suit either of us. So I'm sending you back to Papa Fidel the first flight I can arrange.

— You are? Who you going to use as a catcher? Tio? Tio can't handle the left handers.

— I know that, but I know I need your shit a lot less than that. You got off bad-mouthing me on Telemundo even before the ink was dry on my contract. I don't need that kind of shit.

— You can't send me back home. I got a contract.

— I don't give a flying fish fuck about your contract, Orestes. You been dogging me from the first day in Havana and I don't need to put up with your shit anymore.

— You can't do that.

— Watch.

There were four or five in the room when we were saying these things. They were eating pizza. The place still smelled faintly of sulphur fumes.

Orestes eyed me and I did the same to him. He wanted to see the bluff in my face, but there wasn't any. I figured it out coming over with the exterminator that I had to do something to get their attention, sort of make an example of someone. Do a nice thing like get rid of the roaches and bring them pizza and beer and then drop the hammer on one of them, the trouble-making son of a bitch.

— I don't wanna go back.

— You been doing everything you can to go back except buy the ticket yourself. I'll buy it for you. I don't need someone like you on the team. There's no *I* in *team.*

— What?

— There's no *I* in *team.*

— What does that mean?

"There's no *I* in *team,*" I said in English.

Orestes looked around him and spread out his hands like I was a crazy person. That's what hanging around with George gets you.

— It means your ego is too big for this team.

— And yours isn't? What do you know about managing?

— About as much as you know about playing against real big league hitters, Orestes, which is nothing. You guys are the toast of Havana, but you want to notice no one is noticing that. They're dogging you, the whole league is dogging you. You all got this attitude and Orestes has got it worst of all, and if I got to put up with playing with you for the next season, then I don't have to put up with your snotty shit. You're all a bunch of spoiled kids and you all don't play baseball nearly as well as George was led to believe.

I hadn't intended the thing to turn into a speech, but it turned out that way. I stood there, looking around at them. Nobody said anything for a moment, not even the clown Tio. Maybe it was dawning on them that this was serious shit.

Raul took a step out of the circle.

— Señor, please.

I waited.

— Everything is so different to us.

His voice was soft, his eyes were soft. Was this a con? I thought it might be, but I listened. But Raul responded with silence.

— How you think it is for me? Last year I was wrapping it up. Sixteen years in the Bigs and going home when I got a chance to play another season. I took it. I even took it when I found out my teammates were going to be a bunch of kids from Cuba who'd never been out of the country before and might not be any good at this game. I took it because I like to play ball. It's all I ever knew how to do. So maybe I regret it now, but it's too late for that. I got to play and you got to play.

— Señor, please. (Raul held out his hand in an expressive way.)

— We are afraid.

— Afraid of what?

— Afraid of everything.

— Well, that's a lot.

— The players from the other teams call us names, we are clinging to each other because there is no one else to hold on to. We have been picked by El Supremo, we did not choose ourselves. We have families in Cuba, we have kin who have gone to Miami, yet the people — Cuban people — in Miami hate us because we are Communists. I am just a baseball player, Señor Ryan, like you are. Just a baseball player. My fiancée waits for me in Havana. My heart is heavy, I cannot even sleep at night. And what is this place we are in? New York. It is large and frightening and there is no one but ourselves to depend on, so we become . . .

Here he used both hands to squeeze an imaginary thing between them.

— Tight. Together. Us. Orestes is afraid as we all are. We are like soldiers when the president sent them to Angola. One was my uncle. He did not want to go to Angola. We had to look at a map to see where this place was. And he was so frightened. Until he was killed.

— Nobody's gonna get killed.

— But you see, Señor? Don't send Orestes back, don't send any of us back, we can play this game. There is just so much to . . . get used to.

Yeah, shit, yeah. I saw it. I was running around getting the red ass about Orestes and I saw it the way they saw it. Now, I was fairly sophisticated when I came up to the Bigs — I mean, I didn't spit on the floor or get sexually aroused by hogs or nothing. But I was just another shitkicker kid from Texas and the city dazzled me fairly good. So, yeah, I saw what it was they were facing, first down in Lauderdale and now up here in the city.

— All right (I said).

What a tower of Jell-O I'd turned out to be in my first big managerial confrontation. "But you guys gotta learn a little English, just work on it some."

"I can speak English a little," Tio said then. This surprised the shit out of me, it was like your dog turning to you all of a sudden and telling you he wanted to go out and wee-wee.

"Shit, Tio, you been fucking with me all this time?"

"English I speak like you speak Spanish," Tio said.

"Anybody else speak English?"

"No," Orestes said.

"No?"

"Not really," he said.

"You son of a bitch, you speak English, too?"

"Not really," he said again.

"You fucking around with me, Orestes?"

"*Que?*"

"All right, let's have a show of hands here. Who speaks English?"

One or two hands. But Raul said:

— They speak English a little, but not too much, and they are ashamed to speak English badly.

— As badly as I speak Spanish.

— Exactly. (Raul smiled brightly.)

— If I got to make a fool of myself trying, it's up to you to make fools of yourselves.

— We can try (Raul said).

— All right. Orestes, I'll hang on to the plane ticket for now but don't go bad-mouthing me or the team anymore. In fact, try to stay away from reporters because they just want you to say the wrong thing. And you don't want Castro reading a bunch of shit that appears up here in the paper. I just want us to be able to field a half-ass decent team and not make us ashamed of ourselves.

"Half-ass?" Orestes said.

— That means one buttock short but at least still in the ball park.

"Half ass?" Orestes said again in English.

— Nothing. Forget it.

— Thank you (Raul said then).

— For what? George is going to end up paying for the pizza.

— For the cockroaches, to make them disappear.

— They come back, you let me know.

— Thank you (Raul said again).

And then there they were all of a sudden, thanking me.

Even Orestes stuck out his hand and smiled for the first time that I could recall. It was all getting so warm and runny that I had to get out of there or I might have bawled. I'm a bawler at heart and it always shows up when I watch old movies, which is why I try never to be in the same room with anyone else when James Stewart comes on the small screen.

That might have made the end of the bad day sweet, but the bad day wasn't over. When I got back to my studio apartment in Fort Lee around nine at night, there was a message on the recorder from Tommy Tradup.

"Well, hoss, you managed to get old Sparky deep-sixed, you scab-loving son of a bitch," Tommy said. He was using his six-stinger tone of voice. "But wait'll we get in New York next week, you son of a bitch, you're gonna find out you traded your bowl of grits for a sack of shit, you Commie son of a bitch. Just remember."

Damn, that was a downer. Man hates to get cursed out by ex-teammates on his own damned answering machine. And I knew that no matter how drunk Tommy was when he cussed me, he'd remember it the next day. And the next. And the next. The Yankees had a little personality problem with the rest of the league, it seemed to me.

I contemplated this while I made myself a can of chili labeled Texas-style. It wasn't, it even had beans in it, but I settled in to scarf it down and drink a couple of cold ones while I watched *Three Godfathers* with John Wayne.

That's one movie I cry all the way through.

It was better than crying for myself.

19

We opened in Yankee Stadium against the Kansas City Royals and Tommy Tradup.

Only about 41,000 folks decided to come out to see the new style Yankees and about 10,000 reporters from just about every newspaper and radio and TV network in the country.

Of course, being about 16,000 empty on opening day did not at all improve George's temper, but he had to expect some losses. The tabloids were pounding him every day, and the White House, which had engineered this whole thing to start with, was very quiet, letting George twist out there on his own. You'd think George would have figured it out, but that was pure George, charging through no matter what once he got an idea in his head about something. He wanted to give another pep talk in the locker room before the game, but I told him it would upset the troops, better to give a pep talk after the game.

He was none too happy with me, either, and I hadn't even managed a single game. It seems the city building inspectors were now all over him about a swarm of roaches infesting the lower floors of his building and he'd found out about the sulphur bombs and threatened to sue the exterminating company for stirring the critters up. And he was withholding money from me for all the pizzas I'd sent up to the team, as though pizza was going to break his piggybank. It's bad enough to wet-nurse kids, but when you throw in an emotionally retarded owner, it's even worse.

I closed the locker room door after we'd taken our practice stabs and told the troops what to expect.

— There is resentment out there, boys. Comes from the crowd and from the other team. Now, Stotko is pitching today and he's about half-man and half–pit bull, which means he's totally insane. I expect what he's gonna do is try to scare you.

"Pit bull?" asked Orestes because I had rendered that term in English.

It was the way I spoke Spanish. When my lingo didn't keep up with my thoughts, I just changed horses and blurted out English in the middle of the Spanish stream.

I made a face and a barking sound and Orestes was amused.

— So, boys. Just remember this. This is just baseball and we all play it the same way. But this is no game. Those boys over there on the Royals are mean and mad and they'll do anything to win. So we got to do the same thing.

— I hate royalty (Tio said).

— That's it, Tio. Think of them as kings and queens and grand dukes and such. Just knock their crowns off. And Ramon Suarez, when you go out there to pitch, I want you to knock the third son of a bitch on his ass. Number three. Aim for his head. His name is Tommy Tradup and he says that your mothers are all whores.

Tomas just blinked at me a moment. Raul said:

— He said that?

— To me personally one night in the Palm Aire Hotel bar in Fort Lauderdale.

— He doesn't even know us, nor we him.

— I told you, Raul, that's the way they are. They think they're royalty, that's why they call themselves the Royals. They think you're all a bunch of ignorant peasant scum.

— That's not right.

"Fucking A, it's not right."

— I will knock his head off (Suarez said).

— Pitch right for his head, Suarez. Don't take no shit.

That puzzled them a moment.

Then Tio said, in English: "Don't take no shit."

"We don't take shit from anyone," I said.

Yeah. "No shit from anyone!" Tio said.

"No shit!" they shouted in ragged chorus.

No shit. No shit. It was a mantra they repeated all the way down the tunnel to the dugout. No shit, indeed.

With those inspiring words to fire them, we waited through the opening ceremonies.

George screwed those up royally. Royals and royally. I don't know how these thoughts crawl into his little brain. They're like tapeworms or something.

The teams lined up on the foul lines and we were introduced over the loudspeakers and every time a Yankee name was misprounounced, half the crowd booed and half laughed. I didn't like that at all. But it got worse.

George played the fucking Cuban national anthem.

I didn't even know what it was at first, but I saw the players standing very stiff and I figured out what it was. The idiot was playing the Cuban anthem! What had he been thinking of? This was the worst thing since they'd hung the Canadian flag upside down when the Blue Jays got in the World Series that first time. But at least Canada was a friendly country.

The boos were roaring along now. But that wasn't all. It was more than just the music.

George had posted a Cuban flag in left field, I swear to God. I wanted to run right out there and tear it down, but I couldn't move. I decided I would never move again, in fact.

When the Cuban music ended, you could have cut through the boos with a butter knife, it was that thick.

A couple of guys — turned out they were from the Cuban community in Miami — ran out on the field from the third base boxes carrying a Cuban flag as it used to be before Castro. This meant nothing to no one until it was explained the next day in the *Times* but when the security guards caught up with the guys, the crowd was now more pleasantly restless. After all, they had paid good money to see a ball game, not a political disturbance.

Finally, they played our anthem and the crowd let out a cheer. You would've thought it was a bunch of American Legionnaires cheering the troops as they headed off to Desert Storm. I am not a creature of excesses, and excess anything makes me on edge. Ditto for excesses of patriotism. The crowd was telling the boys that they weren't wanted here. I had a team full of Jackie Robinsons, and it was bad enough for Jackie Robinson when he was one guy out there, but a whole team. I stood with my hand over my heart just the way I was taught to say the Pledge of Allegiance in second grade. The rockets' red glare and the bombs bursting in air gave proof through the night that our flag was still there. The thing is, I kept thinking about the old joke about "Jose, Can You See?"

When it was over, I handed the lineup card to the other manager and the umpire at home plate while the kids went out on the field. The ump was Hugh Bailey, and he said, "You got yourself a real handful, huh, Ry?"

"Semi," I admitted.

"Man, I'm glad I'm not you," Hugh said.

"My eyesight's too good," I said.

"Starting off, is that it, Ryan?" Bailey said.

"You started it, Bailey. Not that I'm gonna sweat your balls and strikes because you never gave the Yankees a break in your life."

"You call these spics Yankees?"

"You are a racist motherfucker," I said.

"They're Communists, for Christ's sake."

"Your mother probably fucked them," I said.

"You son of a bitch."

But what could he do? We hadn't even had our first fight.

Skip Patterson, manager of the Royals, sneered a little. "Well, when we get through, your boys will be on the bus back to where they came from."

"Beats having to make a living in Kansas City," I said to Skip in a friendly way.

"Okay, boys, let's let the players duke it out," Hugh said after he'd started all this shit in the first place. "The Cuban anthem? George must really be losing it," he added.

"I'll tell him you sent your best," I said to Hugh. I turned and walked back to the dugout and descended. I had every intention of going right into the tunnel, back to the locker room, changing clothes, cab it to Fort Lee, pack my shit, and jump in the Park Avenue and not stop until I was halfway to Texas.

Of course, I didn't.

Ramon Suarez is a fastballer and Billy Bacon had taught him a few things in spring training, but I didn't know if he'd really caught on. This was a real game in a real stadium in a real big city and spring training is playing around in Florida for the senior citizens and every other loafer who doesn't have something to do in the afternoon. I had my toes crossed.

First Royal up smacked the first pitch into center. One bounce and caught and in. Welcome to the American League, Ramon.

The second batter grounded into a sure double play except the second baseman dropped the ball as though he was surprised by it. The crowd was booing when it wasn't laughing and we were only six minutes into the game. I looked at my watch. I looked out at the Cuban flag. Someone was trying to pull it down and there were security men all over the place. This was about as wonderful as I could have imagined it in my worst, wake-up-sweating, damn-that-tequila nightmare.

Tommy Tradup swaggered to the plate and I remembered then what I had told Ramon. This was not the time or the place to knock down the hitter, not with two men on. I signaled out to the third base coach, Billy

Bacon doing double duty, but he was staring at the flag incident unfolding in left field. Didn't anybody pay attention to baseball anymore when they went to a game?

Ramon threw right for Tommy's head on the first pitch.

Bam. Tommy hit the dirt in a sprawl, the pitch missing his noggin by about two inches. Orestes was standing at the plate in his catcher's gear and shouting at the downed Tommy Tradup.

I may have overdone it in the locker room when I told Ramon to knock Tradup down.

Tommy got up and went for the pitcher on the mound.

Ramon stood there, watching him like a toreador. Maybe he had some inkling of what was going to happen next, because I didn't.

Orestes ran out behind Tradup and tackled him and began pounding him in the face.

This commenced what we call a "brawl."

Both benches emptied and the outfielders came in at a gallop and everyone collided about ten feet short of the pitcher's mound. The object of a baseball brawl is to cram fifty players into a space the size of a phone booth so that no one can hit anyone very hard or seriously. I guess it was up to me to go out and restore order and that was my intention. Unfortunately, this time I abandoned my usual laconic stroll to a fight and it was still going on when I got there. The next thing I knew, I was in the pile of writhing humanity and someone caught me on the chin with his spikes.

The fight lasted fifteen minutes, which is a long time as baseball brawls go. The umpires in the league are all the size of your average New York City cop on a loving diet of jelly doughnuts. They bullied their way into the meltdown at the core of the fight and began flinging ball players off the center the way you tear the leaves off an artichoke.

Well, I was certainly ready to call it quits the minute my chin came in contact with someone's spike. I was bleeding, and I realized that if I'd gone back to Fort Lee instead of staying in the dugout at the beginning of the game, I would not have been nicked.

But there I was and Hugh Bailey was banishing me from the game even though I didn't get a lick in. Bailey did the same with Skip on the other side and the same with Tomas, the second baseman, and the same with Tommy Tradup and two or three others.

On my way down the tunnel, I grabbed Sam the equipment manager. I told him to quiet the boys down and not let anyone else get into a fight.

He didn't want to go in the dugout to act for me, but I made him. We were the only two that could tell the players what to do in Spanish and I was banished from the game.

Quite a game, as it turned out. I watched it on TV in the locker room, drinking a cold beer, sitting on the training table. Something about the fight seemed to have inspired the kids and they came out playing ball.

The Royals didn't do much after the fight for the next four innings. Ramon, who was not thrown out of the game, held them down while Raul and the boys pounded on them.

In the bottom of the fourth, we put two on with one out and then Raul came up to the plate. He has a funny stance, a little bit of a bend to his back leg, and he never waggles the bat, just lets it sit on his shoulder until the pitcher goes into his windup. Then he draws the bat back, nearly horizontal with the plate, as though he knows exactly where the ball will come.

Turns out he does.

He cracked it a good one and it went to dead center, which is located somewhere near Scarsdale. I have described Raul's line drive ability, haven't I? I swear the thing took off like a clothes line from his belt to the upper deck, without any loft to it at all. Just dead on.

I had to shake my head because Raul didn't have a doubt. He was trotting to first, watching the ball fly out of the park, and suddenly the restless boos and scattered cheers were united. George was right. Everyone loves a winner and Raul made the Yankees a winner with that one blow in the middle of the game. Not just for the game but for what this new-style Yankees team was going to mean.

"Hot damn!" I shouted to my TV set in the locker room and the set hollered back with a chorus of cheers. Even the announcers were excited. Raul went four for four, including the game-winning home run, and Ramon scattered five hits for no runs in a nine-inning performance I wouldn't have expected out of anyone less than Jack McDowell.

They tumbled into the locker room after the victory exactly like the kids they were, yelling and laughing and slapping at each other and even high-fiving, something they had been learning in spring training. They even slapped me around in that good fellowship way in which men note happy occasions.

It was infectious, I have to say. The only damper was when George came in to deliver his postgame pep talk.

"Men! Men! Settle down! That was a great victory out there and we showed the City of New York what we were made of today!" George shouted above the din. Someone threw a wet towel at him and that provoked more laughter, but George was unstoppable. "I think this is the beginning of a beautiful relationship!"

"I bet you say that to all the girls," I said.

"Translate, translate," he shouted at me.

— Señor Owner wants to say the pizza and beer tonight are on him and he wishes you Merry Christmas.

That stopped them a little. Even George, who said, "*Navidad?* Did you say, *navidad?*"

"It means reborn. I said the spirit of the Yankees is reborn."

"*Navidad,*" George said again, turning the word over his tongue.

When the troops were bedded down with their TV sets and beer and pizza, Romero came through and did his count. He was wearing a leather coat he'd picked up from a discount house on lower Broadway and the seams hadn't started to tear yet. Then Romero left and it was my turn. I bid them all good night and went down in the elevator and back through the lobby of the East Side Hotel. It was a little past seven and the lobby was full of pregnant women and their babies toddling around in diapers. The place smelled of old age and fear and neglect and loss of hope, or maybe hope never found the front door. Two blind old men played checkers over a coffee table in one part of the lobby. It was terribly sad, all of it.

I hurried to the street and went over to Second Avenue to get my car from the parking garage. George owned the parking garage and I had a deal. Drove crosstown to the West Side Highway, then up the West Side to the GW Bridge and back across to Fort Lee.

I spent twenty dollars in an Italian restaurant for a plate of tortellini and sauce and a couple of MGD beers. They had highlights of the game on the TV above the bar and everyone was watching. The first highlight was the brushback and the second was the brawl. But the rest of the highlights consisted of Raul Guevara stroking the ball all over the park.

"That kid knows how to hit," the barman said to no one.

"He looks like Reggie Jackson," said a guy at the end of the bar.

"Yeah, but this ain't October," the barman said. "You think they found a real player down there in Cuba?"

"If I had a dime for every April hotshot the Yankees ever brought up, I'd have enough to pay my bar bill," the customer said.

"Well, they won," the barman said, still staring at the set.

"One game."

"That's the way they win them, pal, one game at a time."

"Tell me in September," the customer said.

"I dunno, maybe that guy Ryan Shawn ought to get kicked out of every game," the barman said and laughed.

It was certainly a thought.

20

Charlene called me around ten that night. I'd had the phone machine on and it had recorded three or four hangups. I mentioned this to her.

"I don't like leaving messages on machines, Ryan. It's like being kept waiting."

"I would have called you as soon as I got in."

"Where you been?"

"Putting the troops to bed," I said.

"My, my, does a manager do all that?"

"Manager do what a manager gotta do."

"They say on TV you got cut."

"Got a spike in the face. Don't worry. I'm still handsome as I ever was."

"I really didn't believe you were going to go through with this," Charlene said. "Someone at the hospital says to me today that they wanted to know how I felt about you being on a team full of wetbacks."

"And you said?"

"I said you liked it just fine."

"And they said?"

"They didn't say nothing more to me if they knew what was good for them."

"You don't have to get in no fights on my account, Charlene."

"Oh, I don't, do I? I suppose you never thought of the effect this was going to have on our relationship, did you?"

"I know I didn't want you getting all balled up by it, Charlene. You got your life and I got mine and the only thing that's important is that we got each other."

"We've got each other. Do we, Ryan?"

"Don't we?"

"Well, I know you got baseball and what I got is people feeling sorry for me that I got you."

"Well, don't let people's pity get you down. It's a game and it's a salary and after next September, I'll be back in Houston to stay and we can be thinking on opening up the health food place."

"Ryan Patrick, what if I was to say right now, 'Just quit.' Would you?"

I paused for a long moment. "No, Charlene, I wouldn't. I've come this far, might as well see the thing played out."

"I didn't say quit, I said 'what if,' but you gave me your answer anyway, didn't you?"

"I guess I did," I said. "I love you, Charlene Cleaver, right down to the soles of your pretty little feet."

"But not that much," she said. She was getting in a mood or she was in a mood. Depended on when this all started with her.

"Well, I just wanted to see if you were all right and it appears you are."

"I miss you, Charlene. We play the Texas Rangers beginning of May on the West Coast trip."

"I know when you're next in Texas, Ryan, I can read a schedule."

"I know that, Charlene. I just want to say how much I miss you," I said in my quiet, gentle way.

"Oh, Ryan," she said.

Well, there it was. She was doing Scarlett O'Hara and I was doing Bronco Billy. Different themes.

"I do want to be happy," Scarlett said.

"I want you to be happy."

"I really hate what you're doing."

"What am I doing?"

"Everything wrong," she said.

Well, that doesn't lead to a whole lot of discussion. So I kept quiet and waited for her.

"Well, Ryan. I got to go now."

"Stay and talk a while."

"You miss me?"

"I told you that."

"Well, you can say it again."

"I miss you, Charlene."

"All right. Well, I got to go now."

"Charlene —"

Click.

I could call her back, but what would be the point of that? She was in a mood and I suppose someone had said something to her that was worse than she'd told me and it had made her mad — angry — and the next thing had led to the next thing and now I was about two thousand miles too far away from her.

I knew how she felt.

I could even have sympathy for her point of view. It's a terrible thing when a man gets all involved in something as basically silly as baseball. I used to look at baseball uniforms from a different perspective, and they looked dumb to me. That bothered me because I was wearing a uniform, too, so I put the thought out of my mind. Baseball is full of things like that. Take a catcher's gear — the mask, the mitt, the crotch pad, and the chest pads — the whole getup is as basically silly as a woman wearing a corset with little clips holding up her stockings. On the other hand, you don't think of things like that when you're seeing them the way they're supposed to be seen, sort of in context.

My head was full of this kind of thinking. Always is, when I'm trying to figure out what it is exactly that Charlene wants. She wants me to quit the game but she wouldn't have any use for me if I did — I know that — so what was it that she wants?

Hell with it. I opened a can of beer and turned on the TV and started watching my old friend Clint Eastwood. He would have been as puzzled by Charlene as I was, I knew that much.

21

The players got their first death threat of the season delivered by messenger to their rooms in the East Side Hotel. It was Day Two of the season, as the more pretentious sports writers like to put it.

The threat was wrapped in a box of candy that, when Orestes read the threat, no one ate. (Later turned out the candy wasn't poisoned and the cops in the crime lab ate the evidence.) The threat was in Spanish, which was good thinking because I'm not sure the boys would have understood it in English. It said they would all die very soon and die most painfully if they did not go back to Cuba where they came from. Something like that.

Of course, the boys didn't tell me about it for a couple of days because they were still trying to decide if they trusted me. But when Tio was almost run over by a cab when he decided to take a midnight stroll around the East Side after a game, they spilled it. (Turned out the cab driver was just a regular guy showing a regular cabbie's contempt for any and all pedestrians, not just Cubans.)

This is a wonderful country because we have a lot of experience dealing with death threats. George took it very seriously and so did the cops. So did the FBI, which was called in on the matter. Everyone had a good time, particularly the tabloids, which went to the sleaziest of extremes, speculating this was a plot by Castro to embarrass the United States. As if he needed any help.

The death threat made me sick to my stomach and I thought it would do the same to the kids, but I was wrong. Maybe, being an American, I take death threats more seriously than they do. Maybe it was their Cuban macho.

Whatever it was, they greeted the Boston Red Sox visiting town in the next series like the poultry man greeting a crate full of chickens.

George, in his cynical way, had been right about filling the ballpark when you have a winner. The old loyalty days are over, for players as well as fans. Give them a winner and they'll show up. George started getting celebrity requests for tickets and "Larry King Live" had him on to talk about his breakthrough in Latin American relations.

It was cold in the Stadium for the Boston series, which consisted, naturally, of night games. But still the people came out and cheered and applauded and drank George's four-dollar beers. I did tell George to lose the Cuban flag and anthem and he had the good sense to do it after the *New York Times* ran an editorial saying the flag was "inappropriate."

We banged Boston the way we banged Kansas City. Suarez was learning. He was a fastballer and I was trying to teach him a slider the way Deke had taught me. And I was teaching him about the plate as the plate is in the Bigs.

The batter don't own the plate. He knows it, which is why he blusters so much. It's a hard thing to hit that little ball coming at you at 95 miles an hour in the best of times. It comes down to instinct, and when you're a little light on instinct, which most hitters are, you bring in other tools. Like intimidation.

The rubber is 60 feet 6 inches from the crown of the plate. That works both ways. The hitter, after all, does have this big stick, and when he takes his practice swings, he is showing the top end to the pitcher and threatening him with it. So the pitcher has got to see the ball as a threat, too. Show the hitter who really owns the plate and the boxes around it.

— I could hurt someone (Suarez told me when we were practicing one afternoon in the bullpen).

— Hurt him or he's gonna hurt you.

— I don't want to hurt anyone.

— There's only been one player ever got killed by a pitched ball. Think about it, Ramon. Only one in all these years. Hell, that's statistically insignificant. (Needless to say, the last two words were in English.)

— I don't know (Suarez said).

Somehow, he got the idea. Foxgrover from the Red Sox teed off on him one second inning, and by the fifth, Suarez had learned. Foxgrover got plunked on the left wrist and trotted down to first, holding the injured appendage and shouting curses at Suarez. The ump shouted a warning and Suarez just nodded. Statistically insignificant.

After two series, we had yet to lose a game and sat atop the American League East at six and oh. Raul Guevara was hitting .489 and *Sports Illustrated* tried to jinx us by putting Raul on the cover.

Everyone in the locker room had his own copy of *SI* that week and I tried to calm the boys down by telling them it was a long season and you figured even a good team loses more than a third of its games. These guys were bullet-proof on nothing stronger every night than pizza and beer.

And they were filling the park. It was still cold in New York in April and night games take it out of you sitting in your long underwear through three hours, but the house was filling up. George was humming "My Way" night and day while he checked the receipts.

There was a lot of security at the Stadium normally, but now there was more, reinforced by a detachment of the Finest and a sprinkling of FBI guys casing the layout. The FBI also wanted metal detectors at all gates, so the Stadium began to look more like an inner-city high school. The president had surreptitiously laid on a contingent of Secret Service men who are trained to look for assassins. The whole thing made me nervous as hell.

Still, baseball was baseball. When you're into the game, it's the only thing there is. You're aware of the crowds, of course, and cheers are better than boos, but there is this other thing. You are on a field and your teammates are with you and this other team is over there, pros just like you are, and they are watching you. Watching. You want to be good because your salary gets paid on your pitching ERA or batting average, but you also want to be good exactly the way you wanted to be good in high school ball. You just want to stick it to the other side.

Ballplayers tend to be the least sentimental people on earth. It's a tough haul, getting to the Bigs, and staying in the Bigs is tougher. After you retire, you're still hanging around to catch some of the atmosphere, but mostly it's because it took so much out of you to become a Big, you ain't got nothing left. You sell used cars or golf a lot but, shit, that's just waiting to die. It's the reason old ball players have that empty look to them behind the suntan and face-lift and golf pro shirts.

We lost heavy the first away game in Cleveland's pretty stadium. Ramon Suarez was shellacked in the second inning and he just couldn't believe it when I pulled him out and put myself in. It was like I was sending him back to Cuba by banana boat.

— Just go on, Ramon, this is no big thing, you just ain't got it tonight.

— I have it tonight and every night, those whores, those Indians.

— No slurs, now, Ramon, just go on and siddown, will you?

Bill Donnelly came out to the mound with his mask in hand and said, "What's the matter, Ryan? He don't wanna go? Or you gonna have two pitchers on the mound for the next batter? It doesn't say anything in the rule book about two pitchers at a time." That's umpire humor and it's good to ignore it whenever its ugly head pops up. It just encourages them.

"Bill, just gimme a minute, willya?"

"Hurry it up," he said.

Orestes, also on the crowded mound, just glared at him. An ump had thrown him out of the first game when all he'd been doing was protecting his pitcher from the charge of Tommy Tradup.

— Tell him, Orestes.

— You gotta go sit down, Ramon.

— Why? What have I done?

— You allowed two runs and the bases are loaded, Ramon. Do what the man says.

— He just wants to come in and take my victory away from me.

— Oh, grow up, Ramon (I said).

Shoulders slumped, little Ramon went back to the dugout. The crowd booed him in a cheerful way and he stopped at the dugout steps and gave them the finger. That quieted the booing, of course, the way it always does.

I tried to warm up, which is practically impossible in Cleveland. April is still winter there and that breeze coming off Lake Erie would freeze a well-digger's ass in mid-shit. But I limbered up as much as any thirty-eight-year-old man can limber up.

It did no good.

After three more runs, I took myself out of the game and appointed a reliever named Rosario to see if he could bandage up.

He did all right the rest of the way, but we didn't. Raul hit two real long flies out and one triple, but that was pretty much it. Our first loss in the season and on top of that we were in Cleveland. Everyone felt pretty low on the bus back to the hotel and I wasn't in a mood to cheer anyone up. Romero did his count on the bus instead of coming back to the hotel. His new leather coat was starting to split. He was putting on weight, too.

We had pizza again that night. The capacity of youngsters of any nationality to eat pizza is an amazing one. They never wanted anything else, just pizza. They ate it like they could eat it for breakfast, lunch, and dinner. I think it was the only thing they really liked about America. I tried to rack my brain for a substitute, but there was none. Until you're thirty-five or so, pizza is the greatest food in the world and then your stomach begins to tell you different and you go on to more sophisticated things, like chili.

It was a long, grim northern Ohio night. Came the dawn and there were snow flurries in the air.

And that's the way it went through the first road trip. Life on the road is like a sort of dream you're walking your way through. I've talked to salesmen I've met in hotel bars who tell me the same thing. Life on the road is like always playing hooky and the rules of living are all different. You've got no real responsibility after you do your business so you act irresponsible and it takes a lot of willpower to keep that under control. On the one hand, you can go around and feel sorry for yourself or you can go around and party your brains out. It takes willpower to know when to stop partying and willpower to know when it's no good moping in your motel room watching "The Equalizer" reruns.

I saw the kids were mostly in the self-pity mode and I kept trying to think of some way out of it for them.

Pizza was good for them and easy to get anywhere in America. Then we swung by Comiskey Park in Chicago and the White Sox were just the tonic we needed. We beat the shit out of them, three straight.

Deke Williams came to the games and came by after. He was down in the locker room and he was palavering with the kids in Spanish.

"Where'd you pick up Spanish?"

"Sheet, hillbilly, you can't own a chain of restaurants and not pick up Spanish. Who the hell you gonna get to work for you except Mexicans?"

Deke threw a party for the team on the third night and it was a good one and the boys got laid, those that wanted to get laid, that is. Myself, I didn't party around because I was thinking of Charlene. And Raul. Poor old Raul, mooning about his Maria, he went home early and I think he didn't even get drunk.

Like I said, aside from Deke in Chicago, the rest of the road trip was a cold and lonely affair. I had to do something, I thought, because the kids were moping all the time when they weren't playing baseball. America was big and scary and, in spring, mostly cold. I had to do something. Actually, I had to do it for myself because they'd depressed me, seeing them mope their afternoons away before a night game, sitting in the lobby, writing letters to their mystic, mythical homeland. Homeland.

It got me to thinking along a different set of tracks.

22

We came home to New York on the last week of April with a decent 8 and 4 road record, which meant we were still leading the East with a 14 and 4 record. Raul was hitting .461, which seemed to disappoint him because it wasn't perfect.

One other thing.

I was the one who told the boys to write home at least once a week and made sure that their mail got through. As sure as I could. I arranged it to be sent by Federal Express to Havana in big envelopes and what happened to it from there, I don't know.

On the other hand, I didn't expect they would take to writing letters home with such eagerness. It was making them all indrawn. Most of all, Raul.

Well, Raul wrote home every night.

They were letters to Maria Elena Velasquez.

He would sit by himself at the desk in his motel room and just write and write and write, long and loopy, his sentiments paraded out on a page word by word and then page by page.

I knew a little how he felt, but I couldn't tell him that. I was in love once or twice when I was his age and it hurt bad, being away from home on the road with the team. After a while, I just cauterized the hurt and it healed up. That's why when Charlene makes me crazy trying to figure out what she wants, I settle myself down with a can of MGD and a stiff dose of a Clint Eastwood movie. But Raul was into pain and making himself hurt night after night, alone in his room, writing to his Maria from all the strange places we went to on the road.

I think the road must have been nicer in the old days when they played day games and the teams rode in a private railroad car. Nowadays it's a jet plane waiting on the runway after midnight and flying halfway to dawn to another city where another bus takes you into another hotel in time to crawl into bed as the sun comes up. It would make a well-adjusted man lonely and most ball players, as far as I can see, are not well-adjusted to begin with.

Back home in New York the team bus took all of us over to the grim old East Side Hotel. I went with the troops up to the twelfth floor. Romero came by and did his dreary counting of heads and then disappeared. I wasn't seeing Romero around that much anymore. I figured he'd found out there was social life in the Big Apple.

The first thing the players did, even before using the bathrooms, was turn on all the TV sets to the Spanish station.

The airwaves were suddenly humming with Spanish voices. Kids are the same the world over, they can't see a silent TV without turning it on and they can't wait to ruin their perfect hearing with car speakers or a Sony Walkman turned up to "DEAFEN."

I looked at the set in Raul's room. It was Clint Eastwood, but he was talking in Spanish the way he never sounded in English. It was strange and fascinating, like contemplating baseball uniforms. To top it off, it was *The Good, the Bad and the Ugly,* which was an Italian western to start with.

The day was bright and cheerful and cold outside the unwashed windows of the East Side Hotel. We had a day off before the night game tomorrow. I knew the kids would just laze around in their rooms all day, drinking beer and ordering up pizza. I had something else in mind.

— Raul, go down and get the others and tell them to meet me downstairs in front of the hotel in five minutes, will you?

— Why, Señor Shawn?

— We're going on a little excursion.

— Nobody wants to go on an excursion. We're tired of traveling. We just want to rest.

— You can rest later.

— I don't want to go anywhere.

— Look, Raul. It's more than just going somewhere. It's spending George's money.

That awoke his interest. He sat up in bed where he had been lounging and stared at me.

— Does he know we're spending his money?

— No. That's the beauty part of it.

— Is it a lot of money?

— A little here and a little there and pretty soon, we're talking mucho dollars.

The troops assembled with Latin alacrity, which means they were only twenty minutes later than my five-minute deadline. Hell, I ain't much of a clock-watcher either, the way the New Yorkers are.

They take time very seriously in New York City, which is why their watches cost so much. I've been making do with a Timex for fifteen years and, aside from replacing the battery every two or three years, it works fine and I will compare my time with your time any day of the week.

But I don't count on clocks, and there are times in Texas when minutes are hours and days just last forever. Those are the good days.

I had chartered this bus in George's name. I could have used the team bus but that would have gotten back to George through the usual front office grapevine, but this way, he wouldn't know he'd even hired a charter bus until he got the bill. The troops boarded it with groans and complaints that ceased when they saw it was stacked high with pizza and beer. The driver was a cheerful Puerto Rican named Julio who fancied himself in show business, or at least the dispatcher at the bus company said he was highly entertaining.

And so we took off at one minute before one in the afternoon.

The first stop was the Empire State Building, which Julio announced was the tallest building in the world. This has not been true for some years now, but it certainly looks like it should be the tallest building in the world.

Julio also told us that it was so tall that an airplane had crashed into it once in the 1940s. I didn't know if that was true or not but it made a good story.

We all went up to the first observation deck, which is out in the open and can give you a dizzy spell if you're so inclined. The city really sounds loud up there like someone in the apartment below has turned up the bass speakers and let the sound crawl up through the walls. It was also just beautiful, a toy city laid out there just to be played with.

The boys liked this a lot and they babbled together like pups in a cardboard box nuzzling up to their mom. I was even smiling because, actually, in all the years I played for the Yankees, I'd never been up in the Empire State Building myself. In fact, for the first two years, I thought it was the Umpire State Building because that's what my road trip roomie, Doak Runyon, used to call it. What did I know then? I was just a kid.

Well, when it got good and shivery up there — the wind was whipping us pretty good and most of the kids just had light jackets — we all went back to the elevator bank and waited on a car.

Back in the bus, the mood was a helluva lot more cheerful and I thought this tour thing I had dreamed up was a good idea. Julio the driver started up his spiel again like a demented disc jockey as we cruised along down Broadway toward the tip of Manhattan.

Julio said we were near the Bowery now and that it was filled with bums wearing bowler hats who were dead drunk every morning by eight A.M. Julio and I must have read the same history books, which were slightly out of date. But we didn't see no bowler hats. The kids didn't seem particularly interested in slums. They had seen slums. Some of them doubtless lived in slums. Slums are only interesting to sociologists and city planners and the occasional slumlord. To everyone else, they're boring and everyday enough to be not worth commenting on. I thought Julio blew it there.

When we got down on Wall Street, the traffic was ferocious the way it can be and we weren't going very fast, but the pizza and beer were holding up and a couple of the kids were actually craning their necks to look up at the tall glass buildings. Julio picked up his beat:

— This is the financial heart of the world, this is Wall Street, which you Communists hate so much. Take a look, this is America's center, you might say the center of capitalism. Like the Kremlin was to you people until recently, that's what Wall Street is to us. We even named a newspaper after it.

Julio, I should mention, was playful and I hoped the kids would respond in the same way. They didn't seem resentful except for Orestes, who was afflicted with terminal resentfulness, I'd concluded. Tio said to me:

— Señor Shawn, I thought the center of capitalism was in Washington.

— No, no. That's just politics. The politicians we keep there just spend the money we make here.

— I see.

Well, we made it down to the water and that ship museum they got there. The kids liked that, but it was too damned cold walking around and we all got back on the nice, warm bus and went to the ferry terminal to take a boat to the Statue of Liberty.

It was a bad day for a boat ride. The wind rippled the harbor into waves big enough to make that digested pizza start thinking about an upward exit. Only one of the kids — Tomas — got sick though and I was proud of them.

As we approached the gray lady, I just got goose-bumpy all over. I'd never actually been out there before. Like a lot of New Yorkers, I guess I didn't have time to be a tourist all those years I was playing.

The kids were quiet, sort of respectful, but I didn't expect any deathbed conversions to capitalism. In fact, I didn't think I could have handled one if I'd got one. What would I have told Romero when he counted heads? Besides, what would I have told George? He had it all worked out with the Cubans to send the kids home at the end of the season and it wouldn't have done any good to have one of them suddenly start singing "Yankee Doodle," especially in Castilian Spanish.

When we bumped up to the island in the harbor, we went on shore and to the base of the statue and read the Emma Lazarus words. I tried to render them in Spanish, but there wasn't much poetry in the way I said them, not the way she wrote it down.

— It says to the world to give us your poor and your hungry and all the others just so they want to be free.

— Free to be hungry? (Orestes said.)

— No, it means give us the lowest class of your society, meaning in the rest of the world, just people down on their luck who want a chance to be free. Send them over here and we'll take care of them, it says.

— That seems very foolish (Orestes said).

— What if other countries took your offer? (asked Tio).

— They have (I said). That's why my great-granddaddy come over from Ireland where he couldn't make enough spit to swallow. That's why we got all kinds of people here in all kinds of colors. See, the end of it says something like, if you're looking for freedom, I hold up my light to show you the door — the golden door — that opens into freedom.

— This sounds good, but I don't see it (Orestes said). Look at our hotel. There are naked babies in the lobby, fat women sitting around with nothing to do all day, there are prostitutes and old men and I swear on my father's grave there are drug addicts everywhere. You call that freedom?

— Sure it's freedom. They're free to fail, I said.

— Some freedom. That's freedom with no purpose. You say this says to come to America from wherever you were from because you got nothing where you were from and you can have nothing here just the same.

Orestes was just looking for an argument, I knew that, but I hated to come out second best when I am in the process of defending the American way of life, especially to a half-smart catcher from Cuba who is on the punk side of twenty-five years of age.

— Orestes, being free means being free. It says no one will stand in your way. You can get an education and go out and make something out of your life. It says that no matter who you are or where you came from or who your daddy is or even if you got no daddy at all to speak of, you can be anything you want to be as long as you're willing to work hard for it.

— Señor Shawn, that is so much shit of the bull. I may be young and I may be an ignorant peasant, but I know the smell of the shit of a bull when I see it.

— You saying I'm full of shit, Orestes?

— You're full of shit.

"How'd you like to chew your teeth, you little Commie shit?" I said in English.

— Señor, Señor. Don't get into a fight with Orestes over nothing (Raul said). Come on, let's go back to the boat, it's freezing here.

— It isn't over nothing, he said I was full of shit.

Raul shook his head.

— Act your age, Señor.

He had a point. What was I doing this for except to be a good fellow with the kids and sort of let them settle into New York a little more, make the place seem more like home?

I had thought about it on the road trip, watching the kids write their letters to moms and wives and sweeties, thinking how it had been tough on me the first year with the Yankees. The married players all lived in the suburbs, up in Scarsdale and like that, and the unmarried ones were for partying every night down in the Village or SoHo. Me, I just crawled into a TV set in my room in the El Dorado Hotel every night and drank a six-pack of beer watching John Wayne or old Clint or Jimmy Stewart do the right thing. I was a little shy about partying with so many girls hanging on each arm, reaching into my pocket for their champagne bills.

To me a good time is taking a girl out to a two-step bar and listening to a little country music on the stage and drinking beer and eating peanuts. Or going to a pig roast in someone's yard or getting in my Buick and driving down to the Gulf Coast for no other reason than that it's there.

I know that makes me sound dull but I've begun to think it's my natural color. You can't shine shit, you know.

The ferry took us back to Manhattan and it was time for the afternoon rush hour, which gave Julio plenty of time to regale us with stories of old New York and how the Anglos had cheated the Indians and, later, cheated the Puerto Ricans. We ended up back at the hotel after hearing a long, stirring argument in favor of Puerto Rican independence, which I, for one, had come 'round to supporting just from listening to Julio's playful grievances all afternoon.

I signed the driver's slip and agreed on the time and slipped him a twenty as a tip, which he didn't think was enough.

"This is an insult," Julio said.

"Fine," I said. "Give it back, then."

Julio, insult intact, slammed the door in my face and took off for parts unknown. I myself was tired enough of the team by now to wish for my robe and slippers in my little studio apartment in Fort Lee. But Raul pulled my sleeve.

— What do you do now, Señor?

— I disappear.

— Where do you live?

— Over there in New Jersey.

— You are not married.

— No, I've escaped that. Just seriously in love, but I keep it under my hat.

— It is terrible to be in love and not be married.

— The cure is to get out of love. Or get married, same thing.

— I would rather die of my affliction than be cured of it. (Raul smiled.)

Now, that's what I mean. That was a sweet thing and it was well said, the way these Cubanos could do when they put their Castilian tongues to it. I may not be able to speak Spanish that well, but I'm a big fan of the language. I gave Raul a smile then that was probably just a tad too middle-aged and cynical, but that was the way I was suddenly feeling.

— Come on, Señor. Come have a beer with me before you go home. You cannot go anyway while the traffic is like this and I have found a nice place.

— I thought you didn't have time for anything except writing to your girlfriend.

— My intended.

— Your fiancée, then. Romero know you cruising around the Apple, looking for fun?

— I look for a place like home. To hear my own voice speaking.

— You found one?

— I found one.

He looked at me, waiting. The city throbbed around us, unaware of us, our Spanish-speaking voices just one more bit of garlic in the stew. Or jalapeño.

Sure, I thought. What the hell?

It was an interesting decision on Ryan Shawn's part, in light of what happened next and next after that.

23

While the kids scattered, some to their rooms and some down the street to the McDonald's, I went with Raul. I went not because I needed a buddy and not because I longed to keep on trying to speak Spanish in a civil way but because I was curious as to what Raul had found on his own in New York City and what he thought was a nice place.

Turned out to be a bar on Third Avenue called Tapas. I guess I must have walked by it a hundred times and never saw it.

It was in a storefront with the bottom half of the window painted black. "Tapas" was written in orange neon in the window and that was the only light coming from the place. We stepped into the foyer and there was a heavy black curtain that opened into the main — and only — room.

The bar filled the south wall — mirror and bottles behind and drinkers and glasses in front. There was a jukebox and it was wailing some kind of foreign shit, guitars and such. Not country-western and not anywhere near Waylon.

It was dark and smoky.

The voices were in Spanish. On the north side of the room were tables with white paper table covers. On the faded, yellowish wall were posters of bullfights in places like Sevilla and Barcelona and Madrid. I followed Raul to the back of the dining room where there was a regulars' table. Every good joint has one — a table without a covering, usually round, usually full of the usuals.

They greeted Raul with laconic enthusiasm, sort of the Spanish-speaking equivalent of "how ya doin'." Raul was offered a chair but he stood and I realized he was going to introduce the gringo.

— This is Ryan Shawn, the manager of the Yankees.

They looked up at me. One was heavyset with clear blue eyes and a dark suit. His tie was neatly affixed to the top of his white shirtfront and he wore a jeweled tie clip. The second man was going bald on top and had large hands with a lot of calluses on the fingers and palms. The third dude was younger — about thirty — sort of hidden back in the shadows of the lamp lights.

"Hey," I said in English. I didn't stick out my mitt in the all-American greeting because it didn't seem to me anyone wanted to extend himself to reach forward.

— He wants to follow you to see if you are in touch with the counter-revolutionaries? (said the man with the tie clip).

— Tell him the Irish bar is at the end of the block. He can celebrate St. Patrick's Day there.

This came from the younger guy in the shadows. There was a mean edge to it.

I didn't say a thing.

Raul said:

— I invited him to have a drink with me.

— You should make him pay, Raul. He makes much more money than you do by spying on you.

— Castro's pet.

I didn't know who said the last thing. I just smiled in my lazy, Clint-Eastwood way, not taking offense, and I said:

— Raul, I ain't welcome. You have your beer with your friends and I'll just go home to Fort Lee.

— Suburbanite.

This came from the tie clip.

— Yeah, well, we can't all afford to live in the Big Apple.

— You can (Tie Clip said).

— Not me. I'm just a country boy, got to go to sleep with the cows.

— He sleeps with cows.

This got a laugh, even if it wasn't such a nice laugh. It broke the ice. But Raul wasn't having any of it.

— He is my guest.

Raul said this exactly the way Errol Flynn might have said it before slicing up the Sheriff of Nottingham or something.

— Sit down, sit down (Tie Clip said, gesturing to empty chairs). Any friend of Raul's is welcome here. Have you been here before, Señor Shawn?

— Not really.

— You like Spanish food?

I sat.

— Oh, tacos and shit like that, yeah.

— This is not tacos and 'shit' like that. (This was from the young guy in the shadows.)

Tie Clip gave the young guy a look and then turned to me.

— You speak Spanish.

— Come from Texas.

— I thought so. Mexican accent.

— And you speak like a Cuban.

— Bravo. I am Cubano. My name is Jose Marti Riccardo.

— Any relation to Ricky Ricardo?

That stopped up the conversation a moment and then Tie Clip smiled. He had a weary face and bright eyes and he leaned forward and took my hand without me realizing it was ready to be taken. We did a shake. His hand was soft.

Introductions all around. The young guy was Estavar something and it turned out he was an interpreter at the United Nations, rendering into Spanish things said in English and Italian. The other guy with the big, calloused hands and the hair going to bald was another Jose, this time named Martinez and he was a limo driver who hustled as an illegal taxi on the side. He gave me his card and said he knew where Fort Lee was and he wouldn't complain about taking me there. This was a good thing to know and I thanked him.

I had beer and it was San Miguel, which is not the same as Miller GD but had its own cool. Raul had a beer and then there was a plate full of things like octopus or scampi and other things like that. I am not much for fish that looks strange but I thought I should dip in, even if I was going to get poisoned by it. The others were into their cups — Jose Marti Riccardo was into rum and Coke and the other Jose, the driver, was drinking Tio Pepe brandy — and we weren't going to catch up with them.

— Señor Shawn is the one who came to Cuba to get us to play for the Yankee team, Raul said.

— I know. You forgive them, Señor, they are not baseball fans here but I read the baseball news every day in the *Daily News*. (This from Señor Riccardo.)

— Football, huh?

Estavar said, in cold, precise English, "I suppose you mean American football but that's a stupid, barbarian game. I mean football."

"Soccer," I said.

"Football," he said.

— Call it what you want.

— You should speak English, you don't speak Spanish very well.

— What do you do in your spare time, Estavar? You a diplomat?

That got a smile from the other two — not a laugh, not near a laugh, but a smile — city, clashing with security forces in the biggest and Estavar leaned into the light a little and I could see his face. Why is it I know every punk's resentful face and why do they all look the same? He could have been a beered-up pickup truck cowboy on the road to Galveston looking for a pool cue fight just as well as he could be a UN translator sitting in a Spanish bar on Third Avenue.

— Ignore Estavar, Señor. I love baseball, I am a Yankee fan for thirty years since I came to New York. I once caught a Reggie Jackson home run with these bare hands.

I liked Tie Clip. He was sprawled back in his wooden armchair, enjoying the booze and the smell of cigarette smoke forming brown clouds over the tables. There were a few eaters, but I found out the rush came around nine at night. This was a Spanish place and it was a shabby bit of old España, trying to keep alive thoughts of home, even if the customers came from different homes in the Spanish-speaking world. I bought a round when the girl came again and no one turned it down, not even Estavar. Everyone saluted and we laid it back into our throats.

— Señor (began Jose Riccardo), are the Yankees very good this year?

— I don't know.

Raul looked at me then.

I looked at him. "I dunno," I said in English. I looked at Riccardo. "Trouble is, everyone feels their way the first forty games of the season. Everyone is trying to figure everyone out. Teams change every year. Players who are dipshit in one league find a new life in another league. Trades and combinations. Not to mention twenty-four brand-new ballplayers on the Yanks that nobody ever saw play outside of Havana."

"The element of surprise," Jose Marti Riccardo said thoughtfully. "Yes. I see that."

Raul said:

— No, no. Much better than just a surprise.

— You, Raul, are the greatest surprise of all (Riccardo said). What a beautiful hitter, I want to cry when I see you hit the ball.

I pulled tickets out of my wallet, good box tickets of the kind that are a manager's perk. I threw them casually on the table.

— Come on out and see us.

— Much thanks, Señor.

Riccardo palmed the tickets and then examined them and said again "much thanks." He doled one out to the driver and offered one to Estavar.

— Baseball is a tedious game (Estavar said).

— It has its moments (I said).

— Why are you insulting me? (Raul said).

— I am not insulting you, Raul. I am insulting this gringo.

"Shit, hoss, you can't insult me. I'm insult-proof." Said it easy, just like it reads.

Estavar said, "You work for Señor Castro, the pig. You work for the CIA."

"Hold on, I work for George Bremenhaven, which is even worse."

"The pig who raped Cuba."

"George gave these kids a chance to play in the Bigs."

"Bigs?" said Riccardo.

"The major leagues," I said.

Raul held up his hand.

— Let's speak Spanish.

Riccardo said:

— Is this a good man, Raul?

— He is doing what he has to do.

There was a shrug in that answer as well. I saw the way this was going. It wasn't Raul's fault but it was like the time that Pedro Quininos and I went down into this Billy Bob bar on the road to Galveston with me forgetting he was a Mexican wearing a sombrero and the next thing you knew, we were playing Zorro with pool cues with half the cowboys in the place. Sometimes you forget where you are when you come out of the workplace and go down home.

— Raul, I've got to call it an early night. I appreciate the beer.

— No, no, Señor Shawn. I buy you a beer. I must, before you leave.

— And have this. It is octopus (said Riccardo).

I thought it was. But I took it anyway. It was chewy and I chewed. Sort of like Doublemint gum with all the sugar gone out of it.

More beer came. The juke played this woman singing in a falsetto and there were feet dancing on the record as well as that throbbing flamenco guitar.

"Whaddaya you do, Mr. Riccardo?"

"I am a courtroom interpreter," he said.

"Like criminal court?"

"Yes. I am on call in the branches in Manhattan to interpret for the clients who do not speak English."

"Lots of them, I guess."

"Lot of them. We also have a Korean interpreter, Mr. Kimm Soo Long, and there is the Polish lady, Mrs. Gzenewski."

"Polish? I didn't figure on Polish."

"You only think the lawbreakers are Spanish, is that it?" asked Estavar.

"No, I figured the Spanish speakers played ball for the Yankees," I said. Little shit was getting me hot.

Raul leaned forward then. He fixed his eye on Estavar. He held it a moment, just like an actor. I swear his eye was going to do an Eastwood twitch, but he just held it there on Estavar, his strong wrists gripping the edge of the table.

"Mr. Shawn gave us his free day. To show us this city. He took us to many places. He didn't take us to the courts." He said this in careful and totally unaccented English. "We saw the Statue of Liberty."

"Ah, the statue. *Muy buena,*" said Riccardo.

Estavar said, "He wants you to defect. Why don't you defect and get it over with?"

Raul blinked. The language was too fast for him.

— Defect (repeated Estavar in Spanish). He is trying to lure you to defect. To show you how much there is in America and how little you have in Cuba.

— I will never defect. My fiancée. She is in Havana.

Riccardo appeared uncomfortable. He tapped the tips of his fingers together. He said:

— Please, please. This is a place for pleasant thoughts and pleasant words. Señor Shawn is not an agent provocateur. I have seen him play many times.

Now what the hell did that mean? Did he mean there was something about the way I pitched that said I couldn't be whatever he said I wasn't?

— Look. I don't want anybody to do anything except play ball. We're going to Texas next week and swing through the West Coast and all I want to do is play ball and get through this season.

— And win the pennant (Raul said).

I looked at him.

He stared at me.

— Well, yeah. Everyone's got a chance.

— We have more than a chance.

— You got a chance, Raul. We ain't anywhere near winning the pennant.

— Look at what we have done.

— Look at Suarez. He don't pace himself as a pitcher. He's throwing his arm out. He'll be a cripple by July. Look at Tomas at short. He keeps getting surprised by the ball.

— The grounds are very alive, Señor. He is used to dead grounds. Dead. The infield, I mean.

So that was it. Raul had just solved a mystery for me there. Sure, the kids were playing on semi-manicured grass with a few crab weeds in it. The ball didn't have the bounce in Havana it had in the Bigs.

— Raul is hitting well (Riccardo said).

— He might be a spring phenom.

— No, he's the real thing. I can see Reggie Jackson when I see him swing.

— The second go-round, the pitchers will be seeing him again, figuring out how to pitch to him.

— They can't pitch to me (Raul said).

— That's what they all say.

— Another round.

The last came from Riccardo who sprinkled the infield with his index finger and made a circular motion. More beers and I sat still and took it like a man. Raul was waiting for the waitress to leave to have another fight with me. I was ready.

— Raul, I don't want you to get your hopes up. The season is a hundred and sixty-two games long. You got to pace yourself. Baseball is funny, it's like life, you got your ups and downs. The best team ever is gonna lose a third of its games, that's a given. So we still have a lot of losing to do. It's how you come back from the losing that determines the winning.

— True words, Señor. Very true words (Riccardo said and he burped. His eyes were getting glassy but it was the only sign of intoxication, not counting the burp). I had a case today in which this poor *hombre* robbed a woman at an ATM machine. He has had bad luck ever since he came to New York two years ago. His wife left him with their baby and she is on welfare in Brooklyn and he has not had a job except in the Roy Rogers on Broadway washing dishes. He has no money and he could not stand any more losing. So he robbed a woman at an ATM on West 88th Street.

I stared at Riccardo. He waved his hand in dismissal and sighed.

— He was given two years at Attica. This is the end of the season for him.

I sat there and didn't say anything.

Raul said:

— It is unjust, all the poverty that drives men to these crimes.

"Hey," I said, getting the words in my personal fog machine. "Poverty is poverty. Only thing is here that not everyone is poor so it stands out. I didn't see a lot of rich people in Havana."

"You saw people sharing their fate," Estavar said.

"I don't have to be poor again to know I was," I said.

"You're making a million dollars this year, it says so in the *Daily News*," Riccardo said. He said it softly.

"Damn right," I said.

"The American way, reward the Anglo and keep down the Hispanic who does the work," Estavar said.

"You're a fucking Communist," I said.

"No, I am," Raul said.

We all looked at him.

Riccardo tapped him on the back of his hand. "Raul, little one, you are just a ball player."

"No, they say I am a Communist."

"That's just a way of talking," I explained.

"It is true. We do the bidding of El Supremo. And we do this for Cuba."

"Where'd you pick up your English?"

"My fiancée is fluent in English," he said. "She helps me."

"Then you could talk regular all along?"

"I am not happy with English," Raul said.

"That's what the Irish say," I said. Trying to keep it light and falling on my own joke again. If jokes were sharp, I'd be in bandages.

"You were not born when I volunteered for the Bay of Pigs," said Riccardo. "They said I was just a boy and they would not let me go. My uncle was killed there and my father was put into prison. He died."

Raul closed his eyes a moment, as though to absorb the tragedy of what Riccardo said. Then he said to me:

— You should go home now, Señor. I'm sorry.

I did it with some dignity, I thought. I got up slow and extended my hand to Riccardo and shook it and then to the other Jose who had the limo and then did a wave to Estavar because I wasn't going to let the snot reject my handshake. Then I rested my hand on Raul's shoulder.

— I don't want nothing from you except to make it more comfortable for you. For Tio, Suarez, the others. I know this is just like one long road trip to you, but autumn will come before you know it.

— And we will not win the pennant.

— I didn't say that. I just said, you got to expect losses along the way.

— If you expect to lose, you will lose.

— I didn't say that. I didn't say you should expect . . .

— I know what you said. This is not baseball, Señor. This is a show, some kind of a circus show. This is not baseball. The others on the other teams, they know. They feel they are shamed because we are on the field against them. What are we? Boys from Cuba no one ever heard of.

"Shit and double shit, Raul," I said. Then, in Spanish:

— I don't want you to get down.

— I am down. All the time. All I want is to be with my beloved one.

— Maybe that's all I want, too.

He looked at me. The others looked at me. Damn. I didn't figure on giving anything away. I took my hand off his shoulder.

— You got a girl, I got a girl. You handle it. You make your living. You're on the road, you have to do what you have to do.

— You love someone?

— I love someone (I said, thinking to make him feel better).

— And you . . . "handle" it? How do you handle it?

— You watch westerns on TV and drink beer when you can and when there's a game, you play the game. That's what you do.

— And it is not more important than that?

— It's more important, Raul. You just "handle it."

Estavar guffawed. He brought up his hand half-clenched and made a frigging movement with it.

"He means like this, Raul."

But Raul was staring at me.

"You can do that, Señor? Handle it when she is someplace far away, waiting for you?"

"It's what you have to do."

Raul shook his head and looked away.

— If you can do that, then I feel sorry for you, Señor.

— Why?

He looked back up at me.

— Because, Señor, then you are not in love at all.

And I had to get out of there, right then, back into the glitter of the shabby street with the shabby cabs humping over the patched up pavement, letting the cool night air slap me around a little.

Lovesick little puppy.

Shit.

I lurched down the sidewalk toward the parking lot.

Handle it! I wanted to scream at him.

But I didn't make a sound.

24

So where did a twenty-three-year-old punk from Cuba get off taking pity on me, a grown man with years of experience who has won a hundred and sixty games lifetime and spent sixteen seasons in the Bigs?

Charlene Cleaver did not even enter into this equation and there I was, trying to make him feel better, trying to make all of them feel better by getting them out of their rooms and their fucking Spanish language TV shows and their pizzas and showing them the Umpire State Building and all. Where did they get off?

I went across town to the West Side Highway and up to the George Washington Bridge. The Hudson River was the color of ink and there was a light enough rain to make the wipers go thunk-thunk every ten seconds or so. I turned on the radio and listened to some fucking jazz interpretation of country and turned it off and just tapped the wheel with my fingertips, trying to remember when I was young enough not to be able to handle things.

Left El Paso when I was eighteen and went up to Arizona on a baseball scholarship and I just knew I was going to the Bigs someday. I knew everything when I was eighteen. I remembered Daddy driving me to the bus station for the long haul north. I didn't even have a car at Arizona the first two years. I was poor. Daddy saw me the first year in the Bigs and I cherish that, only wish Mama had.

I handled everything.

New Jersey slouched glittering and dark across the oil on the waters of the Hudson. New Jersey is like a midget hitching up its pants to face off the big bully on Manhattan Island.

Part of growing up is handling things. That's what I was trying to get across to Raul, lovesick pup.

Handled Sue Joan Moffett at Arizona. She wanted to keep house and teach kindergarten and make babies. She was God's gift to cloudy days, sunny and golden all over with breath like a pine forest. Didn't have to figure her in my plans, though. I guess I made it plain enough that she and I were just for fucking and not for keeps. She made her babies with someone else. She was a phase of my life.

Of course, you might say my life was becoming just a series of phases. And now Charlene, with Raul putting it in perspective. If I wasn't a love-starved calf like him, then it wasn't the real thing, is that it?

I hung a right at Route 4 once over the bridge and then went up the Palisades Parkway to the Clyde exit and back over the Palisades to the other side of Fort Lee. Fort Lee takes getting used to, which is why cab drivers don't like to drop you off there.

I parked in the Holiday Inn lot and thought about having a nightcap in the bar there but then thought better of it. Just my luck some asshole would want to bend my ear about the team. I lurched on down the walk, which was all coated with rain, and into my apartment building. I had the key out on the way up in the elevator.

Same old home sweet home. I threw the keys on the table and turned on the kitchen light. I punched up the answering machine and rolled back the tape because the red light was blinking.

"Where are you, Ryan Patrick? This is ten o'clock at night and you're not even home yet and I know you don't play today, so I've had to go take a room at the stupid old Holiday Inn down the street from you. I don't even know where I am, but I do know it's costing me $109 a night because you weren't home. I hope you're satisfied." And the receiver slammed.

I shook my head very slowly in case it was loose. Then I tasted some of the beer to get the taste of Wild Turkey tamed down. Then I dialed information and asked for the number of the Holiday Inn.

I must have been drunk because it seemed like a good idea to call Charlene at two in the morning and tell her I was suddenly home. A sober person would reflect on that before taking action, but I was a man of few words and they were getting fewer.

I called the room of Miss Charlene Cleaver and let the phone ring and ring and ring. This also seemed like a good idea. She might be sound asleep and only my patient ringing of the phone sixty or seventy times would be able to rouse her.

"Mfphm?"

"Charlene? It's me," I said. I thought I said it cheerfully.

"Mfphm?"

"Charlene, are you sleeping?"

That brought on a witty silence for a moment. And then she said, "No, why would I be sleeping at two in the morning?" I had to laugh then because Charlene is just great when she's being ironic.

"I just got in."

"Where were you?"

"With Raul Guevara. We found this great bar on Third Avenue called Tapas. It's like a Spanish place. Like in Spain, not Mexico. Met some of his friends there, fellow named Riccardo. He's a court interpreter for people who don't speak English. And this punk name of Estavar, sort of an asshole. Another guy is a limo driver, I might be able to get him to pick me up at the airport when I get in from road trips."

"You found this great bar? And you got drunk with one of your wetback ball players talking all night, to some guys about whatever fascinating stuff you men talk about? Oh, yes, and the courthouse interpreter, whatever that means."

Now, there was something of the ice princess in the tone of her voice but nothing could stop me now because I had passed over the threshold from merely charming to being bullet-proof.

I said, "Why don't you come over? Just get a cab and come on over and we can have a good talk."

"I don't want a good talk, Ryan. I want to go to sleep."

"Well, okay. If you don't want to come over, okay. But I was just asking you over. I missed you, honey."

"I flew two thousand miles to see you."

"You didn't let me know, I would've been here."

"I got in at five in the afternoon and I took a cab down here from Newark Airport —"

"Actually, it's up here from Newark. Newark is down there if you read a map rightside up."

"Shut up!"

I did. It was something in the tone of voice again, but this time I was listening.

"And I waited and waited and waited and then I went to a coffee shop and had a bacon, lettuce, and tomato sandwich, which I never eat, never, never, never, and then I waited some more and then I decided about nine o'clock that you were just dead somewhere, lying on a street in New York

City, being run over by taxicabs and I came here to this Holiday Inn that I walked six blocks to get to."

"It's more like four blocks, Charlene, don't exaggerate. I keep my car there in the parking lot."

"Shut up!" she said.

"Why'd you come up here? Is something wrong?"

"Yes, something's wrong. Why would I come up if there wasn't something wrong?"

"What's wrong?"

"I'm going home in the morning. This is stupid, I wasted my time off to spend all this money on coming up because I needed to see you and you're spending all your money and time getting drunk with a greaser in a bar when I thought you were dead in the middle of New York City."

"I don't like you to use that language," I said.

"Well, go fuck yourself!" she said.

Don't get the wrong idea about Charlene. She is a sensitive and caring person and she does not use slurs in ordinary conversation or use bad language unless extremely provoked. It was probably something about it being two in the morning that set her off, that and spending $109 for the privilege of sleeping in a king-size bed in the middle of northern New Jersey.

Just think of how provoked she would have been if she had been in Manhattan shelling out 300 bucks a night to listen to the serenade of the garbage trucks.

"Charlene, what's wrong, honey? I didn't know you were coming so I don't think you can blame me if I was trying to reach an interpersonal relationship with one of my players. He's very troubled. He's got a girl back in Havana and he's so lovesick that I was worried about him."

"What about you, Ryan? You had a girl back in Houston. I bet she never came up in the conversation, did she?"

"As a matter of fact, you did, quite often."

"I won't have my name tramped through the mud of a New York saloon," she said.

"It was not tramped. It was brought up. Raul told me how much he loved this little girl named Maria Velasquez and how much he missed her and I told him how much I missed you. He even asked to see your picture." I made that part up.

"You don't even have a picture of me," she said. "You got as much sentiment as wet adobe."

"I said I didn't have a picture of you because I didn't need none. I carried your image in my heart."

"You said that? Was this before or after you got drunk?"

"Before," I said.

"You're a liar. You'd never say that sober."

"I love you. I think I've been sober saying that."

"*They* arrested Jack Wade for income tax evasion," she said.

Plunk. Just like that.

"*They* arrested? Who arrested?"

"The FBI. I think."

"The FBI arrested Jack Wade?"

"Oh, I was so scared for you, Ryan. I just know he's gonna rat on you and drag you into this."

"Rat on me for what? He sold me a car once."

"He said he gave it to you."

"Jack Wade is a car dealer, Charlene. He don't give away anything he can sell. Sort of like being a whore."

"I was so sure you were in trouble —"

I was getting sober in that painful way that is like sliding down a three-story razor blade on your tongue. I shook my head loose and it hurt. I held the phone very tight against my ear.

"Charlene, I ain't in no trouble. I never had no deal with Jack Wade."

"He told me that you and him was thick as thieves."

"Jack Wade is a liar like all natural born salesmen. Also a thief, apparently, though I don't hold income tax evasion as a major crime the way the government does."

"Then you're not guilty?"

"I ain't even been accused of anything to feel guilty about. Except by you, honey, and I just told you I loved you."

"Oh, honey."

Honey and honey. It made me smile. "Hurry on over."

"It's two in the morning, honey. I can't get no cab."

"Shit, then stay where you are. I'll come over."

"Oh, Ryan. You're drunk, aren't you?"

"Yes, ma'am, I am. Took a cab home all the way from Manhattan, driven by a homicidal maniac, cost me fifty bucks." The lies were coming as thick as . . . well, thieves. "I saw the Statue of Liberty today for the first time."

"Why?" Charlene said.

"Took the kids out on an excursion. Went up to the eighty-seventh floor of the Empire State Building, too. Never did that before."

"Why?" Charlene said.

"Show them the city, try to make the kids feel at home. They're all so homesick, writing letters all the time they were on the road trip."

"You never wrote me a letter."

"I don't write, we ain't in Cuba. I can call you just as easy."

"You didn't call me all week," she said.

"I missed you," I said.

"If you missed me, you'd have called me."

"Not necessarily."

"You were too cheap to call."

"I ain't cheap. I'm careful."

"I just spent $413.98 on an airplane and fifty dollars on a cab and $109 plus tax to sleep in a big old bed in this Holiday Inn. I'm on the side facing that big old bridge there. Don't these people never sleep? Traffic bang bang bang all night long. I can hear it now."

"It's the garbage trucks," I said, making a logical connection.

"Ryan. You stay put and so will I. I want to go back to sleep. I want to see you, but I don't want to see you in the state you're in."

"I'm carrying on a perfectly rational conversation," I said.

"You talk like a drunk."

"I never drink anything but beer."

"Then you must have drunk a barrel tonight."

"Drank. Drunk is what I are, drank is what I did," I said. I was so incredibly witty by this point that it was all I could do to stop from laughing.

"I'll call you in the morning," she said.

There was a final note in that and I didn't fight it. If a lady says enough, it's good enough for me. "Sorry about Jack Wade," I said to her.

"Mmm," she said. "I'm glad you're not in trouble."

"So am I," I said.

"Are you sure you're not?"

"I'm sure," I said. I didn't want to think too much about that IRS guy asking Jack about dealing with me. I figured that handling these Cuban players and all, I was working with the government.

"Good night, Ryan," she said then.

"I love you," I said then.

And then, of all things, I thought about that sad look of pity in Raul's eyes.

Shit.

Just like that, I figured I would have a hard time getting to sleep.

Women can do that to you.

25

The doorman in the lobby called me around nine in the morning and told me Charlene wanted to come up. That gave me about two minutes to run into the bathroom, stand in the shower, wipe myself off with a clean towel, and present my hungover presence at the front door.

Charlene had two coffees in paper cups in a bag and a large muffin of the kind that roughage is made out of and is totally inedible. She also had her green dress on, which is more than a heart can bear at nine in the morning. If I had to work with Charlene every day, I'd have my ass hauled in on sexual harassment charges inside of a week.

"You look terrible," she said.

"Just took a shower," I said.

"I didn't say you smelled terrible, I said you looked terrible," she said.

I scratched my chest just to have something to do when Charlene pushed by me after I tried to kiss her. "Whiskey breath," she said.

I went back into the bathroom and closed the door and put a half-pound of Crest on my teeth and then rinsed the whole lot of them in Listerine. I even brushed my hair. There wasn't much I could do with my eyes, though.

I put on my robe and went back into the rest of the apartment, which is just one big room off a Pullman kitchen.

"Ryan, you ever get tired of living in one room?"

"Sure I do. But I don't see the need for a bedroom when all I'm gonna do is sleep in it."

She had sat down at the kitchen counter and opened her coffee. I did the same with mine.

"Brought you a muffin. Banana-apple."

"I'll drink some coffee first to get lubricated," I said.

"You look like you were good and lubricated last night. I didn't know you had a drinking problem."

"Charlene, I just went out with one of my players and we were over-served, is all." I took a sip and scalded the tip of my tongue.

"Charlene, why'd you come up here? To tell me about Jack Wade?"

She opened her purse then and threw it on the counter. I picked it up. It was an envelope addressed to Ms. Charlene Cleaver of Houston, Texas. I opened the unsealed envelope and took out the sheet of paper.

It said:

> Ms. Cleaver:
> That awful man has been pestering me again and it is more than I can stand, knowing that he is two-timing you at the same time he is sweet talking me . . .

It went on in this vein but I skipped through it to the signature.

> Roxanne Devon.

I stared at the signature for a good ten seconds. It was a loopy hand-writing, the kind that sophomore girls practice. She didn't draw smiley faces instead of dotting her i's, but it was in the same category as that.

I put the letter on the counter and took another slug of coffee.

"What do you want me to say?"

"Tell me what you want to tell me," she said.

"I do not know nor have I ever known anyone anywhere named Rox-anne Devon."

"Tell me another one."

"Charlene, we don't play until eight tonight so why don't you and I go over to Brunswick, New Jersey, and go through the phone book and try to see if we can run down this Roxanne Devon."

"You probably know she probably doesn't even live in Brunswick, New Jersey. She just mails her letters from there," Charlene said.

"Why would she do that, Charlene? If she don't live someplace, why would she go there to mail poison letters to some woman she don't even know in Houston, Texas? Tell me that."

"Jack got arrested day before yesterday and yesterday I get this letter in the mail and I ain't heard from you for a week."

"We been on the road. In Cleveland and Chicago and then Kansas City. I don't think of nothing on the road except the baseball games I still got to play."

"So you don't think of me, is that it?"

"I think of you all the time, Charlene."

"I don't want you to think you got to lie to me," she said.

"Why would I think that?"

"It's not like we're married," she said.

"I know that."

"'Course you do. Got this bachelor apartment in this fancy building with a doorman. I bet I ain't the first girl that doorman announced to you. He didn't seem surprised by me or nothing."

"Lewis ain't been surprised since he got a draft notice to report to Vietnam in 1965," I said.

"You think you can talk your way out of anything."

Now she was making me pissed and I had a headache to boot. I got up and went to the icebox and took out a carton of Tropicana and poured some into a glass and drank it down. Orange juice makes me feel better every time I drink it. I poured another glass and then looked at Charlene. "You want some orange juice?"

"Stop stalling around," she said.

"Charlene, you are making me crazy. I don't know who's sending you these letters, but I think we ought to go to the police about them."

"And air our dirty linen in public?"

"We don't have no dirty linen, Charlene, because these letters are fake and the work of that madman I work for, George Bremenhaven."

"So you said once."

"And so I say again. You just sit there while I put on my duds. We're gonna go see George right now and have this out. You want me to quit, I'll quit. Today. On the spot. I told George to stop messing around with my personal life and this is going too far. I'm gonna pop him one."

Charlene just sat there, her mouth hanging open.

I went to the closet and grabbed a handful of clothes. Normally, I'd dress right there but I was doing a modest turn, so I went into the bathroom and closed the door. Shaved first and then brushed my teeth again with another half-pound of Crest and then slipped on my clothes. When I came out, Charlene hadn't moved, even to closing her mouth, hanging open.

"Come on," I said, grabbing my keys.

"Where we going?"

"George's office."

"Where's that?"

"In the city. That big place across the river."

"You mean, New York?"

"Only city I know of around here."

We grabbed a Fort Lee cab with Lewis's help and the next thing, we were tooling across the GW Bridge. It was a nice morning and there was a warm breeze blowing up the Jersey coastline right into the middle of Manhattan. I was hot, hot at Charlene and hot at George for causing me problems when there were enough problems trying to learn managing in Spanish.

Traffic was heavy and it took us a half-hour to get to the big sandy-colored building on Park Avenue. I thought Charlene was a little intimidated by everything about the city and that pleased me. When she's in her own domain, which is Houston, she pretty well takes charge, but this was a different kettle of fish altogether.

We took the elevator up and the doors popped open and we were standing in front of the glass doors that said: BREMENHAVEN PROPERTIES. That described George's day job. We marched right through, with me holding the door for Charlene. We were in the presence of sweet Miss Viola Foster, whom I have described before.

"Oh, Mr. Shawn, how nice to see you," Miss Foster said. She looked at Charlene so I made the introduction and asked if George was in.

"I'll see," she said. This meant he was in, but since secretaries are told never to give anyone a straight answer I didn't blame her any for lying to me.

She went to George's door and opened it after a timid knock and went inside.

"Come on, Charlene," I said to her and grabbed her by the arm. We went to the same door and I opened it.

George was at his desk and a man I didn't know was sitting in an armchair to the side of the desk. Everyone looked at us, startled.

"I gotta talk to you, George."

"I'm busy, Ryan —"

"I don't give a shit because I'm quitting as of now."

"You can't do that," George said in his imitation of a reasonable voice. It makes him sound like Adolph Menjou. "Mr. Sills, I apologize —"

"Hey, no problem, Mr. Bremenhaven. I never did get a chance to meet a real ball player before. You must be Ryan Shawn, I've seen you pitch many times." Sills got up to shake my hand and gaze admiringly at Charlene.

"Sorry to bust in on you but George has a habit of slipping out side doors when he don't wanna see someone and I know he doesn't wanna see me," I said, milking Mr. Sills's pinkies. "George, I'll make this short and sweet. You have gone one trick over your limit and that's the last straw. I'm quitting as of now and you can get some other chump to baby-sit those kids."

"Where would I get someone who speaks Spanish?" George said in that reasonable tone of his. He was just sitting there at the center of the room but everyone else was standing.

"There's plenty of people in baseball speak Spanish," I said.

"But you're an Anglo," he said. "I trust you."

"You are a racist arrogant asshole," I said. "I told you not to play your tricks on my girl but you just don't know when to say no, do you, George. You just keep nudging, don't you."

"Miss Foster, you can leave the room. And take Mr. Sills with you. I'll call you this afternoon, Sills."

Sills didn't seem to notice his reduction in rank from Mr. Sills to Sills the Hired Help. I figured he was a government man then. Like Baxter earlier. But he was looking at me funny, just standing there. "That's it, Sills," George said.

"Mr. Shawn," — Sills had changed from the fan to a government agent in that moment — "I hope you reconsider . . . everything. And I hope you don't quit." Then he beamed at me, beamed at Charlene, and beamed his way out of the office. Miss Foster closed the door behind her.

"Now, what's on your tiny mind, Ryan? And who's the broad?"

"You keep a civil tongue, you son of a bitch. This is Miss Charlene Cleaver is who and you sent her another one of your nasty little letters allegedly from a Miss Roxanne Devon."

George rose from behind his desk and came around and took Charlene's hand in his and gave a little bow to go with it. "I am charmed, Miss Cleaver, really charmed to meet the woman Ryan here has gone on and on about for more than a year."

Charlene lowered her gray eyes at that and let George hold her pinkies a moment too long. She said "Thank you, Mr. Bremenhaven" the way Scarlett O'Hara would have.

"I don't think any description of you would have been adequate. That's a lovely outfit you're wearing, Miss Cleaver."

What was he going to do next, sniff her? I got between them and said, "George, you snake, I got a good mind to punch your lights out —"

"Why, Ryan? Why? What have I done to deserve this?"

"You sent Charlene another poison letter from your alleged Roxanne Devon of Brunswick, New Jersey, who does not exist anyway."

"I had an Aunt Roxanne once. She was my favorite aunt, favorite person in the family. She's gone now," George said. He wasn't even talking to me, he was aiming all the charm at Charlene. Imagine a charming frog and you can vaguely imagine George. It was sickening.

"I'm sorry for your loss," Charlene said.

"Charlene, he's the son of a bitch who was behind sending you those letters so that you'd get jealous and give me up so I could go on playing baseball for this son of a bitch for peanuts."

"We don't know that for certain, Ryan," Charlene said.

"Ah, the benefit of a doubt. I am honored," George said, oiling across the floor toward her.

"Well, I'm quitting, George. You get someone else for the game tonight. I'll be halfway to Texas before the ninth inning," I said.

"And leave everything I've been trying to build?" George said. "Where's the gratitude, Ryan? Where's your sense of patriotism? Do you think Norman Schwarzkopf would have quit?"

"We ain't in war, George. It's baseball. You ripped off a bunch of green kids from a foreign country and you make it a noble cause. You're pathetic, you're so low."

"I'm paying you over a million dollars. If I can't appeal to your sense of duty, let me appeal to your wallet."

George usually had me there, but not this morning. I had a hangover, and Charlene showing up on my doorstep with that phony letter did not improve things. Imagine me saying a million dollars wasn't that important. I was on the verge of doing just that when Charlene spoke up.

"How do you know that Mr. Bremenhaven had that letter sent to me?"

"Because it's exactly the kind of rotten scheming trick George does all the time. You can't trust him, Charlene. Don't look him directly in the eye, either, or he'll try to steal your soul on you."

"You took all the players on a tour of New York and you said I authorized it," George said in his reasonable voice. "You think I'm going to pay for all that?"

"Yesterday I was working for you, but that was yesterday," I said.

"Ryan, you took them to the Statue of Liberty, for Christ's sake. You trying to get them to defect to make me look bad?"

"I was trying to get them to be a little less homesick."

"What's the Statue of Liberty got to do with anything?"

"You might have been owed an explanation if I still worked for you."

"I've got a contract."

"It's not worth the paper it's printed on. I don't have to put up with this shit, George. Charlene is starting to believe there really is a Roxanne Devon, which I know and you know there is not."

"Probably just a fan. Lots of girls go to baseball games and want to sleep with the players. Groupies. I hate to say that so boldly, Miss Cleaver, but it's a sordid fact of the life in sports. What with this age of disease, with AIDS and all that, we try to tell the players to be careful, but you know, they're really like children."

"I ain't no child, George, and I don't fool around with groupies."

"I wouldn't either if I could have the company of a woman as beautiful and charming as Miss Charlene Cleaver. Why haven't I met her before this, Ryan?"

"Because I try to keep the sordid side of my life separate from her. Like knowing you, for instance."

"You see what I put up with?" he said to Charlene.

I waved a hand between them to get their attention. "Yo, George. Me. Ryan. I quit."

"Don't let him quit on me, not at this crucial juncture, Miss Cleaver. This is more than about baseball. This is about trade and freeing the Cuban people from their yoke of tyranny. This is about America reaching out its hand in friendship to a poor, backward nation that yearns to breathe free —"

"You stole that from the Statue of Liberty," I said.

"I didn't steal, it's in the public domain," he snarled. Then he turned back to Charlene and gave her what he thought was a dazzling smile. The problem was that Charlene was getting herself dazzled despite my best intentions. I would have thought just being in the same room with that Gila would have sent her straight into a faint, but it was having the opposite effect.

I said, "Show him the letter, Charlene."

She said, "Oh, I don't want to show him."

"Show him the fucking letter that got you upset enough to come two thousand miles to bug me about it at nine in the morning," I shouted.

"Don't shout," Charlene said. "I won't be shouted at by any man."

"Charlene, you want me to quit and I'm quitting —"

"Miss Cleaver, Miss Cleaver, is that what you want? You want Ryan to walk away from his duties as a player and as a manager of the most revolutionary concept in baseball since the new playoff system?"

"We had talked about it, Mr. Bremenhaven," Charlene said.

George looked at her sadly. I know his sad look, although it is a very subtle shift away from his cold-blooded let's-screw-someone look. But I have studied the man for years up close.

"Then I surrender," he said, lifting his hands. "No man ever stood in a woman's way. If you think it's the best thing for Ryan to turn his back on the game at the peak of his career when golden opportunities are waiting for him, then I can't argue with you. I would never argue with anyone who obviously has Ryan's best interest at heart."

"Mr. Bremenhaven —"

"George. Please make it George." .

"George. I just don't know what to think. Ryan came to Houston this past winter and he said you were poisoning things against him, first with Jack Wade who was gonna give him a job selling cars and then by sending me these notes from Miss Roxanne Devon of Brunswick, New Jersey. But now poor Jack has been arrested for income tax evasion and I was afraid that Ryan was involved in it, too, because he said you sent the IRS man in the first place to see Jack Wade aand spook him about hiring Ryan."

George, to his credit, took this all in as if it made perfect sense. He just nodded his head like one of those toy dogs that the Mexicans carry around in the rear windows of their cars.

"Miss Cleaver. I'm sorry that your distress made you travel two thousand miles on the spur of the moment but I am also pleased that it gave me the opportunity to meet you. If I were a younger man, I would be willing to fight Ryan Shawn right now for the sake of having a chance to try to win your hand. But" — he shrugged and sighed — "I'm an old man and I've had my day. I just hoped that, at the end of my day, I would be able to make some gesture, some little step forward for the game that has been so good to me and for the country that I love."

"He means he fired his fifty-million-dollar payroll and picked up twenty-four homesick Cuban kids for next to nothing and then went out to sell the country that he was doing it for the good of baseball," I said.

"My country has asked me to make a gesture of friendship to the Cuban people, to show that we can all live in the world in peace and harmony —"

"If George owned 'Sesame Street' he'd put it on pay-per-view TV," I explained to Charlene.

"I met the President and I spent the night in the White House. In Lincoln's bedroom. I saw Lincoln," George said.

"Really?" Charlene said.

"He nodded to me as though he was saying I was doing the right thing," George said.

"He just wanted you to free the slaves who work for you," I said.

Charlene gave me that "shush" look and said, "You really saw Abraham Lincoln?"

"His ghost," George said modestly. "That's when I knew I was doing the right thing, reaching out the hand of friendship, not to Fidel Castro, but to the wonderful people of Cuba."

"How come you never told me any of this, Ryan?" Charlene said, turning on me.

"Charlene, the only person George ever helped was George, and if he ever reaches out his hand of friendship, make sure you've got your wallet locked up."

"Is this the way you talk to someone who's made you a major league baseball manager?" Charlene said. "I'm surprised that Mr. Bremenhaven puts up with this."

"George," George said.

"George," Charlene said.

"I get abuse all the time. I get it from the fans and from the press and from the players. I'm everyone's favorite punching bag, but I try to do my best as God lets me see to do my best."

"I think you owe Mr. Bremenhaven an apology, Ryan. You've been very rude."

"Charlene, you want me to quit the team or don't you? You don't make this easy."

"I just don't want you to take me for granted, Ryan — think I'm just the girl in the Houston port of call. I don't give a fiddle for whoever this Miss Roxanne Devon is, doesn't even have the courage to tell me where she lives or give her phone number or nothing."

"Whoever she is," George said, "Ryan would be crazy to even think about giving up a woman like yourself."

"Thank you, Mr. —"

"Just George. Everyone calls me George."

"George," she said.

"So why don't you apologize, Ryan, and shake hands with the man? He *is* paying you an awful lot of money and I don't think you have any complaint."

This was ridiculous and I was damned if I was going to shake hands with a snake in the grass like Old George, but I saw that I was doing it any-way and George was slapping me on the shoulder in that hearty rah-rah way of his, saying, "Ryan, maybe it was a good thing to take those spics around New York yesterday. I just wish you'd have let the press know, they could have followed you, it would have been great publicity. Tell you what, let's do it again tomorrow, the Statue of Liberty thing. Were they im-pressed?"

"They were cold. It was cold yesterday."

"We don't want anyone to catch cold."

"Then why don't you turn up the heat in that welfare slum you own on the East Side?"

"Ryan Patrick, you watch yourself!"

"Honey, he does own a slum hotel on the East Side. That's where he keeps his ball players. They got nothing to do all day, they're trapped in a city they don't understand, and they don't speak very good English to boot. All they know is that Castro wants them to play baseball for the Yan-kees."

"We might get a segment on 'Good Morning, America.' I met Joan Lunden a couple of weeks ago at Le Cirque," George rattled on.

"George, we ain't going to see the Statue of Liberty again. You want to put these kids on the news so that Castro gets a hard-on for them? Then what are you gonna do about next year when you want them back?"

"Castro has a contract."

"George, I just told you to shove your contract up your ass and I ain't even half as mean as Fidel Castro," I explained.

"He can't do that to me," George said.

"George, he was gonna bomb the whole fucking country once until Kennedy stood up to the Russians. Castro is not afraid of George Bre-menhaven looking cross-eyed at him."

"Well, we have a contract. There's levels and levels to this thing you wouldn't understand, Ryan."

"I'm sure there are, George," Charlene said. "And I'm sure we've taken enough of your time over nothing. Ryan, say good-bye to Mr. Bremen-haven — George — and let's get out of this busy man's way. I was pleased to meet you, George."

The slimy shit took her hand again and milked the pinkies a bit longer than was seemly, but Charlene didn't seem to mind. He did his little Adolph Menjou bow again and said, "Would you be my guest in my pri-vate box for the game tonight, Miss Cleaver?"

"Well, I was thinking about getting back to Houston."

"What do you do in Houston, Miss Cleaver?"

"I'm a nutritionist at Rice University Hospital Center," Charlene said, still letting him hold her hand.

"Fascinating," George said. "I really would like it very much if you would be my guest tonight. We can have a little dinner catered in and watch Ryan and his boys jump on the White Sox."

"You gotta get back to work," I said to Charlene.

"Oh, Ryan. I have time off coming and I've never been in New York City before. It might be fun, George. I would like to be your guest very much."

I happen to know that Charlene Cleaver, like most Texas men and women, despises baseball. The sports calendar for them begins in September when footballs fill the air and their clogged little thinking compartments. I have heard Charlene do a rundown on the Oilers or on Rice or any team you want to mention and give you the strong points and weak points without dropping a stitch along the way, but when it comes to baseball, she does this big yawn and prepares to wait the game out. She's seen a few games over by Arlington just because I was playing for the Yanks, but that's as far as it goes with her. And now she was volunteering to be in the company of a living turd like George through an entire evening of baseball played in 40 degree weather. Figure it out and send the answer to me by Federal Express.

"Tell me, Miss Cleaver —"

"Charlene."

"Charlene, would you mind terribly if the meal is vegetarian? I've given up meat, for the most part —"

"Oh, I love vegetarian cuisine," she said. "Ryan tries to eat better than when I first met him, but sometimes he just goes pig crazy like this one time this winter at a barbecue —"

"I know, I know. When they're young, they think they'll live forever."

"George, last time I saw you in Los Angeles you were tucking into a sixteen-ouncer from Kansas City," I said with devastating accuracy.

"No, Ryan. You might have seen me eating meat a couple of years ago, but I've learned sensible eating now. If you don't mind, Miss Cleaver, you can have meat if you wish —"

This man was hitting on my woman by pretending to be a vegetarian. I knew what he was doing, he was just practicing. I knew that Charlene wouldn't fall for him, but he just wanted to stick the knife in me to see if I was well done. I would have admired it if it wasn't personal.

We got out of there with our wallets unpicked. I took Charlene in a cab down to the Village and bought her lunch. I was so mad at things in general that I ordered a beer and a plate of ribs.

And no salad.

If Charlene noticed, she didn't say anything because she saw the way I was. She ate her fish and salad and her veggies and I just watched her.

"What an exciting place this is," she said once.

"Where?"

"The city. It just seems to throb with life," she said.

"You ought to hear the garbage trucks at one in the morning."

"Oh, don't see a negative in everything," she said.

"Charlene, you came to New York all because of a phony letter written by one of George's stooges and so I go over to punch out George and quit the team and give up my baseball career, all for you I might add, Charlene, and you end up making a date with the son of a bitch."

"It's not a date, Ryan. He's just very, very charming and you paint such a negative picture of him," she said.

"George Bremenhaven is a menace to society. He is also the worst thing to happen to baseball since the Black Sox threw the 1919 World Series. You can't believe a word he says, and that's on his truthful days. Vegetarian. I wouldn't be surprised if he gets his kicks watching them slaughter pigs in a rendering plant."

"That's disgusting," she said.

"George *is* disgusting, Charlene, I can't believe you agreed to go to his box in the Stadium tonight, I really can't."

"I'm just doing it for you, Ryan," she said.

"For me? For me? Don't do it for me, for pity's sake."

"For your career," she said.

"My career? Nine o'clock this morning you were accusing me of keeping a babe on the side in New Jersey and I was willing to quit the whole thing to satisfy you. Now you're going to be courted by a swine like George Bremenhaven to advance my career. What career, exactly?"

"In baseball, maybe even in politics someday. You are part of a great experiment, trying to bridge the gap between our two countries."

"I'm the manager because I speak Spanish and it's cheaper for George," I said. "The kids are playing decent ball, but it's a long season and it'll get worse before it gets better. These kids play like kids, they get all het up by the game and it's fun to to watch them win, but when they have to lose — and everyone loses sooner or later — they won't have anything to carry them through the bad period. It can get very bad, Charlene. That's the thing about baseball — it's a very, very long season."

I could see that Charlene didn't believe a word I was telling her. Her evening with George had temporarily turned her against me and she was seeing the old, shiftless ball player that I used to be before maturity set in.

But, dammit, she was making me mad, with her thinking I was someone I wasn't anymore.

So I shut up and ate my meat to spite her.

26

Charlene and I went back to Fort Lee by cab again around 3:30 P.M. to beat the rush hour. The cabbie cursed my directions but still managed to find the Holiday Inn for Charlene. She gave me a peck of a kiss and a bye-bye and a pickup order for six P.M.

I walked back to my apartment building. I took the elevator up and shoved the key in the lock and opened the door on my little world.

Except it wasn't my little world at that moment.

There were two men inside, one of them Baxter.

I didn't even say, "What are you guys doing here?" I just stood in the door and waited a moment.

"Come in, Ryan," Mr. Baxter said.

I let the door close behind me. I dropped the keys on the table and just stood there.

"We have to talk to you."

"You coming from George?"

"No."

"Then what do we talk about?"

"About you. About what you have in mind. We want to talk about that little trip yesterday."

"What trip?"

Baxter said, in a calm voice, "To the fucking Statue of Liberty is what."

The second man said nothing. He studied me like a pitching coach in Triple A.

"What are you doing? You proselytzing for the U.S. of A.? You want one of those pups to defect, is that it?"

"I don't want nothing except to play ball and get through this miserable season," I said. "Why? Something wrong with going out to the Statue of Liberty?"

"Yeah, there's something wrong," the second one said finally. He spent his words like a tightwad peeling them off a roll held by a rubber band.

"Who are you? He's George's lackey, but who are you?"

"The fucking G is who," the second one said.

"Ryan, you were not the man we would have picked for your job."

"Thank God you're not scouts," I said.

"This is a very, very delicate business. You were the one who told that kid, Suarez, to bean Tradup in the first game."

"Who told you that?"

"We know things, Ryan. That's why we are who we are," Baxter said. This was definitely not the Baxter the Lackey I saw in George's company. I took off my jacket and threw it on the bed and went into the kitchen and popped a can of Miller. I didn't offer them one.

"Three brawls in the first ten games. This unsettles certain . . . expectations we had," Baxter said.

"What kind of expectations?"

"We're trying to open a door here. To the Caribbean. These are good ball players, right?"

"They're half-good," I said.

"Good enough to play in the major leagues?"

"They're there, aren't they?"

"You said last night they weren't that good. Did you mean it?"

I tried to think back. And then I flushed. I felt my red face getting redder. "You bugged my conversation with those guys in that Tapas place?"

"Did you say it?"

"Fuck you," I said.

"Hey, fuck you," said the second guy, the one with no name.

"Yeah, that's putting it crudely, Ryan, but there it is. Fuck you. We arrested Jack Wade day before yesterday."

"What's that got to do with me?"

"Everything. You were going to work for Jack this winter. He was bringing up cars from Mexico and he was keeping a separate book on them. Shiny American cars, made in Mexico, but he was selling them without a tariff stamp and without telling the government or the auto maker about it."

"I thought we were all free traders now with Mexico."

"Not free like that, Ryan. You were part of his operation."

"I never worked for him."

"He gave you a car."

"He sold me a car. I got the bill of sale."

"Is that right?"

"Fuck you guys, both of you. What is this about?"

"About your players, Ryan. You just manage them and let them do what they have to do and we'll send them all back intact to Cuba come fall. They can't win the pennant, can they?"

"Everyone has a chance," I said.

It was the wrong thing to say.

"No, I don't think they have a chance," Baxter said.

"It's a matter of time will tell," I said. That's what I tell baseball writers.

"It wouldn't look good for major league baseball if a team of rookies, a team of Cuban rookies, won the American League East. Or, God forbid, the pennant."

"Why?"

It was a lonely little question. I couldn't figure out these guys.

"You said in your best judgment that the team wasn't good enough to win the pennant."

"I was trying to knock Raul into a realistic approach to the game. To the season. It's a long season."

"We're trying to . . . make friends in an unlikely way. With Cuba. For the post-Castro era, which is inevitable. We can pepper the big leagues with Cuban stars, that's okay. But we can't have a Cuban team win the pennant. And we are not making friends, not any of us, when you encourage your players to play dirty and get into fights."

"I don't encourage fights."

"You encourage them to bean opposing batters."

"Well, yeah. Sort of. You got to establish respect."

"Fuck respect. What if one of those kids kills someone? It would set us back fifty years."

"It's statistically unlikely. Only one guy ever got killed getting beaned in the whole history of baseball."

"That means it can happen again. We don't want it to happen to the Yankees."

"George didn't say anything about that —"

Without a cue, Baxter started screaming, "Fuck George Bremenhaven, starfucking asshole. He's got his own troubles. He wants to be useful. He's got income tax problems, he's got property problems, he belongs to us. He doesn't know shit about what we're trying to do here."

"What are you trying to do?"

"Open the door. Feed Fidel a little honey and sugar until he keels over someday and we can get on working with the next crowd in office."

"This has got to be more than just giving Fidel $2.5 million to let his players play here."

The second man said, "Bright boy."

"Maybe it is. But your role, Ryan, is to keep your head down and let the players play and keep them away from distractions that might give them happy feet."

"I thought that was Romero's job."

"He's not competent. The Cubans sent him as a chaperone. You think he's a competent chaperone?" Baxter said.

"He buys knockoff leather coats that ain't worth a shit," I said.

"He's less than worthless," the second guy said.

"You want me to fix games?" I said to Baxter.

"Not at all. That would be tinkering with the Pastime. Not at all. You said it yourself. These are kids, first time up. They can't carry this off."

"Remember the Philadelphia Whiz Kids?" I said.

"No," Baxter said. "And I don't want to remember anything except that the Yankees had a decent year and didn't do anything to embarrass us, or Cuba, or the game."

"Keep talking like that, they'll make you commissioner."

"You think this is a joke?"

"Since you guys are busy spying on me, tell me this — who sent those letters to Charlene? From Roxanne Devon."

"Who?"

"You know who."

Baxter blinked. "We don't read people's mail."

It was my turn to blink. I sipped my MGD.

"You got the picture, Ryan?" Baxter said.

"Why let all these Cubans in in the first place if you were just wanting to go halfway?"

"I don't make those decisions."

"Come on, Baxter."

"Maybe it got out of hand. Maybe Bremenhaven smoked the people at State. Maybe Castro came up with the idea as a non-negotiable demand. He's been stonewalling us for thirty-five years and this is the first chink we've seen in the wall he's built up. He's crazy abut baseball."

"Just crazy, I'd say," I said.

"This is the hand been dealt. We don't want brawls on the field, we don't want the Cubans to wear out their welcome —"

"What welcome? Empty seats at first. Then death threats."

"There's always a contingent."

"We neutralize opposition."

"This is baseball," Baxter explained.

Baseball.

"So what it comes down to is you want them to play and play semi-hard but not so hard that it might upset anyone."

Baxter and the second one just stared at me.

"And you give me the booga-booga about Jack Wade just to make sure I know where I stand."

Again, silence.

And that's when I really started to get hot. And no one knew it at the time but that was the start of the whole thing for me. This goes back to fourth grade and fighting for a girl and getting whupped by my Dad and getting into a fight over a Mexican in that Billy Bob bar on the road to Galveston. And George himself.

It was everything and nothing but it was settling down into my craw and these two boobs from the government wouldn't have understood it if I explained it slow.

"You got the picture?" Baxter said.

"It makes me sick," I said.

"Sensitive," said the second guy.

"Fuck you, No Neck. I ain't throwing games."

"Nobody asked you to."

"You practically did."

"Did not."

"Did too. Double-did too."

"Cracking wise," said the other.

"Yeah, cracking wise," I said. "Someone has to be." I tried to cool down then, I really did. "It don't matter anyway."

"What doesn't?"

"Making threats. You think I could get them to win the pennant if I knew how? I never been on a team that wins the pennant."

"That's to the good," Baxter said.

To the good.

27

Did I say it was a long season?

You play twenty or thirty games in spring training and then you do the regular season, which is 162 games long spread from the cold winds of April to the cold winds at the end of September. Then the playoffs start. There are eight teams in the playoffs, which start with a best three of five series and then go into another best three of five series to determine who gets in the World Series. Finally, in the absolute freezing cold of October, depending on which part of the country you're in, we have a World Series, which is the best four of seven. By this time, the other sports are up and running. Hockey is in the exhibition season and so is pro basketball, and pro and college football is already about half over. So when I say that baseball is a long season, I am talking about a lifetime.

The kids were kids until they hit their first big slump. We lost five in a row and the boo-birds were out in force every night.

I tried shifting them around, but nothing was working. All you can do as a manager is take the heat from the media and try to keep up the confidence of the kids. It was tough, but that's why I get the big bucks.

George.

George really hit it off with Charlene, but thank God she had to go back to Houston and work. I had enough trouble trying to handle George without her being around.

George was doing his crazy act during that losing streak. He fired me twice in a row and then undid it before game time when the reality set in. I've seen George fire lots of people, and when he fired me twice, it was like I was watching someone else or reruns. He ranted and raved and said I was a worthless son of a bitch and that I had shit for brains and the rest of it. I figured if I could make the firing stick just once, I would be home free because he'd have to pay off my contract. I didn't want any more government guys in my life.

But it didn't stick. The only constant during the streak was Raul Guevara. It seemed the sadder and lonelier he got, the better he hit. He was batting .436 and there was talk in more than one newspaper that he would be the first man to hit over .400 since Ted Williams did it in 1941. Even when we lost a game, he hit. I tried to cheer him up more than once and we spent a couple of afternoons on off-days at the Tapas bar, listening to stories of old Havana from Señor Jose Marti Riccardo. I got an education from that old man, and even though I knew the FBI was listening in on the conversation, I didn't give a fuck.

The other thing about the losing streak was that Baxter and the other guy probably thought I was doing what I was told to do. I admit I made a few bonehead errors. Managing is like baseball, a game of probables and inches. I left the starters in too long and then spent too long trying to cheer them up afterward.

One night, pissed off, I let them have it.

"You, Raul. You come up here and you translate."

We were in the clubhouse right before a game with the Orioles. It was warm and it smelled like spring in old Camden Yards, which are really not old but look like they should be. We were on a four-game skid and I was getting sick of it, of the players and of myself.

Raul came by me, but he looked around at the others in an embarrassed way.

"I want to tell you the truth," I began, like a liar. "They love you out there."

Raul looked startled, but he translated.

They looked startled, too, and Tio smiled as though he was looking for love.

"They love a loser when you're playing their team."

He translated.

"They love to see you act like a bunch of dumb hayseeds. Peasants. Plowboys."

A rough translation this time.

"You play like girls," I said.

This was to appeal to their macho.

They weren't smiling now.

"Pussies," I said.

Raul rendered it.

"You think you're big league because Uncle Fidel made a deal with George to ship your asses up here. But George just wants to break the union and you're nothing but scabs who couldn't carry a Triple A jock-strap."

This took time and I had to correct Raul and he finally said "Say it yourself" and sat down. So I tried to stem-wind in a foreign language:

— Pussies. You eat pussy, you are pussy. You spread your legs out there. Whores, that's what you are, because you get paid for it. Worse than whores. You don't even work that hard at it. Tomas, you play like your grandmother.

Tio was on his feet. I didn't notice he had a bat until just then. If I had, I would have picked someone else.

— You know what happened to me in New York? They told me that you were losers. Two men from the government. From Washington. They said it was all right. They said they didn't want a bunch of pussies from Havana to ruin the game by winning the pennant. Well, I told them not to worry. I said there was no way you could win a pennant because you were all pussies. I said you would lose to anyone and everyone to uphold the honor of the United States of America and the honor of baseball. Castro says you are the best. Well, if you are the best, then Cuba sucks eggs. The worst team in the league is better than you pussies and I'm sick of you. Sick. But I'm not worried. George is going to have to fire me for real one of these days and then I go home to Texas with my money and I never have to see you again.

Raul stood up again.

— Señor, you do not believe what you say.

"Fuck I don't."

— Who told you these things? That we were meant to lose?

— Baxter for one. Romero for another. (I was rolling.) And George said it would be all right by him if you lost because he's got income tax troubles. If he wins he has to go to jail. I mean, if you win. Which you won't.

— You mean, if he wins, he goes to jail?

"Fifteen years minimum," I said.

Some of them shook their heads. They understood going to jail for in-comprehensible reasons.

— Then we should continue to lose?

— It's the best thing for the country.

— The country?

— U. S. of A. America.

— But what if we do not lose? (Raul asked).

— You start winning and you bring shame to America and I won't stand for it.

— You are pretending.

Yes, I was. I was thinking of how hot I still was at those goons that came to my room in Fort Lee and I was trying to bring the heat over to this, but it wouldn't work. So I tried to show them.

— Raul, I'm benching you tonight.

Silence. I expected an outburst, but there was silence.

— Bench?

— Bench. As in, on your ass.

— Why, Señor Shawn?

— Because you're the only chance we have to win. Look at them. Pathetic. Tomas plays grounders like he's a croquet wicket, right between his legs. Pathetic. You might make it, Raul, and I can't take a chance.

— You betray us?

— Only for America.

Raul shook his head. "No, you want us to win."

He was even smiling. Thank God he was the only one. So I wiped the smile off his face the only way I knew how. I gave him the shot I should have given George when this all came up last fall.

Raul went down in a rattle of bats. The others were on their feet, but they weren't coming toward me. I stood over Raul and said, "Suarez, when you're pitching tonight, the one thing I don't wanna see is any more of that inside stuff, you understand?"

— Señor, you taught me to pitch inside.

— That's when I thought you were going to be a ball player. Forget it now. Have a good time, don't take any chances out there, they might turn ugly on you. On all you pussies.

Two brawls that night. I had to pinch-hit Raul in the eighth and he homered and won the game. The lovely Baltimore fans decorated us with beer cups and Cracker Jack boxes as we went back to the dugout after the ninth. I gave them the finger and that got me thrown out of the game. The League was not amused and I was suspended for a game. The *Baltimore Sun* said that the Yankees acted more like Caribbean Pirates, not the Pittsburgh kind.

Raul was only semi-fooled, but he treated me cool for days after that. It was just as well. I had enough heat in me for the whole team and the entire State Department. I was so fed up that I called up Charlene on the road just to fight with her and got my wish. That sobered me a little because we were going to Texas again and I wanted to see her in the worst way, so I called up in Chicago and made an apology and a half, and she half-took it.

We warmed up toward the end of May and found our winning ways again. I saw Charlene for three straight days when we dipped down to Arlington to play the Texas Rangers, but Raul managed to spoil that, too.

Charlene came to the second game and I got her good seats behind the dugout, which she didn't appreciate probably because she didn't really appreciate baseball. She wore dark slacks and a light blouse with a red bandanna around her neck. She also wore sunglasses that worked for her, even though it was the middle of the night.

Raul wanted to know if this was my girl so I introduced him to Charlene. He said he was honored and he kissed her hand, which charmed the hell out of her and she sort of giggled the way she does. And she took off her sunglasses to see him better and, I suppose, let him see her pretty eyes. Raul took it in, inhaled even, and then smiled at her.

Then he said to me in perfectly understandable non-Ricky-Ricardo English, "You must marry this beautiful woman before another man steals her heart."

Well, you could have knocked me over with a feather. He was like a talking dog, is all. Charlene was so honored that she batted her eyes and waved every time Raul came to bat or trotted to the dugout. She said she wanted tickets for the next game. I told her they were all sold out, which was not true because you can't sell out baseball in Texas.

June is when the pitchers are supposed to lose their edge because the hitters are always slower in coming along. I didn't think it was possible for Raul to hit any better, but he did, raising his average to a phenomenal .452, which is scarcely human.

We had a doubleheader in Boston and Raul went nine for nine. Nine for nine. He didn't have no home runs, though, because of his line-drive style of hitting, which hit the big Green Monster wall in left and merely turned into doubles. I saw the bright side of things, nine for nine, and congratulated him, but he was just too angry and upset to get happy.

— That fucking wall, I hate that wall, why do they allow a ballpark with a wall like that?

— Because it's always been this way, I guess.

A team from *People* magazine went down to Havana and did a profile on Raul and his family and friends and even included a nice picture of Maria Velasquez.

This, in retrospect, was probably a mistake. Castro loved the publicity and Raul's family and friends loved it, too, and so did George. Anything Castro and George could agree on was bound to be trouble for someone.

Raul got a copy of *People* in New York and wore it out reading it over and over. He tore out the photograph of Maria and placed it in a Woolworth photo frame and put it on his desk in the hotel room. And commenced to write another stem-winding letter to Maria back home.

One night, I tried to shake him out of his melancholy by taking him to the bar in the Ed Sullivan Theater building where they shoot the David Letterman show. I just wanted to get him out of the hotel and I didn't want the FBI to be hearing what I had to say to him because I was going to tell Raul the truth about being lovesick.

This was time for a little heart-to-heart with Raul and I was up for the occasion. We didn't start with the birds and the bees, because I assumed he knew about that stuff, being a hot-blooded Latin and all. But I went right into the honey pot and pulled out love.

"Love, Raul, is not everything." It was a start. Pretty blunt, but you have to start somewhere. I waited for his response.

"It is the only thing," he said. His English was picking up, but I couldn't point out that he was really quoting Vince Lombardi on football.

— Raul (I said, going back to Spanish), love is a great thing. It is beautiful. It is nice and gets you through bad moments. When you are in love, you can eat bologna and like it. When you are in love, you notice sunsets. When you are in love, Raul, you wear purple shirts because your girl likes them. Love is full of crazy shit like that. I know, I know, I been there. But it is not the only thing, the way you make it. You make yourself sick with love and that is not good. Beer. This beer is a good thing. We drink beer and we feel good. But if we drink too much beer, we feel bad. Why do we feel bad? Because it is too much. Too much love is bad.

— I cannot help myself, Señor Shawn. My body is on fire with love every moment of the day every moment of the night. I dream of love, I think of love, I stare for hours at her photograph in *People* magazine.

— Look, Raul. When the season is over, you can go home and get married. Then you can have all the love you want and it'll be right there waiting for you. It wouldn't be the worst thing for you now to relieve . . . well, to get rid of your tensions.

He smiled at me.

— You mean, to "handle" it?

— Well, that too. It's not for me to tell you what to do but you got to give yourself a break, Raul.

— You are so cool, so North American. You have a beautiful woman in Houston in Texas who loves you, but you go about your business as if it didn't matter. You do not write her, you told me that yourself. Do you expect her to wait and wait and wait? I have met her. A woman like that does not need to wait and wait. She is not ugly. You are a fool to let her be alone without you in Texas.

I was suddenly getting a clue. There were a lot of hoofprints and it wasn't that clean a clue, but it was a clue nonetheless. Raul was talking about himself. The truth is, I figured it out too late. He was a hot-blooded Cuban, he knew that the country was full of hot-blooded Cubans just like him and that Maria Velasquez was a looker. He was talking about his own anxiety, which is why he was up half the night writing letters and verses to Maria, to keep her distracted from all the male humanity around her.

Which led me to think about Charlene again. Not that Charlene couldn't wait a bit, she was thirty-five years old and she could control herself when she had to. Besides, she was English, I think, and there wasn't a trace of Latin in her.

Still, she filled out that green dress she wore like someone inspired, like someone who never even read the *Wall Street Journal.*

— Señor, what are you thinking of?

— I was just thinking.

— You were thinking of your woman.

"Along those lines."

— And I am thinking of my beloved as well.

— Yeah, well. Here we are on Broadway in New York on a hot June night and there's not much we can do about it, is there? Except get drunk.

— I don't want to get drunk.

— Fine, then don't.

— You get drunk sometimes so that you will feel nothing. But I want to feel the pain of love.

— You talk like an asshole, sometimes.

— I talk to you of the pain you understand. You are not so wise or clever as to hide this from me.

— Sonny, you're twenty-three years old going on twelve. I am a grown, mature man. How did I get mature? Aging had a lot to do with it. When I was younger than you, I had a little girl named Sue at Arizona State who was just about the lovingest thing you ever saw. All golden and sweet and pleasing in her nature. I mean, she could cook and sew and keep house and wear sexy underwear and there wasn't a bed made that could stand up to her. This was the Olympics, you understand? And she just thought I was the greatest thing invented since flour tortillas.

— And?

— Well, I was going to school on baseball scholarship and the scouts were giving me the eye and I was going to the Bigs. I just knew I was if I gave it a chance. So that's what I did.

— What did you do? About Sue?

— I dropped her.

— You dropped her?

The way he said it, I just looked away. Through the window of the saloon. Up the street. Cab making a left turn. Bus stopping. Guy selling shit on the street. Homeless guy in a doorway, drinking something. Fascinating things. I just kept looking away, trying not to see Sue, as she was a long time ago.

— She didn't fit in with my plans. First thing you know, I would have had kids and a house to worry about. I wanted to be free to play baseball and play it as best as I could.

— Oh, that is the saddest story I have heard in a year. That is just so sad.

— Why is it sad? She married someone else and probably has achieved every goal she ever set for herself.

— Except to marry you.

— Well, you got to make sacrifices. That's what I been trying to tell you about growing up. Every day isn't going to be Christmas, Raul. Everything is a trade-off. You get this, but you give up that. You want that, you have to give up this.

— But love is not a commodity.

— Tell that to the hookers on Eighth Avenue.

— This is not prostitution. Love is not sex, it is not debased.

— You sure you're not a secret Jesuit infiltrated into Cuba by the Church? You talk like a priest.

— Ah, I can't talk to you. I can't talk to you anymore. You have told me a sad story of your own life and you do not even see the sadness in it.

— I didn't say I didn't see the sadness in it. I said being sad is part of the price.

He stared at me then as though he was seeing my skull under the cover of skin and it horrified him.

Then, very slowly, he shook his head and there were tears in those doe eyes. He stood up and put out his hand and rested it on my shoulder.

— You don't even understand, Señor Shawn. But you have made me understand for the first time. Made me understand for myself and for my beloved Maria.

— Understand what?

But he just shook his head and took his hand off my shoulder and turned. He went to the door. He stopped and looked back at me. Then he went through the doorway into the steam of a New York summer night.

I just sat there a moment and thought about Sue as she was, nubile little thing. She was making someone happy somewhere.

And Charlene.

I wanted to call her just then, but I was in a saloon on Broadway in the middle of Manhattan and what could I say to her anyway?

And there was a worse thought.

What if she was out when I called?

28

The All-Star break in the season came the second week of July and none too soon for me. When you're thirty-eight, going on thirty-nine, 162 games is just too many. I looked forward to the break. I planned on flying down to Houston and picking up Charlene for a short trip to Vegas. I don't gamble to make it count, but this guy on the White Sox can get you five nights in a nice hotel on the Strip and comps to the Siegfried and Roy show, the one with the white tigers, and some funny money to play with for less than three hundred dollars. Besides, I needed to recharge my batteries and I was missing Charlene very much.

The team was a semi-solid second, three behind the Red Sox in the American League East. Raul had been second in the voting for the American League All-Star team and the team manager had picked him as a sub, so Raul was scheduled to be at the big game in Cleveland while me and Charlene would be at the gaming tables on the Strip.

That was the way it was supposed to be. I admit I was feeling lax. I hadn't seen Baxter since that afternoon in my room in Fort Lee. I wondered whether he was fretting about how well we were doing. There had been six more certified brawls. The New York papers had turned around and were starting to love us. We were the Scrappy Yanks, the Go-to-Hell Gang, the best thing in baseball brawling since the Gas House Gang operated in St. Louis in Dizzy Dean's day. I was balancing everything, the players who were not pussy (Tomas had picked up his fielding percentage after someone explained to him what a croquet wicket was), George, who still called me at one in the morning, and Charlene in Texas, who didn't know what to think about it all.

I just wanted her to think about me in Vegas. Our little hideaway.

It was nice, the first day, with us gambling a little on the video poker machine and taking a swim in the outdoor pool. It felt good to relax and Charlene was just this side of legal in her bathing suit, which made me very proud of her. Everything was going to be nice. So I thought at the time. It lasted most of the day and the night.

Then it happened. I got this frantic phone call at four in the morning in our room at the Mirage Hotel. It was George. Who else would call me at four in the morning? I said something to him that wasn't polite and slammed down the receiver.

"Who was it?" Charlene said. She was naked and mussed. We had had a wonderful evening and a half crammed into one.

"Who do you think would call me at four in the morning?" I said. "Your friend George."

"You keep saying that. I met the man once in my life and he was thoroughly charming."

"And Hitler had cute bangs," I said.

"Really, Ryan —"

The phone was ringing again. I turned on the light this time and picked up the receiver.

"Ryan, how dare you hang up on me?"

"George, I'm taking a few days off."

"I'm in fucking Cleveland," George said.

"Was it a good game?"

"It was a good game, who gives a shit if it was a good game or not? The important thing is he's not here. He's gone. Vanished. *Vamenos.*"

"Who's vanished?" I said.

"Raul Guevara, you son of a bitch. This is some trick of yours, some sneaky little way to get back at me for sending those Roxanne Devon letters to your broad."

"I knew you did it —"

"That was part of the fun, you knowing. But now this isn't funny, this is serious, and I want you to stop playing games and produce that Cuban cocksucker before I get the FBI to tear you a new asshole, asshole."

"You're stuttering, George."

"Is he there? Is he there with you right now? You gone queer for him, is that it? I don't care if you two want to play daisy chain, just tell me he's there in bed with you right now and I won't say a word. You know what Castro does to queers? He cuts off their gonads and fries them up for breakfast, you cocksucker! Give me that shit about poor little Raul sitting all alone in his room pouring out his heart to his alleged girlfriend in Havana when all along you been taking him out to your queer spots in the Village and hanging around with your sissy friends and —"

"George, no one is here."

"You lying son of a bitch! Put him on!"

"It's for you," I said to Charlene. I gave her the phone.

"Hello," she said.

"Who the fuck is this!" George screamed.

"Don't you shout at me, ain't no man ever going to shout at me and get away with it!" she shouted.

"I mean, is this you, Charlene?" I was standing next to Charlene and heard him yelling.

"Yes, it's me, who'd you think it was?"

"He told me he sent the Roxanne Devon letters to you just to stir up trouble," I said from my side of the bed.

"Is that right, George? Did you send those letters to me?"

"Who gives a shit about letters, you bitch! Put loverboy back on the phone," George said.

She blanched and put her hand over the receiver. "He called me a name I can't repeat."

"George is like that," I said. I was glad she was seeing the snake for what he really was.

"Aren't you going to do something?"

I took back the phone. "George, did you call Charlene a bad name?"

"Fuck you, fuck both of you. Ryan, Raul has disappeared off the face of the earth. He was supposed to be in Cleveland for the All-Star game. No show. I call the East Side Hotel. Nobody's seen him. I send over my friends from the Twenty-third Precinct and they roust the place. They find two wanted armed robbers and a welfare queen the state has a warrant for, but they don't find Raul Guevara. Fucking cops are worthless. I send them to that Tapas place and the bag who runs it said she hasn't seen him for days. She's lying, that fucking whore! I'm going crazy, Ryan."

"I know, it sounds like it," I said. I couldn't keep the pleased tone out of my voice.

"Ryan! You gotta find him, you're his best buddy!"

"You just said I was queer for him."

"A figure of speech, Ryan. Ryan . . . Ryan, you gotta find him."

"I don't know where to look for him. You hit the only two places I know he ever went, the hotel room and the Tapas."

"What do you mean, he ever went? It's a big city, the greatest city on Earth, he must have had dozens of places — Girls, where did he go for girls, Ryan?"

"He didn't go for girls," I said.

"Boys, then. Where'd he hang out to pick up boys? You can tell me. I won't tell anyone. Down on Christopher Street —"

"George, you'd inform on your mother if there was any woman willing to admit she was your mother, which I doubt."

"Tell me he's with you."

"He's with me and Charlene right now. We're doing a double reverse in a few minutes, also called a Charlene Sandwich."

"A fucking orgy! I knew it!" George shouted. "You really are best buddies, but you aren't fags! Great! Just put him on the line a sec. I want to hear that spic's beautiful Spanish voice one time."

"I'm sorry, George. We've got him bound and gagged. That was from our last assignment together."

"Ball players are sick, sick people. But hey, live and let live is all right by me. Ryan, tell me that he's all right."

"He's all right."

"Are you telling me that because it's true or because you're just telling me that?"

"Guess."

"You son of a bitch, you're fired! Fired! Get your shit out of the locker room by this afternoon."

"I don't keep no shit in the locker room. Baseball players are thieves."

"Then don't let me see you again, you cocksucker! I am going to file suit against you and don't think I'm going to pay you, not for what you've done to me. The FBI is going to be on this case. On your case. Kidnapping is a federal crime."

"You're a walking federal crime, George," I said. I said it very calmly because that upsets George even more.

"Where the fuck is he, Ryan?"

"You fired me. So I won't tell you. Good night, George."

I replaced the receiver and just sat there. Charlene was leaning on one naked elbow close enough to let me smell her. She smelled sweet, which is her natural odor.

"What happened?"

"Raul took a walk."

"George doesn't know where."

"No."

"You know."

"Yep."

"He told you."

"Not in so many words."

She worried her lower lip with her upper teeth a moment and just looked at me before she said anything.

"He went home."

That's what I like about Charlene. Under her mere beauty, she is smart. I'm about the only mistake in judgment in her life and that can be explained.

"Yep."

"Back to Cuba."

"Yep."

"Why?"

"Boy's in love. Wants it to stay that way. So he figures that he'd better hitch up with his girlfriend while the hitching is good. Hitting way over .400, he can go home even if Castro don't want him to go home and he can be a national hero and get married. The boy thinks. He doesn't have this love stuff down, but he works at thinking."

"What love stuff?"

"Maria Velasquez is a beauty and he thinks she won't wait for him."

"He got any reason to think that?"

"Not that I know of. Just insecure. I tried to talk to him but it wasn't any good."

"Tell him what?"

"That she'll wait for him."

"Why would she?"

"Why wouldn't she?"

"You think all a woman's got to do is sit around and wait?"

"No. But waiting is a sign of maturity."

"I'm mature enough, thank you. I got mature in crow's feet on my eyes. I don't enjoy waiting. Certainly don't enjoy waiting on a man who keeps you waiting just because he thinks he can get away with it. Ever notice that a man won't wait on a woman, but lots of women wait on a man? Says he'll meet you at one and he comes in late and you're supposed to la-de-da all that, but you keep a man waiting, they practically accuse you of something."

"I don't recall keeping you waiting, Charlene."

"You really don't, do you?"

See, this was turning ugly the way it can and I knew it, but it was like putting the brakes on a ship just about to plow into the dock in the Houston Ship Canal.

I was saved by the phone.

I picked it up again and said, "Hello."

"Ryan, I unfire you." The calm George. "I want you to find Raul."

"I think he went home, George."

"Why would he do that?"

"He's in love, I told you all that."

"He went home because he's in love?"

"Home is where his girlfriend lives."

"Then he's coming back here?"

"No, I don't think so."

"Get him, Ryan. Get him for the love of God and baseball. We are talking about maybe the greatest hitter in the history of baseball and he's going back to Cuba? How did he get out of this country in the first place?"

"I don't know. He's got relatives in Miami."

"I want their names. I'm turning them over to the FBI. This is subverting the foreign policy of the United States government."

"Aw, George. Don't do everything ass backward. Tell the people you know in the government what's going on and what happened and let them sort it out. If Raul don't wanna play baseball in the U.S., we can't make him."

"Why wouldn't he want to? This is the greatest country in the world, isn't it?"

"In parts," I said.

"Castro wouldn't go back on his contract, would he?"

"In a New York minute."

"He can't do that to me."

"I don't think this involved Fidel Castro, I think this was a Raul Guevara production. He's hitting .452 and he can go back to Cuba as a national hero, and what's Fidel gonna do about it? Put him in jail for not wanting to play ball in New York?"

"But we're the New York Yankees."

"Yeah, well, sometimes people don't get choked up the way you do about it."

"You gotta go to Havana, Ryan. You gotta go get my boy back."

"He ain't your boy, George —"

"I paid for the son of a bitch, he belongs to me!"

I held the phone a little away from my ear because George was starting to give me a headache.

"You gotta do it, Ry. We start up again in two days, we need that boy in the lineup. He's gonna be the batting champ, the man who hit over .400 first time since Ted Williams. He is a New York Yankee."

I liked George's appeals to patriotism because it meant I had him over a barrel. I was learning Sid Cohen's lesson.

"George, if I go down to Havana and talk to him, you gotta do something for me."

"I do everything for you now."

"No, no, George. You know what you gotta do."

"What do I have to do?"

"You have to tell Charlene."

"Tell her what?"

"Tell her what you just told me."

"Why?"

"It would make me happy," I said.

"You mean about Roxanne Devon?"

"Yep."

"All right." Just like that. George doesn't even have loyalty to himself.

"And one other thing."

"What, for Christ's sake?"

"About that steak."

"What steak?"

"The steak in the Century Plaza Hotel."

"For Christ's sake, Ryan, this is childish."

"You're the childish one, George. You keep giving people a hot foot because you never grew up."

"All right, all right. I'll tell her."

"Tell her everything," I said.

"All right already."

I handed the phone to Charlene.

She was the ice princess in tone as she said, "Yes?" Like Catherine of Russia, except in English.

Charlene listened. And listened.

"That was a rotten thing to do to me. And to Ryan. You ought to be horse-whipped," Charlene said. "And you even lied to me about eating meat? Well, you're going to be the one that ends up with prostate problems, not me." She handed the phone back to me.

"Okay, George. You got to clear me through so I can fly legal to Havana."

"Oh, I can do that."

"And Charlene. We are interrupting our vacation for you, so the least you can do is fly Charlene to Havana with me."

"Does she have a passport?"

"You got a passport, honey?"

"No," Charlene said.

"She don't have one, George. Get her one, willya?"

"Ryan! I —"

But I was in the process of hanging up again and Charlene was in the process of settling herself on her side in that big king-size bed under the sheets and, hell, as long as we were awake, why waste it?

29

Señor Martinez, who had been my guide before when I first went to Cuba, was at the Havana airport when we landed. And so was Catfish Williams.

"Hey," Deke said to me as I came down the steps to the tarmac. Charlene was behind me because I think she was a little intimidated by everything. The only foreign country she had ever been in was Tijuana, once, and that isn't really foreign when you can practically take a streetcar there from San Diego. In less than twenty-four hours, she had been passported by Mr. Baxter of the State Department and certified for travel to a foreign country with which we had no relationship. It would take that much to intimidate Charlene about anything.

"Hey," I said to Deke. And "hey" to Señor Martinez, who was looking less than comfortable.

"Señor Shawn, who is this lady?"

"This is Charlene Cleaver. She and I had our vacation interrupted to come down here, so I thought it was best to bring her along. Besides, she's never seen Cuba before."

"Charmed, Señora Cleaver," Martinez said. The "señora" was out of respect because she was not a young girl anymore. I don't know if that would have pleased Charlene or not so I didn't bring it up.

"But what's he doing here?"

"Señor Williams is an American businessman," Señor Martinez said.

"We used to play baseball together," I said.

"I know this," Señor Martinez said. The knowledge did not seem to make him any happier.

There were the usual security people hanging around, but things had changed some. First, this was high summer in Cuba and it was hotter than a two-dollar pistol. It had been warm and humid in February, but this was a joke. I was soaking wet and only thirty seconds off the plane. Charlene wore slacks and a blouse and that blouse was into serious clinging already and her hair was wet. Texas is hot in summer, but Texas is also air conditioned from one end to the other.

"Saw your star outfielder came home and I thought you'd be chasing after him," Deke said, slapping my arm and smiling. He was also keeping his eye on Charlene even while he was greeting me.

"It's common knowledge, is it?"

"Everyone knows everything in Cuba, just one big happy family down here —"

"What are you doing here, Deke?"

"Like the señor says, I'm an American businessman."

"I thought we didn't have business in Cuba."

"Hell, it's opening up right and left. Opportunities are knocking and Deke is opening the doors. After I saw you in Chicago I figured that if this thing was good enough for the New York Yankees, it was good enough for Catfish Williams."

"What was good enough?"

"Whole country is gonna open up sooner rather than later and I want to put in my bid."

"On what?"

"Fish, man. I sell fish, you remember. Lots of fish. I could become my own supplier of fresh fish, not just for myself but for other franchises. These people been living in a vacuum the last thirty years."

"Is any of this legal?"

"Hell, yes. Got my certifieds from the State Department even. Even met with the Minister of Fisheries last night, we had a good old chat."

"Charlene, this is Catfish Williams. I told you about. From Chicago."

"I was wondering if you were going to introduce me."

"I'll introduce you but that's as far as it goes," I said.

"Shit, man, you got me wrong."

"I seen you on the road for too many seasons," I said.

"Well, there's that."

We were such a jolly party, standing there in customs while the guys in sunglasses and long white shirts hanging out of their pants went through our bags. They spent their time on Charlene's bag and they were pawing through her clothes like they were pawing her. I don't like customs people even when they don't do anything offensive because they treat everyone like a crook. The U.S. customs are the worst, I think, but I haven't been that many places. The Canadians are polite but cold, exactly the way Canadians are themselves, so I don't attribute it much to customs. The

Mexicans don't give a shit. But those U.S. customs people are convinced you're smuggling dope into the country, even if you're coming in from a three-game series in Toronto on your way to Cleveland. What the hell would you smuggle from Toronto to Cleveland?

These Cuban guys were getting a kick out of their job and there wasn't anything anyone could do about it. Mr. Martinez just stood there, looking nervous, and Catfish just stood there, looking horny. Charlene, however, had had enough.

"Put them clothes back the way you found them, I didn't pack them careful just to have some dumb cop get 'em wrinkled."

One of the guys in sunglasses stopped. Looked up at Charlene. Looked at me. Looked at Catfish. Then closed the bag and made a big chalk mark on the leather.

The other sunglasses did the same with my bag and then we moved along to Passport Control. This was a counter with two more sunglasses behind it and they studied our passports for a long time, as well as the attached visas. Then they did that passport thing with a stamp pad and a pound-pound-pound all over a blank page. When it was done, they had bent my passport and I unbent it a little and slipped it into my shirt pocket.

Mr. Martinez was still driving a Trabant, but Deke had hired himself a 1958 Buick Roadmaster with the long snout and the buildup of chrome on the front end that made it look like a Patton tank, if a tank had chrome.

"Y'all can't fit in that sardine can there, I can take Miss Cleaver with me back to the hotel," Deke said in his honey-colored voice.

"On the other hand, you can take both of us to the Comrade Hilton," I said.

"What do I look like, your driver?"

"You driving Miss Daisy, you're driving me," I said. "I owe you a lot baseball-wise, Deke, but I don't owe you as much as you think."

"You're very short on trust," Deke said.

"I trust you plenty about a lot of things but not about that," I said.

So Señor Martinez followed us to the Comrade Hilton in the heart of Havana. The Roadmaster had air conditioning, but it didn't work. Deke rolled down all the windows. Somehow, the wet hot breeze was less than refreshing, like being slapped with wet towels in a steam bath.

Summer didn't bring out the best in Havana. There were a lot of smells in the air that were not pleasant and the sewers reeked. The bougainvillea were all blooming and there was a sense of jungle creeping over everything.

Even the little yards seemed like jungle, as though no one had the energy to cut back the grass. The buildings gleamed in the wicked afternoon sun. The people on the crowded streets were dressed in the minimum and their faces were weathered by sun and heat. It was all very depressing to me and I wondered if Raul was finding it the same way.

"Where is Raul?" I asked Deke.

"Why ask me?"

"Because you'd know," I said.

"Well, I understand he's being interviewed by the security police."

"How'd he get back here?"

"No one knows. He was picked up on a beach on the north coast yesterday morning. He said someone brought him in from Miami by cigarette boat and this got him in trouble right away because the crack Cuban navy doesn't like to admit it has any cracks in it," Deke said, and laughed. He drove with one hand on the steering wheel. He wore one of those African shirts with a lot of colors in it and no collar. He also wore a big Panama hat that made him look like a character out of *Casablanca*.

"So he hasn't seen his girlfriend yet?"

"Maybe he has. The rumor is she was picked up herself by the security police. This is one helluva city for rumors, sport. The thing is you can't hardly believe anything you read in the papers, but you can go with the rumors, they're almost always right on the button."

"How long you been here?"

"Couple of weeks."

"You met Castro?"

"El Supremo? No, he ain't had the time to *parlez* with this nigger yet. But I'm edging closer all the time. The Minister of Fisheries was a big deal. I told him about catfish farming and he was very, very interested. These waters are loaded with fish, sport. The fishermen are all about a hundred years behind the times. The Russians used to trawl around here, but the Russians are persons non grata. You know what it is to get in on the ground floor of something? When you told me about George Bremenhaven making cozy with the administration and Congress in Washington, I started pulling my own contacts."

"So that was all bullshit about the government being on my case and you not wanting to be in contact with me no more," I said.

"Hell, sport, I saw you plenty when you played the White Sox on that last trip, introduced you to some fine ladies," he said.

He did that for Charlene's benefit, I knew. Why does everyone want to get me in trouble with Charlene?

Charlene spoke up for the first time. "Is he playing around, Deke?"

He just smiled at me and I gave him a look. I wasn't amused, no matter how funny he thought he was being.

"Naw, naw, Charlene. Boy's in love, I can tell when he just sits there and this fine fox is coming on to him, all shivery and satiny, you know, in a red dress that starts where most legs leave off and he just drinks his white boy's beer and starts talking about you."

"He talks about me?"

"Can't shut him up on the subject," Deke said.

Well, that was all right. Charlene purred her pleasure and seemed to unwilt in the heat right before my eyes.

We met Martinez back at the hotel and the woman behind the counter signaled for a bellman to take our bags up. Separate rooms. Hers was 501 and mine was 560. At least it was the same floor.

My theory is that power makes you into a puritan. That's why Communists talk a good game, but when it comes down to it, they're as straitlaced as any hard-shell Baptist. There was no reason for me and Charlene to have different rooms except that was the way to make it more difficult for us.

Her room was even bigger than mine.

We decided to meet in the lobby after taking a shower. It was easier said than done because the water in my shower wasn't working. I turned on the tap on the sink and a little brownish water came out and I scooped it and slapped it on my face and toweled down my wet hair. I looked like hell. I changed my shirt and slapped English Leather all over me, even under my armpits.

Charlene said her shower hadn't worked either and Señor Martinez explained it was because of the heat and the need to conserve water. Here we were on an island surrounded by nothing but water and they didn't have enough.

Martinez said he would take me to the government house in his Trabant. He also said that Miss Cleaver could not go along because he had no instructions concerning her.

Unfortunately, Deke Williams said he would escort Miss Cleaver around Havana to look at the sights and there was nothing I could do about it except trust them both.

The afternoon sun lingered. It was after seven, but the sun didn't show any sign of setting. The street life was, if anything, even more intense now with little open air markets here and there where farmers were selling their products. A little bit of capitalism had been creeping into the country for years, and now it was more or less sanctioned as not being a threat to communism, which shows you can rationalize about anything.

We went back to the same grim building I had been taken to the previous winter for my big audience with Castro. I was hoping the pleasure would not be repeated.

We went down a hall and another hall and then through a double door and into a large room hung with paintings and dominated by a long, old-fashioned wooden table. Red velvet chairs were pulled up around the table. Señor Martinez and I sat down in two of them and we waited.

We waited about a half-hour. Time is not of the essence in Cuba, I figured. One day is much like another, so why hurry them along?

The room was cool but not air conditioned. The windows were open on one side to catch the early evening breeze. There were beautiful flowers growing outside the windows and they smelled sweet almost to the point of intoxication.

About eight, the doors opened and a man in army fatigues came in. He was alone and he carried a clipboard. He stared at me and then at Martinez and sat down.

"How can we help you, Señor Shawn?" he said in English.

"I kind of would like to see Raul Guevara and have a chat with him," I said.

"That's impossible."

"Why? We were on speaking terms just the other day in New York City. We play on the same team."

"The Yankee Imperialists," he said.

"No, just the New York Yankees. We haven't invaded any country that I know of, although the team used to barnstorm in the off season. But they don't do that anymore."

"The person you spoke of does not wish to speak to you."

"Is he all right?"

"Of course."

"Then why can't I see him?"

"It's impossible."

"Who are you anyway?"

"Colonel Colon," he said.

"Well, Colonel, I came all the way down here and interrupted my vacation just to see Raul and I don't see the point of you stalling around. He's got a contract to play baseball for New York and he's only halfway through the year. So he can't just tear up his contract like that."

"A contract to be a slave? To work as a slave?"

"Playing baseball is not working as a slave. The hours are short and we stay in first-class hotels. At least, on the road," I said, thinking of the roaches in the East Side Hotel. "He's got all the pizza he can eat and Miller beer he can drink. I don't know of any slave that would have it that good."

"There's no point in discussing this," Colonel Colon said.

I leaned forward the way my agent, Sid Cohen, does when he's face-to-facing and I folded my hands together just the way Sid does. I even borrowed Sid's tone of voice. "Sure there is, or you wouldn't be here," I said. It was a quiet voice, very reasonable. "Raul is a homesick boy and that's something no one counted on, that he'd just go home. It's an embarrassment to everyone, including the Yankees."

"Poof. I don't care what embarrasses you Yankees."

"You ought to. Señor Castro let himself be engineered into making this deal in the first place and now it looks like he wants to go back on his word. Besides, here you've got the greatest hitter maybe in the history of the game, the most famous thing to come out of Cuba since the cigar, and you want to let it go? That doesn't make sense to me."

Colonel Colon just sat there for a long moment and then got up with his clipboard and marched out of the room. I looked across at Martinez, but he was just looking miserable in general and didn't want to make eye contact with me.

So we sat in the room for another while. Evening arrived suddenly, the way it does the closer you get to the equator, and it was still warm and humid. I got up from my velvet perch and walked around the table a couple of times, just to do something. I also hummed a little of "The Yellow Rose of Texas," one of the few songs I know all the way through.

At 9:40, the double doors opened again and this time it was the big man himself surrounded by his toadies. He came right up to me and stood there, staring at me with those cold brown eyes. Then he said, "Have you learned to speak Spanish yet?" I said in Spanish:

— I practiced a lot.

— It doesn't show. Your accent is appalling.

— I came to talk to Raul.

— I know.

— And the girl.

— That is not the business of the manager of the Yankees.

— It is when it affects the play of my best player. Maybe the best player in all of baseball.

— The best player to ever play the game.

— All right. Have it your way.

— A Cubano, the greatest ball player in the world, the greatest who ever existed!

— I agree a hundred percent.

— Hah! He would not have thrived except under our system, under our nurturing guidance.

— Well, I don't know about that. Ball players are just natural sometimes.

— He is the triumph of Cuban manhood, its finest flowering.

It was obvious to me that Castro was winding the stem on one of his speeches and I wanted to slow him down. So I said:

— You gonna let them get married?

That stopped him.

He stared at me and I thought he was going to order someone to shoot me. I thought it was that close.

Instead, he said, in English, "Why shouldn't they?"

"Exactly," I said. "Maria can join Raul in New York for his triumphant first season. She'll become America's sweetheart. Maybe she already is. And it will be because of you, because of Fidel Castro's big and generous heart that the two newlyweds will set up house together."

"And will come back to Cuba to live at the end of the season."

"Of course, of course," I said.

"And show the North Americanos that Cuba has heart, Cuba is more than strong, it has . . ."

Words were failing him. I helped him out.

"It has romance. Cuba is for lovers."

"Exactly," he said and he had to hug me, he was so overcome by emotion. The English Leather on me clashed with the Old Spice on him, I guess, because he pulled back almost immediately and sniffed at me.

"What do you wear?"

"English Leather," I said.

"I don't like it," he said.

"I left my Old Spice at home. Bought it at the airport on my way."

"It doesn't suit you," he said.

— Orlando, get a bottle of Old Spice, pronto.

Orlando ran out of the room and a moment later ran back in with a bottle of orange liquid. Castro handed it to me and I did what I had to do, even if I felt silly standing there in a room full of men slapping scented alcohol on my cheeks. The Old Spice strove mightily to overcome the English Leather and when it was sufficiently stinky for Castro, he resumed our dialogue.

"If Maria accompanies Raul to New York, she must be treated to all amenities."

"We'll get them a suite at the Plaza Hotel."

"*Bueno!*"

"Get them a car."

"What kind of car?"

"What kind should it be?"

"A Buick. I like Buick, I always have."

"A Roadmaster," I said.

"Good, good."

"And more money," I said.

"What?"

"More money. We ought to hold up George Bremenhaven for more money. The kid is only getting $109,000 a year. He deserves a lot more."

"How much more?"

"Let's say two million," I said.

"Two million dollars?"

"Well, it's not as though it's my money," I said. "I'm sure George will spring for it and for the suite at the Plaza and everything. All we got to do is see if Maria wants to marry Raul as much as he wants to marry her."

"There is a complication," Castro said. "The parents are not certain —"

"Oh, come on, Supreme Leader, what's the point of being dictator if you can't dictate? If she wants to marry Raul and I know he wants to marry her, what parent is going to stand in the way? Particularly since you are the boss. Hell, you ought to marry them yourself."

That was pure inspiration. It just popped out of my mouth. It surprised me as much as it surprised Fidel. He switched languages all of a sudden for no good reason,

— Very, very good, what an excellent idea. I will give them my personal blessings.

— It'll be the wedding of the century.

— Of all time. The world will see that Cuba has a great soul and is a great romantic country where love is still honored and cherished.

— Wonderful (I said).

And it was, when you thought about it. I would get Raul back, Raul could stop buying out the stationery stores, and George . . . Good old George. Good old greedy, mean, rotten George Bremenhaven. Well, I was sticking it to George and the only thing that made it less fun is that he didn't know it was all my idea. And sticking it to Baxter, not to forget him and the fucking State Department. I wasn't going to lose, not for them, and I was going to make George pay for it as well. What if we did win?

It was the first time I'd really thought about it.

What if we did win the pennant? The fucking American League pennant? Twenty-four kids and one old boy from Texas who just won the damned thing? Think people howled about Toronto winning the Series? There'd be a howl on this one for sure. The government would be embarrassed, George would be out a major stack of change even by winning and would have to come up with real money to hold on to his players for next year. For all I knew, George didn't want the price tag of winning a pennant. It would surprise some sports fans to know that it works that way in certain franchises. As long as they can fill the park, they don't really care that much about winning because winners want more money, expectations rise, and pretty soon everyone is telling you how to run the business. I don't know what Castro was getting — really getting — but it was a damned sight more than $2.5 million. Maybe winning the pennant would be the way to square everyone's account. Or my personal account with people shoving me around like a chump. Starting with George and his Roxanne Devon shit. Maybe that Baxter guy with the State Department would be pissed off, too. But George. The thought of George actually winning the pennant and having to deal with a boatful of winners. It almost made me smile.

I owed the veggie-eating son of a bitch for a lot and payback was going to come a drop at a time.

30

Part of the world made it to the midnight wedding in the presidential residence.

There was Fidel in his newly pressed fatigues and a bunch of other guys, some in fatigues and some in suits, including Señor Martinez, who seemed to wilt every time Castro looked his way.

There was Dr. and Mrs. Velasquez, too, and Raul's family and a bunch of foreign dignitaries, including the Swiss ambassador who handles all the American business in Havana because we don't have an embassy there anymore.

Did I mention CNN? And Telemundo? And Miss Charlene Cleaver who had changed her dress after finally getting a shower at the Comrade Hilton?

Deke Williams could have been there, but he got very shy about being around cameras, which makes me feel that whatever he was doing in Havana was less than sincere.

George was in New York, but he was there in spirit. He was paying for it. When I called him and told him about Raul wanting two million for the rest of the year, I had the happy thought for a moment that George would collapse with apoplexy. His arteries were stronger than I gave them credit for and he merely went on a tirade that ate up three minutes of international phone charges. Then I dropped the other shoe, about the Buick Roadmaster that would be waiting to whisk the honeymooners to their suite at the Plaza Hotel on Central Park South. I was sounding like Monty Hall throwing in the prizes, and Raul never had to answer any questions.

The only real question was whether Maria loved Raul as much as he loved her.

Let me tell you, seeing Maria in person, up close, and not hugging and kissing someone on the tarmac at Havana airport, well, it's something. She has eyes and ears and a nose and the rest of it, but it has been put together so beautifully that you would be content just to look at her, never mind the other stuff.

About a half-hour before the midnight wedding, I met her in an anteroom of the president's residence. She was dressed in white, and I believed it was appropriate. Her eyes glittered because they reflected the lights of all the candles in the rooms. Candles were romantic and they also cut down on electricity.

I asked her in Spanish if she really wanted to marry Raul, because I didn't want to get involved in something where someone had to do something against her will.

Her mother was there, frowning at me and frowning at my Spanish. Her father was in the next room, working on his courage with a glass of iced rum and ersatz Coke.

— Yes.

— Okay, just so you're not doing anything against your will.

— And you are the man with the saddest story, is that true?

I blinked at her.

— The story of walking away from love because of a foolish game.

— Baseball. It's what I do. It's what Raul does.

— Oh, he can do whatever he wishes to do, it doesn't matter to me. I only want Raul. But he said you were very sad about so many things that it made him feel even sadder when he was in North America.

"I ain't sad about much," I said in English.

"Good. Even if you deny these things, it's good to be so sure of yourself," she said.

"You speak good English," I said.

"Of course. And French. And Russian."

"Maybe you can teach Raul some more, so I could have a part-time translator in the field," I said.

"Interpreter," she corrected me. "Is Raul really so very good?"

"You don't follow baseball?"

"To please him, I follow but I have no judgment."

"He's the best hitter anyone has seen in fifty years or more."

She smiled at that. She had proud eyes and they glittered so fine in the light of all those candles that I could guess she came from royalty just by looking at her. She had the fine look people who have nothing to prove have. She could have worn jeans and still sat on a throne.

"And he'll make a lot of money."

"Money is not as important as love. Tonight, I have love fulfilled and that is more important," she said.

"Well, I hope it never rains on your parade, is all," I said.

"My parade? Raul wrote me about you and about how you always speak of the parade. You are obsessed with parades."

"That's all there is. It marches by and you're there and you see it or you don't and you miss it. The parade don't need you to make a parade, it just invites you along."

"I have my own parade," she said then. I must admit, I sure admired her for saying that to me, even if I thought she was wrong. Actually, I was beginning to think maybe I was the one who was always wrong.

So there we were, Charlene and me and all those swell people and Señor El Presidente himself signing the marriage license and starting to spout extemporaneously. He was marrying Raul and Maria, but he was also using the occasion to speak of the crisis in the dairy business and the need to increase exports of meat products to the former countries of the Soviet bloc in Eastern Europe. This led him naturally into a ditty about the friends of Cuba and the enemies of peace, you were one or the other, and then into a mild diatribe about the United States government and its corruption.

I have been at tent revivals that were shorter.

About 1:30, I was getting tired of standing and Charlene looked like she was just out on her feet. CNN had run out of tape and Fidel didn't seem to notice that the TV lights were turned off. His toadies, naturally, were used to this sort of thing and just stood there like good little soldiers and took it.

Finally, after we detoured through the chaos in Russia and the need to cement relations with China, Fidel decided at two that he had spoken long enough. He put his hand over the hands of the joined couple and he said that in the name of the people of Cuba he blessed them and their union and that the Cuban people wanted Raul and Maria Velasquez-Guevara to be man and wife and all that that would mean.

I didn't really know what time I got back with Charlene to the Comrade Hilton, but it was late and I was dog-ass tired so that even the sight of Miss Cleaver in her nakedness did not do much for me. Come to think of it, I guess I didn't do much for her. We collapsed in a mutual pile on the bed in her room — it was bigger, I mentioned — and slept under a sheet in the manufactured coldness until noon.

Deke came by around then and roused us with a pitcher full of Bloody
Marys and fresh bread and butter. Charlene put on her blue silk robe,
which was not enough covering but we were both yawning and stretching
and nobody seemed to give a shit one way or another.

Deke said he'd called Chicago early that morning and the story of the
wedding was on the front pages. The president had said he, himself,
blessed the young lovers and hoped it would symbolize a new era in
American and Cuban relations.

"Our president or the one here?" I asked.

"Ours, man. I told you, I'm in on the ground floor, brother. Democrats
in the White House, got brothers to help me out, ain't like when they got
Republicans in; Republicans all the same, white. We get these relations
normal between us and Deke Williams will be the king of catfish as well
as shark, tuna, and whatever else is growing around this island."

"I'm happy for you," I said.

"And it was all due to you comin' through Chicago feelin' so down and
miserable last fall."

"Me?"

"Sure, man, you told me that George was going to deal with Cuba for
ball players long before anyone else in the world knew about it. So I was
a jump ahead, got my congressman with the inside skinny on this shit, and
he laid it all out for me. I just had to give him ten percent of found."

"Of course, a bargain."

"And when I set up Catfish Travel, man, there isn't any way I ain't
gonna be making money comin' and goin', you might say. Sell packages to
people that want a different kind of honeymoon."

"As long as they aren't particular about showering all the time," Charlene said.

"Oh, honey, when Catfish gets cookin', there's gonna be water like
manna running down here," Catfish said.

"Why don't you ever do anything like that, Ryan?"

"Like what?"

"Think ahead. You told Catfish that George was going to deal with
Cuba and he figures out a way to make money out of it for himself."

There she was going on again, holding up another ridiculous example
of what it was I should be doing. She held up George to me until he called
her a bad name, and now, just met the guy yesterday and she's holding up
Catfish Williams as an example of American enterprise in action. Why
couldn't Charlene at least give me credit for playing baseball or something?

Catfish beamed on while Charlene drank her breakfast and gave me this "why don't you amount to something" look. I was pretty sick of her and of Havana and I knew I was sick of Catfish Williams and his big schemes.

Martinez got us all out to the airport in a large DeSoto, which meant I didn't have to ride with Catfish. The newlyweds were there as well, holding hands and giving each other the look that means everything turned out just fine. Parents and kin were also there, weeping and gnashing, and it was all giving me a headache. I got on the plane way before takeoff and just sat by myself up front.

The twin-engine job took off around three and we bumped up a few thousand feet so that we could see the waves forming in the Caribbean.

Ninety minutes or so later, we landed at Mexico City and went through more bullshit and then we were airborne again on Mexicana, headed for John F. Kennedy on Long Island. Out there, we went through the customs and passport rigamarole again. Charlene was irritable and so was I, but at least the airport was air conditioned.

We got into New York at eight, just in time to miss the rush hour. George had sent a limo out to JFK and the press was jammed in the terminal, asking questions and shooting pictures and tape.

We pressed through the flesh with me holding one hand on Charlene's arm and the other on Raul, who was attached to Maria. We were all being battered around by news people. I got a tape recorder in the nose and a microphone in the mouth.

Charlene had had enough. "Will you people show a little common courtesy?" she inquired in her loud way, and the answer was no, not much. She ended up punching a TV reporter in the chest, and a nice little punch it was, too.

I shouted out that the newlyweds were heading for a honeymoon suite at the Meridian Hotel where they would hold a press conference. This was just a small lie, not like some I've told, but I don't think anyone believed me anyway.

I just wanted to fade with Charlene back to my little apartment in Fort Lee — but I thought I'd better check with the driver of the limo when we got out of the terminal. I didn't trust George, and that was the only instinct I was going on. I came around by the driver's window and he rolled it down.

"Where you supposed to take them?"

"East Side Hotel," the limo driver said.

See what I mean? You shake hands with George, you'd be smart to count your fingers afterward. Anyone willing to dump a $50-million payroll and replace it with a bunch of Cuban kids who have to live in a slum is not worthy of much trust. "Gimme your phone," I said to the driver and punched in George's number.

It rang six times before Miss Foster picked it up. I told Miss Foster that I wanted to speak to George. She said he wasn't in. I said, "Well, you can tell George it was a nice try, but we're going to the Plaza the way it was arranged and I'll send him the bill."

She hesitated.

A moment later, George came on the line. "You son of a bitch, you're trying to rob me. I own the East Side Hotel, it's got some nice suites in it, just as nice as anything in the Plaza."

"Any resemblance between the Plaza and your hotel is minor. Like they both have doors and windows. We're going to the Plaza."

"Not in my limousine, you're not."

"Then fuck your limo, we'll take a cab. You're trying to cheat your way through this, but it isn't going to work, George. No cutting corners. And that goes for the new contract you're going to offer Raul. No contract, no workee, *comprende*, Señor?"

"You put that spic up to this, Ryan. I can fire your ass."

"Fire away, George. I ain't gonna fight with you. Send the checks to me in Houston, Texas."

"Is the media there?"

"All over the place. We had to fight our way through the terminal."

The mood shifted, just like that. George was back to his old bonhomie routine.

"Great, great, great. I was on the 'Today' show this morning."

"Why, what did you do?"

"I talked about the welfare of my ball players coming first."

"And then you want to put them in a welfare hotel."

"All right, all right, but this isn't a permanent arrangement, Ryan. You know what a suite in the Plaza can cost? Maybe I can work out a deal on this. All right, put the driver on the line."

I handed the phone to the driver. He listened, said "All right," and replaced the phone.

"What did he tell you?" I asked, checking.

"Take them to the Plaza Hotel. Get them registered."

"Okay, man," I said, letting the weight of the world fall from my shoulders. I was so damned tired. "You take care of it, buddy, and here's an extra ten for your trouble. This couple is from Cuba, you know. The woman speaks good English so if you got trouble getting through to the kid, talk to her."

"What do I look like, a babysitter?"

Said it in that chip-on-his-shoulder way that drivers in New York acquire with their licenses. Ten dollars is no longer enough to earn politeness from anyone in New York.

"This kid is Raul Guevara, he's hitting .435 for the Yankees."

"The last time I was at a baseball game, the seats were a dollar," the driver said.

"Yeah. Well." I wasn't going to win anything with this guy and I might as well admit it. But not before I passed him four tickets for good seats for the next game. That mollified him somewhat more than the sawbuck. Then I went over to the newlyweds and slipped an envelope into Raul's hand. "It's $500 to keep you in pizza and beer until your next check." Normally, I don't go around slipping a little something extra to ball players, but Sid Cohen told me to do it and said I'd get the money back from him.

Raul opened the envelope and felt the greenbacks. He looked at me and said:

— This is from you?

— Let's say it all comes from George eventually.

— And this, this limousine.

— George is being very, very generous.

Maria broke in then:

"Are they always like this, these news people?"

— This is them on a good day. Get on in with Raul. The driver is taking you to the Plaza and he'll get you registered there. You got any problem, call me. (I had already written out my New Jersey number.)

They got in the limo and I slammed the door on them. Charlene said, "We should have bought some rice. When we were in Havana."

"Yeah, I should've thought of it." Throw rice in Havana, you'd have a food riot on your hands.

Raul rolled down his window.

— I am glad you came to Cuba to resolve this. You are a better man than you think you are sometimes.

— I am a tired man, Raul. The driver of this limo is taking you to the Plaza Hotel, which is very nice. You will get a suite of rooms there and you're on your own until I call you tomorrow. We've got to get my agent to be your agent and get you a decent contract. Remember, sign nothing. If George wants to talk to you, don't understand him. Sign nothing. Nothing."

"He understands," Maria Velasquez-Guevara said.

Married eighteen hours and I already saw where this marriage was heading. She was going to be the driver and he was going to be the guy in the backseat.

"Thank you, Señora," I said.

She smiled then. "No. Thank you. For all that you managed to resolve for us. I have always wanted to see New York City."

"Yeah, it's something."

"And I have my Raul," she said, holding his arm.

"Like I said, I hope it never rains on your parade."

"And I hope you find some sunshine for yours," Maria said to me.

Damn. Was she smart or what?

Charlene and I clung to each other through the crowd of press that kept asking me dumb questions. We went around to the cab line at the side of the terminal and when I mentioned Fort Lee, New Jersey, the dispatcher shook his head and called up a Yellow. You could tell them Coney Island, which would take them about six hours to get to, and get away with it, but just a hop across the Hudson River to Fort Lee, you'd think you were asking to be driven to Alaska.

George was going to love reading about himself tomorrow in the *Post.* I had told the reporters that he was going to negotiate a new contract for his hitting star and that the agent was Mr. Sid Cohen of Los Angeles. That'd upset his ulcer. He hates agents in general, but he really despises Sid Cohen. This makes Sid's job much easier when it comes to dealing with George.

Charlene and I and our suitcases settled into the Yellow and took it into Manhattan and then up and across the Bronx to the GW Bridge and then over to Fort Home Sweet Home Lee. This time, Charlene came directly to my domicile where the shower works real good and there are plenty of big, fluffy towels to make you feel wanted.

I ordered up Chinese food and a six-pack of Miller's from the restaurant down the street and we took turns using the bathroom. Travel in a foreign country can make you appreciate an American bathroom. Try it sometime. When the food came, I almost felt like a real human being again and that the last day in Havana was just a dream. Except for the Old Spice I had splashed on my face that still clung, or at least, I still smelled.

That reminded me of the the two-hour oration at Raul and Maria's wedding and that just made me tired again.

I know we ate. I know we had a beer each. And I know we didn't actually say very much to each other. I pulled out the sleeper from the couch and turned on the TV and climbed in bed.

I was sound asleep before Clint Eastwood shot his first bad guy.

31

The year of the Yanquis.

Nothing succeeds like success, especially in New York where being Number One is the only thing.

The season had started out with everyone making fun of George and his crew of Cuban kids. The kids had stumbled around and gotten to know one another in spring training down in Lauderdale. Then George fired old Sparky and made me the manager, the only qualification I had being that I spoke some Spanish.

But somewhere along the way, the team started looking respectable. I can't tell you exactly why. Well, it was Raul hitting the moon, of course, but it was a lot of other little things.

The people once came up to the Stadium in the Bronx to laugh at the Cubans and boo them and hold up their "New York Yanquis" pennants and boo George in his box. But you don't boo a winner and the team was a winner and the boos were gone.

We went on a nine-game winning streak after the All-Star break and pulled up in first place in the East by five games. Everything was going well; the kids had their defenses down and their offenses up.

Something else. There was still a lot of hatred out there somewhere for the Cuban players and some people began to resent it. You only kick a guy when he's down so long and then a contrary streak hits some people to build them up. After all, the kids weren't Communists; they were just Cubans. If we could end up loving Russians, we could end up loving Cubans. And some people began to feel that way. We still brawled because the other teams saw the Cubans as a direct salary threat and I don't blame them any more than I blame strikers beating up busloads of scabs coming to replace them. Feel sympathy for the scabs, too, if you want to know, because when a man has got to eat, he sometimes has to do whatever it takes to eat. I know that isn't very principled of me, but I ain't a principled kind of person.

As I said, it was going well. We were winning. And when we lost a game, the gloom didn't sink in deep, not into the bones. The club was as loose and cheerful as it could be with a pennant race rounding the turn and heading into the stretch.

Well, mostly.

It was inevitable that Raul would tail off some, hitting the phenomenal streak and all. But he couldn't seem to get back into the rhythm of the thing.

The other thing was how happy he was.

We had a good long home stand in August and Raul was just one big grin, ear to ear. It was Maria, of course, and Maria was in her natural element in New York. I've talked some about the style that Cubans have — a certain way of walking and talking that depends on the way they carry it off more than what the substance is. Well, that style fits in well in New York, which means that Maria fit in well.

They ate out every night and found some elegant restaurants that I had never been to in all my years playing for the Yankees. Of course, I live on a more modest scale and tend to watch my pennies turn into dollars, but Raul and Maria were having none of it.

Sid Cohen negotiated the kid a two-year $8-million contract, which must have looked like all the money in the world to Raul. Even to Maria, whose parents were better off in the Cuban scheme of things.

The couple was an item around New York, as the newspaper people say. They were wined and dined at parties and they even met the mayor at Gracie Mansion.

Pretty heady stuff and I was trying my best to let Raul enjoy it all without lousing up his game. But I must have been doing something wrong.

He was hitting .387 by the middle of August and going south all the time. He hadn't hit a home run in three weeks, either.

Despite all this, the Yankees were holding their own because of the play of the other kids, who were stepping up big time. I realize that last sentence is full of sports clichés but that's the thing about sports, it lends itself well to clichés. Especially baseball, which has been played so long that it's got whiskers on it.

After our extended home stand we had to go on the road to bat the ball around with the cities in our part of the country. We started in Boston, did two games with Toronto, went down to Camden Yards in Baltimore, and then had a four-game series with the Miami Marlins.

It wasn't all peaches and cream on that trip. There was Rush Limbaugh and a piece in the *American Spectator* about Castro cutting a secret deal with the State Department and using the great National Pastime to subvert American interests in the Caribbean.

Among the glitterati in New York that didn't play, because everyone there pretends to be a liberal. But it got us boos in Chicago and in Milwaukee and Cleveland and even a couple more death threats.

That's when Mr. Baxter paid me a second visit.

It was around midnight after a home game and I was bushed and alone in my room in Fort Lee when he knocked at the door. I opened it for him. He was alone this time.

He came in the room, inspected it, and sat down in the single armchair, the one I use to do my thinking in when I stare out the window at New York's skyline over the bridge.

"You all mean to win this thing?"

I just sat there and said nothing.

"I asked you a question."

"Saw the president is up in the polls. Can't be the worst thing."

"The worst thing is what they're saying on radio about him."

"I don't listen to radio except for country music."

"We do. We have a plan here, Ryan. I didn't tell you that."

"Planned on us doing well, but not that well."

"The other players aren't happy."

"You *are* the commissioner after all."

"We can't fuck with baseball. National Pastime."

"You aren't. We're winning."

"Ryan, what if I told you that Jack Wade wants to make a deal with us? Tell us about how you get those cars from the Mexican assembly plants and drive them over the border."

"He would be wrong to say that because it doesn't happen."

"Well, you know. It takes a while to sort through things."

"Listen, Baxter. I can't help it if we're good."

"Not that good. Raul Guevara is faltering."

"He's still hitting .378."

"He's going south. How about some other people going south?"

"You want to fix the games?"

"No, no, no. I never said that. I said you can play to your potential. But your potential is not to give Cuba a propaganda victory. Let them say they have the best baseball players in the world. We could take a lot of heat on that. It might affect our standing in places."

"Like what?"

"Mexico, for starters. Or upset Costa Rica."

"I would hate that to happen."

"You think it's been easy to enforce this embargo on Cuba these last thirty-five years? We're not going to give away the Caribbean now because of some baseball players."

"You mean the Yankees can do that? Lose Mexico?"

"It complicates things. Raul has already signed an eight-million-dollar contract. What if Castro sees the further economic possibilities? And the other teams, what if they want a piece of Cuba? This thing snowballs and Castro can just freeze us out. Trump up some crazy charge about the U.S. trying to steal their young manhood or something."

"That's your problem, isn't it? I'm just a country boy and I play ball the only way I know how."

"You really want to be part of a federal indictment?"

I thought about it some. Then I put my can of beer on the table and just looked at him before I said, "How'd you like to go through that window? That one right over there you've been admiring the view out of? How 'bout if I just pick you up and throw you out that window?"

"How 'bout if you get halfway smart? We talked to George this afternoon. He's waiting for a call from you."

I should have known.

I picked up my phone and punched in the office number. It was George without any interference.

"Hey, George."

"Ryan?"

"Me."

"He see you?"

"Sitting right here."

"He explain things?"

"In his half-ass government way."

"He's got me in a box, Ryan. Tell me. Are we going to win the pennant?"

"Time will tell," I said.

"Ryan, I never asked you for anything."

I closed my eyes.

"Ryan, I don't want you to fix anything, I really don't."

"I know. You just want me to not make things work quite as well as they have."

"Ryan. This just makes me sick."

"What are they going to do to you, George? Income tax?"

"Ryan, we're all in this together."

"Yeah."

"All right, Ryan?"

"Yeah," I said.

I hung up.

"What about it, Ryan?"

"When the government wants you, they gotcha."

Baxter didn't smile. If he had smiled, I might have really thrown him through that window. But he didn't smile. It was all business. He just nodded, got up, and let himself out the door without another word.

The odd thing about the last series — the one down in Miami before we came home — was the reaction of the Miami Cuban population. Everyone knows how anti-Castro they are and we were getting some heat at the beginning of the season because the kids were, well, Castro's kids.

But all that was by the boards now. Cuban pride was too great and our four-game series in Miami was a triumph, in that we won three of them and won the hearts of the Cubans in Dade County.

Raul didn't do much for his batting average on the trip, but he seemed cheerful about it. Maria was up in New York, but it didn't seem to bother Raul the way it did when she was in Havana. I guess getting married does that to you.

Which brings up Charlene and me.

I was missing her.

Half the nights, I would end up in my room on the road and call her and run up these big long-distance bills just to say nothing to her.

Jack Wade was trying to make a deal on his income tax problems and it turned out that had all been George's fault, too, the way I'd thought it was in the first place. Seems George sicced the IRS on Jack Wade to give me the dog and when the IRS found something seriously wrong, they kept on keeping on.

In a way, I felt responsible for what happened to Jack because it probably wouldn't have happened if he didn't want to give me a job selling cars for him and George Bremenhaven needed me instead to speak Spanish for him.

We got back in New York the first week in September for a fourteen-game home stand.

We lost the first two to Cleveland. Raul went oh for 10. He was hitting right around .310 now, and it was looking worse and worse. So George came down to me in my office off the locker room late one afternoon and exploded.

"What the fuck am I paying this kid eight million dollars for? He's like every ball player I ever dealt with, as soon as he gets the big bucks, he quits on me."

"I don't think it's that, George. I think he's just adjusting to . . . you know, being married."

"And that was your bright idea, too. I should thank you for that, my weekly bill from the Plaza Hotel."

"George, he wasn't gonna come back if he couldn't bring Maria with him. It seemed like a good idea. Besides," I said, turning the knife, "you wanted good but not best."

"Oh, that was a pipe dream anyway. We're in second place now. Second is good. Build on next year."

"You're plain rotten, George. You work so many deals you can't even keep track of what you want and when you want it."

"You know what's a good idea? Keeping ball players in cages like you cage dogs in a kennel and let them out once a day for exercise."

"Players ain't dogs, George."

"No! Dogs got more loyalty! Raul is stinking up the team."

"We're still in striking distance of first place," I said.

"It's that woman! He's too fucking happy! Players are like artists, they need to be miserable to do their best work."

"I've known happy players —"

"You give a player job security and a contract for life, the next thing is they aren't hungry anymore. I want hungry players, that's why I dumped my payroll last year."

"Well, I don't see —"

"I called Cuba, I called that cocksucker in the beard and he didn't take my call. I ended up talking to some colonel and I said Raul is screwing me. You know what he said? He said it was about time someone screwed the Yankees!"

"He didn't mean the team, George, he was talking in general about *yankees*."

"He meant me! That son of a bitch is sitting in the Plaza Hotel charging room service and fucking his brains out while he slouches around the park hitting just over .300."

"A lot of ball players would like to hit .300," I pointed out.

"It's not good enough for me, though! I've got standards! And I gave him all that money, him and your fucking agent Sid Cohen!"

Managers and general managers get paid to take this kind of abuse from time to time, especially from owners who like to interfere with the team. Owners figure there's no fun in just owning a team unless they can mess with it or throw little temper tantrums or let their wives redesign the uniforms or such.

So I just took it from George and let him sputter along until it was game time and I had to excuse myself to make out the starting lineups.

I didn't really give George any satisfaction, but it didn't bother me, either.

Thinking back on everything that happened next, I should have paid more attention to George's tirade. When a lunatic is giving you signals about himself, you should listen alertly.

32

Raul went oh for 21.

That's when I benched him for his own good.

He wasn't particularly upset by it but we had a long talk about his decline in hitting.

— I don't understand it, either (he said).

— I think maybe the motivation is gone.

— I don't see how.

— Well, you got yourself married. That makes you happy. I'm happy that you're happy and Maria is happy. But sometimes, to motivate ourselves, we have to be a little bit unhappy.

— I was unhappy before, but I didn't like being it.

— You were hitting .452 before.

— You think it's because I am happy to be with my wife?

— Well, you two have become party people. You're always turning up in "Page Six" in the *Post* and other places. You might just be burning the candle a bit too much.

— I understand what you say. Perhaps you are right. Maria is so much in love with this city. She is dazzled by everything and I want her to be happy.

— Stay home some nights and watch television. Order in pizza.

— Maria does not enjoy pizza.

— Well, maybe she would do it just for you.

But I could see that Raul didn't think so, and, if truth be told, neither did I. Like I said, I did my best by benching him for a couple of games. I figured it might motivate him a little more.

Instead, it got me a visit down at the Stadium from Maria herself. She was dressed to the nines in a little wisp of a thing like Saks is always selling on page three of the *New York Times*. I must say, as I have said before, she is an extraordinarily good-looking woman and quite a forceful presence in a small, windowless, uncheerful room like my manager's office underneath the stands.

She lit into me the way Charlene sometimes does when I order ribs. But this was not about eating.

"You embarrass Raul when you will not let him play and you embarrass me. I don't want to answer questions about why Raul cannot play. A man called me twice from a newspaper this morning. What do I know about baseball? Why are you trying to disgrace us?" Those are the words as I remember them but not the tone. The tone was fast and furious. She was just letting it all out.

Like I said, if you're the manager you have to take that shit from the owner from time to time, but I was damned if I had to take it from the player's wife. Especially after all I had done for her and Raul.

"Look, Miz Guevara, since Raul and you set up house in the Plaza, his batting average has dropped about a hundred seventy points. I don't make no connections, but I do think it might be a good idea to spend a few more days hanging around the house and not doing the party party party all day and night."

"Are you telling Raul and me how to live our lives?"

"Yeah, something like that. I figure it's only fair as long as you feel compelled to tell me how to manage my baseball team."

"You don't manage except to insult a proud and sensitive man like Raul."

"I don't recall Raul sending back any of his paychecks — his new and improved paycheck, I might add — while he's been hitting zeros."

"Raul was a happy youth in Havana. He had no desire to come to New York. But now that we're here, we intend to enjoy the amenities of the city," Maria said in that foot-stomping way of hers.

"Fine, Miz Guevara. You do what you got to do and I'll do what I've got to do," I said. She had riled me, I have to admit. I also thought that maybe by building a fire under her, she could light up Raul.

I even went so far as to mention it to George.

His Gila monster eyes fixed on me for a long moment before he said anything. Then, "It sounds to me like our problem, all of our problem with Raul, is right there before our eyes. That little señora is ruining our ball player."

"Well, I don't think she's ruining him. He's just got to find a way to balance his life. You know, the game and his social life and all," I said.

George just stared right through me.

"I wish she'd go back to Cuba where she came from."

"We can't do anything about that."

"Why not?" George said.

I didn't like the way this was going. "Look, George —"

"I've got friends in the State Department. We can expel her as an undesirable alien."

"George, you already put the fix in to get all these Cuban ball players, you can't start putting in the fix to send one of them home —"

"I can do whatever I want," George said.

It was pretty ominous from where I was sitting. I know Baxter said this and that, but I didn't really understand who had who by the balls. George was upset because the team was faltering. He was upset because he had signed a two-year, eight-million-dollar contract with Raul. Raul was the draw at the box office and I had benched him. Raul was flashing in the pan, so to speak. That made George look like a fool and George didn't like it. That could set George off in a bad direction. I know people like that. They're into control, and sometimes they get their wires crossed.

33

I don't know what follows what in what happened next, a lot of it is still a mystery and some of it is probably top secret. I don't want to know my government's secrets as long as they don't involve me.

But it did end up involving me to an extent.

Now, I can say I don't know who George talked to about the Maria problem, aside from me. He might be whistling smoke about his famous connections. Then again, he is a man who once saw Abraham Lincoln in the White House, so what do I know?

What did happen is that two men went over to the Plaza Hotel around nine, two nights after George and I talked.

We were busy playing the White Sox in the Bronx. I had even un-benched Raul in the hope he might see the light, but he didn't do a thing his first two times at bat.

Now it seems that on the floor of the Guevara suite was a new maid named Elena Sanchez. She's the one who goes into the room and puts that candy on your pillow and other things.

Elena was Mexican, as it turns out, and she was in the Guevara suite, putting in new towels and such.

Miz Guevara was out, not at the ball game, naturally, but dining in the restaurant in the hotel.

This probably explains how it was fouled up, but it doesn't excuse anything.

The two men — I will get to them in more detail later — went into the Guevara suite on the fifth floor of the Plaza just as Miz Guevara was dining on her turtle soup and Mr. Guevara was striking out his second time at bat.

What was only explained much later was that Miss Sanchez was wearing the very same little black dress that had so impressed me when Maria wore it down to my office in the Stadium.

The details get very murky here. Maybe Miss Sanchez shouldn't have been trying on Miz Guevara's dress, but it doesn't seem that much, if you ask me. When you live in a hotel, you expect that your life is going to be a little less private than when you live at home.

I went over this with Charlene after the season and she said she once caught a maid trying on her fur coat the time she was at the convention of nutritionists in Las Vegas. It seems to me that nutritionists shouldn't meet in places like Las Vegas because it tends to take away from the seriousness of their conventions, but that is another matter entirely.

Well, what it came down to is that the two men went into the suite and they grabbed Elena Sanchez. She cried out something to them in terrified Spanish a moment before they maced her.

The Spanish only added to the kidnappers' impression that they had the right person. Because that's what they were going to do, kidnap Maria Guevara and hold her.

They would have done it, too, except for the circumstance of Miss Sanchez being in the right suite at the wrong time in a $325 little black dress from Saks.

They took the struggling woman down a service stairway and gave her a shot of something that rendered her halfway unconscious.

Well, I didn't know any of this was going on at the time and neither did Raul. We were just playing baseball and beating up on the Sox, despite the fact that, once again, Raul went oh for 4.

The game ended around eleven and I cleaned up and changed into civvies and drove home to Fort Lee. I guess I put the car in the lot at the Holiday Inn around 12:30 A.M. I just went up to my apartment and flaked out, which is why I was in bed sleeping at 2:30 when I got a call from Maria Guevara. I had guessed it was George calling because of the odd hour so I said something like, "What do you want now?"

"The police have come," Maria said. "They are searching our rooms. This is such an insult, they say that we have kidnapped our maid. We have no maid!"

"Whoa, Maria. Where's Raul?"

"He is here as well. A policeman is speaking to him, but Raul doesn't understand."

"I don't understand!"

"They are going to arrest us. This is terrible, this would never happen in Cuba. I wish we had never left Cuba," she said, and it was not the Maria of stamping feet and cold disdain but a rather young woman on the edge of panic. I said something to calm her down and said I would be right over.

You can make good time in New York at 2:30 in the morning. It took fifteen minutes to get from the parking lot of the Holiday Inn to the Plaza Hotel — although it took a bit longer to get in a parking garage.

The cops were still in the suite with Raul, who was looking sick and haunted, and Maria didn't look quite as stylish as the last time I saw her.

I told the cops who I was and one of them said a maid in the hotel had disappeared during her shift.

"Why are you figuring it was here? Or that it involved these people?"

"The maid was Mexican, been here only a month, and she worked this part of the fifth floor," a cop named Brennan said. "So we went up and down the floor and knocked on doors. This is where we found her maid's uniform."

"Her uniform?"

"Yeah. In the closet."

I looked at Maria and Raul and then at the uniform the cop held in his hand. It was gray and the kind of dress that maids always wear. Except there was no maid inside it.

"Raul was at the park, we had a game —"

"I know, I know. We won 3 to 1 but Raul went oh for 4," the cop said. He was either a fan or a good questioner. "He said when he got home here, his wife was asleep and he just crawled into bed without waking her."

You could see the way the cop looked at Maria just then that he was thinking about the act of crawling into bed with her.

"But this doesn't make any sense, what would they have to do with someone disappearing?"

"Look, Mr. Shawn, it's this way. Someone has disappeared, leaving behind her dress. It just doesn't happen in the normal course of things. And Mrs. uh Guevara says she didn't notice the maid's dress in her closet."

Why was I having a sinking feeling?

It had something to do with something that I didn't really want to think about. But there I was, thinking about it, and the cop was watching me think.

The cop said, "What's on your mind?"

"Nothing. What if the maid was in this suite just when someone was coming in looking for someone else?"

"Someone else who?"

"Someone who speaks Spanish."

The cop saw it. He looked at Maria in her terry cloth robe and then at Raul and then at the dress in his hand. He held up the dress in front of Maria and she took a step back.

"This could fit you," he said.

"I'm not a servant," she said with a little of her old fire.

"You have any clothes missing?" the cop said.

Maria looked oddly at him and went to the closet and looked through the dresses hanging there. She had accumulated a decent-size wardrobe for only being in New York seven weeks. It was a testimony to the shopping power of rich women.

"My black dress, the dress from Saks," she suddenly said. "My black dress is gone. The maid must have stolen it!"

"A guy comes into this suite, say when Mrs. Guevara is eating downstairs, and he sees a Spanish-looking woman in a dress and thinks it's Mrs. Guevara," the cop said. He shook his head.

"What are you going to do?" I asked him.

"We're all going to have to talk downtown with Immigration. I don't want to get in the middle of this," the cop said. I knew the feeling.

"The police want to talk to you some more down at the police building. It's down near where we saw the ships that time, Raul." Then I realized that Maria would understand and not Raul. She didn't bother to translate.

"This is terrible, they can't arrest us."

"They're not putting you under arrest, they just need to talk to you some more —"

"But this is terrible, this is like in the days when people disappeared —" She stopped, her hand on her mouth. "Oh my God, someone wanted to kidnap me?"

"Or kidnap whoever was in this suite. Maybe it was a sex thing," the cop said. I thought it was a bit too cheerful a way to put something like that because it sure wasn't reassuring anyone.

Raul, who had been looking on helplessly from the sea of English swimming around him, said to me:

— What is happening, Señor?

— The police want to talk to you and Maria more about this down at the police station. It's all right, Raul. I'll call George and get a lawyer down there.

— Why do I need an attorney?

— It's the usual thing.

— For someone under arrest.

— They just want to talk to you. A woman has disappeared and they need help to find her.

This went on for some time. I sort of shepherded the couple around to find their clothes and get ready to go with the police, telling them everything was going to be all right and asking the cops exactly where this station house was located where they would be talking to the Guevaras.

I left the hotel and then grabbed a cab. I went to the Tapas bar on Third. It was getting ready to close, but Jose Marti Riccardo was still there. He must have been drunk, but he was still ambulatory and coherent.

"Señor Riccardo, the cops have picked up Raul and his wife and they're talking to him down at police headquarters. You think you can go down there and interpret for them?"

"Oh, I heard about Señora Guevara. She doesn't need me," he said.

"She's a kid, Jose. She needs someone who can talk to the cops for her."

I told him what happened.

"Who would do something like that?"

I gave him a hundred dollars in twenties.

"Of course I will help," he said. "I know many of the police. They are friends."

"I hoped so. You call me when it's over. I don't care when it's over, you call me."

"*Gracias,* Señor," he said. "But I'll need cab fare." I gave him another ten. I had just about enough to get back home with.

I didn't get to call George until after four. I admit there was pleasure in waking him up, but it didn't overcome the sick feeling I had felt rising inside me the last hour or so.

I told him what had happened.

"You mean someone kidnapped the hotel maid thinking she was Raul's wife?" he screamed into the phone. I had to hold it away from my ear.

"That's about it," I said.

"Who could be that stupid!" he shouted again.

"Hey, George, I don't know from stupidity, I just know that Raul needs a lawyer."

"Why, what are they going to do? Arrest him? He was at the ballpark when this happened —"

"Nobody knows exactly when this happened."

There was a pause then.

I thought of Jack Wade and the IRS and notes written to Miss Charlene Cleaver by Miss Roxanne Devon of Brunswick, New Jersey.

I was definitely feeling sick.

"Nobody knows, do they George?"

"Can you imagine nincompoops kidnapping the wrong person? All because she was Spanish and that was who they were looking for? Can you believe people would be that stupid?" He was screaming all this at full throttle. It didn't seem that he actually wanted me to answer any of these questions.

"George, you didn't —"

"I didn't what? What are you accusing me of?"

"George, you wouldn't have done this, would you?"

"Done what, done what?"

I just shook my head. It was a stretch to go from sending phony letters to Charlene, to siccing the IRS on Jack Wade just because he offered me a job, to something like this. On the other hand, who would have believed all that stuff about Richard Nixon if it hadn't have come out the way it did?

On the third hand, I was talking to a slumlord and a baseball team owner rolled into one, a deadly combination.

"George, the maid is named Elena Suarez."

"Yeah, yeah, yeah, you told me —"

"George, are you going to get a lawyer to help out Raul? I mean, if they're talking to Immigration, then maybe this is a big deal."

"The big deal, you son of a bitch, is that Raul is hitting .295 and dropping and I want to win the fucking pennant. That is the big deal. And this bitch Maria Guevara is ruining everything with her fucking social engagements and driving my star hitter crazy in bed every night!"

"George, you don't want to win the pennant."

"Who told you that?"

"Your friend Baxter."

"I took care of Baxter, the little shit. He thinks he can fuck with me, I got friends he never even heard of until they came down on him."

"Now you want to win the pennant?"

"I wanna look good. I want the Yankees to look good."

"George, you got to get a lawyer —"

"I'll get him a lawyer, I'll get him twenty lawyers, the stupid son of a bitch. Can you imagine someone kidnapping the wrong fucking person, a fucking maid?"

34

I am glad to report that Miss Elena Suarez was released unharmed around four in the morning in the terminal of Newark International Airport.

She reported that her kidnappers were big men but she was not very good on descriptions because they had kept her blindfolded, driving around half the night in New Jersey.

This let Raul and Maria off the hook but it caused all kinds of problems for poor Elena, which I thought was unfair. The hotel fired her for interfering with guests and that revoked the viability of her green card status in the United States. So I did the next best thing, which was to ask Charlene Cleaver to get her a job at Rice University Hospital, where she is to this day.

Next thing, I had to straighten out Raul and Maria.

I thought and thought about it during the off day. And I figured that the only thing that was going to work was shock therapy.

I called Raul into my little office at the park and we shut the door, to show I was being serious.

And then I told him.

Maybe I was describing something that had never happened the way I described it, but I was betting I was pretty close to the truth. The more I thought about it, the more it seemed to me that George was behind this crazy thing. I couldn't prove it and I didn't want to prove it. I just wanted to straighten out Raul's head and it seemed this might work.

"I will kill him," Raul said in English.

— No, no, no. You kill him and you'll go to prison and you will never see Maria again. And don't tell this to Maria or she might get some of her Cuban connections to shut down our operation. This is all very, very delicate, Raul. You and I are tiny little pieces in a big puzzle. The United States government and the Cuban government got some stakes in making this crazy idea of George's work and they aren't going to let us blow the whistle on it.

— You mean I must fear the government?

— A little decent fear of the government never did anyone harm. Elephants sometimes don't mean to step on you, they just don't see you in the way.

— Then what must I do to satisfy myself?

You see, this Cuban macho honor thing was rubbing off on my doe-eyed boy, Raul.

— The one thing you know how to do. Hit the ball.

— But then I am doing that for George.

— No, Raul. You are doing it against him. It is your best revenge. If you hit the way you've been hitting, George is eventually going to have to pay you millions more. Same with the other players. The worst thing that could happen to George would be to win the pennant, because he's only got a one-year contract with the rest of the players. He'd have to negotiate big bucks or explain to the City of New York that he was going to cheap out the pennant-winning Yankees. You see? You can have him over a barrel.

— I would like to put him in a barrel of lobsters and watch him try to crawl out.

— He can't crawl out of this if you don't let him.

— Why should I trust you?

It was a good enough question. I might have asked it myself if I was talking to me.

— Raul. George doesn't want to win the pennant.

— He doesn't?

— It's all about you and the boys. He had a cute idea, to get rid of his old payroll and pay you peanuts. It worked out and he made money on the deal. And he did some favors for friends in Washington, who are a bigger deal to him. But if he wins the pennant, he turns everything upside down. You guys aren't supposed to be good enough to win the pennant. You're kids. Peasants. You don't know shit. This whole thing is put together with bubble gum and bailing wire.

— Bailing wire?

— Baseball. Structure on structure, all of it without foundations. What do you think a ball club is worth? What do you think a seat goes for? Four dollars for a beer. This game was just a game, but now it's something else. It's a business. Winning a pennant is nice, but it causes all kinds of problems. Show me a team that finishes second and I'll show you a happy owner. Besides, that stuff I told you guys once is true. What would happen to baseball in America if a bunch of Commies came here and won the pennant over all those high-priced Anglos?

— This is giving me a headache.

I thought of Mr. Baxter. He had planted my headache. I said:

— You want to fuck George, then win. You want to fuck these arrogant sons of bitches who run this game, then win the pennant. You want to fuck the government in Washington, then win the pennant.

— And then what?

— Then what? I dunno. Maybe you could go back to Havana and raise kids and I could go home to Texas and say I finished it out by winning a pennant despite the greedy cocksucker owner I worked for.

Raul's eyes glittered then, exactly as I wanted them to. I saw all my motivation was going to have a good purpose.

That night, he went 4 for 4, including a three-run homer to win it in the ninth.

It was the stuff of heroes.

After the game, we drank beer in the locker room and sprayed it on each other as though we had just won the pennant instead of moving up a half-game in the standings. George stayed away, which was all right because I think Raul might have forgotten himself and killed the bastard right then and there without thinking of the consequences.

The next day, Suarez caught the fire. I let Raul give a locker room speech to the troops because I was speeched out. He was very good. He disparaged George and he said that George wanted us — the team — to lose the pennant because the CIA had told him to do this. He said the CIA said they were unwashed filthy scum of Havana and did not deserve the American pennant.

It was a lot better than I could have done.

Emotion is a funny thing. It can set you up for a fall or make you play out of your shoes. Suarez knocked down the first batter and you could see he meant it. When the batter charged the mound, no one came out of the other dugout. The Cubans had taught them about brawling, I saw. The Cubans take fighting seriously and this was September and it wasn't worth getting your calf sewn up because some crazy Cuban bastard decided to chomp on you in the middle of a civilized baseball brawl. When the dugout finally, reluctantly, began to edge out toward the field, the umps had it all cleaned up. And ejected the hitter this time and left Suarez alone.

Naturally, Suarez knocked down the next guy and then he was gone. Ump was Bailey and he threw his hand out toward the dugout so hard that he wrenched his shoulder. He was steaming, everyone was steaming, and Suarez threw down his glove and spit on the mound, and that did it.

I had used Santana (whom I have not mentioned before) the night before and thought it was my turn. I didn't want to pitch, but there it was. I went out to the mound and took the ball from Tio and we did our warm-up.

I don't know why.

I was feeling it myself, getting fired up by Raul's oration.

It made me thirty-four again. Maybe thirty-three.

The other things crowded into my head, too. I was worried about Baxter from the State Department or wherever and I was worried about Charlene and Raul and Maria and everyone. I was thinking about all these distractions and I went through the pitching like it was something else, the way I think and drive sometimes on a hot night when I have an urge to take the highway down to Galveston. Driving makes the thoughts run free, and this night, pitching was doing the same thing. I know that there isn't a pitcher on earth who's gonna admit it, but sometimes you pitch on automatic. It's like some hitters just hit and can't really explain why they knew they were gonna hit the ball when they did. They'll never admit it, but it works that way, just like driving down to Galveston.

I laid it across and I knew exactly where it was going every time. Caught the spot and everyone could see it. The old gringo was doing fine. I laid them down, one two three, for five innings before my arm came back to normal. It hurt a little in the sixth and a lot in the seventh. That's when I started to think about the job at hand, what I was doing on the mound, rather than figuring out what I was going to do to get myself out of my various messes.

I was sitting in the dugout, watching us bat, holding ice cubes in a bag on my elbow. Seems no one wanted to come over and chat with me, and that was all right just then. I didn't want to talk to them, either.

Raul lined a double down the first base line — for a rightie, he owned that line the way left-handers dream of — and I just sat back on the bench feeling the ice on my elbow. I had already taken a steroid before the game but doubling up steroids doesn't give you twice the satisfaction.

Tio was next and he singled to left, but Raul went around third like there was no tomorrow. Did I say it was 0-0 at that point?

Raul slid home and the tag was on the money, but the umpire didn't see it that way. Maybe he was afraid of us. Crazy Cubans were scaring the league first and now the umpires. They fought in brawls like brawls meant something — kneeing, scratching, biting, all that. An ump got a black eye in the brawl in Chicago, and even though he didn't know who did it, he blamed us.

I hung on to win the game. I thought that's what I was doing, hanging on. With all my thinking about other things, I wasn't really that in touch with what I was doing. So I just did a day's work, kept lining them up and putting them down. Heave-ho, heave-ho. Hung on to put them down.

I got a clue when the dugout exploded out onto the field as the last guy, Charley Hough, flied to center. The kids were running at me and I thought I had missed some slight that was going to be the pretext of another brawl. I held up my hands and shouted in Spanish:

— Get back, get back, we can't afford another fight!

But they kept coming, laughing and smiling, and they pounded me on the back and arm and it hurt like hell.

"Get the fuck off me!" I shouted.

And then I got it.

Turned back to the scoreboard and blinked.

	1	2	3	4	5	6	7	8	9	10	R	H	E
W. SOX	0	0	0	0	0	0	0	0	0		0	0	0
YANKEES	0	0	0	0	0	0	0	1	-		1	4	0

I had pitched a no-hitter without even realizing that was what I was doing. A relief nine-inning no-hitter.

A fucking no-hitter.

The crazy bastards carted me off the field on their shoulders. I bumped my head first on the lip of the dugout roof and then on the entryway into the tunnel and then a third time on the door leading into the lockers. The third time, I started bleeding, but who the hell cared?

Me. Thirty-eight years old. A no-hitter in relief.

And we slipped into first place around midnight when the Orioles lost their third in a row. I was totally drunk by then and my arm felt like the *Hindenburg* going up in flames, but I didn't give a shit. I had called Charlene and even she was cheering. Damn. Thirty-eight years old.

Raul was drunk, too, the first time I ever saw him drunk. He was plastered with sprayed-on beer and his eyes were glassy and he kept hitting me on my sore arm, but I didn't feel the pain that much.

I wisely left the car in the lot and took a cab at one A.M. back to Fort Lee, across the darkness of the Bronx. Even the driver was nice because he recognized me and didn't sneer at my five-dollar tip. Not so that I noticed.

And then, in my room, I just sort of collapsed. The phone was ringing, but I didn't give a shit. I passed out and when I woke up, it was morning already and I had three day's growth of beard on my tongue.

I stumbled to the shower and stood in it while the hot water rolled down my throbbing arm. I was definitely too old for this game.

By eight, I had eggs eaten and coffee drunk and I was drinking a can of beer to wash down a couple of aspirins. Aspirins and beer for breakfast; the breakfast of champions.

The doorman called up at nine.

"He say his name is Mister Riccardo, he say he know you."

Riccardo.

I had my robe on and nothing else. I opened the door. Riccardo was dressed for court with his neat suit and the tie clipped down with a tie pin. He carried a bag with him.

I showed him in, sat him down, and offered him a beer.

He looked at me funny.

"You want some vodka, I keep vodka."

"Please," he said.

I poured some on ice and asked him if he wanted something to kill the taste, like orange juice. He didn't.

I sat down at the table across from him.

"Señor Shawn, you were magnificent last night."

"Yeah, you see the game?"

"I saw the game. We were in the bar. We were all very happy."

"Yes," I said. "How come you don't look happy."

"Señor . . ."

I waited.

He played with the handle of his bag.

"What's wrong, Señor Riccardo?"

"You will think badly of me," he said. "I am ashamed of myself."

"For what?"

"For being the spy."

"Spy?"

"Do you know when we talk? At the table in the Tapas? Do you know that I spy on you?"

I just sat there. His eyes were small and miserable.

"Spy for who? For Castro?"

"Not him," he said.

"What do I have to be spied on?"

"You are the manager of the Yankees."

"I got no secrets."

"*Si.* They want to know what you say, everything about you."

"Who?"

"The people. The people I must deal with."

"Who?"

"Our government."

"Ours?"

"*Si.*"

"You were the one who bugged me? When I was in the Tapas?"

"You know that?"

"Yeah. I know that."

"You suspected me?"

"No. I didn't think it was anyone I talked to who was bugging me. I just thought they put in a bug or something, whatever they do."

"No, Señor. They put the wire on me. That is what we call it. I was working for them a long time. I had to work for them. My uncle and father, I told you, they were in the invasion. For many years, I worked for them. For my government. They took care of my mother, my sisters. It was not dishonorable. I hate Castro and what he has done, I —"

"Yeah, but I ain't with Castro. I'm just the manager of the Yankees."

"Señor, last night I saw what you did. It was brave. Very brave. Mr. Baxter, he does not want you to do what you do."

"He told you that?"

"I know things that he doesn't tell me."

"And now what? You came up here to have me tell *you* something?"

"No, Señor. I come to you to tell you there is danger. For you. The State Department does not want the Yankees to win the pennant. Didn't Mr. Baxter warn you?"

"I thought it might be that." I got up, went to the icebox, and got another can of beer. I sat down again. "I thought about it, but last night, I won a no-hitter. I never won a no-hitter before. Never even come close.

And this was just by accident because I had to relieve for Suarez, who was feeling his oats and knocking down everyone that came to the plate."

"Mr. Baxter will warn you again," he said.

"He can go fuck himself."

"You see, Señor. The government . . . I know this thing . . . is not just one thing. This is complicated. Part of the government wants this thing with Cuba to blossom into other things. Others do not. The government is cautious. And you are not cautious. Didn't he tell you that it was good to find good ball players in Cuba but it was not good to . . . to rub the nose of Washington into it?"

"No, not exactly in those words."

"And Señor Castro? If he wins the pennant, this is a bad thing, no?"

"He don't win. *We* win. Us. The Yankees."

"But the men are Cubanos."

"So are you."

"I am an American now."

"And you are Cubano."

"Yes."

"Aren't you proud of the boys?"

"*Muy.*"

"Well? Why do tricks for the government?"

"I don't care much, but last night, I saw much courage from you. I saw you stand up and do right, even if it would bring bad to you."

Principles again. I hate principles.

"Is something wrong, Señor?"

"Just figure I threw that no-hitter by accident, that I wasn't really thinking about it. I was thinking about other things."

"About your men. Who look up to you."

"No, not about them."

"Then what?"

That was a good question. One that I never would have asked myself.

"I dunno. I don't like to be pushed around. I don't mind a little nudging once in a while, but I don't like George pushing me around and I don't like what he did to Señora Guevara or tried to do."

"You think that, too? That it was Señor Bremenhaven?"

"Yeah. Why?"

"Because I think that other people think that, too."

"In the government?"

He shrugged.

"You getting this on tape, Jose?"

He looked at me then with infinite sadness. "I apologize again for all that I have done."

"Hell, that's all right. You ain't done nothing by me, Jose. I didn't say nothing I didn't mean."

"But what will you say when Mr. Baxter comes again? To . . . threaten you."

"I dunno."

"You see, that is courage."

"No, just stupidity. I don't think that far ahead."

"Señor, perhaps I can make an amend to you."

And then he opened his bag and took it out. I saw what he was thinking before he even said it.

35

Baxter and Sills met me at the park at five. I was late because I had to do an interview with WFAN and about half the TV stations in New York and because I treated myself to a rack of ribs at Wollensky's that was this side of sinful. Charlene was going to have to forgive me for that one.

Did I say I sent her a dozen roses by wire? I never did that before. What the hell, I never threw a no-hitter before.

I was wearing my blue blazer and a black knit polo shirt and gray slacks. A guy from the *Daily News* was stalking me and I exchanged pleasant remarks with him for a few minutes before I went into the sanctum of my inner.

The reporter did ask me one thing: "How would you feel leading a team of Cubans to the pennant?"

"I'd feel fine."

"Some people are upset about the idea."

"Bigots. This is the same crowd that didn't want Jackie Robinson to play. I think it's a sin that Toronto whupped us in the World Series. I thought this game was about exporting American ideas. If we export ideas we can't go back on them when they do us one better, can we?"

"You want to explain that?" He held the tape recorder right under my nose.

"America is doing our best and showing others how to do our best. I don't recall that Castro said he invented the game, like the Russians used to do. Now we kiss Russian ass bigtime and we forget all that cold war stuff, which is okay by me, but I think we give credit where credit is due. Take George. I've had my differences with George, but he said to me just this morning that he hoped more American ball players would learn the Cuban work ethic when it comes to knuckling down to the grindstone and doing what they had to do."

"You agree with that?"

"Hell, no. I'm an American ball player, ain't I? And I just threw a no-hitter, which isn't bad for an old relief pitcher, is it?"

The *Daily News* guy laughed and said he would quote me accurately and I said it was more important that he quote George accurately because he knew how George was, always trying to slip out of something. He said he knew. 'Deed, he did.

I went into my cubbyhole and there was the entire U.S. Government waiting for me. I didn't take off my coat or say anything.

"You're trying, aren't you?" Baxter said first.

"Trying what?"

"Close the door," he said to Sills. No Neck did.

"You're fucking with Uncle," Baxter said.

"I'm trying to win the pennant," I said.

"Exactly."

"Exactly what?"

"You forget the conversations we've had?"

"Apparently so."

"I can hang an indictment on your ass tomorrow," Baxter said.

"For what?"

"For what we were talking about."

"Oh, that was just talk."

"It was fucking serious talk, Shawn. Don't shrug that kickshitter attitude at me. You're in deep doo-doo."

"Doo-doo? Kickshitter? Do people in Washington really talk baby talk like that? I thought it was only that president we had once."

"Funny guy," said Sills.

"I don't talk to people like you. Kickshitter. What a laugh," I told him.

"These Cubans are not going to win the fucking American League pennant."

"All right, you tell me why not."

"Because they can't."

"Why can't they?"

"Because."

"Because why?"

"Because of the game. It's an American game."

"So what?"

"Because."

"Oh, why don't you just blow it out your ass, Baxter. I got to get dressed for the game."

"I want you to understand something, cowboy. Fidel Castro let us use his ball players for a considerable amount of consideration."

"Like what?"

"Like oil, for one thing."

"All right, you made your deal, I don't need to know about it."

"But we didn't intend for him to take over major league baseball. George Bremenhaven is a fool. It was his idea to carry the water on this, take in the Cubans in the most liberal city in the country. Well, it worked out fairly well. But they weren't supposed to win this thing."

"You want me to fix it?"

"We want you to look out for your best interests."

"Like what?"

"Stop the fucking winning," No Neck said.

"Is that right, Mr. Baxter?"

He stared right through me. "You're thick, you know that? You could end up testifying to grand juries for years for fucking this up."

"So you want me to fix the game."

"Not fix, not fix. You're encouraging this . . . rabble team. What was the point of that guy's speech last night? Raul?"

"You bugging the locker room, too?"

"We do what we have to do."

I put my hand to my mouth. "Is nothing sacred? You'll be wiring jock-straps next."

"Why can't you leave well enough alone? Castro's got recognition for baseball and that makes everyone feel warm and friendly in Havana, that's all we wanted. Not give the fucking pennant away."

"Nobody gives anything away in the Bigs. You take it, is all."

"You take it and you're in trouble the rest of your life."

"Well, that's as may be. But I'll have my moment of glory." I thought of something then. "Last little bit of sun on my parade before we wind it down."

"You don't want to win that bad," Baxter said.

I just smiled. "Pardner, you don't know what I want that bad. Maybe I didn't even know until the last few days. Maybe I still don't know. But I can feel it, Bax. Can't you feel it?"

We ended the conversation then. They left very sullen.

*   *   *

One other thing.

Raul, Tio, and I went over the locker room and found two bugs, both hidden in boxes. One was in the electrical box and one was in a hot water transfer box on the wall. We drowned the bugs in the shower.

Then the boys gathered around me and I gave them my last speech of the regular season. Riccardo was there, too, as our honored guest, and he got a Yankees cap out of it as well as good box-seat tickets. He also did the interpreting for me because I wanted the Spanish part to come out just right.

Especially when I played the tape.

The tape was real tiny in a real tiny machine. It had been strapped inside my waistband. They make those things real small, you know? Not the kind you can buy at Radio Shack.

First Baxter would talk and then Riccardo would translate and then I would talk and Riccardo would translate and then Baxter would talk and Riccardo would translate and it was quite a conversation. There were parts in it I hadn't picked up on at the time.

When it was over, I thanked Señor Riccardo and he went out of the room and down the tunnel to the stands.

Then I stood up and said, "Friends, the only thing we have to fear is fear itself."

"And those government men," Raul said.

"I spit on them," I said. And then I spit on the floor. "I'm proud of you boys and I don't give a shit what happens out there from now on. We are the team of destiny and you all know it. Even Tomas Butterfingers knows it."

Tomas grinned at me and shook his head.

"The world is going to know it. Everyone stands against us, but we aren't going to lose. Not tonight and not forever. We are destiny, *compadres*. We are the New York Yankees. Forget Cuba and the men from Washington and forget Castro and forget your wives and sweethearts and all the rest of it. That's for tomorrow. Tonight and in all the tonights into October, we are destiny. We are going to win the fucking American League pennant."

They held their collective breaths because they saw I wasn't finished.

"And then, *muchachos,* you know what we're going to do with the pennant?"

Raul smiled. His English was better than most.

"Shove it up their ass," he finished.

"In Spanish, please," I said.

And he complied.

36

It took until the end of September, but the New York Yanquis won the American League East.

Now that baseball is divided up into six divisions, with three in the American League and three in the National, winning the American League East is not the big deal that it used to be. We were tired at the end of the season, but as far as the owners were concerned the season was just beginning. There is no reason to have playoff games except for owners' greed. And the owners would say it all started with the players' greed, so you have to concede a point or two to both sides.

Winning the East was the story of the world for a couple of days. What no one noticed was that I went down to the U.S. courthouse on my day off and had a chat with the U.S. attorney.

He started in about Jack Wade and all that Mickey Mouse stuff and I stopped him.

I had copied the tape, of course. I gave him the copy and he played it.

I just sat there with a can of Sprite staining the rosewood table we were sitting at. When the tape was finished, he played it again. Then he said he thought it was illegal to secretly tape the conversation of two agents of the State Department and I said there was illegal and then there was illegal and fixing baseball was more illegal than making a tape.

He said he would think it over.

(As far as I know, he is still thinking it over.)

George Bremenhaven came down to the clubhouse before our first playoff game to try to put a good face on it. He asked me to translate for him and I was glad to do it.

"Men, I never thought you could do it. No, no, strike that, Ryan. Men, I always knew you could do it."

— Men, he thinks he was fucking you before but now he has ended up fucking himself.

Many smiles all around.

"Men, I know that some of you do not want to return to your unhappy homeland and I can't blame you. I want you to know, I have extensive contacts in our government and you are all welcome here, in America, welcome here even in New York, the greatest city on Earth."

— He wants you to defect. It's the only way he can show face with the other owners.

— Tell him to go fuck his fat Yanqui ass (Tio said).

"Tio said to go fuck your fat Yankee ass," I translated.

George went red all over and shouted, "Tell him he's fired, the cocksucking Commie prick."

— He says you're fired, you cocksucker of a Communist prick.

— Tell him we could not have won without hating him for kidnapping Raul's wife (Suarez said).

"George, Suarez said they could not have won without hating you for kidnapping Raul's wife," I said.

"What the fuck are they talking about? I didn't have anything to do with that."

"Oh, come on, George. Take a bow. It was great motivation. You should get a TV infomercial on motivating ball players."

"I never kidnapped her, the dumb bastards kidnapped the fucking maid," he shouted again.

— He says his goons got the wrong woman.

— He admits it? (Raul said, picking up a bat).

I stood up and stood between them. I said to George, "George, Raul wants to turn your head into a squashed watermelon, I think you motivated enough for tonight."

"Jesus Christ," George said.

"Yeah. Say good night, George." I'd always wanted to say that.

That was just frosting. We kicked serious ass that night and I did three innings of relief as a star turn. Gave up no runs on two hits and two walks, which was my usual speed. What the hell, we won.

And won and won and won.

Raul had ended up the season hitting .381, which was enough to ensure that he would be the American League player of the year but no Ted Williams. We were in the Series and the boys were the toast of Broadway. The only fly in the ointment, if you can call it that, was Romero, the head bean counter. He defected in the U.S. courthouse. Naturally, we had to take him in. I mean, the U.S.A., not us Yankees personally.

I ended up the playoffs by flying down to Houston. I am not an extravagant man so I charged the ticket to George and the team, but I did fly first class because I owed it to myself. My first season as a big league manager (and last season as a player) and I pretty well steered a gang of Cuban kids to the pennant. Hell, I might turn out to be the manager of the year.

I wanted to tell Charlene Cleaver that I wanted her to be Mrs. Ryan Shawn. I had a ring with me that would pop your eye out and I was wearing my best brown suit.

I might say here that I wasn't exactly sure what Charlene would say to all this. (I had noticed that she waxed and waned about me and was seriously concerned about my bad eating habits, combined with her feeling that I might be mentally retarded in places.) But I rented the best Buick I could find and drove out to her apartment with as much confidence in myself as winning the pennant can bring to a manager.

She had made the reservations at Tony's and I carried a great big bouquet of yellow roses for her. She was impressed by the flowers, I could tell, and even though I had overdosed on the Old Spice, she didn't comment on it. I was getting to like Old Spice. Castro was right about that.

I gave her the ring when we got in the car and said that I wanted to marry her.

She said, "Ryan, are you doing this because you won the pennant?"

"I'm doing it because I wanna marry you, Charlene."

"Because I'm not going to go off and marry someone just because he thinks he should be celebrating something."

"Now why would you say that about me?"

"Well, I just want you to know that getting married is different from playing baseball games."

I had six or seven replies to that, but I was smart enough not to offer any of them up.

And she was smart enough to take the ring.

I guess getting married is just about getting smart enough. At least, I hope that's the way it all turns out down the road.

You might just say the sun was shining out on my personal parade and it felt as good as everyone always said it would.

37

The funny thing was we were going to be facing the Cincinnati Reds in the World Series, which led to all kinds of creative headline writing in the sports pages. Some people don't know that the Reds became the Redlegs for a while during the McCarthy years because Cincinnati did not want to look like it supported Communists. Silly, isn't it? Now there were *real* Communists in the World Series.

When baseball is at its best, it is a feelgood game and it gives pleasure in and of itself. I figured the pleasure I felt had spread to Charlene and to my little parade and the sun felt good. And the pleasure had even spread to old George, who probably didn't even know the shit that was about to hit him.

I flew back to New York for the start of the World Series. It was a night game, because television is the tail that wags the baseball bats these days. There were more people willing to watch night games, which meant more money from sponsors for commercial minutes. Which meant that little boys who dream about being ball players have to go to bed without seeing the game because they got school the next day. Which is a shame.

Charlene came along with me because she had some vacation days and she had never seen a World Series.

We went out the eve of the Series with Mr. and Mrs. Guevara and we had a good old time of it, speaking in two languages and a bottle of champagne.

The next morning I went out to the Stadium early to set up for the TV interviews and to get some personal business done. The last thing I intended to do was to spend quality time with George Bremenhaven.

The guy who waited for me in my manager's office was not from the news media, not by a long shot. His name was Johnson and he showed me a plastic identification card that said he was a lot more important than I was.

I went upstairs with him to George's office and there were more people like Mr. Johnson, government people. We were all going to have a chat, apparently. I was at ease. I had a tape and they had the same one and we all knew where we stood when it came to intimidating a poor old shit-kicker from El Paso, Texas.

"Look," I began, "before any of you guys start talking about your secret stuff, I just want you to know I don't know anything about anything and I would just as soon stay out of it."

"Sure," Mr. Johnson said, "except you're right in the middle of the deep doo-doo."

"This is insane," George said, looking fit for the part. "These double-dealing bastards —"

"Shut up, Mr. Bremenhaven," Johnson said. "What we have here is a delicate balance involving several federal agencies and a foreign government that we are trying to establish a working relationship with."

"I don't see that I fit into any of that," I said, starting to get up. I had been all through this with Baxter back in the bad old days.

"Sit down," Mr. Johnson said.

I sat.

"You know Deke Williams," Mr. Johnson said to me.

"Yeah. We were on the team together."

"You met him in Havana in July."

"Saw him there, he was getting into the fish business."

"Is that what he told you?"

"That's what he told me."

"Mr. Bremenhaven has been named in a criminal complaint. We have arrested a certain Salvatore Bucci on smuggling charges and he, in turn, has mentioned that Mr. Bremenhaven paid a certain amount of money to two men to kidnap Mrs. Maria Guevara last August."

"This doesn't have anything to do with me."

"Except that Mrs. Guevara has relayed your suspicions to her parents in Havana who, in turn, relayed them to President Castro. This doesn't make our job in the State Department any easier, you see that?"

"Well, I don't really see what it's got to do with me."

"What it has to do with you is dealing with the Cubans over the next few months. If Castro blows his top again — and he is a somewhat un-stable man — then it mars all the progress we've made by using the Yan-kees and baseball to establish a friendly people-to-people contact with the Cubans. You follow me?"

"Not exactly."

"George Bremenhaven may or may not have been involved in a criminal conspiracy to kidnap Mrs. Guevara. We don't really care and we have no interest in pursuing this. But President Castro cares. And cares deeply. And so does the management of major league baseball, which does not want to lose its antitrust exemption. Am I being very clear?"

"Somewhat clearer but it still doesn't involve me —"

"It involved you, you shit, when you told Raul you thought I'd kidnapped his fucking wife," George said.

"That was just a suspicion based on a character study," I said.

"You're fired. As of now."

Mr. Johnson held up his hand. "No one is fired, Mr. Bremenhaven. You're not going to have the say on that any more."

"And why not?"

"Because you are going to sell the New York Yankees to a minority ownership consisting of Deke Williams, a former Yankee pitcher, and a consortium of Cuban businessmen in Miami, New York, and Chicago."

"I am doing no such thing."

"On the other hand, you could be looking at life in federal prison for kidnapping," Mr. Johnson said. "All anyone has right now is suspicions. Charges. We don't really have to get into this, do we, Mr. Bremenhaven? You can sell the team at a fair price and make a reasonable profit — a very profitable profit — and go your own way. At the same time, Mr. Williams has demonstrated he has the wherewithal to become a black owner of a major league team, something we have neglected to have."

"But what about me?"

Everyone looked at me.

"You, Mr. Shawn, will manage the team in the Series and sign a contract for next year if you're so inclined. Mr. Williams speaks highly of you. As does President Castro. We've backgrounded you nine ways from Sunday and you seem to be a reasonable American man who has no serious flaws we've detected. And you're not to play with tape recorders anymore."

Apparently, we weren't going to bring up that nasty old tape I made with Riccardo's help. So that was all right.

"Yeah, you're right. I like compact discs better. Better sound quality."

"What the fuck is this about!" George screamed. But no one paid him any mind.

"You'd be the ideal fellow to work for a black owner with a Cuban team and Cuban investors," Johnson said to me as though George had disappeared.

"Yeah, that and speaking Spanish."

"And learning not to peddle your conspiracy theories concerning the unfortunate kidnapping of that maid in the Plaza Hotel."

I looked at Johnson and the other government men and then at George and George was staring right through me the way he does. I knew he was thinking his way out of this thing but not finding any way.

"What do I have to do?" he finally said.

"Enjoy the World Series. And please be a good host to Mr. Deke Williams when he joins you in his box," said Mr. Johnson.

"I gotta sit with him, too?"

"It's part of our scenario," Mr. Johnson said.

"This is all your fault, Ryan, you son of a bitch."

Actually, it was, wasn't it? The more I thought about it, the happier I became.

"But what was Deke doing in Havana?" I asked Johnson.

"This is about business, Ryan, and you don't know anything about business. He was there because he contacted us through his senator. We liked his ideas, particularly in establishing an export fish business. And we like our . . . friends . . . to have friends. When George made the mistake of telling you of our scheme in opening ties to Cuba last winter, you told Mr. Williams. He saw the commercial possibilities."

"I told you to keep your fucking mouth shut!" George exploded and jumped out of his chair. One of the security men sat him down. He was shaking with rage.

"Yeah, well. I only told Deke."

" 'I only told Deke,' " George mimicked. "And now that shine is going to take over my Yankees."

"You did it to yourself, George," I said.

" 'You did it to yourself,' " he mimicked. It was getting dangerously childish, so I stopped speaking.

"I hate this son of a bitch!" he explained to Mr. Johnson.

Mr. Johnson said, "You are going to play ball, aren't you, George?"

We all waited.

"Or there is federal court, prison, those things," Mr. Johnson said.

Yeah, well.

George is cruel and mean, but he is a coward at heart. And just think, at the moment when his New York Yankees finally became American League champs, well, I tell you, the thought of it keeps me tickled to this day.

And it was my fault in part, wasn't it? I mean, involving George and Catfish and everyone? I didn't know it at the time, but I think I know it now and that makes it even more fun, thinking about George and his ulcer and the way he couldn't see his way out of a trap that was partly my making.

You see, I ain't an owner and he is.

And that means, when you get to do a gotcha to an owner, why, you go ahead and do it.

Gotcha.

38

Charlene and I got married that fall in the Riveredge Episcopal Church where her mother attends services. We went on our honeymoon in New Orleans, which is where everyone goes for a honeymoon, and Deke popped for the hotel room, which was very nice of him. For an owner, I mean. He also asked me to manage the Yanquis again and I told him yes. Everything was going along on an even keel.

He became an owner in December when the majors approved his purchase of the Yankees from George. And George? Well, what would you say if I told you he ended up as ambassador to Guatemala? Yeah. That's what I thought, too. I wonder if he had to learn Spanish.

Now, in case you don't know how the kids did in the World Series, well, that's another whole story in itself and I'll get around to telling it someday. Let's just say that winning the American League pennant made them heroes in a couple of countries and Sid Cohen got someone to work up an instant book on them.

Every day with Charlene is a different parade, and that's mostly what I got out of that strange year. I was so darned busy not wanting to miss anything that marched through my life that I missed everything else. You know that Charlene knows the names of all the flowers? And that she reads the *Wall Street Journal* every morning just like it was as interesting as a regular paper? And that after church on Sunday, we can talk ourselves into an afternoon nap, just sitting together on the couch and not watching anything on TV? There were a lot of things I never knew were parades of their own and just as interesting as the ones I had been watching all these years.

It goes to show you, don't it?